DAY ZERO:
GAUNT
MAN

This is a work of fiction. Names, characters, places, and incidents are either the product of the author's imagination or are used fictitiously. Any resemblance to actual persons – living, dead or undead – events, and locales is entirely coincidental.

Library of Congress Control Number: 2017938683

ISBN: 978-0-9914702-2-8
10 9 8 7 6 5 4 3 2 1

Covers by Terry Fogarty
Edited by Judith Swain

www.DayZeroBook.com

To my Muse.

ACKNOWLEDGEMENTS

To the people in my life who inspire me, who drive me, who criticize and force me to be better. Thank you to everyone who assisted in making this effort as true as it could be.

A special thanks to the staff of the real Worcester Art Museum in Worcester, Massachusetts for their support and assistance in making this work of fiction as non-fictional as possible. Undead aside, the museum is an excellent location to visit.

DAY ZERO:
GAUNT
MAN

Written by Charles Ingersoll

Edited by Judith Swain

Table of Contents

PROLOGUE

DAY ZERO: GAUNT MAN

PROLOGUE

1

Assessment

+29 Days – 1630 hours

I stared at my reflection in the church's lavatory mirror, my hands curled around the sides of the porcelain sink.

My irises had taken on the tiny gold flecks again. A tinge of red dashed across them as my eyes dilated in the cold fluorescent glow.

I took slow deep breaths.

Thump… thump.

My heart rate slowed.

The red and gold receded.

I splashed away the blood, dirt and sweat from my face.

When I looked at my face again my eyes had returned to their normal dark brown color.

I turned off the water, reducing it to a single drip that would not be staved off no matter how hard I would have turned the squeaky faucets.

Grabbing a paper towel from the dispenser, I wiped my face and the sink top. Spidery cracks had formed where I had grabbed the edges of the porcelain.

2

Follow up

+29 Days – 1645 hours

The bathroom door bumped into the back of my leg.

I instinctively drew my Glock.

Donovan, who had been waiting outside, rushed in and grabbed my shirt. I squeezed his shivering arm and led him back out to the vestibule.

The boy was still in shock.

He needed food and rest.

Joyce looked up from folding linens between the pews and gasped.

Sheriff Garrett and some of his men had returned, their clothes bloodied and their hands scraped.

"Don't worry." Garrett raised his hands in surrender. "We ran into a few FRACs at the Norte Bridge, but we're good. These scratches are from fixing a massive tear in the chain link fence. We added some barbed wire, but it bites hard when you're rushing and don't have the right gloves."

"Well, come get checked out," Dr. Rawlings said from the side aisle, ushering the sheriff's men to a pew. "We don't need any unnecessary infections."

Garrett waited for his men to be seated before walking toward Donovan and me.

"What happened, John?" Garrett asked, looking at the pool of drying blood under Diggs' body at the altar.

I gestured for Garrett's pad.

He handed it and a pen to me.

I wrote down seven words and handed both back.

" 'Diggs was a FRAC. Donovan shot him'," Garrett read the note aloud then appraised the boy. "That the way it happened, son?"

Donovan nodded, his eyes wide.

"Diggs was family." Garrett sighed and nodded back. "And I can't believe the shit he did. But it was the least he deserved after what he did to Gloria. And Lucy. If he was a FRAC, it was for the best."

Garrett winked at Donovan, eliciting a small smile from the boy.

"Take care of him, John," he commented to me.

I nodded and put a hand on Donovan's shoulder.

Garrett departed to Dr. Rawlings triage station, putting his notebook back into his breast pocket.

Donovan showed his resolve and led the way up the aisle. Daisy the ferret clucked inside his satchel. Holly padded along behind us, slowing to drop her white snout to the carpet every so often.

The sun warmed our faces as we stepped outside.

Town Hall still burned.

Plumes of gray and black smoke rose from the remains of the structure. Islanders were busy carrying FRAC bodies across the grass and through a gaping hole in a partially collapsed wall that the fire in the Town Hall had created.

On Mall Street, Monroe was pointing and shouting out orders. He still wore his bandanna like an outlaw. His crew hustled pails of water and fire extinguishers to douse the remaining licks of flames trying to survive on the storefronts.

I bumped into Donovan.

"Shit," the boy muttered, staring at the Searing Bridge. "Shit. Shit."

At the top of the ramp, behind the barricade of cars, pushed a clawing and moaning mob of FRACs. They swayed and bobbed at least twenty rows deep. Their familiar guttural groans rose up in unison.

I put a hand on Donovan's trembling shoulder.

The spectral Gaunt Man shook his head as he came up beside me.

My fingers gripped my Glock.

I hadn't realized I had drawn it.

You're going to need more bullets than that, Johnny, the Gaunt Man murmured softly, his voice laced with an underlying tsk-tsk sound.

"Yeah," I gravelly whispered in agreement, my voice finally returning.

DAY ZERO:
GAUNT
MAN

1

Happy Hour

+47 Days – 1321 hours

Weeks had passed but every day seemed the same.

Waves lapped endlessly against the bridge's concrete piling, unfazed by the passing on of the world.

I sat on the guardrail watching the vast grey Atlantic waters fade into the eastern horizon, rubbing out a new kink in my neck.

Holly curled up at my feet with her snout buried under her white tail. She suddenly lifted her head and sniffed the air, a low growl humming from her throat and her tail slowly slapping against the pavement.

Three men came into view as they rounded a bend in the road. They stumbled against each other in a drunken stagger. Their clothes were torn and muddy as if coming from a music festival mud pit. The two younger and thinner of the trio kept bumping into the heavier set middleman, moaning something unintelligible.

They passed by us without notice, continuing toward Rainier Island.

Holly looked up at me. Her tail wagged with more rhythm.

"Yeah," I slid off the guardrail to the pavement. "Come on."

Holly popped up to her feet, woofing softly.

We followed the dirty drunkards until they were twenty meters from the line of parked cars that served as a barricade between the end of the Searing Bridge and Rainier Island.

I whistled.

The young man on the left slowed and looked up from his feet, not turning.

Holly ruffed at them.

The three men crowded against each other, the middleman finally craning his neck around. He spied the dog and appeared to

8

grin, a bit of something caught in his yellowing teeth. Waddling around, the fat man in the khaki pants and red polo shirt wobbled as he reached down for the dog.

I stepped up between them and jammed my tactical knife into the top of his head. His face fell into a lifeless expression. Gravity dragged him to the pavement as his partners turned to face me.

Holly barked again.

The young duo stared at her, never noticing the razor-sharp machete slicing sideways through the air. The blade took their heads off clean. The men crumpled to the road, the pile of bodies serving as a soft resting place for their decapitated tops to bounce off of.

I crouched and cleaned the dark blood off the machete blade with one of their shirts before returning it to its scabbard on my belt. It was a damn shame that we lived in a world where I couldn't use the Glock 18 holstered under my arm except in extreme situations. It was even worse that I couldn't flip the selector lever down to dispatch the disorderly in fully automatic fashion.

A quick bleep of a squad car siren got my attention from the other side of the barricade. The island's sheriff emerged with his sidearm aimed at me.

"Christ, John," he said, staring at the men at my feet. "You're going to have to stop killing at some point. Do I need to run you in?"

"Nah, Garrett," I said with a shrug. "I'll finish my shift. I'm sure a few more FRACs will be along. They've been coming in sporadically lately."

"Alright." Sherriff Garrett holstered his weapon, giving me a nod before returning to his cruiser.

"I'll be back with Reynolds to relieve you at 4 o'clock," he said before getting in the driver's seat.

"Yep."

I started back to the crest of the bridge.

9

Holly padded behind me, stopping every few meters to sniff at something she deemed of interest. Over the past seven weeks hundreds of FRACs – or as Felix had originally coined them, 'fucking re-animated corpses' – had been killed on this bridge, more taken down at the other checkpoint on the island.

Returning to my original vantage point, I hopped up and resumed watching the crashing waves of the grey-blue ocean.

In spite of the picturesque quiet setting and the faithful Pekingese poodle at my feet, I was still very far from home and feeling very much alone.

Mostly, I was just tired.

2

Hard Truths

+47 Days – 1405 hours

2pm arrived and our shift was finished.

SSDD.

Same shift. Different day.

I bent over to scoop up Holly.

She dodged me and crawled under the barricade of cars instead. I climbed up over a station wagon and met her on the other side. She barked when she saw me, sprinting away to the overgrown grass in the center of town.

Streets and shops surrounded the rectangular plaza. To our left a massive sunken charred pit had replaced where the Town Hall building had stood for over a hundred years. To our right was a white cedar sided church, a single tower with arched ports in the belfry rising out of its gable. Smoke and flame scars crept up out of the windows courtesy of a rocket propelled grenade.

The summer sun had burned out the neglected high grass across the plaza while a gasoline tanker explosion from the Exxon station tarmac had effectively scorched the rest. Several new deaths – this time by natural causes – had upset the schedule of caretaking of the grass.

I was sure sheriff Garrett and Monroe would get things reorganized soon enough. All of the residents had rebounded the best way they knew how after the original infection had spread. Young and old, the members of this community had pitched in to make repairs and bring their community back to a point of livability and normalcy.

The height of the early afternoon sun kept most people indoors or in the shade these days, leaving the plaza barren and quiet.

Holly pounced after a dragonfly on the other side of the field.

I walked to the gazebo.

Although its formerly pristine white paint had blistered and darkened with the scars of flames, the gazebo still stood. It was a testament of the endurance of the town, a symbol of their perseverance.

Sitting on one of the benches under the gazebo's scarred angled roof, I stared at the top of one of the posts. Its corners had been dug into, the grooves a result of the shear from ropes that had been attached to my wrists at the other ends.

The sheriff had been hanging off these posts, too.

A maniacal military officer and his men had strung both of us up as crucified warnings for the other islanders. He paraded them past us at gunpoint during a move from the Oceanside Diner to the Town Hall.

Grim stares and hidden, tear stained faces had been marched past us. Men, women, and children forced to witness two beaten and bloody men hanging from the posts under the gazebo roof.

The Oceanside Diner, once a hub of gossip, good food and warm hospitality was now dark and soaped over. One of the windows had been boarded over with a knotty piece of plywood. Carol was gone. And no one had had the heart or strength to keep the restaurant going in her stead.

Holly yapped as she trotted down the alley between the diner and the back wall of a row of shops. She sniffed at a pair of Bilco doors leading to the basement of the bookstore. The shop owner, Gloria, was also one who the islanders had assumed had left after the outbreak. Unfortunately for her, she had not gone to find her family as many had speculated.

No.

Instead she reappeared on the island as one of the undead, made that way by a sociopath who had used the end of the world as a chance to use his neighbors as experiments to see just how the animated dead ticked.

Lucy.

12

She had met me at that bookstore.

She was a firecracker military brat who gave me no quarter but gave me all of her heart. And in the little time we had together, I had given mine to her.

But it had been short-lived.

Her life had been cut short, another casualty of a world rotting out from the roots.

One of the people I had come to care about.

From inside the extinguished blackened gazebo, I stared at the hollowed out guts of the Exxon station. The steel of the tanker from the Exxon rig blossomed open with ragged split open edges. Its flammable contents had engulfed the station and a third of the plaza itself.

The rig's driver had not been a casualty of the infection but his body had succumbed to the trauma of gunfire. A grizzled Marine Corps vet with a shred of the most times elusive zest for life, Sebastian has been a man after my own heart.

More death.

After my general discharge from the Corps Sebastian had been kind enough to pick me up from a lonely New England highway whose route number I no longer remembered. While my only goal and gift had been to serve my country, my time in the sweltering desert had only served to degrade me to the point where I was no longer an effective Marine.

I was broken.

No career. No voice. No hope.

These boarded up and burned out buildings were a reminder of the death I had brought with me, and the lives I couldn't save. But the people, here and gone, were a reminder of the ferocity of life and how we should embrace it.

They had given me back hope.

In some small measure.

But even with the reminder that there was a life worth living I couldn't stand to walk by constant reminders of death anymore.

It was time to move on.

3

Decisions, Decisions

+47 Days – 1633 hours

"Sgt. John Walken, you're really leaving us?" Garrett asked. "I'd hoped we had warmed your heart enough by now to stay."

He had taken up the habit of squeezing the same handball as his predecessor while sitting behind the desk.

"It's not you, Sheriff," I replied, a twinge of loss already tearing wider in my chest. Deflection was my only tactic. "You're back to 100% health. The fortifications are stronger and holding. New people are coming in who are just as capable as me."

"None of them are as capable as you," Garrett corrected.

"Not sure I agree," I responded.

"You know what I mean, John."

I nodded but didn't add anything to validate his point.

Garrett threw the handball up in the air several times before speaking again.

"Going home?"

"You could say that," I offered. "I need to be somewhere."

"Somewhere? Or anyplace but here?"

"Sheriff," I replied honestly, "I appreciate you and everyone in this town. You all have welcomed me in with open arms, and not just because of the threat of walkers. There's just things I need to attend to, is all."

"I understand," Garrett said, then changed the course of the conversation. "Well, you healed up pretty well."

He squeezed the handball and tossed it back into the air. Its ascent maxed out a few inches before hitting the drop ceiling, coming back down to his waiting hand.

"Genetics, I guess," I lied after we watched the trajectory of the ball.

Well, not entirely a lie is it?

"And we were just starting to have so many wonderful deep conversations, too," he said, ignoring my reply. "You finally get your voice back and you decide to light out for the territories."

"Sorry, Sheriff."

He waved my last comment away.

"What do you need?" he asked earnestly, leaning forward. "You take whatever you like, John. It's the very least we can do for you. The very least."

"I appreciate that, Sheriff." My heart was shot through with a pang of regret. "Just the usual. Guns, ammo, food, gas, water. I already have a transport in mind."

"Done," Garrett smiled. "I'll even throw in a bit of Alpo, too."

4

Last Respects

+47 Days – 1922 hours

After leaving the sheriff's office, I went to the place where I had been spending most of my time. It was the most familiar and melancholy place on the island. At least that's how it seemed to me. I was a part of a lot of the island's recent history, even if the time spent here had been intense and short.

The church loomed before me, the jagged shadow of the broken bell tower resting its cool embrace over several new white crosses hammered into the grass. The burn marks on the hollowed out wall of the spire was a constant reminder of long shifts on overwatch. And, as always, it served as a grim reminder of concussive pain, searing flames, and of death.

I knelt on the hillside in the midst of an increasing number of grave markers. The closest crosses bore the names of Frank and Glenda. The scrawls insignificantly marked the names of the island's former sheriff and his wife. Their deaths were the first of many tragic losses to the community.

Emily Proctor.

Derek Block.

Felix Lareby.

These were just some of the residents who were lost in the early waves of defending their homes against the undead.

Jacob.

A boy who proved he was more of a man than many other men should have boasted.

Sam. Patrick. Doug and Rita. Carol. Steven. Basia.

Not an endless list for someone who has seen death in battle.

A Marine learned to callous up against facing death in the theater of war, but the loss of the innocent cut deeper into the heart and seared longer into the mind.

Erma.

The crosses were sturdy and planted deep. The white paint was stark, shiny and fresh. Sadly, these markers wouldn't brave the elements forever. They will weather and wane, eventually rotting into the grasses far sooner than was right or deserved. Eventually there would be no one to remember or to care.

I slowly dusted off Lucy's marker.

Holly lay on the still settling dirt in front of it.

"So you're really leaving," a voice drifted down from deeper in the shadows at the base of the church.

I looked up.

Sergeant Bowers was familiar with this sacred ground, too. The taste of death was still on his tongue. His hand had been an accessorial part of it.

I nodded.

"Why do you keep coming here?"

"Reminders."

"Reminders?" Bowers spat out. "The daggers from the glares from the living are enough of a reminder for me. Isn't that enough without adding self-imposed punishment like this?"

"Keeping it crystal."

"You must be stocking up before your trip."

"Yes."

"Got your voice back and talkative as ever," he said sarcastically.

A seagull screamed to fill the awkward silence I couldn't fill.

Can't? Or won't? You are a stubborn one.

The unseen Gaunt Man asked rhetorically.

Holly lifted her head to watch the seafaring bird glide out to sea before plopping her head back down onto her paws.

"I rest my case," Bowers said with his hands jammed into his pockets, staring out at the Atlantic and the waves it continued to force into the rocky shore.

"Need company?" he asked.

Accepting Bowers' request would ruin my hope for solitude and my need to leave this island's memories behind me.

"Please," Bowers added with an edge in his voice that caught my full attention away from Lucy's marker. "I really need a ride out of here."

5

Mi Amigo

+47 Days – 2045 hours

There was one last stop to be made after saying my goodbyes to the dead and making my promises to the living.

The gray, weathered cedar sided summer cottage stood on pilings, sand encroaching its underbelly. The air inside the aptly nicknamed Shack was oppressive in the heat in spite of its prime beach ocean front location.

Hopefully, Garrett would remember to air the place out every so often.

I grabbed my packed duffle from the kitchen and stepped through the sliding doors to the deck with the ocean view. A pier jutted out into the waves, a gazebo at its terminus with a lone Adirondack chair placed in the middle of its shade.

The waves beckoned me to stay.

But I could not.

The deck joined the house to a two-car garage with an architectural style same as the house. I dropped my duffle to the deck, unlocked the garage's side door and went inside.

More of the same oppressive heat escaped past me.

A tarp covered something big in the center of the floor. I pulled off the painters' cloth and let it pool at my feet. Dust swirled around the gloomy hot air, caught in the light cast from the door.

Frank's sports utility vehicle, an Isuzu Amigo, sat there shiny and mostly road worthy.

A few repairs would make it ready to go.

Should.

6

Fond Farewells

+50 Days – 0900 hours

Three days later the Amigo hummed like it was straight off the
showroom floor. The eco-features Sherriff Wayne had hoped for
would forever be part of his unrealized dream. Instead, this early
adaptation of the sports utility vehicle ran purely on the all-
American blood of gasoline.

Holly and I drove west on North Plaza Drive into the center of
town, my motley companion curled up on the back seat. We passed
the closed Oceanside Diner and the boarded up library. The
businesses around the plaza had taken on a decidedly bankrupt
small town feel. In this case it was the undead that had destroyed
the local economy, not the closing of a local factory.

We turned left, passing the gaping burnt out wound that was
what was left of the town hall. I grimaced with the memories of a
deranged military officer who had been the architect of the near
ruin of the community. The pit still smoldered with the faintest
wisps of smoke rising from it.

At the ramp to the Searing Bridge, a contingent of islanders
barred my exit from the island.

Shit.

I should've known that Garrett would never let me leave
unscathed.

I pulled up to the barricade and got out of the truck.

Garrett walked over to me and gave me an appraising look.

Bastard, I thought with a grin.

Then he gave me an unexpected bear hug.

I tensed up for a second before returning the gesture.

"You're a shit head, sheriff."

"Thanks, Marine. I'll take the compliment."

Sheriff Garrett backed off, leaving the hulking Deputy Lincoln Reynolds to immediately fill the void.

"Hate to see you go, man," he said, shaking my hand with both of his. "No one will be able to do the things you do."

"Thanks."

"Speak for yourself, lawman," Pete chimed in, his arm still in a sling from the gunshot in the shoulder he received from the battle that Wallace and Diggs had a hand in orchestrating.

He was certainly proving that he was too grizzled and spiteful to be ended by bullets or the undead.

The older gun shop owner's slight frame and scraggly features deceptively hid the fact that he was an all too-avid gunslinger, happy to enjoy target practice against the undead. No one could ever have pimped out a Gatling gun like he had. That weapons system was as exquisite as it was simplistic.

"Be safe," Pete offered with a punch to the bicep before he walked away toward his store across the plaza.

"How could you?" came a voice from behind me.

I turned toward the Isuzu.

Donovan stared at me. His fists jammed onto his slim hips. A familiar satchel slung across his chest. The leather squirmed a bit before Daisy poked her ferret muzzle out from under the flap. It quickly disappeared again as she moved into a more comfortable position inside the bag.

"You're leaving without me," the boy cried.

"It's safe here, Donovan."

"I'll be safe with you."

"You're way safer here than on the road."

"Like with Diggs?" he spat out at me.

I reached out to the boy.

He pulled away, nearly bumping into Monroe and Bowers.

Doctor Rawlings, trailing behind the pair, tried to corral the boy but he proved too nimble and elusive even for the doctor's skilled free hand. As always, the good doctor seemed prepared for another rain shower with an umbrella handle hooked over his forearm.

The boy had lost his family, one of his pets and his best childhood friend. The topper had been that he had been threatened with death on a church altar at the hands of a handyman turned serial killer.

Donovan had killed that man.

I had hoped it would've provided him some catharsis, or at least a sense of vengeance that would burn warmly for him for a while. But only time and experience would cover those mental wounds.

And I wanted him to have a chance to have time to heal. That wouldn't happen on the road with me.

"Let him go," Bowers offered as he patted my shoulder, holding me back as I thought to pursue the boy. "He'll heal."

"Will he?"

"Yeah," Bowers added knowingly. "He may carry hate for some time but he'll heal."

"You good?" Monroe asked as he blocked my view of the retreating youth.

Hate is such a strong word. Despise you, maybe.

"John? You good?" Monroe repeated.

"Are you?" I sighed, focusing on Monroe and his now ever-present bandanna.

"Better now," he affirmed, looking at the exposed and marred foundation of the town hall. "With Anderson gone a weight has been lifted off my shoulders."

"Good."

I still wondered what Anderson had had over this young man. Whatever it was would be forever buried under ashy rubble.

"Yeah," Monroe added, rubbing his chest in a small circular motion. "Much better now."

"Well, at least now you're the town outlaw."

Monroe smiled, the circular motions slowing.

"Hey, John," Doctor Rawlings parted Bowers and Monroe with his furled umbrella to squeeze my wrist. "Sorry to see you go."

"Sorry about Basia, Doc," I offered, finally voicing my regret.

"Do not let that be your worry, son," Rawlings said with resignation. "It was a mercy that needed to be carried out."

"Doesn't make it easier."

"Our actions rarely do. But we must soldier on. No offense."

"None taken," I said, glancing at Bowers. "Army pukes are okay in small doses."

"When they are not taking hostages," Bowers muttered, looking away. "We going or staying, John?"

"We all would rather you stay," Rawlings offered.

Monroe nodded with his support.

"Not an option, Doc," I begged off. "This was always supposed to be just a stop to get some chow."

"Perhaps. But that meal brought you to us when we needed you most. And perhaps you need us a little bit."

Bowers walked away to the other side of the Amigo, hopped into the passenger bucket seat and slammed the door.

"At any rate, young man," Doctor Rawlings insisted, gripping my wrist with both hands, the umbrella handle draped over his wrist. "You will be missed."

The crowd murmured its approval but backed away a few steps. Except Garrett, of course, who stepped up and shot out his hand.

I shook it.

He tightened his grip for a moment, drawing me in close almost shoulder to shoulder.

"You don't need to leave, John," he spoke softly. "We appreciate all you've done but we want you here because you are family."

"I know," I said, nodding and backing out to arm's length.

He nodded back.

I believed what he said.

He and I had an unbreakable bond.

Shared crucifixion tends to do that to men.

The Gaunt Man insisted on chiming in.

I released Garrett's grip.

Monroe, Rawlings and the others looked on with slight smiles on their lips but grim looks in their eyes.

Offering one last look and nod to everyone gathered, I waved and made my retreat to the steel safety of the Amigo.

When I closed my door Garrett twirled his hand in the air.

Reynolds and Monroe jogged over to the bridge entrance and crawled into the open driver's door windows of two of the designated barricade cars parked side-by-side across the road. The cars roared to life. Reynolds backed off the ramp and Monroe followed.

Lincoln stood behind one of the remaining cars with his M4 at full draw scanning the bridge. Garrett moved over to where he stood and waved us forward.

I slowly drove through the opening. Garrett walked alongside as we made our way through. Once we cleared the barricade, Garrett tapped on the roof and leaned into the open passenger window.

"Wish you were staying, John," he said in earnest.

Bowers stared out the windshield.

Holly leapt up and licked the lawman on the cheek.

"Wish we could stay, Garrett," I said, "but you've come a long way. You all have."

"Figured pleading one last time couldn't hurt."

"I know."

"Godspeed, Marine."

"Be well, Sheriff."

7

On the Road Again

+50 Days – 1237 hours

We had smooth travel and empty roads for about six miles.

One of the good things that Diggs' had done when he was alive was to keep the road from the island to the FRAC dumpsite clear. He had been obsessive that way.

Now the Amigo was parked on the grassy soft shoulder.

Two miles past the burned out Exxon station and the gravel turn that led to the dumpsite we encountered our first real obstacle.

Holly looked at us between the seats before padding around the back seat for the best place to curl up again.

Ahead of us, a set of deep double grooves etched out the spongy dirt in a ragged parallel path before veering sharply to the left back onto the asphalt.

A semi truck and its trailer lay on its side blocking the road.

Bowers and I got out.

Holly looked up one last time as the doors closed, woofing and plopping down on the bench with her nose under her tail.

Bowers scouted the far side of the trailer with his M4 drawn. I pulled out my Glock and stepped around the broken glass and chrome trim littering the pavement toward the front of the rig. Leaves and plastic bags were caught on the cabs undercarriage.

I paused at the edge of the cab's front tires.

Slowing my breath, I swung around the crumbled front bumper.

Clear. Good show.

The Gaunt Man continued to be a spectral annoyance.

I guess leaving island couldn't leave all my ghosts behind.

The road beyond the rig was scattered with the wrecks of over a dozen crumpled cars and several intersecting skid marks.

Inside the cab the dead driver was still buckled in his now horizontal captain's chair. His skin was shrunken and grey, his arms dangling down toward the passenger's seat.

"Clear," Bowers announced as he emerged from the other side of the rig.

He set his rifle against the exposed dashboard and ducked his head inside to grab the maps littered against the passenger door amid other debris shaken loose from the crash.

"Poor bastard," he said. "Can't have too many maps, though."

An itch started tingling at the base of my neck.

Still half inside the cab Bowers turned around and stuffed the map into his fatigues pocket.

The driver's hand grabbed at Bowers' collar.

"Shit!"

I drove the Glock's grip over Bowers' shoulder and into the hanging driver's face. Convoy FRAC's grip withered.

Bowers fell to the asphalt.

"Damn it!" Bowers shouted, picking up the rifle and wildly aiming it at the driver.

"Take a breath," I said, grabbing the barrel.

"Why'd he wait to grab at me, John?" Bowers hitched. "Christ!"

"I'm just that quiet," I hedged.

I had to keep mindful that the undead didn't see me like they saw other people.

"Yeah," Bowers exhaled loudly as he leaned against the light bar on the cab's roof. "Like a fucking church mouse."

8

Wide Open
+50 Days – 1314 hours

The rig and the cars scattered beyond it proved passable with a little time and finesse. We navigated along the rutted soft shoulder with only a few lines of paint scraped off by outcroppings of rocks and an overgrown tree line.

Each mile was dotted with more vehicles, each pulled off onto the shoulder or deeper into the tall grass. Some were abandoned with their doors and trunks wide open and their interior picked clean. Others were sealed tight, serving as tombs for its mummified occupants.

Inside one SUV a torn-faced female slapped her hand against the driver's side window, smearing near-dry blood across the window into an almost opaque artwork.

"Crazy that the roads are as clear as they are," Bowers looked out at the blurs of trees and grass as I was able to speed up on a clear stretch of road. "We had a hell of a time with traffic jams coming south with Wallace."

"I bet."

The speedometer needle held steady at 40 as we clipped along Route 5.

Bowers unfolded the map, making crinkling noises as he snapped it open.

"We could hit 128 to I-95."

"Yeah."

"You seem to communicate even less now that you can talk."

"Maybe."

"Are we heading through Boston?"

Sanchez's words rang through my head.

We didn't get to Atlanta. Not even close.

I was amazed that Professor Taylor had thought his group would have a clear path to Georgia. A Winnebago was a huge disadvantage – great for comfort, horrible for tactical advancement and fuel consumption.

"Well?" Bowers inquired again.

"No," I finally answered. "We'll avoid large metro areas."

"Probably smart. Less FRACs on the road. Less ops for refueling and supplies, though."

"We'll make it work."

9

Yankee Division
+51 Days – 0757 hours

"We are going to need to stop, John," Bowers said, the map resting in his lap.

I glanced at the gas gauge as I steered to the soft shoulder around a line of abandoned cars.

Outside of the occupants trapped inside their American steel tombs only one FRAC had appeared on the road, shambling along a swath of gravel poked through with dried blades of grass.

"Strange we haven't seen any people," Bowers said. "We should've seen somebody on the road by now."

Bowers was right.

"People probably hunkered down and burrowed in."

The Yankee Division highway – Interstate 128 - cut through mostly residential packed areas. The north and south lanes were separated by concrete and grass medians.

Too few cars.

Too few walkers.

Too few people.

Darkening clouds moved towards us. Lightning touched down in the distance. A curtain of rain raced across the pavement and engulfed us, pattering off the windshield and roof.

I turned on the wiper blades.

And slammed on the brakes.

"Christ!" Bowers yelled, his hands rapping against the dashboard as our seatbelts locked.

Holly tumbled into the foot well behind me, barking with annoyance before scrambling back up to the bench.

The wipers swiped across the window in a vain attempt to provide a clear view of the road. As the downpour drenched the dust from the road and flooded the grass into a greener darker hue, the Gaunt Man stood in his dry retro black suit, thin tie and dark sunglasses with his thumb out to be picked up.

He smiled good-naturedly.

Did he expect me to pull off to offer him a lift?

"What the hell, John?" Bowers exclaimed. "What's out there? I almost got whiplash."

I glanced at Bowers and in the rear view mirror at Holly who had popped her head up between the bucket seats for a better look before I peered back out into the deluge.

"Thought I saw something."

"Well, warn a brother. Shit, even my mom threw an arm across me when this type of thing happened."

I let off the brake. The truck coasted past where the Gaunt Man had been hitchhiking.

He had vanished.

The rain pelted the truck. I nudged it forward as the wipers worked desperately to keep the windshield clear.

As we slowly rounded a bend I tapped the brakes again and doused the headlights.

A line of FRACs wandered haphazardly in the road like a mother duck and its ducklings, their heads tilted up to the rain. They staggered across the pavement, bumping into each other and emitting that same warble that they always seemed to make during storms.

The low, but penetrating noise filled my head.

"Damn," Bowers said, seemingly unaware of the FRACs' chorus.

They didn't notice us. The rain bouncing off the car was indistinguishable from the rain smattering off the pavement, effectively masking us from their sight. After a few minutes they made their way over the grassy median to the northbound lanes.

After they found their way to the opposite shoulder I flipped on the lights and got the Amigo moving in a southern direction again.

The walkers quickly faded from the rearview mirror.

A mile later the rain let up and disappeared, too.

10

No Escape

+51 Days – 1213 hours

We discovered why the roads were so clear when we drove off the interstate to the service road. National Guard trucks and Massachusetts State Police cruisers had blocked off each ramp.

We got out and approached the cruisers with weapons drawn, systematically checking each of the sedans' door handles.

The second cruiser was unlocked.

Inside, a shotgun was still snapped into its rack mount. Stacks of cardboard boxes lined the back seat, camping equipment stuffed on top of them.

The keys were still in the ignition.

Bowers turned the key over but the battery was dead.

"Oh well."

He released the truck lock.

The latch clicked and the lid slowly opened.

Bowers raised his M4 and circled to the back bumper.

He lowered his weapon as I came around from the passenger side.

A state trooper lay inside with his service revolver in one hand, a disconnected inside trunk release handle in the other, and a splatter of brains and blood on the interior sidewall liner.

"Guess he should have listened to the recall," Bowers smiled.

I rolled the body towards us. We grabbed a few boxes of ammunition, two heavy-duty flashlights, and a first aid kit. I peeled the trooper's fingers back, snapping them off as I removed his service revolver from his death grip. I rolled the officer onto his back again and gently closed the trunk.

This steel tomb was as good as any.

The paint on the trunk hood was bloody and scratched away

with several deep parallel lines.

"Christ," Bowers said, tracing one of the series of marks with his fingers. "Poor bastard. Guess he thought the trunk would be FRAC proof."

"It was."

Bowers took another swipe with his fingers across the flaking enamel.

"I guess it was at that."

A quick scout of the other vehicles proved less unsettling and less fruitful. We returned to the Amigo and offloaded the supplies into the trunk.

Holly's head stuck out the open passenger window with her tail wagging. Bowers pushed her snout back inside to get into the passenger seat.

We backed down the exit ramp and continued west.

11

Fill 'er Up

+51 Days – 1429 hours

We left Boston far to our south.

The quiet of I-128 was unsettling, but the lack of activity made for quicker travel.

"We stopping, John?"

The gas gauge needle had just dipped past the one-eighth mark.

"Yeah."

"As least this looks promising," Bowers said, pointing to the red sign with the yellow clamshell. Several other signs had assured us that there was a gas station at this exit.

Unfortunately, the off ramp to that station was impassable. One car had careened into the outside guardrail. The next sedan had tried to swing to the right but only managed to wedge itself between the bumper of the first car and the inside guardrail.

"Maybe I spoke too soon," Bowers muttered.

"Have faith."

I drove under the overpass and swung around to the on ramp. We crawled past a police cruiser parked across the intersection with a Ford F350 pickup T-boned into it.

"What was that you said about faith?" Bowers questioned. "Christ."

A trooper was crushed from the waist down between the cruiser's passenger door and the truck, pressed against the crumpled grill with his gun still in his grip.

Several shots had been fired into the truck's windshield. The driver's bloody head congealed against the steering wheel, his eyes staring out the cracked side window.

A female passenger clung to him with bullet holes through her shoulder and temple.

The hardcover flatbed top was propped open on its hydraulic arms, showing scraps of supplies long gone.

I squeezed the Amigo past the concrete barricade and the truck toward the Shell station. A sign for an Exxon station loomed from the other side of the overpass.

My stomach soured.

Poor Sebastian.

Shut up.

And Basia.

I pushed the thoughts away.

We pulled into the Shell station. A mix of faded asphalt and gravel surrounded a single white concrete structure with two garage bays.

We parked close to the refueling ports. A burned out sedan with melted tires sat as an empty hunk of metal next to one of the ports. The nearest cover had exploded off, leaving black scars and a depression around the opening. The ground was still damp from the rain in the crater. Large zigzagging cracks from the blast radiated across the pavement.

"Should we try the Exxon?"

Poor Sebastian.

Fortunately, the other two tanks were intact.

"We'll try from the other unleaded port."

"Okedoke." Bowers got out with his M4 and scanned the woods and hill behind the service garage.

A steady chirp filled the air.

"I hate cicadas," Bowers added.

I opened the trunk and took out a length of rubber hose, a pump and a crowbar.

The metal cover popped off easily enough. I ran the rubber hose down into the tank. The rest of the siphon pump assembly went quickly and, once turned on with another hose fed into the Amigo's gas tank, we were in business with the transfer of fuel.

All the while Holly tracked my movements from the passenger window.

The screech of the cicadas became unbearably loud in my ears, making my head buzz and my neck itch.

I pinned the hose into the Amigo's gas tank with the port cover, grabbed two empty gas cans from the trunk and prepped them.

The itch got worse.

I rubbed it away.

"Clear," Bowers announced, taking a quick look through the oily windows of the closed garage. He leaned against the cinderblock wall, checking his six before looking out to the road.

With the Amigo's tank filled, I crimped the siphon hose and dropped the end of it into the first of the extra gas cans.

The gasoline slowly poured in, splashing off the plastic bottom. Fumes assaulted me as the vapors escaped from the can. After filling the first container, I repeated the process with the second.

I made sure the gas containers were strapped in.

The itch in my neck was unbearable.

I glanced up at Bowers who continued to look out to the road.

Movement.

"Down," I yelled as I hurled the crowbar at him.

He dropped to the deck.

Thunk!

The hook of the crowbar embedded into a FRAC's forehead.

It stumbled into Bowers, collapsing on top of him.

"Christ," Bowers pushed off the walker.

I walked over and extended my hand.

"I'm good," he said, letting out a long sighing whistle. Bowers put a hand to the wall for balance and grabbed the stock of his rifle. He checked his corners, gave me a thumbs-up and leaned his forehead against his weapon.

"You got a spidey-sense now?" Bowers asked.

I put a boot on the FRAC's face and dislodged the crowbar from its skull, which seemed nothing more than a softening melon.

"Just good vision," I shrugged.

"And aim," Bowers added. "Don't forget aim."

12

Oil and Water

+51 Days – 1955 hours

Ninety miles west of our fill-up the Amigo's engine started to sputter intermittently. Seventeen miles more and the engine stalled. No more than a mile later we coasted to a stop as the engine seized up for good.

It was dead.

Like the world you live in.

We all exited the SUV. Holly promptly raced off to the grass at the edge of the shoulder to relieve herself. Bowers popped the hood and stared at the engine with his arms folded. Holly came back and plopped herself down at the Sergeant's feet.

I pulled one of the spare gas tanks from the truck and opened it. The fuel had started to separate.

Shit.

"Water in the gas, right?" Bowers asked from the front.

"Yes."

"I guess the explosion at the tanks cracked the tank."

"Yeah."

Bowers dropped the hood, lay out and consulted his map while I put the gas container back. I scanned the empty road before joining the Sergeant.

"Looks like we're close to Worcester," he said, pointing to a spot on the map. "It's a somewhat built-up area but we may have to chance it."

"Yeah."

"Sleep in the car tonight and bug out early tomorrow?"

"That'll work."

"Glad you approve."

An angry but beautiful red setting sun raged before extinguishing behind the horizon, the dusk turning the trees and road a dirty, bloody plum.

"You taking first?"

"Yeah." I replied.

I tapped the handle of the machete, patted down the comfortable weight of the Glock, and grabbed the spare M4 from the trunk. Cradling the rifle in my arms, I followed the broken white line for fifty meters.

Sounds of crickets and cicadas filled the air, their songs competing and layering into a sometime synchronous chatter. At least this time the buzzing wasn't loud on the interior walls of my head.

The purple light dissipated into the dark gray monotones of night.

Standing in the center of the westbound lane, the black enveloped me. It veiled over the holes in my heart, even if only temporarily.

Such a sullen fellow, aren't you?

The Gaunt Man nearly touched my left shoulder. He had put away his sunglasses from earlier in the day. In spite of the dark, he continued to have a luminous charge to his skin.

Why so serious?

"Leave me alone," I muttered.

I would never abandon you to your own misery and self-destruction. You should know better.

The road to the west was now empty.

The Gaunt Man had disappeared again.

Turning back to the Amigo I came face to face with him, nearly bumping into him.

Was he tangible?

I took a swing at his too-pale, too toothy grinning face.

Like the Cheshire Cat of Wonderland, he had evaporated into the ether.

13

Vague Shadows

+52 Days – 0654 hours

My shadow slowly materialized and lengthened on the asphalt in front of my crossed legs as the cold sun crept up. Another day where the earth continues to obliviously spin.

Another pale and barely there shadow lengthened beside me.

"You didn't wake me for watch," Bowers said as he approached. "You didn't sleep at all?"

"No."

"I'm starting to think that I should have stayed under those pallets behind the diner," Bowers said, stretching out the tightness in his back.

Holly padded up to my right, her nails clicking on the pavement. She pushed her snout under my arm, burrowing her way onto my lap. She yawned before curling up and burying her face under my knee.

I stared to the west as I scratched her behind her ear.

The road was empty for as far as the highest crest of the slightly rolling hills.

The itch had started again, making the emptiness grate on my nerves.

"Check the map, Bowers. We need a different way around."

"Sir. Yes, sir."

14

Overpass

+52 Days – 1012 hours

"You still itchy, John?" Bowers asked.

"A bit."

We stood in the middle of an overpass.

A half-mile away several dozen FRACs bumped into each other in small clusters. They did not all move in the same direction but did seem to have a fluid pattern to their movement, like several flocks of birds in flight.

I scratched at my neck.

"Won't be able get through there," I said as Bowers looked through the binoculars beside me.

Be careful what you wish for.

We were too exposed to take the walkers on directly. Moving into the residential areas offered more protection, but had its own set of problems.

Poor sightlines.

Threats of ambush.

"Why do they pool together like that?" Bowers wondered. "Safety in numbers?"

"Don't know."

I tapped the trigger guard on the M4.

Holly stuck her snout through the concrete overpass railing, sniffing the air. A low warbling hummed in her throat.

"Don't worry," I said to her. "We'll stay on the main roads for as long as we can."

15

A Murder of Crows

+52 Days – 1347 hours

The plan to stay on the interstate was quickly abandoned as FRACs started to split off from the main group in our general direction.

A whitewashed concrete wall loomed to our right on the service road, lined with landscaped trees and shrubbery. Black mulch packed around the bases and inside the edged borders. An orange city truck sat on the service drive shoulder, a green tarp covering the bed.

Bowers drew up his M4 and moved to the passenger side. I shouldered my rifle, drew the Glock and side stepped to the driver's door.

The cab was empty of man or monster.

I opened the door.

Holly jumped up into the cab and sniffed around the floor mats, her tail wagging.

The steering column cover had been removed, the wiring exposed. From the charring on the housing it looked like an amateur carjacker had tried to hotwire it.

"John."

I backed up.

"Grab a corner."

We pulled back the tarp from the cab halfway down the bed.

"Christ!" Bowers abruptly dropped the tarp, covering his mouth and nose with the crook of his elbow.

The bed was filled with rotting bodies.

Each was complete with a bullet through the temple.

A fluttering.

Crows cawed and landed on the roof of the cab. They paced

and shifted their weight, eyeing the carrion in the bed.

Bowers shooed them away. The crows lighted for a few moments before returning to their perch, flapping their wings and pecking the air at him.

"Stupid birds."

Bowers went to the passenger door and opened it.

Holly jumped out with a bark.

"Damn it," Bowers exclaimed. "Stupid dog."

Holly raced to the line of trees. She weaved between the trunks of a grove of pines. Behind where she squatted to pee, a series of faint maroon blossoms stained the wall. Each was at roughly two meters from the ground.

.357 hollow point shot from close range.

I looked back at the corpses in the back of the truck bed. No blindfolds. No restraints.

It's almost like they wanted to be shot, isn't it?

Holly finished her business and returned to sniffing at the bushes, oblivious of the fact that the Gaunt Man stood behind her in the center of the killing field.

"What's up, Walken?"

I whistled twice.

Holly bound through the lengthening and slightly dried grass of the lawn, leaving the stained wall behind her.

The murder of black crows cawed insistently at us, anxious for us to be away from the now open buffet.

"Nothing. Let's move."

16

Near Dark

+52 Days – 1901 hours

Another day bled out, casting us into a dying bloody hue.

After leaving the Amigo behind, we had managed to hump over twenty miles. The frequent fruitless stops to find other transportation had slowed our progress dramatically.

The road had been relatively FRAC-free though, with only three undead to dispatch with a quick machete blow to the head.

We came up onto an entry drive. Several cars were parked in a haphazard fashion blocking the inbound and outbound lanes on both sides of a gatehouse. Both drawbars had been cracked off their posts. A flowered curb with a low curved brick wall and raised golden cursive letters welcomed us to The Howard Estates.

Bowers went to the gatehouse.

"Clear."

The cars were also empty.

"Clear here," I called back.

We moved side-by-side to a wooded road curving to the left.

Holly trotted ahead of us.

I turned on the tactical light under the Glock. Bowers did the same with his M4. Our beams bounced off the trees and asphalt in the dimming light of the end of the day.

No movement.

After 250 meters, the road opened up into a roundabout. It circled a dry fountain, with two offshoot streets leading farther into the subdivision. The road to the right led to higher ground with less overgrown terrain.

"Double-time, Bowers," I pointed.

We jogged up the crest. Stopping at the top we both dropped to one knee.

Amstel Drive leveled off and ended in a cul-de-sac. Four large brick homes sat back from the street with cobblestone drives and elaborate spiked wrought iron fences topping brick half-walls.

No signs of life.

No lights.

No sounds.

No barricades on the doors or covering the windows.

I chirped to get Bowers' attention.

"What do you think?" he asked.

"It's a cliché," I replied.

"Too quiet?"

"Yeah."

"We go in this one here?" he asked, tilting his head to the house closest to us.

"Sure."

It was as good a scout as any of the others.

I rolled my neck to chase away the knot that was forming.

It's been a long day.

The driveway gate was secured on chains and rails run through an electric motor. Bowers tried the gate but it wouldn't budge. I pointed to the left side of the gate.

Bowers shouldered his rifle and shimmied up between an oak tree and the jutted out brick detail of the wall. At the top, he swung around his weapon and shone his tactical light into the yard.

He splayed out three fingers then pointed them to the right. Crouching at the top, he waved his light back and forth in a circular motion.

"Yeah," Bowers whispered down, "we got three deadheads coming in from the southeast."

I could have told you that.

I nodded to the Sergeant.

Bowers cautiously straddled his way over the wrought iron spikes at the top of the brick wall and jumped out of sight.

I climbed up without the assistance of the tree trunk.

Holly stared at me from the driveway. She let out a low warning grumble.

"Stay put, dog."

I left her behind and dropped down onto the property next to Bowers.

The FRACs Bowers had mentioned sped up their staggering pursuit.

I pulled out my machete. Bowers drew his knife. The trio crossed the driveway, one of them stumbling a little bit as her heels slid on the cobblestones.

I swung the blade into the closest FRAC.

It sunk into her cheek past her ear, cleanly cutting into the line of ruined mascara that had run down her face. As I pulled out the machete, the FRAC's earlobe and dangling pearl earring fell away as her body dropped.

Bowers drove his knife into the head of the second female walker. She stopped and looked up at his wrist. He pulled out the blade, her blond hair coming up with it.

"Shit!"

He shook the blade trying to dislodge the hair.

Bowers was too distracted to remember the third FRAC.

A man with a sports jacket, polo shirt and faded jeans lunged at the Sergeant. I swung the machete deep into the back of the preppie FRAC's neck. The momentum of the blade caused his head to topple forward revealing most of his neck as he collapsed into the grass at Bowers' feet.

Bowers skittered back, still trying to shake the clump of hair off the knife. I grabbed the hair and pulled it off, tossing it at its former owner.

The Sergeant dragged out ragged deep breaths as we walked to the driveway.

Holly watched us from the gate for a moment before cleanly slipping through the vertical posts. She padded over to the hair and sniffed it. After a growl she trotted after us.

17

House Hunting

+52 Days – 1933 hours

Bowers stood lookout on the driveway.

I picked the garage door lock easily enough.

The interior was freshly painted and empty save for some new lawn and gardening equipment. The floor was sealed in a light gray coating without a drop of oil marring its pristine appearance.

The three of us moved inside.

I locked the door behind us and Bowers moved along the wall to a second door. He tried the knob and gave me a thumbs-up to join him at the door.

He gave me a silent three count, opened the door and rushed inside to the right. I moved in beside him and turned left into a kitchen complete with prepping island and an alcove dining area.

Our lights bounced out the walls.

"Clear," Bowers whispered, coming up beside me with a pat on the shoulder.

Two archways led to the rest of the house.

Bowers flanked right to a formal dining area.

I went straight through into a cathedral ceilinged vestibule with tall oaken double doors. On the opposite wall was another door – an interior one – and carpeted stairs that lead up to the second floor.

I opened the door to discover a master bedroom and bathroom. Both were empty.

I backed out and started up the stairs just as Bowers finished his first floor sweep.

"Basement," he confirmed, shining his tactical light down the enclosed set of stairs.

He quickly disappeared, swallowed by its darkness.

The beam of a spinning broken flashlight came to mind.

I pushed the memory away.

Climbing the steps I came to a landing linking a room three steps up to my left with a mezzanine and a hallway to my right.

The door to my left was open.

Moving inside, I checked the corners.

The room was empty except for a fully made bed and desk.

I backed out and crossed the mezzanine that offered a view of the vestibule and the formal living room below.

The other hallway revealed two more empty bedrooms with a bathroom between them. They were all furnished but unused and empty.

I returned to the first floor.

Bowers stood in the main hallway.

It's staged," he said. "Maybe it's a model home."

I shined my light on a modern decorative table next to the front double doors. Several brochures and a standup display were arranged on its glass top.

The Sergeant grabbed one.

"Phase 1 of the Howard Estates – Wi-Fi – 8-Zone sprinkler system. All stainless steel appliances," he read aloud. "Deluxe living, John. Yep, model home."

"You called it."

We went into the formal but modern living area, complete with a fireplace rising up two stories to the pitched ceiling. On either side were tall narrow windows. In the center of the space was a corner sectional couch with another glass topped coffee table.

Holly had already curled up in the corner of the couch with her head on one of the accent pillows.

"Looks pretty safe to me," Bowers determined.

"No food or supplies."

"True. But all the sleep we could ask for."

We turned off our tactical lights, casting the space into darkness.

Maybe sleep would come.

If Holly's snores were any indication it was certainly possible.

18

Model

+53 Days – 0341 hours

The living room was still dark, the sun not yet ready to rise.

Luckily, one of the byproducts of reincarnation is having excellent night vision.

The sectional couch had nearly enveloped me with its too soft cushions. Unfortunately, they still failed to take me to a more dreamlike state.

But you don't really need sleep nowadays.

Bowers' backpack was still against the couch but he was gone. He had decided to go to one of the bedrooms to sleep to get away from the log sawing of Holly.

I grabbed the M4, headed to the kitchen sink and turned the faucet by habit.

Nothing came out.

Damn model home.

"So I'm stronger, see at night, heal faster, and invisibility to FRACs," I muttered, "but lose the ability to sleep?"

Nice list of abilities. Seems to be an excellent trade, in my humble opinion.

I ignored the voice.

Through the window over the sink, I had a good view of a grove of landscaped Japanese maples surrounded by curved edging and black mulch. The recent hot weather and lack of water had burned the needles and leaves.

Hell of a night, isn't it?

The Gaunt Man leaned against the stainless steel refrigerator, absently picking at his nails and looking at me with an oversized grin.

A fine place you and the Sergeant have decided to play house.

51

I drew up the M4 at the specter. Only the brushed steel of the refrigerator remained at the end of my sights.

That won't do you any good, John.

The Gaunt Man sat at the breakfast table, leafing through one of the model home brochures. He wet his thumb with his pointed tongue and turned the page.

Did you know this house sits on two acres with an eight-zone sprinkler system and motion sensor security lights? It's all very impressive.

I left the Gaunt Man to his reading and went back to the couch. Holly continued to snore.

Plopping down on the couch I closed my eyes.

You can't run away from who you are, John.

I opened my eyes to the pale man with his dark suit at the other end of the sectional. His suit sleeves had started to wear at the elbows and threads had started to fray at the cuffs. He petted Holly's belly but she paid him no mind, continuing to snore.

Did you really think that what happened on the island was a fluke? You certainly cannot think that you will ever be what you were. You came back from a glorious death –

He blinked out and reappeared facing the mantle with his arms outstretched. He spun around in a quick fluid movement.

– better than you were before. Better. Stronger! Faster!

His last words boomed off the angled cathedral ceiling.

He smiled at me with something akin to compassion, or maybe empathy.

"Go away," I said. "I need to sleep."

That's unlikely. You seem in fine health.

"That's up for debate."

Well, all except that itch and buzzing you carry around.

I pressed my thumb and forefinger firmly against the bridge of my nose. A dull pain traveled to my eyes at the inside corners. When that subsided I open my eyes again.

The Gaunt Man was gone, leaving me with only Holly for

company.

Was I ever going to be the same?

Probably not.

The Gaunt Man's dissipating voice whispered.

Maybe I was just slipping further into insanity.

The dread of that thought dug its fingers deep into me as I sat in the dark waiting for Bowers and the sun to wake up.

19

First Light
+53 Days – 0613 hours

I sat in the same breakfast nook chair that my imaginary friend had occupied a few hours earlier.

Soft steps came from Bowers descending the stairs.

"Sorry to have bailed on you," he said as he came in from the foyer. "I had to get away from your dog. She snores too loud for me to sleep."

Holly still slept on the couch, her deep breathing faint but unmistakable.

"See? That mutt is a menace."

The mutt, as he said, is certainly a menace.

Holly was one of the heroes of Rainier Island. She deserved as much rest as she wanted.

Bowers looked at his watch.

"Another thirty before full sun up. Should we bother looking through the other houses?"

The brochure for Phase 1 of the Howard Estates said that the move-in dates could be immediate but scheduled for late August of this year.

"No. Be ready to move in 5."

Bowers went to retrieve his backpack from the foyer, passing the still snoring Holly.

"Get up, you damn dog."

Holly kept her eyes closed but started a low growl.

I got up and looked through the drawers under the kitchen counter. Each was empty and spotless. Bowers looked through the knick-knacks on the shelves. He hefted one brass globe but eventually returned it to its spot.

"Not much to take away," he ran a finger across the black

lacquer. "Except for maybe some dust and allergies."

Outside the landscaped pine shrubs and dried out Japanese maples clung to their last few leaves. It was a battle that would be lost in the next day or two. They had seemed much more vibrant in the dead of night.

Death is always more attractive in the night.

Otherwise the yard was empty.

"Let's go," I ordered.

Holly jumped off the couch and padded to my side. Bowers took one more look around the living room. He ran his fingers across the six-burner stainless range as he cut through the kitchen.

"Goodbye, home I could never afford in life," he sighed.

"Let's go, Sergeant."

We went through the garage, shutting the mudroom door behind us. Bowers took point. We drew up our weapons as we approached the outer garage door. After a mouthed count of three he turned the doorknob and went out.

"Whoa!" from new voices. "Whoa!"

I cleared the doorframe to the driveway, my M4 leading the way.

Holly swept past my leg, barking her head off.

"Hey. Don't shoot. We talk."

A woman stood on the cobblestone drive with her hands up, a .38 Special revolver hanging off her thumb. To her left a man stood with an arm around a second young woman's waist, wielding a knife in his free hand. Both were decked out in fatigued cargo pants. He had on an oversized University of Massachusetts T-shirt. She wore a peasant blouse.

The leader with the .38 stared at us, the pistol still hanging off a silver ringed thumb. In fact all her fingers and other thumb were adorned with silver rings. With her hands raised above her head, her T-shirt pulled up enough to reveal a swirling tattoo at her waist. With curly brownish-blond hair, blue eyes and artsy glasses she did not appear to be the overly aggressive type.

Regardless, Bowers and I continued to keep our weapons up.

"Who are you?" Bowers asked.

"Does it matter?" the leader said. "At least we're not dead heads."

"Can we move this along, Jude?" the tattooed and pierced male half of the couple interjected.

"Stay the course, Lenny," Jude said. "Sorry. Can I put my arms down, please?"

"Yes," I said. "Where'd you come from?"

"Originally?" Jude asked, putting her revolver through her belt. "Or today?"

"Today, for starters."

"Main office."

"Why didn't we think of that?" Bowers said, finally dropping the barrel of his rifle toward the cobblestones.

"Not much left there, man," the tattooed Lenny added.

"We did find some stale chocolate chip cookies and two gallons of spring water," Lenny's equally tattooed girlfriend chimed in. "Wasn't anything else to scrounge."

"Shut up, April," he hissed while pulling her in tight.

"You shut up, Len," she replied with emphasis on the 'you', putting her head on his chest.

"We've been crashing there a couple nights," Jude continued. "Were going to check out the model homes today before we head out."

Holly padded over to Jude, sat on one of her cowboy boots and leaned her face against her leg.

"Hey, fuzzy face."

"Where you heading?" I asked.

"Don't know," Jude shrugged. "West, I guess. You?"

"Sounds about right."

20

Lunch Break

+53 Days – 1121 hours

One dog, one Marine, one soldier, one sarcastic woman and two early twenty-somethings walked in a general westward direction along I-128.

Sounds like the start of a bad joke.

Bowers had been quick to ask Jude and her group to join us at the Howard Estates house. I think he may have been worried that I would have left them behind if he hadn't taken the initiative.

Was I that far gone?

Not yet.

More cars cluttered the road.

Bowers and Holly took point as we approached an overpass, weaving between the increasing traffic jam of cars. The Sergeant checked out each interior, shaking his head each time he finished.

Jude and her group walked cautiously between the cars while I covered our rear. Jude tapped the roof of each vehicle she passed. Lenny and April held hands as they squeezed between a sedan and a minivan. I gritted my teeth and held my tongue, knowing their intertwined hands would be useless for those first crucial seconds if trouble struck fast.

Tired of watching the lovebirds, I went back to walking backward. The trail of vehicles petered off about one hundred meters from our position. Coolers and luggage were still tied down on minivan roofs and sedan trunks but the interiors were eerily empty.

Where did they all go, John?

Hell if I knew. The itching had returned.

"John," Bowers shouted from the hood of a station wagon in the intersection.

We all rushed to where Bowers stood under the darkened bank of turn arrows and stoplights. I looked off in the direction that the Sergeant was zeroing in with the binoculars.

"Can you see it?" Bowers asked.

I could see what was ahead of us as clear as if were happening thirty meters away.

"What is it?" Jude stepped on her tiptoes for a better view.

"People," Bowers responded.

"Explains the empty cars," I answered.

"What are they doing?" April asked.

"I'm sure they were eating at some point," Bowers speculated.

"And now?" Lenny chimed in.

"Now it just looks like a crap ton of FRACs," the Sergeant mused.

21

Hostess

+53 Days – 1203 hours

We watched the FRACs from the relative safety of an embankment fifty meters west of the overpass where Bowers had spotted the herd. They were a stationary group with only a few ambitious walkers staggering around the perimeter.

"There must be over a hundred dead heads," April said. "Why are they all clumped together down there?"

"FRACs," Lenny snickered. "Dead heads is a much better name."

"You think?" April asked.

"Yeah," Lenny confirmed. "Especially when you say it."

"Gag me with a spoon," Bowers whispered as he leaned in beside me. "What do you think?"

"Looks like a last stand," I answered both Bowers and April.

"What do you mean?" Bowers asked, looking over the mosh pit of rotten corpses.

I scratched at the back of my neck.

"Look at the ends," I finally said.

A semi trailer had been parked across the road, separating us from the herd. It was outfitted with the newer style side skirts that kept stray FRACs from squirming under the rig. Another rig had been jack-knifed across the road another quarter mile away. Both vehicles effectively boxed the walkers on the road at both ends, with the tall concrete divider for the eastbound lanes and the steep incline up to our position keeping them pinned in on the sides.

"They lured them inside," Jude speculated.

In the midst of the herd was a Hostess and Wonder Bread delivery panel truck with its sliding driver's door and roll up rear doors wide open. Its white sides were smeared with crimson paint.

Probably animal blood to start with, I would think.

The man in the black suit's voice was a hive of angry bees, dripping with sickly sweet honey.

At least, that is, until they got hold of the drivers.

Several of the FRACs wore National Guard uniforms. One had his rifle still slung across his back although his sidearm holster was empty. The rest was a coalition of every creed, race, age and walk of life. Amazing the solidarity the undead found after death.

"Whatever they baited them with, it wasn't enough to keep the dead heads distracted for long." Jude commented. "It's a shame."

"Better them than us," April said. "Right, Lenny?"

"Hell, yeah," her boyfriend agreed.

"As fascinating as watching these things is," Bowers offered, "I assume we are going far around this mess?"

"Hell, yeah," I answered, mimicking Lenny.

22

Intersection

+53 Days – 1957 hours

By nightfall we had traveled another twenty-one miles.

Jude and her group had kept up without complaint but none of us had been talkative since encountering the roadway pit of FRACs. We hadn't seen another walker since then. Coming across abandoned vehicles to pillage became more the exception than the rule.

"We need to be inside soon, John," Bowers said after walking with me in silence for a few minutes. "Ooh rah?"

"Ooh rah, Sergeant."

Jude, Lenny and April trailed back a bit as we approached another cross street blocked with a three-car accident. Holly ran off to the high grasses again, searching for butterflies, Butterfingers, or whatever she could scrounge up. The only visible part of her was the tip of her white tail.

"Whatcha think about those three?"

"Jury's still out," I said. "Eyes front, Sergeant."

"I see it, John."

The middle sedan's gas tank had ignited violently. All that was left was a frame and melted tires. The station wagon that had smashed into the back of the sedan had caught some of the flames, its engine compartment blackened. The Prius that the sedan had collided with was in better shape, escaping most of the explosion but crumpled through to the rear doors with its rear tires angled out on a broken axle.

Remind you of anything?

"Let's go."

No?

Jude's group came up on the wreckage, Lenny and April

leaning in to check out the gutted steel.

"No casualties," Lenny commented. "That would have been cool."

"Must have walked away from it," April speculated.

Sure it doesn't remind you of something?

I left them behind to gawk.

I thought back to Rainier Island, to Sebastian, and to a certain patch of scorched earth.

Bowers stood off at the curb with his rifle up in the direction we had come.

"What?"

"I don't know," he replied. "I've just been a little jumpy since the mosh pit, I guess"

"We're good," I offered, not a twinge of an itch on my neck.

"How do you know?" he asked, emphasizing the 'you'.

"Intuition," I shrugged. "Let's get that shelter you wanted."

I patted him on the shoulder and whistled for Holly.

She popped up her head, mulch stuck to her snout and a candy wrapper between her lips. With a quick bark, the wrapper fell out and she bolted over. Instead of stopping she jumped up, popped off my thigh and landing neatly on her feet.

"Weirdo." Bowers shook his head.

"Neat trick," Jude added.

"We going yet?" Lenny asked, apparently bored with the carnage.

23

Site

+53 Days – 2157 hours

At the corner of a never-to-be-built strip mall and gas station plaza, a construction site office trailer served as a reasonable roof over our heads.

The drawers to the upright cabinets were open. Folders and documents were still inside, but plenty of papers and blueprints lay scattered across the threadbare carpet. Bowers and I dragged two of the more empty units in front of the door.

There was a laminated particleboard desk with a worn black leather office chair behind it. April and Lenny sat together on an aluminum desk next to it. A long-empty water cooler stood in the corner.

"Jude?" Bowers asked from the barricade at the broken door. "Did you have a destination in mind?"

Jude sat on a ratty plaid couch scratching Holly under her left ear while the dog rested her head on Jude's thigh. The mutt exhaled loudly, licking her chops and closing her eyes.

"Not really sure," Jude replied. "I'd like to say we've got a foolproof plan, but we're just moving until we stumble upon someplace that looks right. I'm sure it's a shit plan compared to what you guys are doing."

"You would think," Bowers chuckled. "I'm sure John has a plan, but I'm just along for the ride. I couldn't stay where we were."

"How come?"

Bowers glanced at me and I shook my head so only he saw. It wasn't my place to reveal his history to the general populace. That was on him. I went back to sharpening my machete on an oiled whetstone, using small circular patterns that produced a

63

comfortable rhythmic grinding sound and a razor sharp edge.

"Truth is," the Sergeant swallowed, "I was part of a decimated Army unit. We were a mess. Our superiors had all turned tail or were killed. Generals disappeared. No chain of command.

"We'd never trained for anything like this. I'm just a reservist. I ain't a hardened warrior like John. It was probably the worst thing we could've done by rushing in to control the situation. Killed more of us than we killed of them."

"So what happened?" Jude asked.

"One day a Lieutenant Colonel comes through the smoke, shoots a walker in the back of the head on the way into our perimeter, and tells us to mount up."

"Well, that's good."

"You would think so, wouldn't you?" Bowers adjusted his rifle and gazed out at the dirt-covered site. "He was a bad commander. Made us do bad things. Bad things that haunt me."

"We have all done shit to stay alive," Jude empathized. "It'll get better."

"It's a little better now that I don't have to look at the people who suffered under us, but I still have a lot of penance to do."

Jude moved her hand to Holly's belly. The dog twisted onto her back for a better angle.

"You from the same unit, John?"

I stopped sharpening my blade.

"Nah. Marines. Discharged."

"Two of my brothers were in the Marines. We lost Matt in combat in the Saudi desert a few years ago. Andy is still out there somewhere, I'm sure. He was stationed in Germany."

"My condolences," I said.

"Just the two brothers?" Bowers asked.

"I had four in all."

"Had?"

"Yeah," Jude swallowed. "The two youngest had to be put down. My parents, too."

"Sorry," Bowers offered after a much too long and heavy silence.

"We march on, Sgt. Bowers," she shrugged. "Some things are just unavoidable."

"Just like Lenny," April giggled.

"Maybe I'm that good, baby," Lenny promised.

Unavoidable. Like the plague.

I snickered to myself, in spite of the poor taste of who said it.

24

Inspection

+54 Days – 0330 hours

Another night spent in a less than hospitable environment.

The darkness in the construction site office trailer deepened into black in the shadowed corners, even with my heightened vision.

Black IS the new black, you know.

It was time to relieve Bowers.

Jude was curled up with Holly on one of the sofa cushions, both using her jacket as a pillow. The other cushion was on the floor used by the spooning Lenny and April. They never seemed to be more than a couple inches from each other.

I went to the two steel cabinets that blocked the doorway where we had set up post.

Bowers was gone.

I must have dozed off. A few days had passed since that had happened. It was actually a relief to know that my body still required some downtime.

Grabbing my M4, I climbed over the cabinets and dropped to the steel mesh steps outside to start my search. Two unevenly spaced boot prints led away from the bottom steps, heading deeper into the construction site.

I turned on the weapon's light and followed the trail, rolling my shoulders to loosen the knots.

Skirting a huge pile of dirt and gravel, I kept the light down on the prints. Halfway around I found the owner of the boots.

It wasn't Bowers.

A FRAC in army fatigues turned toward the flash of light.

He stared at the beam, opening his jaw to let out a gurgled moan.

I clicked off the light.

FRACtigues lost interest, stopping his moan and returning to his previous aimless state.

I shouldered the M4 and pulled the machete.

As I stepped closer I was struck by the stench of his rot. Not a meat smell but more of an earthy composting deterioration. Up close I could see that his eyes were filled with burst blood vessels, the flecks of gold and red nearly lost behind the clouds of extensive milky cataracts. He snapped at the air as if he sensed I was there but unsure as to where. The blackened gums held strangely white teeth, the gums receding after death to make them look more menacing and feral.

His camo jacket's name tape said he was Brenner. His rank insignia designated him as PFC. He cocked his head and looked at something over my shoulder. Brenner clicked his jaws closed, a ticking sound emanating from his throat.

More clicks joined in.

The hairs on the back of my neck stood up.

I sidestepped and clicked on the light.

Dozens of FRACs stared at me from a shallow pit. Their heads were cocked in the same way as the PFC's, each mimicking his clicks.

The pit was barely a meter deep but it was enough to keep the FRACs corralled.

For the moment.

The ticking rose in pitch, a cross between a symphony of cicadas and popping bubble wrap.

In the middle of the crowd stood the Gaunt Man.

He pinched his trousers and pulled up one pant leg. He was wearing the same military-issued boots as Private First FRAC Brenner next to me.

Boots - so much more practical for traveling. Don't you think?

The FRACs moved in an agitated state around the Gaunt Man. He raised his hands and waved them around as if he was a conductor of his own grotesque stage full of marionettes.

Those wingtips were definitely the wrong choice. I feel bad that I have not been able to catch up to you until now.

He stomped the ground with his new footwear. The FRACS shuffled, kicking up smoky swirls of dirt.

A blade swung into Brenner's skull with a wet crack, spraying my cheek with blood.

The force dropped Brenner to the ground with Bowers landing on top of him.

"What the hell, John?" Bowers whispered as he pulled out the blade and got to his feet. "Why you letting these things get that close? It was practically on top of you!"

I aimed the light at the walkers reaching out at Bowers from the pit – and me by association. The Gaunt Man was gone, having made a hasty exit.

"Damn. No wonder you were distracted." Bowers ran his free hand through his hair. "Going in?"

"No reason. They can't get out," I answered. "We're bugging out in the morning anyway."

"Rain runoff could cut out an incline for them," Bowers speculated. "Plus, what happens if other people like Jude come by?"

"Point taken."

I gripped the machete handle tighter and swung it down at the closest FRAC.

25

Sideways

+54 Days – 0503 hours

"You okay, John?" Bowers asked as we walked back to the trailer.

"Yeah. Why?"

"I don't know, man," he commented. "Maybe because a dead head nearly took a bite out of you without you even realizing it."

"I got distracted by the ones in the pit," I lied. "You like 'dead heads' instead of FRACs now?"

"Has a ring to it."

"I'm sure it does."

"Gotta be more careful." Bowers shook his head and changed the subject, wiping specks of viscera off his arm. "You're leading this charge. I'm just following along."

"Isn't that what got you in trouble in the first place?" I asked, regretting my words as soon as they left my mouth.

Bowers stopped short. His finger was on the trigger of his M4 just a little too tight, his knuckle a little too white even in the dark. Thankfully, his rifle barrel was still aimed at the dirt.

I opened my mouth to apologize.

"Jude, I found them," Lenny called out from the blocked doorway.

"Yeah," Bowers smiled at Lenny. "We had a nest of dead heads to clear out. It's all good now."

"Crap," Lenny replied. "How many?"

"A couple dozen," Bowers replied.

Jude poked her head through the doorway. "A little heads up would have been advisable, sergeants. You aren't the only ones out here. Just sayin'."

"Sorry, mom," Bowers said, his smile widening.

"Better be," Jude responded, matching his grin. "You might want to wipe some of that blood off you, too, while you're at it.

"April!" she yelled back into the trailer. "Wake your ass up. The military's back and we're heading out."

"The military's here?" I heard April say faintly. "Finally."

"Not the government, Einstein. Walken and Bowers are back. Just get up."

Jude slapped Lenny on the arm.

"Get her ready, will ya? We're moving out in five."

"Okedoke," Lenny nodded. "Are we going to eat those granola bars now or later?"

"Planning on joining us, gentlemen?" Jude asked us, ignoring Lenny. "As you can see, I need as many experienced triggers as I can get."

"Yeah, Jude," Bowers said as he passed me with a sideways glance. "I'm in total agreement."

Bowers hopped over the barricade of file cabinets, ushering the rest back into the trailer.

I stood alone in the dirt and stared at the uneven footprints that led away from humanity toward chaos and death.

26

Innocent

+54 Days – 0919 hours

I took point as we resumed our course on I-128. Lenny and April walked hand in hand behind me. Jude was next with Holly trotting beside her. Bowers brought up our rear flank, keeping several meters between us. His Ray-Bans and ball cap hid his eyes.

Abandoned vehicles were scattered across the road again. We pulled supplies from where we could, even finding a pull top can of Alpo. While Holly wolfed down the steamy congealed meat-like glob from the asphalt, we divided up three granola bars and two sealed bottles of hot seltzer.

Afterward we traveled for a few miles before walking around a wooded bend into the midst of a larger traffic jam.

Huge gouges of earth tracked up an incline on the right side of the road. A Greyhound had overturned onto the hoods of two other cars, the bus' windshield popped out.

I looked inside expecting to see the driver still strapped into his seat like our friend in the overturned rig. But this driver was gone.

Behind the captain's chair, past the yellow "Do not cross" line, everything had fallen to the left side – now the down side – of the bus. Clothing and toiletries pooled on the spider web-cracked windows, a lone bra hooked over the corners of a sideway seats.

Slinging the M4 and drawing the knife, I stepped inside.

The air was heavy and sour, the smell of old dry sweat and fear clinging to the seat fabric. Staying above the seats and stepping through the discarded belongings on the windows, I worked past the first couple of rows.

At the third row I picked up a walkie-talkie. I turned it on and was rewarded with static. I turned it off and clipped it to my belt.

At the fifth row I stopped again.

A woman in her thirties was crumbled against the bus'
sidewall, her neck severed on the window and her skull partially
crushed on the sedan's hood where the bus had landed. In her
arms, she clutched a small toddler in a death grip.

I touched the little girl's forehead.

She opened her brilliant blue eyes.

My stomach clenched as the little girl strained against her dead
mother's embrace. She mewed and squirmed for a moment before
staring past me. Her eyes had not taken on the red-gold flecks or
clouded over yet, the too-blue irises of a life cut so short
unnerving.

"Find anything?" Bowers called in.

"Nothing worth mentioning," I replied over my shoulder.

The child reacted to my voice, growling and attempting to
escape her mother's grip once again.

I pushed her head back against her mother's chest, my hand on
her forehead. Slowly, and with little force, I slid my tactical knife
under her jaw.

Her blue eyes tilted upward before her eyelids fluttered closed.

I swallowed hard to keep down the recently consumed granola
and hot seltzer.

I slowly withdrew the blade.

Putting it away and touching the undead baby on the forehead,
I said a silent prayer to an absent God before moving on with my
search.

27

Static

+54 Days – 1835 hours

The road cleared up considerably after the bus accident and its unfruitful search. I remained on point, this time Holly sticking with me for a change. In the apocalypse, a hearty meal trumped scratches under the ears from a pretty woman most days.

"Still ain't going to work," Lenny insisted from the middle of the group.

"Try it anyway," April ordered.

"Whatever."

He rummaged through his backpack as he walked.

"You sure you don't have it?"

"You had it, Len."

"Oh. Here it is."

Lenny pulled out a smart phone with a cylindrical charger plugged into it. He pressed a button on the bottom of the face. The screen remained dark.

Bowers gained on them and looked at the device.

"Hope you got the real charger."

"We do, smarty pants," April snickered. "We just need a working outlet."

"Just sayin'," Bowers advised. "I used to buy chargers online and was screwed every time."

"Got the charger, cigarette adapter, and even three of these external battery rechargers, man," Lenny added. "But we've been without an outlet for too long."

"Maybe we'll find you a new backpack with the solar panel built right in," Bowers replied. "Gotta be a mall or an outfitters around somewhere."

"That would be sweet, dude."

I looked at the road ahead. It was clear as far as I could see. The sun had started to drop into the west, taking our chances of trekking another ten miles today off the table.

"Let's keep moving," I called out.

"Hey, Sergeant Walken," Jude said. "I'm starting to think that my idea of looking for better real estate is more thought out than what you got going on."

"Yeah, John," Bowers agreed. "What's the plan?"

Lenny put the phone back into his pack.

Yeah. What's the plan?

The Gaunt Man stood behind the group, his hands on his emaciated hips.

There's no place like home. Maybe you are like a shark? Just keep swimming. Just keep swimming. Or was that Dory?

Just as the first hint of a syllable snuck past my throat, I was cut short.

"– there? Is anyone there?"

The walkie-talkie on my belt squawked to life with a background of static between those faint words.

April and Lenny hovered over to my left, Lenny with his face nearly over my shoulder. Jude held Bowers' arm expectantly.

"I hear you. Over."

"Oh my God," a female voice came back through the radio, getting softer as she started talking quickly to someone else with her thumb still on the SEND button.

"What's your position, over?" I asked when I heard static.

"Need help," another voice, older and male, said. "Surrounded by the dead."

"Acknowledged."

"In an apartment building."

"We read. Over."

I tapped the radio against my chest.

"New plans."

28

Surrounded

+54 Days – 2011 hours

The Gables Apartments complex rose up from a gated parking lot at the end of a cul-de-sac. Retail stores filled out the first floor on either side of the lobby atrium. Several undead wandered around the lot and inside the stores where the glass had been shattered.

Vacant townhouses lined the rest of the block, with a ransacked Snapper Lawn Care Center on one corner and an unmolested bookstore on the other.

"Apparently," Bowers mused, "reading is not paramount after the fall of man.

The only lights in the front façade of the complex came from the edges of a drawn curtained window from a third floor corner apartment.

"Wonder where the other residents are?" Bowers asked.
"Maybe they're sleeping or don't have lights," April commented with a hint of hope.

"Or they could be the ones walking around the lot," Jude replied. "The gates are closed. Most of the cars are still in their stalls. I don't think this is another case of baiting dead heads."

"Damn, you're good," Bowers remarked. "Sure you weren't in the service?"

"Nah. Just astute," Jude said, clicking her tongue off the roof of her mouth and shooting at him with cocked fingers.

"They wouldn't all be in the lot," I said.

"Walken," Bowers distracted me from analyzing Jude's assessment. "We going in or are they coming out?"

With daylight nearly gone we didn't have a strong enough fall back position for an extraction nor did we have near enough

75

firepower for an incursion. Bowers was capable. I believed the same for Jude. Lenny and April seemed way too green for this type of work.

"Walken?" Bowers asked again.

I thought of a particular three-day pass in Tampa where I had been stationed stateside after boot. I couldn't help but grin.

"This can't be good." Bowers said. "Walken never smiles."

29

At the Races

+54 Days – 2147 hours

The four-foot brick and concrete wall around the apartment complex wasn't tall enough to hide me from the FRACs, but it really didn't matter as I hunched over as I made my approach to the gate.

You are so dramatic.

I guess I was being dramatic.

The FRACs didn't sense my presence. As long as I wasn't making noise or flashing a light at them, my movements didn't agitate them or draw them to my position. The fact I concealed my approach was more a protection against being asked questions I didn't want to answer.

The main entry security gate was closed.

A quick test pull did not budge it.

It was jammed shut.

That won't do.

I reached through the vertical rails and grabbed the upper and lower run of the chains. Bracing my shoulder against the gate, I pulled with a grunt. The gear assembly tore through the power box housing. The chain and gears clattered to the asphalt.

The closest FRACs turned toward the noise and snarled but did not expend much more energy to investigate.

I pulled at the gate again.

This time it rattled open, the chain pooling on the pavement.

The added noise caught the full attention of the walkers around the entrance. They shuffled over and paused at the now open gateway before shambling through. I crouched at the wall, Glock and knife drawn.

I aimed the Glock at the end of the block and flicked the

tactical light on and off three times.

Three winks of light responded.

The next sound was the pull of a cord, followed by a coughing, sputtering sound. The muffled noises stopped.

"Damn it," someone hissed in the distance.

The cord was pulled again.

It was pulled twice more.

"Stop," a female's voice. "Give me that."

More FRACs realized they weren't penned in and joined the crowd assembling on the street.

I gripped my weapons a little tighter.

Two more cord pulls turned into the steady rev of a two-cycle engine. It accelerated for a moment.

The tactical light at the other end of the block flashed twice.

I was forced to stand up to respond over the crowd of undead.

The engine's roar drew a steady stream of walkers toward the sound. The sputter receded as the rest of the FRACs staggered to the corner. They passed the sidewalk at the bookstore and out of sight.

The others approached along the wall and crouched beside me, Bowers and Jude with their weapons trained on the rear of the FRAC column. Holly trotted over and plopped down at my feet.

"John," Bowers whispered. "That was pretty cool."

"Except for the fact that the good sergeant here," Jude said, tossing a thumb at Bowers, "has zero skill starting a lawnmower. He must be used to those top-end models with the key start."

"It got started, didn't it?"

"As soon as I took over."

"Oh, man," Lenny grinned. "That self-propelled mower shit was awesome!"

April slugged him in the bicep.

"Hey!"

"Alright, kids," I interrupted, smiling. "Look sharp. We still have to clear the rest of the FRACs in the lot and the lobby. Once we get to the mezzanine, we find the eastern stairwell to the 3rd floor."

Holly growled softly and wagged her tail.

"Ooh rah," Bowers acknowledged.

Jude nodded.

Lenny and April looked at me with wide eyes.

I looked around the corner.

Flip-flopped feet shuffled toward us, accompanied by a gurgling sound.

I stood and raised my knife.

An overweight gray-haired man raised a Beretta 9mm Model 92 at me. His wheeze turned into a phlegmy hack.

"Thanks for coming," he said, a crooked cigarette between his lips. "You the ones here to rescue us?"

30

Candlelight

+54 Days – 2205 hours

The old man proved himself quite capable as we sliced our way through to the building past the last few FRACs still wandering around the parking lot.

With the undead dispatched we climbed through a broken plate glass window into the lobby. Shards of glass crushed under our boots. Bowers carried Holly in his arms, her tail swishing into his hip and her tongue licking his face.

"Knock it off," he mumbled with his jaw upturned away from her slobbery kisses.

The man with the Beretta led the way past an empty elevator shaft. He pointed the way up the central stairway to a mezzanine, his gun still aimed in our general direction.

"Stairwell is to the right," he said as we climbed. "Leads to the third floor."

"You don't need the gun," Bowers reminded the shoddily shoed senior citizen. "We came to rescue you."

"There," the old man said, ignoring the Sergeant and waving his gun toward a metal fire door at the end of the hall. "Be careful. The infected keep getting inside."

I looked through the wired tempered glass window.

The stairwell looked clear.

Cracking open the door I whistled and waited. After thirty seconds I waved the others inside. The old man came in last and I closed the door behind us.

Holly squirmed in Bowers' arms and nipped him on the nose.

"Damn it," Bowers hissed as he set the dog on the landing.

"Match made in heaven," the old man said.

"That wasn't the location I was thinking," Bowers retorted.

"I'm sure," the old man said as he started up the stairs. "Sucks not having a working elevator. Makes me want to move to one of the garden apartments in the back."

Bowers shrugged.

I shrugged back, trailing the man up to the next landing.

The others followed my lead.

After the old man checked the interior hallway through the fire door window, he opened the door and gestured us inside.

The hallway was dark save for a nearly exhausted candle in front of the first apartment to our left. The rest of the hallway quickly faded to black, the candlelight too weak to pierce the darkness.

There came a faint crunching sound.

Moaning wandered toward us from in the darkness.

I drew up my Glock.

Bowers brought up his M4.

The old man put his hand on the slide of my gun.

"Don't worry," he said. "A few of the neighbors are infected and locked in their apartment. They won't be trouble."

"Anyone else alive?" Bowers whispered.

The old man thought this over and simply answered, "Let's get inside."

He knocked twice on the door behind the candle.

"Yeah?" a muffled female voice answered.

"It's us, Melissa," the old man said. "Everything's A-Ok."

Scraping of two slide chains and a deadbolt.

The door opened a few inches with one green eye staring at us through the crack.

"It's okay, honey. Let us in."

The door opened farther.

A woman stood in the doorway with another 9mm Beretta in her hand. She backed away into the apartment, the gun trained on me.

The old man brushed past me and went inside.

"Come in and welcome," he said.

April, Lenny and Jude followed the old man inside.

Bowers, Holly and I remained at the entrance.

"After you, boss." Bowers offered.

Bowers and I peeked into the apartment, checking the corners.

Holly looked up at both of us.

She snorted and trotted inside, leaving us with our guns in our hands.

"Good enough for the ladies," Bowers said before he entered the apartment and left me in the dark hallway.

My neck itched.

"… do you have a working outlet?" I heard Lenny ask.

Soft scraping sounds.

The infected, as the old man called them, scratched for me behind their locked doors.

Come join us…

… They seemed to say. Or at the very least…

… let us out to play.

I picked up the candle, blew out the flame and took my chances with what remained of the living.

31

Scratches

+54 Days – 2345 hours

The old man's living room was stuffy and dim, heavy curtains drawn across the windows of the congested living room. Jude crowded with the lovebirds on a sofa, Holly snuggling up on her lap. The woman who had reluctantly answered the door sat with another woman with similar features, a teenage girl leaning against her. The old man sat in a ratty Lay-Z-Boy recliner. Bowers had dragged in a chair from the dining room.

I stood close to the door.

"Now that we're mostly settled," the old man said, looking at me, "I guess it's time for introductions."

He shifted his weight in the creaking chair.

"I'm Jack Russell," he started.

Holly woofed.

"I get that a lot," he continued with a grin. "These are my two daughters, Melissa and Victoria. Young lady between them is Victoria's daughter – my granddaughter – Summer."

The women each nodded as they were introduced, staring at us with white-knuckled fingers around the grips of the handguns in their laps. Summer looked like she was going to say something but Victoria put a restraining hand on her arm.

"As for the soldier's question," Jack answered, "most of the residents are gone. Either dead or evacuated."

"And the evacuated are probably dead, too," Melissa added.

"We've only seen massive groups of FRACs since we left the coast," Bowers replied.

"FRACs?" Summer asked.

"It's just what we call them," Bowers said, emphasizing the word *them*. "It's an acronym. Fucking re-animated corpses."

"Bowers," Jude warned.

"Been on the road too long?" Jack glared at Bowers. "There are ladies present."

"Sorry, sir," Bowers averted his gaze to the carpet, losing his grin.

"Where have all the manners gone?" Jack asked, his mouth turning up at the corners. "FRAC had a ring to it I have to admit."

"Gramps!" Summer exclaimed.

"Come on, Dad," Victoria added.

"Anyways," Jack continued. "How about you all?"

"John." I offered.

"Sgt. Sean Bowers, at your service."

Never would have pegged him as a Sean. Seemed crazy I hadn't known his first name up to now.

"I'm Jude." She pointed to herself. "And this is April and Lenny. And the fur ball is Holly."

Jack's daughters loosened their grips on their weapons, Victoria a bit more so than Melissa. Jack's granddaughter scooted to the edge of the couch cushion, her elbows crossed over her bare knobby knees. Holly jumped off Jude's lap and plopped down on Summer's sandaled feet.

"Awww," Summer squeaked, scooping the dog up. "How are you, puppy?"

"Where is everyone?" I asked.

"I already said," Jack replied.

"Sorry. Not talking about here." I amended my previous question. "The roads are way too clear."

"I can't speak for what may have happened on the coast," Jack pondered. "Around here, most people were evacuated east to Boston or south toward Framingham. Lots of Greyhounds and Blue Birds transporting people to designated holding areas or safe zones as they called them. After the New England blackout and what happened when people didn't evacuate before the last hurricane, this time most said 'how high' when the Emergency Broadcast System said to jump."

"The buses stopped making pick-ups four or five weeks ago," Melissa added. "The Army transport convoys stopped coming around a week after that."

"Why didn't you go?" Jude asked.

Jack's daughters glanced at each other. Melissa put her hand on her sister's wrist. Summer was oblivious as she scratched Holly under the chin.

"We've been to a FEMA disaster relief station before." Jack swallowed. "Corralled us in the stadium. It didn't end well for our family. I would rather wait it out here."

"The problem," Bowers answered, "is there isn't an end to the wait. The government doesn't exist anymore. At least in what we have seen out there."

"I'm sure they're holed up somewhere waiting for the situation to die down," Victoria said.

"No pun intended," April snickered.

Lenny smiled but gave her a serious elbow to the ribs.

"Stop it," she squeaked, nudging him back before mock biting him on the shoulder.

Jude rolled her eyes and sighed.

"How you surviving here?" I asked.

Victoria started to say something but Jack beat her to it.

"Lots of stuff lying around inside the other apartments. Since most have gone, we help ourselves."

Let us out to play. You know you want to.

Faint scratching echoed in my head. Glass crunched under the bare soles of rotting feet, the blackened blood leaving prints around like that kid from the Family Circus comic strip.

"What about the FRACs inside the parking lot?" Bowers asked.

"Not from here," Melissa said quickly.

85

Jack clucked his tongue a couple times before giving his own answer.

"After the apartments emptied out and we were the only tenants left..."

We're still here.

"... me and my girls stayed put, scavenged what we could. Kept our heads down."

Soft faint scraping came from behind doors beyond the safety of this apartment.

Jack kept talking.

"One day we woke up and found a group of people tented out in the parking lot. Seemed harmless but I wasn't going to let them know we were up here."

More scrapes.

Possibly from whittled down fleshless hands.

"A couple of the women in the group looked pretty ill the first night. They decided it would be smart to break through the plate glass in the lobby and move the sick inside. I saw them on the couch cushions in the lobby."

"They see you?" Bowers asked.

The scratching turned into a repetitive slow knock.

My finger went to the M4's trigger as I stared at the door.

"No. We stayed hunkered down. They rattled around the hallways but didn't try to break into any of the units. I'm sure they took advantage of any unlocked doors."

Come on out. They seemed to call out.

"We peeked out two days later and found them infected and roaming around the lot."

"The women infected the others," Victoria said in a hushed voice.

"She's probably right," Jack added. "They died and came back while everyone slept. Attacked enough of the others to start a cascade of infection."

Knock. Knock. Knock.

I went to the door and listened with my ear next to the metal.

The knocking stopped.

"What's up, John?"

I put a finger to my lips.

Nothing.

The conversation died, all eyes on me.

The knocking outside had fallen silent, too.

BANG! BANG! BANG!

I jumped back from the door, weapon drawn.

Bowers, Melissa, Jack and Jude were standing, too.

"What are you hearing?" Bowers asked in a whisper.

I flanked the entry and turned the deadbolt with a click that was much too loud in my ears.

I pulled the doorknob.

Cleared left and right of the door as it swung open.

I stepped slowly into the hallway.

The darkness from the hall didn't invade the apartment, but the unit's dim lighting didn't penetrate too far into the hallway either, too weak to illuminate the corridor's deep murk.

I took three more steps into the hallway.

My night vision was not so useful without a sliver of light.

Shouldering the M4, I drew the Glock and switched on its tactical light. The LED speared through the dust in the empty corridor.

The air was heavy and stale.

And still.

"Follow you out?" Bowers called out in a low voice.

I put up a fist as I passed the third set of units.

"Roger that."

Scratching from my 2 o'clock.

Leaning in, I listened through the door of apartment 3H.

Help me. Let me out.

I stepped back.

Reaching for the doorknob, I raised the Glock to chest level and exhaled an even breath.

"I wouldn't do that if I were you, Sergeant," Jack said with his shotgun faced in my general direction.

"Give me a reason."

"She's infected."

"Who."

"Elaine Trask."

A moan.

Both our weapons sighted on the door.

The scratching was unmistakable now.

The door shuddered.

"She was a young woman just back from Boston College." Jack said as we moved back the way we came.

"I guess not everyone left, did they?"

"Told you that there were infected in the apartments," Jack said with a sigh. "There are plenty of residents left in their units. Just not in a position to pay rent."

I stopped.

"The other group did break into some of the apartments, didn't they?" I asked, knowing the answer.

Jack looked at me, knowing that I knew.

"Yeah," he admitted. "A couple of the campers tried to scavenge from some of the 2nd floor units. They didn't get too far before the dead got to them and the sick women. By the time it was over, all the campers had turned. And trapped us in."

"So you had us clear them for you."

"Yes."

"So what do you want now?"

Jack lowered his shotgun and shrugged his shoulders.

"I don't rightly know."

32

Bedtime Stories

+55 Days – 0130 hours

The Russell women said their polite goodnights and retreated to the back bedroom, weapons still in hand. April and Lenny had fallen asleep cuddled up on the couch. The rest of us occupied the chairs around one end of the dining room table. Bottled water sat on the placemats in front of each of us.

"So you staying or leaving?" I asked.

Jack turned his half-empty bottle around in his fingers, the label starting to come off. An image of Felix and the Irish Spirit rushed to the front of my mind, but I pushed that memory back with gritted teeth.

Another ghost.

"I needed the infected off my lawn," Jack finally said. "That's been taken care of. I feel safer here now."

"Can you survive indefinitely?" Bowers asked.

"Probably not. But we can hold out for a good while."

"Then what?" Jude asked.

"Guess we'll have to see."

"I know you have a sense of comfort here, Jack," Jude added, "but it can't last."

"And go where? Go find another safe haven?" Jack spit out with venom on *safe haven*. "Or die in a ditch somewhere while we're looking? Or watch one or all of my girls die in that ditch?"

I couldn't argue with his logic. Was my plan any better?

"You know that stadium we went to?" he asked in a lower voice, leaning his elbows on the table. "While we were dealing with thugs taking blankets, water and stale crackers from my girls, my wife was…"

Tears escaped Jack's weathered eyes.

Jude put one hand over her mouth and placed the other on Jack's arm.

Bowers tapped his fingers on the table with a far away stare. We both knew what went on at those sites when law broke down – stateside and in refugee centers around the world.

I didn't need Jack to say more and wished he wouldn't finish.

"She was raped and murdered," Jack whispered, "and I couldn't get close enough to save her."

I swallowed hard, Lucy coming to mind.

"Summer was young and doesn't know what really happened. I want it to stay that way."

We nodded, agreeing to keep his secret.

33

Should We Stay or Should We Go, Now?
+55 Days – 0512 hours

Jack had retired to his own bedroom soon after his dining table revelation. Bowers slept in the recliner, his boots off and his arms wrapped around his M4. Jude sat next to the dozing April and Lenny, petting Holly's belly.

I stood in the center of the dining room, watching the locked door and wondering if sleep would ever come for me.

Maybe death will come for you first? Oh, wait. That has already happened.

After stretching her arms over her head Jude opened her eyes, moved Holly off her lap and walked around the apartment blowing out the candles.

The morning crept in through the slits between the overlapping curtains, sending slivers of light across the carpet to the opposite walls. The dust swam and swirled as Jude moved through it, like the wash behind an Apache.

"You sleep much?" Jude asked.

"Enough," I replied.

"Liar."

Did she know?

"There's never enough," she continued, seemingly unaware of how I tensed up at her faux accusation.

Holly yawned, stretching her body until her legs quivered. She rolled over to snuggle against the arm of the couch. The others did not stir.

"So what's the next move?" Jude pulled out a chair and sat.

"Concerning what?"

"Are we staying?" Jude waved a hand around the room. "Or are we moving on?"

"You do what you like."

"Hey, don't be a dick," she said. "I'll stick with you if you have a plan. I'm not necessarily sure this is where I want to hole up for the duration. It gives me a bad feeling."

"Don't like the undead behind locked doors?"

"Not particularly."

"Agreed." I thought back to the scratching and moaning.

"Hell," Jude said, "if I wanted to play house I would've stayed at the swanky Howard Estates."

"That place was nice."

"Except that the supplies consisted of brochures." Jude looked over at Lenny and April and nodded. "Plus, I have the kids to look after."

"Where'd you find those two, anyway?"

"Shacked up in a Starbucks." Jude smiled. "They made it seem like it was just another day."

"They could be a problem," I said in a lower voice.

"They're harmless," she replied. "It's nice to see that they found each other."

"Maybe. But we need fighters, not lovers."

"With me you get both," Jude said without thinking, immediately flushing red.

Jude quickly stood and put her chair back.

"Anyway, we need to figure out what's next. Let me know."

She went over to the couch and shook Lenny's shoulder.

"Hmmmm." Lenny stirred. "What?"

"Get yourselves up." She leaned in. "We are guests, not squatters."

Lenny grumbled, rubbed his eyes, and started poking at April's belly.

Jude proceeded to slap the bottom of Bowers' foot.

"Don't kick me, Mom," Bowers said without opening his eyes. "I've been awake for a while."

From Jack's room came the creak of mattress springs.

The shuffling and clearing of a throat came out of Jack before he opened his bedroom door. He walked out wearing the same clothes and carrying the same Beretta as yesterday. This morning, however, he also had a Smith & Wesson revolver.

He knocked on the other bedroom door with three sharp raps. "Rise and shine," he said. "It's time to make the doughnuts."

34

Shower and Breakfast

+55 Days – 0645 hours

We stood in the stairwell, the skylight at the top of the shaft giving us the beginnings of the day's light to work by. A large number six was stenciled on the concrete block walls on the landing.

Bowers and I flanked the fire door.

Jack and Melissa stood in front of it.

"Glad you boys are here," Jack said. "Wasn't fair that Summer ever had to do any of this."

Was that Jack's angle?

Maybe he just wanted a few able bodies that take the brunt of the work and risk off of his girls.

"We haven't shopped this floor yet," Jack said, "so it may get a little dicey."

"Great... FRACs," Bowers groaned. "I woke up for this?"

We all exchanged nods before Jack opened the fire door. The corridor was dark, the emergency lights long since dead.

Bowers and I lit up the hall with our tactical lights.

No moans.

No scratching.

No thumping.

The corridor was empty.

I pulled out my machete with my left hand, steadying my Glock on top of the blade-wielding wrist. The Harries technique taught in the Corps was always preferable to the Neck Index technique that the FBI offered.

"Skip the first unit on your left," Jack whispered as he and I moved into the corridor. "It's been vacant for over a year. Go to the second."

We moved to the apartment with a metal 6F screwed into the steel door.

Melissa kept the fire door propped open with her body, her Beretta aimed into the stairwell. Bowers stood just inside the corridor under the exit sign.

"You seem to know everything that goes on around here," I said to Jack.

"I'm a busybody," he said with a chuckle.

He pulled out a key ring from his pocket, jangled one free and slipped it into the apartment door's deadbolt.

"Super's master key," he said.

"I'm sure that comes in handy," Bowers added.

"Sure does."

The deadbolt retracted and Jack pocketed the key. He turned the doorknob and opened the door. It stopped at three inches as the inside chain tightened.

"Well," Jack said. "Definitely in for a surprise."

Jack pressed his cheek against the doorframe and whistled through the opening. He waited five seconds and whistled again.

Nothing.

Jack puckered his lips again.

He whistled like he was calling after a pet poodle.

Still nothing.

"Move," I ordered Jack out of the way.

I backed up a step and rammed a shoulder into the door. The chain snapped and I skidded inside the foyer. Jack and Bowers quickly moved in behind me.

"You know," Jack chuckled, "I do have bolt cutters back at the apartment."

"Now he tells us," Bowers replied, following us in from his post at the stairwell.

The living room and dining room were empty. Swimming dust swirled as he pushed through the space.

"Someone must be here, though," Bowers pointed to large

boxes on the dinette table filled with dry goods, cereal and cans. A hiker's backpack sat against the wall under a window.

"Score," Jack said. "These units are way bigger than ours."

I rubbed the back of my neck.

"Somebody was making preparations," Jack replied.

"Where did they go?" Bowers asked.

"Not my concern."

"It better be your concern," I advised, not liking his reckless tone.

I snapped my fingers and pointed to the hallway and the two closed bedrooms. Bowers nodded and moved to the first room.

He tried the door.

It swung open and Bowers matched its motion with his M4's barrel. He pressed against the door as it hit the wall, swiveling his weapon through the space.

"Clear," he gave a thumbs-up.

Jack went to the second bedroom and opened the door a couple inches. After peeking inside, he opened it more. With his revolver up he walked inside and moved out of view.

I counted to ten.

No Jack.

I gestured for Bowers to check on Jack.

Bowers nodded and poked his head into the bedroom

Jack popped back into view.

"Christ," Bowers exclaimed, startled.

"All good," Jack said.

"Give a guy some warning next time," Bowers retorted.

"Next time."

As they squabbled I stared at the bathroom door. The paint had bubbled and started to peel, but it still looked shockingly light in the dim room.

Jack and Bowers headed over to the dinette and started poking around in the food supplies.

The lightest of scratches came from behind the bathroom door.

Don't forget about us
Lucy's voice echoed.
Why did you leave?
Sebastian's voice chimed in.

I reached for the faceted glass and brass doorknob. My hand distorted through each bevel as I closed my fingers around it.

The scratching stopped as soon as I touched the cold knob.

I turned it and pushed the door open, the hinges letting out a long squeak.

A putrid damp smell assaulted me. I covered my nose and mouth with the crook of my elbow and went inside.

The vanity, toilet and tub were chipped white porcelain. The rest was covered in avocado green tiles. I pulled my knife, drawing back the shower curtain with it.

The tub was filled with blackish water.

Spongy meaty chunks bobbed on its surface.

Lying in the middle of the full tub was a half-naked bloated man. He had a straggly beard and oily hair plastered across his forehead. He lay still and stared past me, not expending any energy. An angry purple slit cut across his right wrist. A slight low wheeze escaped his throat through a tear in his esophagus, patches of flesh sloughing off his chest.

I sighed and held the tactical knife in front of him. His milked over eyes followed the blade like a cobra swaying before the snake charmer. I lowered the tip of the blade to his chin and the FRAC's eyes tried to follow. He uttered a mewing sound for a moment before I slipped the knife under the soft part of his jaw directly into the base of his brain.

Withdrawing the blade, I wiped it with a towel from the rack before returning it to its sheath. Closing the shower curtain I left the FRAC to his wet coffin.

"Shit!"

Yells and banging came from the living room.

I rushed out with the Glock drawn.

Bowers was pulling a small female walker off Jack, using his knife as a lever through the top of its head. The FRAC crashed to the kitchen floor.

"You alright?" I asked.

"Yeah. Yeah." Jack panted with a shaky voice.

"Sergeant?"

"I was looking through the supplies and found a second backpack by the window," Bowers reported. "Jack went into the pantry and she attacked. Christ, she's a damn kid!"

"How was I supposed to know that a child lock on the doors was keeping the infected inside?" Jack asked.

"Are you bit, Jack?"

"Nah. I'm good. Just shook up."

Jack seemed no worse for wear other then some splatters of goo on the shoulder of his shirt.

Melissa arrived at the apartment door.

She turned the barrel of her Beretta at each of us in turn.

"No harm," Jack told her with his hands up in surrender. "We're all good."

"I think Jack has had enough excitement for one morning." Bowers smiled weakly, his own voice cracking.

35

No Harm, No Foul

+55 Days – 0904 hours

"Are you shitting me?" Victoria berated her father as she held Summer in front of her.

"It's fine," Jack said. "I'm fine."

"Relax, Vicky," Melissa said from the table, continuing to inventory the contents of the boxes and backpacks.

"Are you kidding me?" Victoria continued. "Is this how we're going to live? Ransacking every unit in the building? Every unit a possible deathtrap?"

Summer tried to squirm away from her mother.

"Geez," Summer said. "Let me go. Grandpa's fine."

Victoria reluctantly released her daughter.

"And hang on until something bad happens to you?" Her eyes bored into her father. "On the seventh floor? The eleventh? When's it going to end… for all of us?"

Jack stood and motioned for his daughter to stop.

"We'll keep doing what we're doing. That's the way it's going to be. Not another word about it."

He coughed out the last few words.

"Lissa, give me some of that water."

Melissa grabbed one of the bottles from the shrink-wrapped flat. Jude took the water from her and handed it to Jack. He cracked open the top and took two long swigs.

"And with that, I am going to lay down. Sgt. Bowers was right about the excitement part," Jack said, patting Bowers on the shoulder as he passed.

"No problem, Jack."

Jack closed his bedroom door with a soft click.

A surreal hush fell over the room with Jack's departure.

April and Lenny sat on the couch, April's arms around Summer. Melissa continued to inventory the stash of food and supplies. Victoria stood in the middle of the living room glaring at us with wide eyes, her mouth opening and closing as if she meant to say something but thinking better of it. Bowers stared out the window with a finger pulling back the curtain.

"This is your fault," Victoria said with a hiss before storming off to the back bedroom.

Slam!

Jude nudged me with one of the bottled waters from the morning's scavenge. Holly padded along with her, resting against Jude's leg when she stopped walking.

"It's not your fault, John," Jude said.

"Isn't it?" I asked.

"No."

"Should have cleared that pantry," Bowers muttered from the window. "She was so small. Didn't think the child locks around the knobs were keeping anything locked inside."

Not everyone is as thorough as you, Johnny.

I shook away the thought. Jack wasn't hardcore military.

But Bowers is.

Shut up. He's only a reservist.

Is it easier to take the blame than to accept the truth?

Shut up.

"Hey," Jude said.

"What?"

"Shake it off, Marine," Jude ordered. "You figure out what we're doing?"

"Getting clearer by the minute."

"Hope so," she replied, heading back into the kitchen.

I sat on the edge of the sofa with the M4 cradled in my arms. Holly padded away from Jude and jumped up on the couch cushion. She licked my hand before curling up.

Jude came back and sat down next to Summer. She added her

hug to April's.

"It'll be okay," Jude offered.

Summer hesitated – deciding between leaning into the hug or not – then shrugged off both April and Jude's arms.

"Can't everyone just leave me alone?"

She stormed off to the bedroom like her mother before her.

Jude caught my gaze and shrugged. Holly left the cushion next to me and plodded over to comfort her.

Bowers came over.

"Plenty of food, John. And we're high enough off the ground for a good defensive position."

Sure. Now he's a strategist?

Fucking shut up.

"It is," I replied, "but it doesn't feel right."

We're also trapped this high up.

"I don't think anything feels right these days."

I tapped the M4 with my trigger finger. I looked around at the apartment and its new supplies that Melissa was now lining up on the dining room table with anal-retentive precision.

We looked like any other bored family during a power outage and lack of battery-powered electronics to occupy their attention-deficit time.

Well... the cache of guns and knives ruins the Norman Rockwell-esque quality a bit.

Or makes it better.

36

Westward, Ho!

+55 Days – 2010 hours

Night had fallen again.

It was a strange notion that amid the chaos, some things remained constant in the universe, unaffected by the infinitesimal stresses of humankind.

The world still spun. The seasons still kept to their namesakes. The summer was no exception.

Even with the windows and the sliding door open to the questionably named balcony, the heat in the apartment was stifling.

I leaned back in a chair against the entry door.

The others had retired to their bedrooms, Jude and Holly sleeping on the floor in Jack's room with him and his granddaughter. The lovebirds shared blankets used as a mattress in the other room with the sisters. Bowers still hugged his M4 in the recliner, his boots and socks lined up on the floor next to the footrest.

The summer season had come.

It didn't mind that the living suffered without the comforts of air conditioning and ice cubes. Nor did it care that the sun's rays cooked the rotting flesh without actually doing any lasting damage to the undead, adding to a stench that never went away.

Undead hordes – 1.

Humanity – 0.

I missed the Atlantic.

The FRACs had been calling the shots since the beginning. They had divided and conquered as well as any military commander worth their salt. Hurt the enemy. Take away their morale, supply lines, leadership. All you have left is an unorganized rabble. Like Tomahawk missiles without the firing controls or propulsion.

What's the matter, John? Feeling sorry for yourself?

The pale skinned, well-dressed specter sat at the dining room table next to the supplies. He crossed his legs and pinched the crease in his pants with his long, sharp nailed fingers so the pleat sat just right. He flicked away a stray piece of lint for good measure.

Come now. This is the adventure of a lifetime!

"If you say so," I whispered.

I do! Join the Army. See the world!

I closed my eyes to ward him away but he droned on.

Oh yeah, you were a Marine. Sorry. Sorry. You are a Marine. Once a Marine always a Marine, right?

I sighed and looked at him.

He sat ramrod straight, even with his legs crossed. His left hand rested on his knee with his right hand on top. He smiled, his teeth too white and his incisors too long. Without his mirrored sunglasses, his onyx eyes were soulless and unreadable. The laugh lines around his mouth and eyes were contrary to the uneasy feeling he gave me.

Where's your sense of adventure?

I gave him both middle fingers.

I have more adventure in my left pinkie than you do in both your middle fingers.

I turned my back on the man in the 1960s Government Issue black suit and headed into the kitchen. One of the bottled waters was half-empty. I emptied it in three swigs and tossed it into the sink.

Really? Your mother raised a boy who doesn't know how to recycle?

I retrieved the bottle and dropped it in the green bin under the sink.

"Happy?"

So very much. Thank you.

"What do you want?"

The Gaunt Man reappeared on the other side of the dining room table. He gripped the back of the chair in front of him, making squeaky rubbing noises with his digits.

You have to leave here.

"Why?"

Because they're coming.

"Who?"

People a bit worse than who you have come across so far.

I chuckled at the last comment.

After a sea of unrelenting FRACs pouring onto Rainier Island, a psychotic military officer bent on crucifying me, and a serial killer madman looking to turn me into the undead, I couldn't imagine much worse.

The Gaunt Man stood up straighter, somehow taller.

Heed me, John. If you do not care for your well-being, I would ask you to think about the others. The women. The girl.

"And where should we go, smartass?"

The Gaunt Man smiled again.

Why, go west, young man!

37

Hard Choices

+56 Days – 0800 hours

Everyone with a vote sat at the table.

Jack sat at the head of the table with a daughter on both sides. I took up the other end of the table with Jude and Bowers.

Holly demanded a say in the matter. She stood on her back legs and scratched away at Jude's jeans until Jude lifted her onto her lap.

April, Lenny and Summer stayed back on the couch. None of them looked too pleased to have been excluded. Luckily, Jude had agreed that we needed to keep the discussion to the adults and to keep the voices at the table equal.

"I'm saying we need to keep moving," I advised.

"We got a good thing here," Jack replied. "I'm not sacrificing shelter and supplies for the open road. That's suicide."

Victoria clenched her teeth, her jaw flexing. She kept her eyes on her wringing hands.

Melissa looked toward me with something close to disdain at my presumption to bring such an idea to the table.

"There's no way we are going out there," Melissa said, hissing the last word.

Bowers chewed on bubblegum found in the hitchhiker's backpack, content with any forward momentum. Jude looked at me with questioning eyes. I'm sure she was curious as to my sudden decision.

Jack cleared his throat, drank from a bottle of water, and cleared his throat again. He swallowed two aspirin with another swig of water then spoke up.

"I'll keep my family put, thank you very much."

"That's your decision and your right."

"Damn right it is," Jack said before coughing.

A tingling went up the back of my neck, but only for a moment.

"Let's take one more day." I offered as a reply. "You talk it over and we will reconvene tomorrow morning."

"Same bat time. Same bat table." Bowers chimed in.

"You're an idiot, Sergeant," Jude said.

"Maybe a little," he grinned.

"Tomorrow, John," Jack said. "Then we put the matter to rest."

38

Pack

+56 Days – 1230 hours

"You think he'll change his mind?"

Jude climbed through the jagged window frame next to the intact lobby doors. The glass shards reflected the sunlight, dotting her as she stepped through. She tapped a cigarette on a pack in her hand as she walked over to the bench where I sat.

"Well?"

I gestured for her to sit.

"I doubt it," I answered after she settled. "He's right."

"About what?"

"The shelter. The supplies. He's got an apartment building full of food. It would be a while before they run out. Why leave?"

"So we just go on our own, then?"

"Yeah."

"I think Bowers would be happy to stay."

"He just needed to get away from the island," I responded, then nodded to the unlit cigarette Jude held between her fingers. "You going to smoke that?"

"Figured the end of the world would be the perfect time to start killing myself slowly," she answered as she raised it up and rotated it around. "That hitchhiker's backpack seems to have something for everyone. Can't seem to get the courage to light the first one up, though."

She laughed with a little sadness laced in.

I took the cigarette from her and held it up to my nose. The cut tobacco – in spite of all the other additives – smelled enticing. Taking the pack from her, I stuffed the stray back through the foil to rejoin its friends.

"Is this an intervention, Sergeant?"

"Might be."

39

Sibling Rivalry
+56 Days – 1230 hours

Once Bowers returned from his perimeter sweep, he joined us at the bench and we returned to Jack's apartment.

Something shattered as we approached the door.

I rushed in with my Glock up. Bowers flanked on my nine with the M4. Jude stayed at the door with her revolver out.

"It's bullshit," Victoria cried.

Melissa and Victoria were standing in the middle of the living room with the others looking on from the couch.

"He's not going to make it," Victoria cried.

"Stop saying that, Lissa."

Holly cocked her head toward each woman as they spoke.

"Are you kidding me? He's got a fever and has been coughing since noon."

"Stop it!" Victoria screamed in tears, her eyes red.

Melissa pointed an index finger at her sister and closed the distance between them. Her eyes were sharp with emotion, too. The difference was that Melissa carried way more rage inside.

They stopped long enough to look at us.

"Put those things away," Melissa said. "For now anyway."

"Jesus, Lissa." Victoria wept, wiping her eyes with her sleeve. A snot bubble popped out of her nostril and she wiped that away, too.

The itching at the base of my neck had returned – stronger this time. I could clearly hear Jack wheezing through the bedroom door.

"Bowers, check on Jack."

"Roger that."

Jude came into the apartment and closed the door as Bowers moved toward the bedroom.

"What happened?" Jude asked Melissa.

"I don't know what happened on six but Pop caught something up there."

Victoria paced between the hallway and the couch, her hand up to her mouth.

Bowers peeked into Jack's darkened room.

Jack's wheezes became deafening and heavy.

The itch got stronger, starting at the base of my hairline and radiating out. I rolled my shoulders against the tightening muscles.

Bowers came back.

"He's feverish."

"Figured."

"Now what?" Jude asked.

Victoria continued to pace.

Melissa fumed at the center of the living room.

Summer rocked back and forth with her arms around Holly.

April and Lenny sat with their arms around each other, their eyes puffy.

"We wait," I finally answered, "until something breaks."

40

Girls Next Door

+56 Days – 2047 hours

Jack lay under a sheet with a bedspread pulled up to his chest, his breathing labored. His arms were at his sides, doing a good job of tucking himself in. Melissa stood at the open doorway with her arms folded, revolver in hand. Victoria sat in an armchair. She rocked Summer in her arms.

The rest of my party stayed in the living room.

Even Holly had opted to keep her distance.

I sat on an ottoman in the corner, the Glock and tactical knife within easy reach. My itching was now accompanied with a low buzzing.

Victoria wiped away tears and blew her nose, releasing her squirming daughter who quickly put herself out of arm's reach from her mother. Victoria scooted the chair closer to her father's side and pulled his hand into hers.

"You'll be okay, Dad."

Jack continued to drowse, his breathing deeper but no less strained.

Melissa caught my attention with a disapproving snorting noise.

"What?" I did not avert my gaze from Jack.

Neither did she.

"There's no point to this."

"Don't think so?" I replied. "Want me to put a blade into his ear now instead of later?"

Melissa lost a bit of her bravado. She turned a paler shade that darkened the circles under her eyes.

"Asshole." She looked at Jack.

"Make peace with your father," I advised. "It won't be long."

Some of the edges of her impotent anger smoothed off. She tucked her revolver into the back of her waistband, guided her niece back to Victoria and put a hand over her sister's. Summer added hers and they hugged each other in solidarity.

"John," Jude whispered from the door. "Got a sec?"

I glanced at the bedside vigil.

The buzzing hadn't gotten any louder and the itching was still tolerable.

"Sure."

I joined Jude out in the hallway.

Bowers leaned against the wall, his fingers tapping away on the stock of his M4. Lenny was closer to the apartment's door, April rocking back and forth on her heels next to him. Holly slept on her back on the couch, wedged between the cushion and the armrest.

"Ready to mutiny?" I asked.

"Close," Bowers commented.

"You said we would decide with Jack in the morning," Jude acknowledged, "but I doubt he's going to make it to sunrise. And you were suddenly pretty hot and heavy about getting out of here."

Bowers nodded slightly.

Lenny and April had lost their desire to grope in favor of wide-eyed skittishness.

"Get Jack's master key," I ordered. "Get everyone next door."

"And you, Boss?" Bowers asked.

"I'll be along," I said. "After."

41

Death Rattles

+57 Days – 0157 hours

"Just you and me, Jack."

The old man replied with a rattled wheeze.

"You have some strong-willed daughters," I said. "It was all we could do to get them next door. They love you, old man. And Summer may be the strongest of all of them."

I leaned closer.

"Summer was the one to get everyone away from what's coming next."

Jack's chest rose.

"She will be the most adaptable," I mused. "Probably better than all of us. You should be very proud."

Jack didn't respond and his chest did not fall.

I gripped the knife handle.

Not just yet.

The Gaunt Man sat in the armchair Victoria had occupied a few hours ago. He leaned forward at the waist, his face above Jack's. He took a deep breath through his flaring nostrils.

He exhaled sharply as he leaned back.

Gross.

He pressed his fingers together, touched his pale pink lips and made the sign of the cross.

It won't be long.

"I know."

Yes. You do.

Jack shuddered out a ragged breath.

Then went still.

You know you were to have gone by now, John.

113

"Needed a consensus," I said. "Won't leave the girl. You were right about that, at least."

Jack won't be a bottleneck. Not for much longer.

The Gaunt Man stood tall, seeming to elongate enough to nearly brush the ceiling. He loomed over Jack and stroked the dying man's thinning gray hair. With one more long-fingered touch to the old man's cooling shoulder, the Gaunt Man stood up again, straightening his shirt and tie.

The buzzing behind my ears grew louder, like cicadas at dusk.

You have to go, John.

"In a minute."

Not him. You need to escape from what comes after him.

I sat on the mattress beside Jack.

The Gaunt Man blinked out and reappeared behind a chair, his digits curled around the chair back.

Placing a hand on Jack's chest, I waited.

A moment later the buzzing became a deafening symphony before stopping altogether. The sudden silence unnerved me.

Jack opened his eyes.

The blood vessels in his eyes had burst, leaving gold ringed pupils in a sea of red. He strained against my palm attempting to sit up.

I placed the tactical knife blade against his ear.

"Sorry, father."

The blade slid in smoothly up to the hilt.

Jack's eyes fluttered and closed for the last time.

42

Under the Dogwood

+57 Days – 0623 hours

Another hole dug.

Another person lost.

Victoria had asked for her father to be buried beneath a patch of lawn at the rear of the complex near a dogwood tree and a wooden bench.

Jack's family held hands for some time over the mound of dirt. Summer eventually pulled away from her mother and placed a bouquet of silk flowers on the top of the freshly covered grave. Her hand lingered on the flowers for a moment before she walked away across the parking lot.

Melissa squeezed her sister's arm and walked after her niece. Victoria held on for several more seconds before following them.

My group looked at me as the sun's light and heat crawled across the asphalt toward the grave. I could see why the old man liked this spot for his morning cigarette and newspaper.

"We goin'?" Lenny asked.

"Yeah," April added. "It's creepy here."

"Boss?"

"Yeah, Bowers," I said, picking up the spade shovel. "We're going. With whoever else wants to join."

I pressed a dirty nail into a white puffy blister that had risen up in the webbing between my thumb and forefinger. It would probably heal by the end of the day.

We walked to the front of the complex.

Light danced off the shards of glass littering the asphalt, making the entryway a sparkling sea. Holly let out a woof from the lobby stairway. Her tail wagged slightly as she pressed her snout into her front paws, knowing better than to navigate the glass.

I kicked my boots against the first step to dislodge any fragments.

"Come on."

Holly followed me up to the second floor mezzanine.

The others were just coming in the front doors.

The buzzing had returned.

Too late, I think.

But it wasn't the cicada from inside my head.

1500cc motors sputtered in the distance.

Not close, but close enough.

The others made quick time getting to the lobby doors.

"Not sure we should be in the open when they get here," Bowers said in the lead.

"Agreed," Jude nodded as she passed me.

She scooped up Holly and retreated to the second floor to join what remained of Jack's family. Melissa held onto Victoria's arm as she dragged her sister toward the fire door. Bowers stood with me at the top of the steps as Summer, April and Lenny reached the mezzanine. Lenny had one arm on April's back and his free hand on his knife handle.

Good boy.

"Go," I said to Bowers.

He followed the rest of the group into the stairwell.

I crouched on the top step as the motorcycle engines roared louder.

Told you, Johnny.

The Gaunt Man sat on the step beside me, his elbows on his spread open knees.

"Why are they so bad?"

Them? I hear things.

No way to barricade the windows. The lobby would be impossible to defend. Higher ground was better overwatch but limited ammunition would make it a poor tactical decision. The upper level hallways were narrower and more defendable, but

116

could trap us in a siege just as easily.

I backed up the carpeted risers to the mezzanine.

The whine of motors and the sputtering of shoddy mufflers ripped through the air as almost a half dozen motorcycles plus a panel truck rounded the corner past the bookstore.

I retreated to the cool, dim concrete-lined interior of the stairwell. The morning sunlight hadn't risen high enough to blast through the roof skylight just yet.

What's your next move, fearless leader?

Next to the large stenciled M was a firebox with an emergency water hose and axe.

Another brilliant John Walken brainstorm?

"Maybe."

Well, yippee-ki-yay mother…

I broke the firebox glass in case of this emergency.

43

Home Invasion
+57 Days – 0623 hours

The Russell women hugged each other on the sofa. Lenny peeked through the living room blinds at the parking lot below. Bowers did the same from the dining room.

"Got five motorcycles down there," Bowers said, "and a panel truck. They look scrubby but not really road weary. Well armed, too."

Jude and April leaned against the dining room table, April looking more lost than usual without Lenny. Holly lay curled at Jude's feet, her nose under her tail.

"We hide?" Jude asked.

"Bowers?" I asked. "Assessment."

"Don't know, John," he shrugged. "They're scavengers. Lots of gasoline cans… half-filled baskets…"

"And the firearms?" I prompted.

"Each have a handgun strapped. A few shotguns."

"There's a bald black guy in a denim jacket packing an AK," Lenny added.

I went to the window.

The bikes were parked haphazardly across the street, one of the smaller bikes against a sidewalk lamppost. The six men and one woman spread out. Three of the men disappeared into the Lawn Care store. The black man led the rest through the broken entry gate.

"John?" Bowers asked. "It ain't going to take long for them to get to us."

All eyes turned to me.

"Stay dark. Stay quiet." I ordered as I grabbed the master key from the hook by the door.

"I can help," Jude offered.

"Yeah," I replied, "by staying here."

I moved into the hallway and shut the door behind me before Jude could object.

I grabbed the fire axe and leaned against the stairwell door. Faint voices came from below, getting louder.

"...the fuck, Joey."

"What, Donny?"

"Tired of salvage work. Why don't we get to stay put and enjoy the fruits of someone else's labors?"

"Deal with it. You want Duke to know you want off the crew?"

"Hell no! He'd probably shoot me on the highway, siphon the gas from my tank and kick the bike on top of me for good measure. You know he's a mean black sonofabitch."

"Well, there it is. Choices."

"What about that backpacker from last week?"

"Who? The nerd? Dead weight. We have standing orders. You know that."

The pair stopped at the third floor landing.

"Gas. Food. Tools. Entertainment."

I gripped the axe handle tight.

"You ready, Joey?" Donny asked.

"I guess," Joey said sheepishly.

I slid out of sight just as a stream of flashlight pierced the corridor through the fire door window.

"Looks clear," Donny said. "Ok... three, two, one."

The door swung open into the stair well. A scrawny guy with a flashlight and a snub nose .38 passed by. He shined the light on Jack's apartment door. His partner followed, his hand easing the fire door closed with a soft click. A bit heftier than the first guy, he carried his weight as if the apocalypse's weight loss program was showing him good results.

I remained in the shadows.

The thin man tried the doorknob and then pressed the door.

"It's locked," he whispered, "but I don't think the deadbolt is thrown."

"Okay. Stand back."

The heavier man backed up and lunged at the door. He threw his shoulder into it and the door shuddered. He backed up again and rammed the door again. This time the door burst open with splinters flying from the frame. His momentum carried him inside and his partner quickly followed.

I rushed to the doorway behind them.

Jude and Bowers already had their weapons trained on the newcomers. Melissa and Summer stood to the left with their pistols drawn. The looters stood inside the door, their hands partially raised and unsure of what to do next.

"Hey. Hey. It's all good," the smaller Joey said, waving around the revolver and flashlight in the air as he spoke.

Joey's heftier companion, Donny, started lowering his hands to his waist. The pistol grip of a Beretta M9 hung out from the back waistband of his cargo pants.

I grabbed it before Donny did, cocked the hammer and held it to the base of his neck.

"Whoa! Whoa!"

He raised his meaty hands higher in the air. "No trouble."

He spun around and swiped at the Beretta.

I easily stepped back out of reach.

His swing met with empty air. Without any resistance he continued to spin, pirouetting almost all the way around.

"Shit," he exclaimed.

I kicked him in the back, sending him tumbling to the floor.

Joey snickered.

Stepping forward I returned the Beretta to the back of Donny's neck.

"Would you like to try anything else?" I asked.

"Nope," Donny replied softly. "I'm good."

"Glad to hear it," Bowers said.

"What do you want?" Jude asked, gesturing between the pair with her gun.

"Just food and supplies," Joey said.

"And entertainment?" I reminded him.

Joey bowed his head with a frown.

Donny looked sideways at me.

"You should let us go mister," he warned. "We got plenty of men with us."

"We're aware," I replied.

"I'd worry more about what's happening right here, bud," Bowers added.

"How about we call it even?" Donny asked. "We go our way. You go yours."

Bowers and Jude looked at me.

"Hardly. Get the rope and tape."

"Nice," Bowers said with a grin. "That's an idea I can get behind."

44

Choices

+57 Days – 0745 hours

The sixth floor unit was the same as we had left it. The male hitchhiker was in the tub, his female companion still on the kitchen floor next to the center island. Melissa, Victoria and Summer had already retreated to the master bedroom away from the body. Lenny stood vigil at the living room curtain as he had three floors below. April sat on a sectional couch with Holly on her lap, staring at the semi-mummified female on the linoleum.

The rest of us sat at the dining room table.

"We can't cat and mouse this forever, John," Jude said in a low voice, a finger twirling in her hair.

"I know."

"Any reason we're back here?" Bowers asked.

"Because we don't have time to clear out other apartments," I said. "No more surprises here."

"Okay. We do have the master keys," Bowers said. "We jump around until they get tired of looking."

"May not work," Jude said. "They could station people on the stairwells to wait us out."

"We could wait it out longer." Bowers added to his plan. "Plus, we have them outnumbered."

"Only in number," I said. "Not necessarily in skill."

"Can't outrun them," Jude said. "Can't pack enough to be prepared or light enough to be nimble."

"Cross country?" Bowers added.

"A couple dirt bikes out there." I shook my head. "They would run us down."

"Take 'em out?"

"Seems cruel and unnecessary doesn't it, Sean?" Jude asked.

"We wait for an opening," I said.

The rev of a motorcycle cut through the air.

"Guys," Lenny said from the curtains. "They found their friends."

"Get away from there," Jude hissed.

"We see you on the sixth floor," someone shouted from below.

"Damn it," Bowers said.

Bowers and I went to the curtain.

"Shouldn't keep moving the curtains when you're spying on people," the hulking bald black man called up from the parking lot. "Thanks for not killing my boys. That's mighty white of ya."

The motorcycles formed a semi-circle outside the entry gate. All of the riders stood beside their cycles, more weapons now on display.

Probably from the panel truck.

"Thanks for clearing out the Festers for us," the dark-skinned man in denim shouted, "We've wanted to clear out this building for a while. Who knew it could be done?"

A few of the others hooted and whistled.

"You come on out and let us get in there," he said, tugging at his sleeves to make sure they were even. "We don't need any more hogtied comrades down here."

Two of the riders unstrapped gasoline cans from the backs of their bikes and trotted over to the leader.

"Otherwise we may have to scrap the supplies altogether and burn you out." he said. "Your choice."

45

Quick as a Bunny
+57 Days – 0801 hours

Melissa and Victoria had joined us while we listened to the rev of the motorcycles and the leader's demands. Summer had opted to stay in the bedroom.

Everyone looked at me.

"What's the plan?" Bowers asked with his finger pressed against the M4's trigger guard. "We go out shooting?"

"That's not so bright," Jude answered.

"Can't stay here."

"Bowers is right," I said. "We can play cat and mouse for a while, but not for long enough."

"Okay," Jude replied. "So what then?"

We could fight our way out. That was one way to go. We had enough weapons and ammunition. We had the high ground and my expertise at killing at range.

Aren't you tired of killing people?

"So?" Jude asked again.

"Stay put," I ordered, grabbing the fire axe and heading to the door.

"Again with that crap?"

"I'm going out, Jude. Let's see how it goes."

"Great plan, John," Jude said sarcastically.

"And if it goes sideways?" Bowers asked.

April and Lenny huddled on the couch. Summer peeked out from the bedroom door. Holly padded over to the young girl and head butted her in hopes of fresh petting. Melissa and Victoria – miles apart in their worldviews – both gripped their revolvers with white knuckles. Bowers and Jude looked at me expectantly.

"If it goes sideways," I said, "you go sideways, too. Fast as you can."

I gripped the axe handle tight.

"And if that happens, I'll take out as many as I can."

46

Tarantino

+57 Days – 0814 hours

I walked through the lobby door with the fire axe slung over my shoulder. The door hissed to a quiet close behind me. The glass from the shattered windows crunched under my boot. A brown streak of burned out dandelion stems filled in one of the jagged cracks in the asphalt.

The scavengers raised their weapons as I approached the gate, all barrels tracking me.

"Your momma must have taught you well," the leader said.

"Taught me what?"

"To always exit an establishment using the proper exits," he clarified. He definitely was more imposing in person.

I twirled the axe handle like a majorette and let the head spark off the pavement. Dragging it behind me, I stopped at the gate.

"You might want to let that cleaver go, friend," the burly leader warned me.

"I think I'll hold onto it for a while," I replied. "Especially with you having all these friends."

"And the gun?" he asked one of his men.

"Holster's empty," I assured him.

Two of his men flanked me from the other side of the wall.

"Looks clean, Duke," the bearded one from my left called out, his sawed-off shotgun held with his elbow much too high.

"How you want to play this, Duke?" I asked the man in the denim jacket as if we were old acquaintances.

Duke smiled with ultra white teeth at my familiarity.

"Well," he replied, "how about a name from you so I have equal footing? I'm sure your momma raised you better on that point, too."

"I wouldn't be so sure about that."

"Well," he added, "common courtesy isn't a foreign concept, I hope?"

"John."

"Well, John," Duke said, "I made my position quite clear earlier, don't you think? You clear the Festers in the parking lot?"

"No," I shook my head. "The gates were open and the parking lot was empty when I got here."

"I know there's a few more festers in there."

"I know you know," I replied. "They came in after me. Their mommas didn't teach them to use the doors instead of the windows."

He belted out a hearty laugh.

"Anyone else?"

"There's more around. I heard scraping behind a few doors."

"Fuckin' things will be the death of me," Duke spat out.

Joey stood partially behind him, his eyes to the ground.

A woman smirked, holding a Remington 30/30 on me with a too tight grip, her finger pulsing against the trigger. Donny, back in the ranks, held a new Beretta on me in a one-handed grip, the barrel turned slightly sideways. The bearded man to my left pointed his sawed-off shotgun toward the ground, tired of holding the weapon in such an obscene high-elbowed stance. His finger wasn't even on the trigger.

I smiled at Duke.

He smiled back.

"What'll it be?"

"I think I'll stay put," I decided with a shrug. "Thanks, anyway."

"You know I can't abide that," Duke replied, nodding. "Donny and Francis, if you please."

I leaned the fire axe blade on top of my boot.

Donny grinned and moved toward me with his Beretta pointed at me like a hood rat from a bad urban film.

127

The man on my opposite flank – obviously the man named Francis – grabbed the gate and pulled it the rest of the way open. When the gate clanked against the frame, he and Donny trained their weapons at my chest and continued their approach.

I kicked up the flat of the fire axe head.

It struck Francis under the chin.

His head snapped back.

Donny's mouth made an O as he reached for his crumbling partner.

I swung the axe again.

The flat of the blade connected to his ear.

He bounced off the wall as he fell.

"Unwise," Duke's smile faded and a faint crease fell to his brow. "Arnold."

I shrugged, hefting the axe across my shoulders.

Arnold, the bearded man with the seemingly too-heavy sawed-off shotgun stepped forward. Surprisingly, Lady Remington rushed forward, too. She still gripped the rifle too tight.

Arnold didn't hold the shotgun tight enough.

I easily swiped the barrel away from him.

"Oh," he stared at his suddenly empty hands.

I drove the shotgun tailstock into his face.

It cracked into the bridge of his nose, bursting it open with a spurt of blood.

"Shit," Lady Remington exclaimed as Francis dropped to his knees.

Red crept into my vision.

Her knuckles turned white as she started to pull the trigger.

I threw the shotgun at her.

She turned the rifle away to block it.

The shotgun jammed her fingers against the stock.

She hissed and dropped the Remington.

I hooked her ankle with the axe blade and pulled.

She landed hard on the pavement, her head bouncing off the

asphalt.

I kicked the rifle and the shotgun away from the pair and looked back at Duke.

Duke's massive jaw clenched and unclenched.

Joey continued to stare at the asphalt, having backed up a few steps toward the panel truck. The driver had drawn up the AK-47, resting the barrel on the strut of the side mirror.

The fire axe went back up to my shoulder.

Duke brought up his Beretta M9 and pointed it at my forehead.

"I could drop you now and end this foolishness."

"You could."

A shot rang out.

The side mirror on Duke's motorcycle disappeared with a spark.

Duke and the truck driver looked for the source.

Joey crouched against the truck's radiator grille.

The others still lay on the ground, now keeping as low as possible in addition to tending to their injuries.

"Interesting turn of events," I ventured. "Why don't you collect your friends over here and light out."

Duke glared at me, his weapon coming up again.

"Kill me and you'll get shots in the tops of your heads before you can even turn your bikes around."

"He is a hard man to kill," Bowers said as he stepped around the corner of the wall with the M4 drawn tight to his shoulder.

Duke partially swung his weapon toward Bowers.

"Sergeant." I nodded.

"Sergeant," Bowers replied with a grim smile.

Duke looked between us. He hefted his Beretta twice before holstering it.

"I'm not giving up my weapons."

"Didn't expect you to," I replied.

Francis and Donny stirred, crawling over to Lady Remington cradling her fingers and Arnold nursing his bloody nose.

"Help your friends. Turn your bikes around. And be on your way."

"Everyone get up," Duke ordered. "We're exiting."

I backed up a few meters with the axe on my shoulder.

Bowers leaned against the wall, his M4 trained on our visitors.

Francis helped Lady Remington up while Arnold lifted Donny to his feet until they were steady enough to retreat under their own power.

They collected their weapons.

Lady Remington grabbed the rifle by the trigger guard.

"Don't, Deb," Duke warned her a second before I did.

She glared at him, her fingers bruising.

The four of them escaped to the uncertain safety of their bikes. They strapped down the gasoline cans, shouldered their weapons, and put their helmets on. In turn, Twin-Vs and Knuckleheads revved to sputtering life.

Bowers joined me.

Deb glared back at me from her open helmet.

Duke led the column of motorcycles down the block. Joey hopped up into the passenger seat of the truck. The driver started the engine and made a sloppy three-point turn to follow. The column turned right at the corner, only the diminishing sound of opened throttles marking their departure.

After a few minutes, the noise dissipated entirely.

Bowers looked back at the apartment on the sixth floor. The rifle barrel receded and a hand stuck itself out and gave a thumbs-up.

"You're something, John."

"Who's the sniper?"

"Melissa and Jude fought over who got to be on overwatch."

"Jude won?"

"Yep. Paper covers rock."

Bowers looked behind me.

"How long before you were going to bring out the Glock?"

I pulled it from under the back of my shirt and returned it to my holster.

"It was getting close."

"What now?"

"We move while we still can."

47

Congregation
+57 Days – 1950 hours

Bowers, Jude and I stood at the head of the westward service drive. Summer, Lenny and April leaned against the guardrail. Holly had run off in search of privacy to do her business. We could have used any of the cars in the apartment's parking lot but did not find a vehicle that was running or suited the needs of nine passengers, including a dog.

Melissa and Victoria knelt next to the backpacks.

"Come on, Vicky," Melissa said with disgust. "How much shit do you think you can carry? No wonder your back hurts."

Melissa dug inside the pack. She dragged out a winter jacket, a photo album and a rawhide bone.

"Really?"

"I thought Holly would like it."

"She'll survive."

Melissa glanced over at us. I shrugged but took the rawhide off her hands. Holly would like it.

Victoria went to the album and hugged it.

"Pick out a couple and leave the rest, Victoria," Jude insisted. "You won't make it two days with all of that."

Victoria started looking through the pages, eventually pulling out six or seven pictures and finding a zip-loc bag to put them into.

"Keep the bags," I said.

"See, Lissa?" Victoria whined.

"Let's hurry up, ladies," I suggested, listening for the buzz of motorcycles and waiting for the itching under my skin to pick back up.

"Come on, Vicky," Melissa complained. "Even Summer knew what to pack."

Summer smiled from the railing with her feet up on her roller suitcase, its handle extended. She even threw in a wave of the hand to prove how compact and efficient her packing was.

"Come on, Mom," Summer said. "We need to find a car big enough for all of us before dark."

"Are we sure Victoria is her mom?" Bowers asked. "She definitely takes after Aunt Melissa."

Jude smiled before punching Bowers in the arm.

"Ouch! Hey!"

"Children," I said in a firm voice.

The buzzing had returned, as I'd feared.

A horn blared from over the next rise.

Jude and Bowers stopped talking, spreading out across the road.

"What is it?" Bowers asked.

"Let's move," I called out.

Holly returned at a run, stopping in front of me. She started a growl deep in her throat.

"Enough said," Jude confirmed. "Come on, ladies. Let's go."

Summer ran past me with her roller suitcase rattling off the concrete. Lenny picked up the plastic grocery bags for April. They shifted from foot to foot as Melissa zippered up her sister's backpack and helped her into the straps. Once the pack was secured, they hurried as a group toward me. Jude and Bowers closed into formation behind them.

We jogged up to the next rise. Summer, already there, let her suitcase handle fall to the asphalt. As I came up beside her, I could see the half-mile to the next crest and intersection in the road.

More than a hundred FRACs milled along the side street at the lowest valley. They clustered around a convoy of three minivans in the right lane. The closest of the undead were rocking against the vans while the FRACs on the perimeter tried to reach in as far as they could.

"Go around?" Bowers checked our six. "Go back to the last

overpass?"

"They seem pretty interested in the vans," Melissa added. "Can we get to the parkway? Slip through a hydrant cut-out?"

A muffled scream came from one of the vans.

"There's people in there!" Jude exclaimed. "We have to help them."

"Are you insane?" Victoria shrieked in a panicked voice. "We can't help them."

"I'm in," Melissa said.

"Me, too," Summer added.

"I'm related to crazy people." Victoria shook her head.

The Gaunt Man stood at the edge of the mayhem.

He pointed to a panel truck nearest us on this side of the undead congregation. It didn't look stripped - just parked and abandoned. The driver's door and the rollup door were closed. The tires were inflated with good tread.

"If we get that truck running," I said, pointing at it. "Figure it out from there."

A series of pops and flashes erupted from inside each of the closed minivans.

Nine shots rang out in total.

Fresh blood splattered on the inside of the minivans' windows and dripped down the glass, obscuring the view inside even more.

The FRACs slowed their assault and eventually dispersed away from the vehicles.

Jude and Bowers exchanged knowing looks.

"Never mind," I sighed. "Nothing we can do now."

"You're just going to let them die?" Summer demanded.

Jude swallowed as she tried to find the right words.

"They opted out, kid," Bowers said, looking back at the way we had come. "Must have had an exit strategy."

"Yeah," I agreed, a numbness descending on my heart.

I was suddenly very tired.

Not sleepy.

Just worn down.

A single tear fell down Jude's face.

Just one.

None of us spoke for a while, the gravity of what had happened to those people sinking in. We rested from the relative safety of the hill and watched the sun burn a fiery crimson and orange as it sunk behind the slowly breaking communion of the undead.

48

Boxed and Wrapped Up
+58 Days – 0028 hours

We huddled inside the panel truck.

FRACs slapped against the aluminum from time to time, but the majority of the herd had shuffled off in search of new sights, sounds and food.

Why don't the undead flock to you and your group?

I held a finger to my lips as another group bounced off the sides of the truck.

Just keep moving along, please.

Victoria and April whimpered into their sleeves.

Summer sat cross-legged on the wheel well, running her hair through her fingers and staring at the opposite wall.

Holly curled up between Summer's knees, snoring lightly.

Melissa squatted at the back of the enclosure, her head against the roll-up door and her hand on her rifle.

Lenny slept with his grocery bags at his feet.

I leaned behind the driver's seat.

Jude and Bowers sat together behind the other seat, whispering to each other. I made an effort to block out their conversation.

At the other corner of the roll-up door the all-too familiar pale man in the well pressed, although frayed and worn black suit stretched out with his legs crossed at the ankles. His wingtips were glossy in spite of the dim interior.

Beautiful place you have here, Johnnie.

The Gaunt Man interlaced his fingers, propping them behind his head. He looked at the roof.

Shame about those people, isn't it? If only you had gotten to them sooner. That Victoria. Isn't she a piece of work? If only she hadn't slowed down the show with all those decisions about

136

packing and what precious memories to keep.

I sighed and closed my eyes.

His presence resonated louder than anyone else in the truck. The buzzing in my head became a screeching grind – the metallic equivalent of nails on a chalkboard.

I opened my eyes.

The Gaunt Man was straddled across my legs, leaning his face into mine. I twitched, trying to keep from jumping out of my skin.

The whispering between Jude and Bowers had stopped.

Stick with me, kid. I'll take you places. See the world!

His face physically brightened into a glowing luminance. I averted my eyes until it faded.

He was gone.

I put my fingers to the bridge of my nose until the spots behind my eyelids faded.

He was still gone, thankfully.

Everyone stared at me, except the slumbering Lenny and Holly.

"Get some sleep," I snapped, shutting my eyes in a vain attempt to chase the sandman down for myself.

49

Diehard

+58 Days – 1015 hours

The heat inside the truck was becoming unbearable with the sun beating down on the metal paneling. Melissa had opened the roll-up door a few inches while the sleepy Lenny cranked open both of the roof vents. It helped – but just barely.

"Damn it," Jude said, pulling her shirt away from her neck. "It's going to be freakin' hot out today."

Holly lay at the base of the roll-up door, her snout pushed through the gap for fresh air. April and Summer leaned against each together on the wheel well, with Lenny being the sudden odd man out. He looked incomplete.

Melissa decided to go through Victoria's backpack one more time.

"If John gets the truck started you may be able to keep stuff," Bowers said.

"How 'bout it, Sergeant?" Jude asked me.

"Yeah, Sergeant?" Bowers mimicked with a smile.

I got up, not bothering to stretch. My body felt good and my mind clear and quiet in spite of another sleepless night. The buzzing was gone. It had haunted me most of the night, even after the Gaunt Man had made his grand light show exit.

I looked out the windshield.

A few FRACs wandered around the service road, oblivious to our presence. Some still banged against the three minivans, clawing against the closed windows. One bit into the chrome trim above the window in an attempt to rip open the metal, but only succeeded in losing several teeth in the process.

I knelt under the dash, squeezing in between the steel floor shell and the driver's bucket seat. Dislodging the steering column sheath with my tactical knife, I pulled down the cables and cut through the red ignition wire.

Stripping back the two lower wires, I sparked them together. The motor turned over, the radio blurting out static. Jude reached over me to turn off the knob.

"Thanks," I said.

The engine died.

I touched the wires together again.

Nothing.

"Gas gauge needle moved to half-full for a second," Jude advised.

"It needs a jump," Bowers added.

"Thank you, Sergeant Obvious," Jude snickered.

"Yeah," I said, tying the wires together for the moment.

When I sat up I realized everyone had crowded behind the seats to watch the excitement.

Or lack thereof.

"Need a battery," I announced.

"And I need to pee," Lenny added to the list.

I slipped into the driver's bucket seat and tapped the steering wheel. Leaning forward, I watched the gap-toothed FRAC continue to scratch against the lead minivan. The other walkers had completely lost interest and moved farther up the road.

"Let's take care of everyone's needs," I finally said. "Bio breaks and a battery from one of those vans."

"A battery from down there?" Victoria asked. "You're kidding, right

"Nope," I replied.

50

Overbite

+58 Days – 1031 hours

The others stood by the panel truck as I made my way down the service road toward the minivans. The Dentist's Dream FRAC continued to gnaw at the minivan's driver's door, scraping his blackened bloody fingers against the window. He smeared pus around the glass as if he was a kindergartener creating his first finger painting.

I glanced through the windows of the last of the three minivans. The insides of the passenger windows were sprayed with blood, obscuring the view to the interior. A woman in her thirties or forties leaned against the side door, shot through the temple with her hair sticking to the glass. In the driver's seat with a gun in his lap, a male of roughly the same age sat against the headrest with the top of his head opened up and matter dripping from the liner.

I moved to the second minivan.

The FRAC continued to peer into the lead vehicle, this time tapping his head against the window in a slow rhythmic motion.

I pulled my knife and reversed my grip so the edge was down and out.

Down and out – like the passengers in the vans.

In the second minivan – a Ford Aerostar – two small children held each other in a siblings' loving embrace, a splash of deep red on the bench seat behind their heads.

My stomach clenched.

The front passenger seat was occupied by whom I assumed to be the children's mother, her body and arms outstretched to the young ones in the back seat. A red hole adorned her forehead. This driver had a smaller caliber handgun than the other driver.

Dentist's Dream continued at the lead minivan, a late model

Honda Odyssey. I tapped the rear window with the blade of my knife.

The FRAC cocked his head toward the noise.

Dressed in khaki Docker's pants and a Polo shirt perfect for Sunday brunch, he wouldn't have been admitted to any restaurant with his shoeless feet. The one muddy holey sock he still wore would have invited the appropriate scorn of a proper maître de.

As he turned around, his need for proper dental work was on full display under the flaps of his ripped open cheek. A gold-hoop earring clung to a torn earlobe. His eyes were flooded with cloudy cataracts but they seemed to bore through me. He clicked his remaining teeth together, the sound made louder without his cheek to muffle it.

Dentist's Dream FRAC stood in front of me, watching and listening to the clicking blade on the rear window. I stopped the tapping. The FRAC turned his head a little bit toward me, wetness draining from his left eye.

Were those tears?

I thrust the knife blade into his ear up to the hilt.

His clicking teeth stopped.

It was time to get that battery.

51

It's Alive! Alive!

+58 Days – 1101 hours

The death of the Odyssey and its occupants was a morbid blessing.

"Christ, Sergeant," Jude demanded. "There a reason you weren't paying attention to the deadhead?"

"I had it under control."

"Gave that one an earful, didn't you?" Bowers added.

Lenny snickered.

Bowers grinned to his captive audience, proud of his clever puns.

The battery from the truck was already removed – courtesy of Bowers – allowing me to stick the Diehard directly into the motor compartment. I tapped the leads onto the positive and negative terminals and tightened them down with an adjustable wrench Jude had found in the glove compartment.

I left the others to stare under the truck's hood while I went to the driver's side. I reached for the wires, untied them and sparked them together again. The motor roared to life after two cranks. I retied the wires and revved the engine.

"There you go!" Bowers shouted with enthusiasm, slamming the hood closed.

The gas gauge needle did indeed float up to the half full mark. None of the other service lights winked back to life after ignition.

Good news.

"Good to go, people," I shouted over the engine. "Let's get."

"Can I use the cigarette lighter?" Lenny asked.

52

Smooth Sailing

+58 Days – 1128 hours

I accelerated past the minivans in case Summer hoped to catch one last look. We rode in silence along a clear stretch for a couple miles. Our luck faltered again as we rounded a bend and ended up in a line of traffic that littered the two lanes in our path. Some had veered onto the shoulder in a haphazard fashion. The rest were parked almost bumper to bumper.

"Hold on," I called out.

The left shoulder was overgrown, barely wide enough for the truck. The powerful diesel engine roared as the driver's side panels scraped loudly along the guardrails.

Everyone braced as best they could as we went up a sloping incline. In the rear view mirror, I saw Holly skid across the back. She landed against Bowers who had wedged himself in the rear corner with a leg pressed against the wheel well.

"Hey there, pup," he said.

She climbed up onto his lap. Bowers groaned and made a face as Holly leaned a paw against his tender parts. Victoria giggled at Bowers' discomfort, and then squealed and tipped over with surprise as the truck pitched the other way.

Lenny and April hugged each other behind the passenger seat, still dejected that the cigarette lighter charger hasn't worked to charge their phone. They continued to have bad luck with charging that device.

Once we cleared the traffic jam at the intersection, I centered the truck over the dividing line of the two westward lanes. From the empty highway ahead it looked like we were finally in for some well-deserved good luck.

143

53

Jackknife

+58 Days – 1836 hours

The sun had dropped considerably into the western skies, burning a glaze of bright amber against the dust, smoke and clouds thick on the horizon. I dropped the visor against the glare, my eyes more sensitive these days.

"You need my shades?" Bowers offered from the back.

"I'm good."

"Stubborn," Jude said from the passenger seat. "I thought Marines were tough."

"Marines have a softer side," Bowers teased. "Right, John?"

"Umm," was my response.

"Yeah," Bowers continued, unimpeded, "the good Sergeant here has a heart of gold, is loyal to a fault, and loved by all."

I heard a bit of sarcasm laced in Bowers words.

Most likely as a result of my shitty comments from the night at the construction site. Christ, the man helped me to clear a pit full of FRACs in the dead of night. He didn't have special abilities. And he wasn't invisible to them. Bowers was actually a better man than me, by far.

We rounded a bend as I searched for the right words to say to Bowers as an apology.

The words would have to wait.

I pressed on our squeaky brakes.

Our smooth sailing had come to an abrupt end.

"Shit," Jude said as she grabbed the binoculars from the dashboard. "Are you kidding me?"

"What's up?" Bowers asked.

"Looks like we're in trouble again," Jude said.

I put the truck in Park, listening to the engine's bubbling idle.

Two hundred meters ahead, several motorcycles and an idling panel truck were parked across the road. The riders stood beside their motorcycles while the truck driver sat behind the wheel of his vehicle. All had their weapons trained in our general direction.

"Shit is right," Bowers commented from between the seats. "Is it the same gang from the apartments?"

Even though they were over three hundred meters away, I could see them as if they were less than a quarter that distance.

The hulking Duke trained his Beretta on the windshield, centering it directly on the form behind the glass that would be my chest.

Arnold and Deb grinned as they flanked each side of the highway, advancing on us. Her fingers seemed no worse for wear as she gripped a new weapon, a pistol grip M4 Benelli tactical semi-automatic 12 gauge shotgun.

The closer she got with that weapon, the worse the damage would be for us.

Arnold sported wadded up toilet paper in each nostril with a band-aid over the bridge of his nose. He didn't look menacing, but he did look unpredictable.

Maybe more unpredictable than Deb was.

Maybe.

"Step out of the truck," Duke called out through a blowhorn. "Ain't looking for trouble here."

Arnold and Deb had closed to within a hundred meters.

"Everyone get to the back," I ordered.

"No way," Jude objected.

"Screw them," Bowers said. "We can take these clowns."

"Now," I hissed. " Melissa, open the back."

Melissa rushed to do what she was told.

"Hold on."

I slammed the truck into reverse and jammed the pedal.

The truck's rubber squealed as we sped back around the bend, out of sight of Duke's men and the pursuing Arnold and Deb. I

145

reversed another hundred meters before slamming to a stop at the edge of the road beside a crop of evergreens.

"Everyone out!"

Everyone jumped out of the back with their bags and headed to the tree line. Holly leapt into Jude's arms. Before Jude could give me more than a pleading look, I slammed the truck into Drive and hit the accelerator.

What's the plan?

No idea. Just keep them away from my people.

I love it when a plan comes together.

I got up to forty on the speedometer when I approached the pursuing Arnold and Deb.

She fired at the truck.

I accelerated to sixty.

Buckshot sprayed across the hood.

A second shot took out the passenger mirror and window.

Several shots from Arnold blew out the driver's side rear tires.

The steering became unbearably heavy.

I quickly found myself drifting to the right.

Trying to muscle the truck back to center I only succeeded in bending the steering wheel.

I careened to the right.

A breakdown lane and a slight berm loomed ahead.

I corrected as hard as I could against the skid.

The steering wheel snapped away from the column.

The truck swerved left.

The blown out tires overbalanced the truck, tipping it onto its left side.

The windshield cracked.

I slammed against the steering column then the door, losing my breath.

Metal sparked against the concrete.

The truck stopped.

I lay against the door.

The engine still raced.

The asphalt glared inches from my face.

Tempered glass embedded into my arm and cheek.

My shoulder was dislocated.

My head swam.

Murky.

A tire iron scraped against the edge of the windshield.

Leather gloved hands.

Peeling back the glass.

Fresh air swam in where the windshield was missing.

"Hey, hero," Duke squatted down, hands on knees. "Whatcha been doin'? Haven't seen you in like forever."

I smiled, in agony.

"Yep," Duke continued. "Been too long."

His hand cocked back.

"Night, sweet prince."

Black.

54

A Night at the Museum

+58 Days – Evening

Humming filled my ears and vibrations coursed through my body.

I didn't wake to dusty floor planks and magnified ants this time. My blood didn't boil razors.

Small favors.

My arms were tight against my back with what felt like zip ties. My Cobra watch was missing from my wrist. My holster was light and empty.

My Glock was taken… again.

A bump in the road shot pain through my shoulder and upper arm.

Yeah.

Definitely dislocated.

The enclosure was familiar but larger. It smelled of balsa, old paint and Styrofoam. I spent enough nights in a cramped panel truck to recognize another one.

"'Bout time you woke up."

Duke sat across from me on the opposite wheel well. His face flickered in intermittent light but he stayed mostly in shadows.

"Wait until the boss sees you."

"The boss?" I muttered.

"Yeah," Duke replied, wiping a spot of lint off his right sleeve. "He's gonna like you."

"I'm sure." I paused as another bump shot pain through my shoulder. "I'm a charmer."

He laughed good-naturedly.

"We're here," the driver called back.

"Cool," Duke acknowledged, rubbing his smooth hands together. "Show time, John."

The truck braked sharply before slowly backing up. It came to another abrupt, jarring stop.

"Damn, Dwayne."

"Sorry, Duke."

Duke slapped the roll-up door.

A few seconds later, it flew fully open.

Deb was there with her fingers tight around the Benelli's pistol grip. She would be foolish to use it in such close quarters.

Duke reached over and pulled me up by my dislocated arm.

I exhaled roughly.

"Probably dislocated," Duke assessed. "Must hurt like a bitch."

Another of the marauders, Francis, grabbed me roughly under the other arm. They half dragged, half-walked me across a concrete loading dock and then through one of two large blue roll-up delivery bays. Joey glanced my way and looked quickly away like a dog who knows its been found out for doing something bad while the master was not at home. Donny glared at me from a large planked crate, only outdone by Lady Remington Deb who trailed next to us with her Benelli.

"Good weapon," I said. "Your choice?"

She raised the barrel to my gut.

I nodded back.

Arnold stood against a large reinforced concrete column smoking a cigarette. He was struggling to exhale the smoke with the wads of red tissue stuffed up his nose.

He didn't have a very friendly face, either.

They all looked like they would love to hurt me.

"No hard feelings?" I asked as I was escorted past.

He snorted out smoke in my direction.

We went by more wooden crates, packing blankets, and bubble wrap. I tried to shake off Duke's hands-on assistance.

"I'll still keep a hand on ya," Duke warned, "if you don't mind."

I was handily led through the warehouse toward a set of hydraulic double doors. Duke smacked a panel on the wall and the doors hissed open. We walked through to a tiled and ivory painted corridor. Ahead was an elevator.

Duke pushed me to the right to a connecting corridor. Steel doors with placards lined either side, but my captor hurried me along too quickly to read any of them.

At the end of the hallway was a fire door.

We went into a stairwell, and up.

One flight up we emerged out through another fire door and turned a corner into an atrium of stone, concrete, mosaics and tapestries under a set of skylights. A series of columns supported arches under covered mezzanines on either end.

Very impressive digs, I must say.

On the long wall above an alcove leading to a gift shop with a brass revolving door was a massive mural. It depicted a lavish dinner scene with an eclectic mix of alcohol, food and oddities. In the background was the lower half of a huntsman with a bloody stag. Even staring at it, I couldn't take all of the imagery in at once.

On the floor was a large inlayed mosaic cordoned with brass posts and railings. It had a series of vignettes surrounding a central theme of...

"Come on." Duke dragged me to set of steps opposite the mural. Steps ascended to both ends of the space.

Duke pushed me toward the left mezzanine. It balconied the main space on three sides, ending against the wall with the mural and leading into gallery spaces behind the wall.

At the top of the landing we made two quick rights and a left into another dimly lit hallway.

On our left was a gallery exhibit space behind a wall of glass emblazoned with the name 'Knights!'. Duke pulled me through the doorway into a gallery space displaying suits of armor from various medieval eras and locations. On the opposite wall, several massive framed portraits looked down on me.

Duke pulled my arm and led me through one of the two open archways in the wall to a larger gallery space. The waning sunlight from the main space fell away, replaced by flickering torch light in the exhibit. Plexiglas cases held a variety of broadswords, chained maces, spiked gloves and shields.

Surprised the cases haven't been cracked open for the weapons.

In an adjoining space were two curved rows of standalone cabinets filled with military helmets from the Middle Ages era. Lording over the exhibits was the silhouette of a brooding hulking caped crusader from a more modern period – The Batman.

"I'm a big fan of the Dark Knight, too," Duke told me. "Michael Keaton was the best of the bunch, I'd say."

Christian Bale, in my humble opinion.

He guided me to the left of the life size statue on the high pedestal.

"You know he wore black sneakers as part of the costume?" Duke asked. "Crazy, right?"

Duke didn't wait for a response.

Behind The Batman statue another space opened up serving as the elbow between the exhibit space we walked through and a second chamber to our right. A long tapestry ran like a red carpet from our feet to a wooden platform.

On a throne of oak and iron upholstered with cushioned velvet and strips of what looked like a lion's mane sat a bespectacled man. He was slight in frame, with thin features and a close shaved buzz cut.

With the immaculate conditions of the museum, it was curious that a man who was not a king sat on a throne meant for viewing from beyond velvet ropes.

"Whom do we have here, Duke?" His voice resonated in the chamber, strange from his thin lips.

"Just a knave to you, my liege," Duke said, "but a thorn, none the less."

"A thorn, you say," the man replied, letting the '*th*' slide off his tongue.

"Yeah," Duke shuffled his feet, a strong hand still on my bicep. "He took out a few of the men during a supply run."

"Took out? I hope not the lovely Debra?" he asked with genuine concern.

"Yes, she got roughed up a bit with the others because of this guy," Duke amended.

"Ah. So no casualties then?"

"Oh, no," Duke corrected, "No casualties."

"Duke," the man said from the throne, "it is important we use the correct words. Words always have meaning. Let us not forget that for the next time, please."

"Yes, sir." Duke deferred. "My apologies."

"Oh, kind sir," the throne sitter confided to me, "you may have stirred the hornet's nest. Debra is a feisty one."

Duke smirked.

"Do you have a name, sir?"

"Said it was..."

"Let the man speak for himself, Duke."

"John Walken," I said.

"Well, Mr. Walken," the seemingly self-appointed king replied, "welcome to the wonderful Worcester Art Museum. I am the leader here. You may address me as Roy."

"Quite the monarchy you have here, king," I said.

Duke drove me to my knees, his hand still tight on my bad arm.

I hissed in pain.

"Duke," Roy said. "Do not be so harsh to our guest."

"I would be careful with this one."

"It is alright." Roy came down from the throne and stood in front of me.

Duke pulled my bloody head back by the hair. Roy leaned over, his face inches from mine.

"You seem like a smart man, Mr. Walken," Roy whispered, searching my face for something. "Unfortunately, Duke may be right that you may be too smart."

Roy stood again, straightening his white dress shirt.

Just as prim and proper as the Gaunt Man.

"Duke, please escort this young man to the Chapter House."

55

Chapter House

+58 Days – Evening

Duke escorted me out of the 'Knights!' exhibit to the mezzanine and back down the wide stone steps to the center of the main atrium floor. The smooth wall of stone was replaced with a more chiseled and chipped style under the mezzanine, as if transported directly from the perimeter walls of a British countryside castle.

Duke pushed me ahead.

Double arched windows were cut out of the stone, trimmed with more angled stonework and set on a center row of five columns.

Beautiful craftsmanship.

Donny stood at one of the narrow openings, holding a length of heavy chain. It led through a ring mounted at the top of the archway and into the space beyond.

Five meters away, at the other open archway, was Donny's sweep team partner from the apartments. Joey also held the end of a chain.

The back of my neck felt as if fire ants had nested under the skin, burrowing through to the muscles.

Duke grabbed my arm in an upward grip.

The pain nearly eclipsed the insects and their homesteading. Almost.

He stopped me in front of an entryway between the windows that opened into a darkened red hued rectangular room. My shoulder muscles tensed and bone ground against parts of the socket where it shouldn't.

"Ok," Duke ordered the men. "Do it."

I heard Joey and Donny reeling in the chains. The ring clicked against every link as the lines were pulled back in. After several drags they stopped and braced their weight against the lines.

"All set, Duke," Joey said.

"Thank you, boys."

"Welcome to your accommodations," he said as he pushed me forward through the doorway toward a pile of chains lying between two stone columns.

On the far side of the dim chamber was what may have been an altar or mantle. On both sides were stained glass windows with shuffling silhouettes of additional guards standing in front of them.

My shoulder ached with sharp fire. The fire ants bit and crept their way both deeper into my neck and up into my skull.

Duke jammed a boot into the back of my knee.

I dropped to the stones at the center of the room.

The guards at the windows rushed forward to meet us.

Before converging on me their bodies went rigid and their necks snapped back like junkyard dogs at the end of their ropes.

They moaned and reached out at us.

Roy had employed additional guards but they weren't of the hot-blooded living variety.

The FRACs strained against the tight end of chains attached to collars around their necks. They reached forward at us with less than a meter between their ragged fingertips and us.

Duke drove a knee into my hunched back, dropping me closer to the stone floor. Quickly, my wrists were shackled to the chain attached to a ring mounted in the floor.

More chain links clicked through rings.

Another FRAC came up behind us.

Duke jammed a shoulder into the suited walker, dropping it to its ass.

"Damn it, Joey," Duke yelled. "Reel that shit back in."

"Sorry, boss."

The FRAC was dragged back to the interior open window as it tried to get back to its feet. After several pulls on the leash its body was pinned against the wall.

"You good now?" Duke barked.

"I got it," Joey replied between grunts. "I got it."

A last FRAC strained against the other inside arched window, obviously held by Donny with more resolve. The blonde female was dressed in a skirted suit with a red satin blouse. On her blazer was a gold WAM nameplate with the name Libby. She had a tear in her forearm below where her blazer had been ripped away.

"Comfy?" Duke asked, flexing a bicep and running his other hand along the pronounced muscle line.

"I'm good. Thanks."

Duke stood and glanced at Libby and the other business suited walker.

"You got them, boys?"

"Yeah," Joey called back.

"Coming out." Duke moved back into the corridor. "Ok."

The chains went slack.

I tested my chains, rattling them.

Libby and Business Suit FRAC rushed at me, the stained glass walkers still at the end of their lines. Duke wouldn't realize that the FRACs were reacting to the noise of the chains and the stench of human sweat and urine where I was shackled, not me specifically.

When all four were straining against their chains, Duke spoke up. "Enjoy your stay."

He left, the echoes of his work boots quickly fading away.

56

Self Help
+58 Days – Evening

Joey and his friend bullshitted for a while and eventually left. I suppose their shifts ended.

The FRACs finally wandered off to their corners dragging their slack chains behind them. They had strained toward me for a while after Duke left the room, reacting to the chains each time I rattled them.

Based on the strong acrid smell of dried urine and sweat, I was not the first prisoner to be sentenced to the center of this room. But dried excrement wouldn't have made the walkers continue at the end of their chains. There was a Pavlovian response to noise and movement that was only enhanced by the remains of a human scent.

Another fine mess you find yourself in, Johnny.

Inside the Chapter House, several strangely shaped pews were pushed and stacked against the sidewalls keeping the center of the room clear. The Gaunt Man sat atop the stack, leaning precariously forward with his elbows on his knees.

The walkers stood up taller.

The Gaunt Man hopped off the artsy pews and pressed a red-tinted hand against the stained glass.

Beautiful.

He splayed his fingers. The light from outside made him into a one-dimensional cutout of black. The walker chained at that window made no move toward him, only standing silent and still.

Did you know that a chapter house is part of a monastery or cathedral where larger meetings are held? In medieval times the rulers of the land would come to a place like this to take audience with the locals, peasants and the like.

The Gaunt Man tapped the stained glass one last time before facing me and turning luminescent again.

"Ain't you the fount of knowledge?"

I try. I am only as smart as the people around me. Libby is a very knowledgeable woman.

He wandered around the room. Once he completed a full cycle, he scratched the side of his head.

You ready to bust out of here?

I raised the late Middle Age era shackles.

Eh. I could get out of them.

"Yeah. But you're not real."

Aren't I? Well, that's unfortunate.

I dropped my arms, the heavy iron chains thunking to the stone.

My dislocated shoulder twinged with pain but not as bad as before. I rolled my shoulder.

The pain flared.

Getting my feet under me, I squatted and tested the length of chain under the shackles. With almost a meter of chain on both sides of the ring mounted in the floor, I could stand with my arms loose.

With a deep exhale I drove my shoulder into the stained stone tiles.

This time I couldn't help but let out a yell through gritted teeth.

The FRACs stayed still.

I lay on the floor.

Almost done, my boy.

I dragged to my feet again, my arm dangling and throbbing.

Grabbing the shackle's chains in each fist, I looked at the Gaunt Man who stood watching and nodding his approval. I let out a long breath, spittle flying from my mouth.

One… two…

I dropped onto my shoulder again.

I clenched against the second scream rising in my throat, but failed to keep it suppressed.

This time the FRACs joined in with their own moaning voices.

Maybe they did so in solidarity.

Or maybe it was because they hadn't fed in a while.

57

Ten-Hut

+58 Days – Night

"How's it going in there?" Duke called out from the corridor.

I looked up from the work on my shackles. Libby FRAC and business attire FRAC were dragged back to the archway, the chains skimming across the stone floor, their freedom reeled in.

Duke made his appearance at the entrance.

"Enjoying our hospitality?"

"Not five-star accommodations," I replied. "Should let management know."

Libby strained against her collar, reaching out toward Duke at the entrance. Business attire FRAC stood complacently at his own archway.

He seems sad.

Probably still upset at that beating Duke gave him.

I shook my head at the notion.

The two bound walkers at the stained glass windows slowly advanced, links of chain skittering across the floor.

"What's the deal, Duke?"

"Whatcha mean?"

"Seriously?" I asked. "You have a man ruling from a throne in a museum."

"He is eccentric," Duke replied with a snort. "I'll concede to that."

"So?"

"So what? Got a good place here."

"Even if you don't seem to be above taking prisoners."

"You downed four of my men."

"All still breathing, correct?"

"Yeah," Duke shrugged. "But Deb is not a big fan of yours at the moment. I would steer clear of her if possible."

"Really?" I asked as I raised my shackled wrists.

"Well," Duke agreed with a laugh, "you have a valid point there."

"So this is my penance?"

"Gotta be taught a lesson. Made an example, if you know what I mean." Duke sighed and leaned against the wall. "What do you want me to tell ya? We're safe here. Isn't that enough reason?"

"You could've let me pass on the highway."

"Actually," Duke replied with a grim smile, "I couldn't."

He turned to the corridor and waved his hand. I instinctively raised my hand to wave back but was stopped short by my shackles.

The chains on the walkers had slackened again as Duke's men let go of their leashes. Links rattled on the stone as the FRACs approached, milling within a few meters of me.

Libby looked at me, or more accurately, at the spot where some humanity had been formerly chained.

She clicked her teeth together.

Abruptly they turned their backs to me and stood silently, guarding me against the deepening darkness.

58

Admin

+59 Days – Night

A painful prick stung my side.

I awoke to blackness in the Chapter House.

Libby and the other interior wall FRAC who I had named George had been pulled back to the archways. Their black forms flailed against their restraints, their arms pin-wheeling.

The glint of a blade thrust out of the darkness.

I blocked it with my shackled wrists.

It thrust out again, sparking off the iron.

"Shit head!" Lady Remington – Deb to her friends – said, arcing the knife down again.

I dove under their thrust and drove a shoulder into her belly.

She exhaled sharply, staggered and fell back on her ass.

The knife skittered away.

"Damn it," she yelled.

She got her feet under her and felt around for the blade.

"Christ, Deb," someone called out from behind the window, my line of sight to the window columns making it impossible to see out to the main atrium. "These festers are getting really agitated. Hurry up."

"Yeah," the other guard chimed in.

Finding the blade, Deb switched the knife to her left hand and rolled her right hand into a fist.

She swung a powerful roundhouse punch to my jaw.

Pain lit up my face.

She backhanded me with the same closed fist.

My lip split.

The FRACs chained to the outside walls lunged at her but were audibly snapped back by the collar.

She backed up and made a running kick at my chest.
Something cracked.
I rocked back, using the chains to stay upright.
"Shit, Deb. They're getting squirrelly."
"Tie the chains off then," Deb hissed, turning to the archways.
I spit coppery blood, a wheeze escaping my throat.
Deb switched the knife back to her strong hand.
The FRACs strained against their chains as she advanced.
"Stop," I said as a warning.
Deb smiled and raised the blade anyway.
"Stop!"
Her smile faded as she lowered the knife to her side. I guess
my bravado clipped the strings of her hateful vengeance.

The FRACs also stopped pulling at their restraints. The stained
glass walkers wandered back into the darkness, their chains
dragging and clicking on the floor behind them

"Okay, Deb," the first guard called out. "They calmed down a
bit."

"Hurry up," the other one said. "Duke's gonna kill us."

"Calm down, pussies," Deb replied.

She redirected her angst back toward me.

I guess my bravado had had no effect after all.

She is a driven woman.

"Where were we?"

"Mid-torture, I believe."

Her bobbed brown hair skirted inches from my face.

"If I was in the mood for messing you up, I would have
brought the Benelli and some rock salt. Or just more buckshot."

A tingle spread across my cheek, my jaw line swelling.

"Are you this far gone?" I asked.

She stared at me with her head cocked and brow raised.

"What did you do?" I took a different approach. "Before, I
mean."

She backed up a step.

"Worked in a fucking office. So?"

"You ready for this, Deb?" I asked, breathing through the pain. "This is a different form of administration than you're probably used to."

"No less than you deserve."

"Maybe," I shrugged. "But is saving face that important?"

"Survival and respect are fleeting," she said as she backed up another step toward the corridor.

"So is life," I added. "Just think about the necessity of it."

She raised and pointed the knife at me.

"This isn't finished," she warned, backing to the door. "And, yes, it's necessary."

She stormed off across the atrium.

"We done?" one of the handlers asked.

"I guess so," the other responded.

"Cool. I'm heading back to post."

They dropped their chains and walked to the main stairway.

I sighed and spat out blood.

You seem to be a very important person, Johnny.

I exhaled with pain and sunk to my knees, sure that a rib had cracked.

You'll be right as rain in no time.

Couldn't say that the Gaunt Man was wrong to either comment. Unfortunately, the level of my importance seemed to correlate directly with the amount of suffering and pain I was to be subjected to.

I plopped my shackled wrists onto my lap.

This seemed to be my new station in life.

59

South Lot

+59 Days – Morning

A klaxon sounded.

Emergency lights flickered to life.

The Chapter House brightened, the tinted residue from the stained glass windows across the floor fading.

The alarm squawked twice more before going silent.

Joey, Debra, and two other guards ran past. Their sneakers slapped against the floor, sending up an echo through the main atrium and into my prison cell.

"Get the staves," Duke's voice boomed from the stairway landing. "No firing. I'll pistol whip the first one I smell GSR on."

"We got infected on the south parking lot," someone yelled.

"Well," Duke called out, "Where should you be, then?"

He descended the steps and strolled over to the doorway.

"Idiots," he said as he peeked through the opening. "Almost every one of them."

"I told you to watch out for Deb," he leaned against the wall, glanced at my face, and smiled. "She's really taken a shine to you. Or is the word shiner?"

"Thanks for the warning," I replied. "I'll live."

"For now," Duke said, his grin fading.

"Having security issues?"

"Nothing we ain't prepared for. Don't worry your sweet head about it."

A series of muffled gunshots.

"Fucking idiots," Duke shook his head.

"You sure you don't want help?"

"We have it well in hand," he replied. As more sporadic rifle shots rang out he sighed and added, "But I'll let you know."

165

60

Houdini

+59 Days – Morning

Lady Debra Remington had done me a favor.

Her knife strike against the shackles had nicked off the hammered top of the hinge pin. Even several hundred-year-old restraints couldn't last forever. Using my pinkie finger, I forced the pin halfway through the hinges. Grabbing the exposed pin with my teeth, I pulled it out the rest of the way.

One more gunshot popped in the air, closer than before.

I spat the pin and the metallic taste out, the pin tinkling off the floor.

With one wrist free, I pulled against the other restraint. Skin scraped off, the welling blood providing lubrication enough to finally slip the shackles off.

The FRACs drifted over with the scent of fresh warm blood but did not become agitated.

"Randy," Duke yelled, coming back into the atrium. "Swear to Christ! Knock it off!"

Several of Roy's marauders walked past, looking worse for wear. They were bloody and sooty. Some came back with tar staining their hands and clothes. The man named Randy – the driver of the WAM panel truck – and Joey carried several long spears between them.

Duke moved quickly across the corridor and slapped Randy on the back of the head. Randy rocked forward; his grip on the spear handles keeping him on his feet. Even Joey pitched forward a few steps.

"What'd I tell you about the gunshots? Goddammit!"

"Sorry, Duke."

Randy shrugged up his shoulders to protect himself from another of his boss's meaty-handed hits. "The festers got too close for the spears."

"Then you choke up on the handle, asshole," Duke said, letting the stave bearers go past without another word or another slap.

Leaning on the entryway wall, Duke tapped a cigarette out of its pack. He clicked open a Zippo with a Confederate Flag emblem and flicked its flame to life. It lit up his face with wavering orange and yellow, a single drop of light sparking off his eyes.

Duke looked at me, letting the Zippo's flame dance. "You shitting me?"

I sat cross-legged on the floor between the stone columns, the bloody iron shackles in a pile of chain next to me.

He snapped closed the lighter and walked into the Chapter House. Libby and George staggered toward him. Duke punched George in the face, caving in the bridge of his nose and dropping him to the floor. George did not stir. By the time Libby got to the end of her chains, Duke was past the extent of her reach.

"Why you still here then?"

I raised my torn and darkened wrists.

"Maybe I still need some first-aid."

What do you really need?

I didn't rightly know.

"You're definitely a crazy shit, aren't you?"

"Maybe."

"Get up."

I did as I was told. Duke still towered over me by six inches.

"What's your play?"

"Three hots and a cot."

"You don't need to be here to get that."

"Maybe," I answered. "And maybe you need the help."

Duke's glare bored through me. I could almost hear the gears turning as he mulled over the situation.

Another of Duke's guards shuffled by, a spray of viscera on his shirt and his eyes staring at his feet as he walked.

"Let me see what I can do," he nodded slowly.

61

Hard Labor

+59 Days – 1243 hours

Duke led me to the delivery bay where I had been originally brought in.

"Is this where we part ways?" I asked, adjusting my newly returned Cobra watch around the bandages on my wrist.

"Always a mouth on you," Duke replied. "Just wait here."

You should make a break for it.

The Gaunt Man was probably right. But they still had my Glock.

You have such a hang-up about that weapon.

We'd been through a lot, that Glock and I.

The two-way radio on Duke's hip burst into static life.

"Coming in," the voice over the radio advised.

"Understood, over," Duke replied, the radio held close to his mouth.

A truck with WAM and Worcester Art Museum written out on the panels appeared. A large concrete and stone building loomed behind the vehicle on the opposite corner.

I took one step toward the edge of the loading bay platform.

It is just one step toward freedom.

I caught a glimpse of Duke moving his free hand toward his sidearm. He didn't say anything, still holding the radio up to his mouth. I stretched and looked up at the blue skies, white wispy clouds drifting through the stratosphere.

I don't think they are in the stratosphere.

Shut up.

A flash caught my attention.

On the edge of the atrium roof, a man looked down at me from the other end of a rifle. Even if I had overpowered Duke without

169

catching a bullet in the gut it was more likely that I would catch one in the back of the head by one of his snipers.

"Stay back," Duke warned, grabbing a handful of collar and pulling me back from the edge. "Dwayne can't park worth a shit. That's why we keep Randy 'round 'cause he's a better driver.'"

The museum truck revved as it reversed down the ramp toward us. It drifted side to side, nearly clipping two of the parked cars on its passenger side.

"Jesus," Duke said.

He is definitely right about that one.

Dwayne was indeed a poor truck driver.

He straightened out at the last moment, still managing to skim dangerously close to a concrete retaining wall that connected a series of steps to the locking dock.

Brake lights glowed for a moment before the truck's bumper unceremoniously bounced off the delivery dock's rubber mounts.

"Jesus." Duke shook his head with his reiteration.

The ignition cut off.

The driver's side door swung open and Dwayne hopped down from the cab.

"What's up, McDonald?" Dwayne said with a huge smile.

"How many times have I told you to cut that shit out," Duke growled. "I am this close to bashing your head in."

"Couldn't help it," Dwayne replied as he ascended the steps to the dock. "Plus, you're gonna thank me for what I brung ya."

"Excuse me, mister," Dwayne said to me.

I stepped back another meter.

Dwayne swung open the roll up door latch lock and hefted up the door. It rattled up its track, exposing a trailer full of palletized propane tanks of different sizes.

"You can have it your way, Boss," Dwayne beamed.

"Well, Dwayne," Duke replied, "you definitely did good this time around. Nice haul."

"I figured you would appreciate the size of my haul." Dwayne winked at me.

Duke smiled but left his ultra white teeth behind his lips. He rapped his knuckles on a few of the tanks, each sounding back with a dull but deep reverberation.

"All nice and full for ya," Dwayne said with pride.

"How did you get them loaded?"

"Nursery farm had its own loading dock and a hand jack. Just need ours to get this stuff off loaded."

"That's why I brought you Mr. Walken here." Duke pointed at me.

"Hey, Mr. Walken." Dwayne nodded.

"Hey back," I replied.

"So," Dwayne asked Duke, "Mr. Walken is going to get the hand jack?"

"No," Duke replied.

"No?" Dwayne repeated.

"No, Mr. Walken is your hand jack," Duke countered, elongating the 'is'.

Sounds dirty.

"Get it done," Duke ordered before returning to the bowels of the museum.

After Duke disappeared into the interior shadows, Dwayne looked at me.

"Well," Dwayne said, shrugging and scratching his head, "I guess you're the hand truck."

"I guess."

"Well, let's get it done," Dwayne said, using his fingers as air quotes to mock Duke one more time.

Dwayne went to the panel truck and grabbed the handles on a propane tank perfect for the everyman's backyard barbeque. The cords in his neck stood out as he attempted to lift it off the palette.

"Christ."

He wiped his hands on his jeans, stretched out his arms at the elbows. After one more stretch at the waist he bent over the propane tank.

"Come on, you son of a bitch," he warned the tank.

He lifted it a few inches off the ground and waddled it off the wood and onto the concrete platform.

"I took the bulk of the labor out for ya," he winked. "I think you can take it the rest of the way."

"Ok," I replied. "Where do you want it?"

"Inside is fine. By that first rack over there."

I grabbed the handles of a second tank, lifting it off the palette with ease. Although full, it felt empty. I lowered it a bit and pantomimed how Dwayne had carried his.

"Heavy, right?"

"Yeah," I lied.

Nice to have all that newfound strength, isn't it?

I passed Dwayne as I headed into the receiving area. When I was out of his peripheral vision I dropped the act and handled the tank with one hand. It still seemed way too light.

"Am I supposed to leave you out here by yourself?" Dwayne asked as he struggled with his second tank.

"Yes," I replied.

I didn't think it would matter if it were true or not. I wasn't going anywhere with the sniper on the roof.

And you want your gun.

There was that, too.

"Cool," he said. "I gotta take a piss."

He hurried away inside the receiving area.

I looked up at the atrium roof. If I stood at the very edge of the receiving area I could still catch a glimpse of the end of the rifle barrel.

Could use the truck as cover.

I could but the incline up the driveway to the street or the steps to the upper parking lot would still make the back of my head a perfect target. I could rush to the wall but the sniper could lead his shot right into the top of my head.

It could work.

But it wasn't worth the risk.

There would be better opportunities.

You hope.

Yeah. I hoped.

With the overwatch position partially obscured I grabbed two more propane tanks and moved them inside with the others. I off-loaded twelve tanks before I heard the slap of Dwayne's sneakers on the painted concrete floor.

"Shit!"

I had returned to hefting one tank at a time as Dwayne came into view around the corner of a steel storage rack.

"How did you get all those tanks inside?" he asked with a sense of amazement. "I was only gone to piss, not drop a deuce."

Now what, smart guy?

"Easy enough, Dwayne."

I rocked one of the tanks, careful not to lift it. Pushing it at the top, I tipped it over onto its side. I gave it a push with my foot and we watched as it rolled across the loading dock and into the receiving area.

"Son of a bitch," Dwayne said. "That's some smart shit, right there!"

"I have my moments."

"I guess you do. Since Duke has got you out here being a human hand truck I guess that means that you are new and are getting hazed."

"That's what I figured."

"Well." Dwayne smiled and shrugged. "Let's stick it to Mickey D and get this shit done ahead of schedule."

"I thought it was McDonald?"

"Anything along those lines works for me," he replied as he strained to tip one of the taller tanks.

"Do tell," I pried lightly as I helped to lay Dwayne's tank on its side.

"Thanks. Christ these things are heavy," he wiped sweat off his forehead. "Duke reminds me of Michael Clarke Duncan. You know? The actor? Except Duke is probably more in love with himself."

"Yeah." I smiled. "I can see that."

"Right? So I tried calling him that but it just don't roll off the tongue, you know? So Michael Clarke Duncan became MCD, which became Mickey D. Once you get there you have all of the fast food taglines to play with. Genius!"

"Works for me," I replied, rolling my shoulders to alleviate a knot that was forming between the blades.

He kicked a tank and watched as it stopped rolling before it made it halfway across the dock.

"Damn it."

He walked over to the stationary tank and gave it another kick. This time it managed to get enough momentum to cross the threshold of the loading bay door but petered out before it had a chance to clink off the other tanks.

"Good try, man," I said, hoping to not sound sarcastic.

"It's all good," he replied, flexing his biceps.

His mood quickly changed.

"Argh!" Dwayne yelped.

A walker grabbed at the leg of his jeans from the edge of the dock, partially obscured by the corner of the truck.

Dwayne hopped on one foot, trying to break free of the FRACs bony grip.

The dead man wore a Boston Red Sox ball cap and had a blackened toothy grin on his face where his lips used to be. He hissed at Dwayne.

"Let go," Dwayne cried. "Come on!"

174

I picked up one of the propane tanks with one hand and swung it around. It smashed into the right side of the walker's head, driving it against the side of the panel truck.

Its head caved in with a wet splat.

Where was the roof sniper now?

As the FRAC collapsed to the road below us, its death grip dragged Dwayne with him. He hopped toward the dock edge.

I swung the tank again.

The tank reverberated as it crushed the walker's wrist against the edge of the platform, slicing it off from the rest of the arm.

Dwayne fell backward, the walker's hand still clutching his pant leg.

"Shit, shit, shit," Dwayne shouted in shock.

I tossed the now bloody tank back on the palette. Gripping the severed hand I ripped it off Dwayne's clothes and dropped it on top of the body below us.

"Thanks," Dwayne said shakily.

"No problem," I replied, extending my hand out to lift him back to his feet.

"Those things get all over. Like cockroaches."

"Yeah." I nodded. "You good?"

"It's all good," he said with a nervous laugh. "Price of living in the new world."

He took a series of deep breaths and shrugged his shoulders to work out the tension.

"Still good?" I asked after his meditative calisthenics were finished.

"I'm good. Let's get back to work. I don't need Duke on my ass for slacking. The excuse of fester attacks don't seem to hold water anymore with him."

"Lead on, boss."

He smiled at that, his chest pumping out and his chin tilting upward a bit. We worked in silence for a few minutes, getting back into the rhythm of the off-loading.

"You been here long?" I asked as we kept working, making sure that I moved two tanks for every one of his.

Making his life easier?

Yep.

"Man, I don't know," Dwayne said, scratching at his stubble. "Seems like forever but I guess it's been a month."

"You from around here?"

"Born and bred. It was just by chance that Duke and his guys picked me up when they did. Hell, I didn't even know there was anyone in this place back then. I could've made it down here on my own before that, had that been the case."

"They scoop you up?"

"Actually, they saved me from a bunch of festers while I was out in the streets getting supplies. Once it was all over they offered to take me in if I was interested."

"And here you are."

"Exactly. As long as I pull my weight like everyone else, it's fine. Roy was very clear about that."

"Roy?" I asked carefully. "The guy in the throne room?"

"That's him."

"What's his story?"

"Not sure. I think he worked here when WAM was still open. He seems to know how to keep things running, though."

"What do you think of the walkers - the festers - in the museum?"

"In the Chapter House? It's scary but effective, I guess. Only the worst offenders get that treatment."

"Worst offenders?"

"Yeah, you know," Dwayne clarified. "Stuff like stealing, desertion, dereliction of duty. Crap like that."

"Does it get much use?"

"Just enough to be a reminder for everyone, I guess."

See, John? You were just an example for the others.

"I see," I said. "Interesting."

"You were the last one in there, right?"

"Yeah."

"Was it horrible?"

"Yeah," I lied.

Although it wasn't a lie, was it? The FRACs cared nothing for me. They didn't see me at all. But the living still saw me. Duke and Debra both had taken a shine to me. The Chapter House wasn't the spot to be if armed men and women thought it justified to exact retribution through violence and pain.

Survival of the fittest seemed to be the preferred choice for the living, much more tangible than faith in one's fellow man.

It has always been survival of the fittest, John. Faith is just an illusion for the weak.

62

King's Court

+59 Days – 1450 hours

Dwayne and I had emptied the panel truck and chatted for a while before Duke returned with two other men and the hand truck that I had substituted for. While the two new men watched me, Duke corralled Dwayne and led him away to talk. Although several meters away from me I could make out pieces of the conversation; Dwayne was giving his blessing to Duke that I was a 'good egg'.

They returned.

After barking orders to the others to put away the propane tanks Duke led me outside again past the rotting corpse and up the steps to the upper parking lot. Once there we went through a PVC gate into an enclosed courtyard with a manicured lawn. Curving paths led to sculptures and benches. There were brushed aluminum tables with umbrellas, chairs scattered around them.

To our right was the rest of the building I was familiar with. Ahead and to the left was a two-story wall of glass, completing the square enclosure with the PVC fence on the fourth side where we had walked in.

Children wandered around inside the corridor that connected the main museum to the more institutional wing.

"That's the learning wing." Duke noted. "Come on, keep up."

Duke took a sharp right into the museum and quickly walked me through a welcome center and a café-style dining area. A sharp left past a security check-in station and through another set of glass double doors led us to a rich oaken stairway. We walked down the center flight to a corridor that led to an exhibition hall on our right. It had been converted to sleeping barracks.

"Inside." Duke pointed to an empty spot in the corner of the hall. "Enjoy."

He unceremoniously turned and left, leaving me to enter the barracks on my own.

Inside there were two rectangular spaces filled with cots, sleeping bags and a few people. The first space had a wall at its center, effectively making a ring. The second smaller rectangular space was connected to the first with a large cutout in the wall. Asian calendar paintings lined the walls.

The spaces were warm, the scent of stale sweat and body odor drifting throughout. There was even the faintest earthy hint of mildew from camping equipment not aired out.

Most of the cots held someone's belongings. I went to the corner that Duke had pointed to. There were no personal belongings or people in that area.

Three hots and a cot.

Duke had been true to his word. The cots were more military olive canvas than weekender camping nylon. Even the blankets were rough wool in a green hue, most likely Army surplus.

The few people in the gallery kept to themselves. Each had a look of what old timers called shell shock, the distant and simple cousin of the more modern and politically correct post-traumatic stress disorder.

I sat down on one of the cots. Blood was soaking through the gauze on my wrists in a few spots. The powers that be must have decided that I hadn't earned a pillow or a wound redressing.

Joey and Randy entered into the exhibit gallery, followed closely by a now tissue-free Arnold.

Joey looked my way and stopped short, his face going pale.

Randy ran into Joey, pitching the smaller man forward a few steps toward me.

"Watch where you're going, retard," Randy advised as he angled away to his own cot.

Arnold stopped to watch his colleague's frustration.

Joey continued to stare, his mouth only working out a few soundless words.

"Don't worry, Joey," I said, palms out. "No trouble. Not even a fire axe. See?"

I gave Joey a big grin to put his mind at ease, producing the opposite effect. He quickly turned away, bumping straight into Arnold's chest. Randy came back and grabbed him by his slim shoulders and steered him toward the other side of the exhibition hall.

"Watch out, idiot," Arnold warned Joey, wandering away to his own cot.

The others in the gallery paid little mind to what just occurred, obviously used to blowups and scuffles.

"Mr. Walken," Roy called from the hallway, his slight frame seeming to take up more of the entry than it should have.

The others now stared at me.

Guess the King usually doesn't talk to the peasants.

"Walk with me," Roy said. "If you please."

I got up from my new digs and joined him in the hallway.

"Quite a feat of will, young man."

"I do alright."

"Quite right," he said with a laugh, shaking his head. "Quite right."

"What's the deal here?"

"Ah. A man with pressing questions," Roy replied as we walked the short corridor. "An inquisitive man."

The corridor quickly opened up to a square space with a deep rich lacquered oak staircase. On our left was a glass door leading to a library. To our right was an exhibition hall for Modern Art with the title 'You Are Here' over the glass double-door entrance.

"Join me, please," he asked as he pulled the glass door open to the library and waved me through with a stiff bow.

The interior stood in stark contrast to the exhibition hall. Instead of modern and sleek, the library seemed filled with the weight of age and knowledge. A long light brown lacquered table sat in the open space, surrounded by four high back leather chairs on each long side and a chair at both ends. Bookshelves and several card catalogs lined up in rows under an open mezzanine with more shelving.

Roy waved a hand at the table, pulling out the chair at the far end for himself and sitting.

I pulled out the chair to his immediate left.

"A very strong collection," Roy said with pride. "You may be unaware that this reading room was originally the museum's Sculpture Gallery."

"Fascinating."

"Truly it is," Roy beamed, unaware of my sarcasm.

"Fifty thousand books. Forty-five thousand slides."

I clasped my fingers together and leaned forward with my hands on the table.

"You have a good place here, Roy. Well organized. Defendable."

"Quite right."

"You are the man in charge," I stated, emphasizing the 'are'.

"I am," Roy smiled. "Master of my domain, as it was."

"You built all this?"

"You could say that," Roy added with a grin. "It pays to know the area."

"I would imagine."

"Impressive how you got out of the shackles," Roy acknowledged, nodding to my wrapped wrists. "And even more impressive that you chose to stay in the Chapter House with the atra mors."

"Didn't have anywhere pressing to go."

"You were heading somewhere before Duke came across you, I would imagine."

"Home is a fairy tale," I shrugged, "and nomadic life is overrated."

"What about your friends?"

"Not much loyalty there," I lied. "Just served to slow me down."

Now it was Roy's turn to lean forward, his hands together and his arms on the table.

"A shame, really," he shook his head slowly.

"It's a matter of survival," I offered. "Something I am sure you are familiar with."

Roy looked around the library, admiring the collections on the shelves.

"Did you know," Roy said, ignoring my last comment or maybe filing it away for future use, "that the end result of the Terrible Death of the 14th century was the increased value of the workforce, bringing peasants from the countryside into the cities, and was the genesis of the decline of the Feudal system?"

"Learn something new every day."

"This pestilence has done the same - in an accelerated fashion, of course. People rushed to the city centers in their ignorance and haste, to their demise.

"And the new working class? We now have a breakdown of classes. Doctors, the police, housewives, and students – you name it – all have the same job to do. Of course, a doctor has more value elsewhere than walking a perimeter, but those who come here pull their weight and contribute to the system as a whole."

"A life lesson, I take it."

"Correct."

"So," I had to ask, "why the torture?"

Roy's facade cracked for a moment, but his lips pursed into a thin solemn line.

"I apologize for the way Duke and Debra treated you," Roy said with bright eyes. "You were a probationary prisoner, but I cannot condone what Debra did. She is a willful woman, to say the least. Her punishment will be doled out."

"Why was I a prisoner to start with? You could have left me on the road."

"True," Roy admitted. "But the way you treated Duke's men left him in quite a state. I made the decision to allow Duke to save face and for me to vet you out. I stand by that decree."

"And the atra mors as watchdogs?" I asked, adopting his nickname for the dead.

"They serve a few purposes. We do not have the manpower or facilities to hold prisoners indefinitely. Plus, we get the added bonus of testing your mettle, so to speak. The atra mors act as pretty good defensive system. Don't you think?"

"Yes," I admitted.

"The chains are short enough to keep the occupants safe from any real harm." Roy beamed at what was apparently his own genius.

"Why the theatrics?"

"Theatrics?"

"A king on a throne."

"Ah, yes, well…"

Duke knocked on the door, interrupting Roy.

Roy called him over with an insistent wave of the hand.

He walked over to Roy and whispered something in his ear.

Roy nodded twice.

"Mr. Walken," Duke said. "You're needed outside."

"As I said, Mr. Walken," Roy added. "We do value our workforce and their contributions to the system. Please follow Duke."

"Come on, Rambo," Duke snickered. "Let me get you that fire axe."

63

The Music Man
+59 Days – 1523 hours

True to his word, Duke allowed me to have my axe. We both leaned against a tree trunk, isolated on a grassy patch on the northwest corner of the museum's property. The intersection of Salisbury Street and Lancaster Street met behind me.

Good to know where I was on a map.

A small parking lot separated me from the museum atrium.

Three sets of heavy metal double doors carved out simple entrances in the middle of the facade. The second story of the façade was windowless and covered with two rectangular 'Knights!' exhibit banners flapping in the breeze.

Above the banners, on the roof, a sniper stood on the roof with a scoped mid-range rifle. I wasn't sure of the shooter's skill, but I was sure his presence was meant to keep me on a short leash.

Like the FRACs in the Chapter House.

Someone whistled.

From the middle door Duke pointed to the other corner of Salisbury Street where it intersected with Tuckerman Street.

I guess it was time to earn my keep for the accommodations.

Duke still had my Glock, knife and machete. But the fire axe would suffice. Its heft was substantial and comforting on my shoulder.

Five FRACs staggered up the curve of the driveway from around the far corner of the museum, wandering into view as they stumbled across the parking lot.

At the head of the undead parade was the Gaunt Man. He reminded me of Robert Preston in *The Music Man*. Although he wasn't regaled in a marching band uniform, the man in the black suit still tipped a salute my way as he made his way up onto the walk towards the steps.

I glanced at Duke. He was still stabbing the air with a finger.

The Gaunt Man, pantomiming the twirl of a baton, gave me a wink.

You may want to step in, Johnny. Wouldn't want them to realize the walkers can't even see you, do you? Please be gentle.

I sighed and spun the axe head in my grip.

Sprinting across the parking lot, I hurdled a low bush and launched myself at the nearest FRAC. I landed a boot on a former meter maid's knee, the leg bending out at ninety degrees. He collapsed to the sidewalk.

Still an admirable job, even for a man.

The flat of the axe head found its way into his skull.

John! You are ruining the parade. What would Al Roker say? I said 'be gentle'!

"Shut up."

I pulled the bladed head back and swung it around to my left. The axe cleaved into the face of a young woman. Her flaxen hair, dry as straw from weeks in the sun, flipped back with the axe's impact.

My stomach clenched.

She had been barely out of her teens.

I pulled the blade out as she dropped.

An older man, who seemed ready to sit on a park bench to feed the pigeons, came up behind the girl.

As he stumbled around the girl's body, I punched through his weathered wrinkled face. The center of his face imploded into the concave shape of my fist.

He fell onto the motionless girl.

Now in the center of the pack, I drove a shoulder into the back of a heavyset black man. Although I was not a Boston Red Sox fan, he showed his support by wearing the team's jersey. He pitched forward but remained on his wobbling feet.

I hooked his ankle with the axe and pulled. Gravity took him and he crashed on top of the growing pile of Old FRAC Pigeon Feeder and the girl with the split face.

The axe continued to do its job as I embedded the blade into the top of Sox fan's head.

Thunk.

The Gaunt Man sat on the steps with his arms crossed over his knobby knees. He shook his head with disapproval.

He was a good man. A family man.

I grabbed the last FRAC in a headlock. The pant-suited middle-aged woman struggled against being restrained.

Go ahead, I guess. Do what you have to do.

My pulse quickened.

Red blurred my vision around the edges.

I tightened my grip on Polyester Pant Suit FRAC.

She continued to flail, slapping her hands against my forearms.

I let out a yell and twisted her neck.

Sinew snapped.

Muscle tore.

Her head tore completely away from her shoulders.

That's one way to get "a-head".

Disgusted, I hurled her bloody top at the Gaunt Man.

It sailed through his insubstantial form and knocked into Duke's leg.

He kicked it away.

I pushed away Pant Suit FRAC's decapitated body as her head bounced down the stone steps to the sidewalk.

"Jesus," Duke said. "You're a piece of work."

"We good here?" I asked, ascending the steps.

The red tint in my vision faded.

Duke turned sideways in the doorway, but put an arm across the doorframe.

"I'll take that axe back," he ordered with a hand out. "And you may want to clean up. You got some Fester goop on ya."

64

Bambi

+59 Days – 1601 hours

I washed up in the basement level restroom.

Steam from the water fogged up the mirror over the sink.

The museum had hot water two months after the infection hit.

Roy was indeed resourceful.

Or clever I would say - at the very least.

The red tint in my vision had disappeared completely.

The Gaunt Man sat on the toilet in an open stall behind me, having followed me in from the front steps.

"You could close the door," I complained.

But then I wouldn't be able to admire you from afar.

Ignoring him I flexed the arm that had ripped the head from a woman's body. Leaning closer to the mirror I couldn't see any swelling in my shoulder – neither from the dislocation or from driving it into the Chapter House floor.

You're a fast healer now, Weapon Z.

The beating at Deb's hands was healing well, too. No swelling on my cheek. The cut on my lip was gone. The kick to my chest only showed faint yellow and purple bruising. And my rib, which I know had audibly cracked, was knitting together again with only minor discomfort.

I dried my face and hands. Throwing the paper towels away in the empty receptacle, I put my shirt on and left the washroom.

"You talking to yourself in there?" Duke asked from his post at the base of the stairs.

"You keeping tabs on me?" I asked.

"Of course," Duke answered. "You don't think you got free reign of the joint, do you?"

"I figured at least the Asian exhibit wing," I replied. "More square footage."

"I knew you were a smart ass."

"Glad to not disappoint," I replied. "What now?"

"Back to the Hiatt for five-star accommodations before dinner."

"What's on the menu?"

"Venison, white boy."

65

Quiet, Please

+59 Days – 1815 hours

Hiatt Hall was nearly full now, filled with chatter. Even with the noise, some of the residents lay on their cots and stared at the ceiling. Some slept.

Debra looked like a solitary island in a busy ocean as she stood in the middle of the hall with one hand on her hip and the other on the Benelli. Joey was using his arms to help convey the story he was telling.

She hefted the shotgun to her shoulder and set her sharp eyes on me, pushing Joey and his animated monologue aside.

"Really?" She spewed as she closed the distance and pointed the shotgun barrel at my chest. "Roy will let in any piece of shit these days."

The choppy seas of conversation calmed. The others who had been staring at the ceiling were now staring at us.

It's time for the show.

"You should have seen him earlier on the front steps," a lanky long-haired man said. "Tore a fester's head clean off."

"Shut up, Roger," Debra hissed.

"Roger that," Roger replied, putting an elbow over his eyes.

" 'Roger that'," Joey chuckled.

"Shut up, Joey," Debra warned.

Joey mimed locking his lips and throwing away the key. When no one reacted to his wit, he shrugged and left the hall with slumped shoulders.

The others didn't bother to feign sleep or disinterest.

"See you're healing up," Debra observed. "I guess I'm losing my edge."

"Your edge is just fine, Debra."

"Don't fuckin' talk to me like you know me."

Deb smoothly lowered the Benelli's barrel as far as my groin.

I wanted to cover my crotch with my hands, but opted to raise them in the air instead.

"Don't cross me."

"Wasn't planning to," I replied, hands still up.

"Better not be."

"How would you like to be addressed?"

"As seldom as possible," she said. "Otherwise, Ms. Staff."

She turned away, the weapon's stock pressed against her thigh. At least it wasn't pointed at my manhood anymore.

"That's a good weapon," I commented.

"Yeah," she answered. "It was my husband's."

66

Flag Pole Sitta

+59 Days – 2000 hours

Dinner in the museum cafe was indeed venison stew, although a stew usually consisted of vegetables and potatoes. The best offered was a thick broth and a surprisingly fresh tear of bread.

Debra – Ms. Staff – continued to glance my way from a table on the opposite side of the room, only half listening to the conversation taking place at her own table. Her Benelli – her crutch – lay across her lap and a bowl of the stew sat untouched in front of her.

A shadow fell across my left side.

"Mr. Walken?"

Joey stood beside me.

"What?" I asked.

"Can I sit?"

I looked at the other tables. Most of the chairs were filled. I nodded.

"Thanks," Joey said with a grin, pulling out the wooden upholstered chair. "Ah man. Sitting with a legend. Shit, yeah!"

He plopped down and banged his bowl and spoon onto the table.

"Sorry, man," he apologized, still smiling.

"You going to keep grinning?"

"Sorry. Sorry. Can't help it."

"Why is that?"

"The way you took off that fester's head. Popped it right off the body. Sweet!"

"Glad I can entertain you."

"Wish I could have seen it. Roger told me. He was on the roof when it happened."

Roger was one of the snipers. Good to know.

"Sorry about what happened in the apartments," I offered in exchange of the freely given information.

"You did what you had to. We all do, right?" he shrugged. "I was mad at ya for a while. But that's more 'cause of pride than any lasting damage."

"Where you from?"

"Me?" he asked in surprise.

"Yeah. You."

"No one ever asks me anything around here."

"Well?"

"Sorry." He shook his head. "Just surprised. Duke usually talks with his hands... against my noggin."

He snickered before continuing.

"Came out of Boston, actually," he scratched his neck. "One of the few who was too stupid to listen to the EBS, I guess. Everyone was heading into Bean Town while I was cycling out."

"No car?"

"Ma never let me get my license. She... died."

"Condolences."

"Thanks. She was a good woman. I wish she would have listened to me instead of ignoring me like usual."

"You're here," I offered. "Alive."

"Yeah."

Joey looked around the cafe. Some of the others had finished and departed, their bowls stacked in a bus bin by the kitchen door.

Ms. Staff stood and wiped her lips with a paper napkin. She slung the shotgun, picked up her bowl and put it away with the others. She walked to our table.

"Hey, Deb," Joey said.

"Shut up, Joey."

"Ms. Staff," I said in greeting.

"Mr. Walken." She nodded.

She leaned over as if to kiss me on the cheek.

"See you on the playground tomorrow at 3pm."

67

Helping Hand

+60 Days – 1458 hours

I sat in the courtyard garden on a bench meant to face a sculpture to reflect on. My bench was positioned in front of an empty pad of concrete and the glare cast from the learning annex's two-story wall of tempered glass.

Behind the windows came a muffled gurgling chorus of moans.

The cicadas in my head buzzed.

A faint strobe of red pierced through the sun glare on the glass.

The hairs on the back of my neck stood at attention.

I rubbed the sensations away as Ms. Staff and her Benelli arrived.

"You're prompt, at least," she admitted.

"One of my few redeeming qualities," I said.

"Whatever, hot shot," she replied. "Let's go."

"Where?"

"To church."

Ms. Staff went to the gate, unlatched it, swung it open and brought up her shotgun. She cleared her corners.

"Clear. Come on."

I hefted the fire axe.

Still missing that Glock of yours?

Yes, I was.

Following her out, I closed and latched the gate behind me. We crossed the handicap parking lot and stepped onto Tuckerman Street. We moved south to where the street intersected with Institute Road and headed east along the sidewalk.

A standalone insurance office/single family home sat quiet and dark, boarded up with planks nailed haphazardly on the windows.

On the south side of the street was a huge concrete building that took up the entire block.

"That's the Worcester Memorial Auditorium," Ms. Staff said. "Never been inside."

At the midpoint of the block, the United Congregational Church stood out as a red-bricked sentry against the unwashed and undead masses. It looked like several low-roofed structures had been added to the property over the years.

We continued to the corner of Grover Street and advanced up the steps to the church's small gabled brick main entrance. Its doors were red with wrought iron details. To the right of the entry, a typical urban New England bell tower spired out of the shrubs and grass. The brick was used in ornate relief, topping in an open arched belfry and a steep gabled roof.

Ah, memories of home.

Shut up.

FRACs staggered across Institute Road, flooding in from the wide sidewalk in front of the auditorium. I counted thirteen in all.

"Ms. Staff."

She looked back from the doorway, a key to the padlocked doors in her right hand.

"Shit." She hissed as she tried the key in the bottom of the lock again. It wouldn't fit. "Damn!"

The walkers stepped onto the near sidewalk.

I moved to the center of the angled low-walled patch of grass between the sidewalk and the street.

"Blades only," I advised, "if possible."

The FRACs charged toward Ms. Staff's curses and the clanking of the chains against the church doors.

I let out a piercing whistle.

The walkers snapped their necks toward the sound.

I gripped the axe in my hands and whistled again.

Two of the FRACs stumbled over the two-foot capped granite wall, falling face first into the grass. I walked over and plunged the axe blade into the back of their heads in quick succession.

The others closed in.

Three of them lifted their legs enough to make it over the wall. I swung the blade sideways, crushing the skull of the first one and sending him sidelong into the other two. Their legs caved and they landed in a pile. I pulled out the axe head, stepped on the second FRAC's skull, and drove the handle into the third.

Eight FRACs left.

A shadow fell to my right.

Ms. Staff launched at a walker with her knife leading the way. The blade landed with a wet thud into the bald dome of an overweight waste management worker. Her momentum and his dead weight dropped them in a heap to the ground with her on top.

Lucky man.

Another walker sunk a hand into her hair and pulled her up.

She freed the knife, pivoted under the FRACs arm and drove the blade up through the soft tissue under his jaw. His body went lax, but still clung to tangles in her hair as he fell.

She ripped his hand away, clumps of hair coming with it.

A woman in a sundress reached for her from the other side.

I punched her in the square between the eyes.

Bone cracked.

Sundress FRAC's eyes rolled back as she dropped to the grass.

Five left.

I pulled Ms. Staff to her feet.

She slapped my hand away.

To get even I buried the axe into a young man with a vintage Petra T-shirt.

Sorry, God.

I had to smile at that.

The rest of the walkers had made it to the lawn.

196

Ms. Staff killed another FRAC courtesy of a blade in his ear. She pulled out the knife and backed up to the sidewalk.

Three walkers left.

Ms. Staff gasped as she caught a foot on the edge of the pavement. She flailed for balance before sprawling hard to the ground.

Her knife skittered away.

The stock of the shotgun clattered against the concrete.

Two of the walkers lunged at her with outstretched arms.

The last of the FRACs grabbed at my axe.

I punched the blade through his face.

The other two were nearly on top of Ms. Staff.

I hurled the axe.

It split the back of one of the FRAC's heads, driving him on top of Ms. Staff.

I grabbed the last walker in a flying headlock. Our momentum drove his mouth onto an iron railing.

He bit into the metal involuntarily.

I got up and drove my heel into the back of his head, sending the railing deeper into his brain and shutting him down.

Picking up Ms. Staff's knife, I went back to her and pulled the axe head FRAC off of her. She slowly turned over, looking around with wide eyes.

"Clear, Ms. Staff," I said, "Your knife."

She grabbed it and put it back into her scabbard.

I continued to hold my now empty hand out to her.

She repositioned the Benelli on her shoulder and looked at the piles of dead walkers before focusing on my hand.

She clasped her hand in mine and I lifted her to her feet.

"Thanks," she finally said. "We're done here. I don't think Roy gave me the right key."

68

To Russia, With Love

+60 Days – 1803 hours

We made it back to the museum just as the sun started its slow descent in the afternoon sky. Once the gate was latched behind us, Ms. Staff made her way to one of the benches and sat down. She leaned forward - elbows to knees - and put her hands behind her neck. Then she let out a ragged breath.

I sat down on the bench next to her.

The garden was empty otherwise.

She brought out and looked at the key to the padlock.

"Definitely not the right key," she said as she turned it over.

"For a different door, maybe?"

"Not what I was told."

Strange.

Roy's words, 'her punishment will be doled out', rang through my head.

She wiped her face with her free hand. "Thanks, by the way."

"No problem."

"Guess I'm glad that you can kick ass."

"Doesn't hurt."

The shotgun went back across her lap. She absently started stroking the stock.

"What did your husband do?"

"Boston PD," she said. "Didn't make it out of the city after the outbreak."

"Where were you?"

"At home. We lived in Lexington west of the city. We made a stand for a while. Holed up in the bedroom after the first wave. "

"We?"

"Me and my daughter," she answered.

She tapped her chin and looked at the closed vinyl gate.

"Do you think Moscow got hit like we did, Walken?"

"No idea."

"Hope so," she wiped away a tear with her ragged sleeve. "Would ease my mind."

"Why?"

"Want to believe her fate would have been the same whether we had adopted her or not.

"It would seem that this thing must be global by now."

"Yeah?" Ms. Staff stood. "Good."

69

Armaments

+60 Days – 1914 hours

Ms. Staff and I returned to Hiatt Hall. She moved to the other end without acknowledging me or shedding another tear.

"Hey, Deb," Randy called out with a wave.

She simply glared at him.

He dropped his hand and gave her a thin smile. "Talk to you later then, I guess."

As she walked past Randy's cot, he flipped her the middle finger. His smile brightened and he looked around. When his eyes set on me, the grin disappeared into a frown and his middle finger withered back into his fist.

I dropped to my cot and leaned my head into my hands.

Two black workboots invaded the space in front of me.

Duke held my holstered Glock in one of his meaty hands. My knife, tach light and machete fit easily in his other.

"Heard you did Deb a solid today," he said. "I think I may have seen a genuine smile from her for a change. Could have just been a trick of the light. One never knows."

He didn't wait for a response, instead dumping my weapons onto the cot beside me.

"Roy says you deserve your armaments back." Duke rolled his eyes at Roy's choice of words for a gun and knife. "I aired my grievances on the issue but Roy says you understand the chain of command and the 'values of the system'. All that happy horseshit."

"Understood," I replied, patting my Glock. "I will put these to good use. Although I was beginning to like the axe."

"Yeah, well," Duke replied, "the axe is still available if you want to keep using it. You know where to find it."

"Thanks," I said, "for everything."

"Yeah." Duke said, rubbing his large hands together and flexing his enormous biceps. "Just be sure to remember what side your bread is buttered."

"I do love butter."

"You better. Not loving butter would make you a Communist."

70

Eggs Over Easy

+61 Days – 0733 hours

The next day started the same as the last. We filed out of Hiatt Hall once the chains came off the doors and walked up the center steps to the upper level through the common area to the cafe. Everyone dragged out their chairs and sat down.

A woman and two men I had not met before came out from the kitchen with brown plastic trays with bowls and utensils. The smell of warm powdered eggs drifted off another tray.

They doled out the only breakfast option to everyone present – over three dozen of us in total.

Duke and Ms. Staff came in and looked around for a place to sit. Joey ducked by both of them, grabbed a chair and plopped down beside me.

"What's up, John?"

"Not much," I replied. "You?"

"More and more festers every day. That's all I know. Roy had a few of us out leading them away."

"Stow it, Joey," Duke ordered as he sat down. "John doesn't want to hear about your morning shifts."

"Better than hearing about my morning shits."

Ms. Staff smiled thinly at me as she sat down.

"Shut up, Joey," she said to him, but not with her usual venom. She even threw a wink my way. "What's for breakfast?"

"Smells like powdered eggs," I answered.

The kitchen crew continued passing out the bowls, only two tables away. The Gaunt Man appeared behind them, a grim look on his face.

Duke asked, "Did you check the west… ?"

Duke's question faded out as the Gaunt Man walked to each table with his hands behind his back, wrinkling his nose up at the steaming bowls of food. When he approached the third table, he brought up his hands.

Dangling by their swollen pink tails between each finger of the Gaunt Man's closed fist rats squirmed and spun. Their white paws scratched against each other, red eyes bulging from their sockets.

"...yesterday," Ms. Staff replied from behind a veil of warbling fog.

The servers arrived at our table.

The Gaunt Man shook his head from one table away.

The rats' bellies split open. Their bloody intestines dripped into two of the bowls at that table.

We were served our food.

The Gaunt Man shrugged.

Duke added salt to his eggs.

Joey spurted packaged ketchup onto his.

Deb pushed hers around with her fork, wrinkling up her nose.

I choked back bile and pushed my bowl away. It clattered off Joey's bowl.

My chair fell backwards as I quickly stood up.

Joey jumped, his bowl and blood red and yellow eggs dumping into Duke's lap.

"You kidding me?" Duke scowled. "Damn it, Joey."

"Sorry, Duke," Joey apologized before throwing me under the bus. "John scared the shit out of me."

The Gaunt Man nodded with solemn approval, the rats no longer in his fist.

"You alright?" Ms. Staff asked from very far away.

All of the bowls were filled with pulsing pink entrails. Randy scooped a fork full into his mouth, the ends dripping bile on his lips and chin.

Someone laughed at another table, tossing a tail into his mouth by hand, oblivious that the tip was still twitching. Others were still digging in, not reacting to the horrors in front of them.

I bumped into someone.

"Excuse you," he said, "asshole."

Ms. Staff looked at me for another second before pushing her own bowl away. Duke picked up the bowl from his lap and wiped off as much of the faux eggs as possible before tossing the mess back on the table.

"Can't even enjoy a shitty meal," Duke grumbled.

Joey raised a hand and opened his mouth to say something.

"Shut up, Joey," Ms. Staff and Duke said in unison.

71

Dumpster Diving

+61 Days – 1234 hours

My next shift paired me with the ever chatty and sometimes informative Joey.

"Stoddard Garden Court. I come out here sometimes to get away from the others."

"I can imagine," I replied, thinking back to the ocean side gazebo and Adirondack chair that I had left behind. "How about the others?"

"Roy's been here since I got here," he replied as we walked through the courtyard. "Definitely been here longer than Randy and Duke.

"Deb can be a little mean." Joey raised his hands. "Don't get me wrong, she's a great lady. But she can be…"

"Stoic?"

"Sure," he replied uncertainly." That's as good a word as any, I guess."

Across the courtyard, inside the education wing, several of the children pressed against the glass. The same red strobe pulsed off the interior walls.

"What's up with the kids?" I asked.

Before Joey could answer a rat caught our attention as it padded along the top of the PVC fence line on its way toward the museum.

My stomach churned.

I guess I shouldn't have skipped breakfast.

"Damn things," Joey exclaimed. "All over the place these days."

I picked up a rock and launched it, hitting the rodent broadside and sending it off the top of the fence with a pained squeak.

"Nice shot."

More faint scratching came from behind the fence. I moved toward the sound, drawing my Glock.

Joey trailed behind me, gripping a machete with both hands.

The scratching continued.

It was definitely coming from outside the fence.

Unlatching the gate, I pulled it open and cleared the parking lot.

"Come on."

Joey followed me, peering through the bushes and across the lot.

At the far end of the parking lot a dumpster overflowing with garbage bags sat against the fence.

Scratches.

And thumps.

I moved wide left until the dumpster was directly in front of me. Joey stood near the open gate, unwilling to come any closer.

Approaching the dumpster, I heard the scratching more distinctly. There were also multiple squeaks and an irregular thumping sound. The dumpster was cock-eyed, half on the asphalt and half against the fence.

A walker was pinned behind the dumpster, several bags of garbage strewn around him.

His university lab coat flapped in spite of the still air. A rat fell to the grass from under his coat, scurrying away under the fence as soon as its paws hit the ground.

"Damn!"

Joey raced back inside the courtyard.

I stared at the FRAC. The glasses he wore were still propped on his nose courtesy of a band around the back of his head. The laboratory technician turned and slapped a mutilated gray hand against the side of the dumpster, producing a dull *thumm*.

Another rat disembarked from under the tail of his dress shirt, this time from a ragged tear above his belly button. It hit the ground like its comrade and scampered away, but not fast enough to escape a pulpy end at the heel of my boot.

I kicked it away, letting it land somewhere under the dumpster.

The FRAC tried to move out of the corner but was stymied by the pile of black Hefty bags that had fallen in behind him. After another failed attempt at escape, he returned to bumping around in a tight constricted circle between the metal and the PVC.

Pulling the knife, I wedged into the same space with the walker. As he made another tight turn to face me, I plunged the blade upward through his soft pallet. As his un-life dimmed to a single pinprick – like a vacuum tube television of the 20th century – his head and his body weight dangled from my knife. I pulled out the knife and let his body land on the garbage bags that had imprisoned him.

Two more rats escaped the carcass, opting to rummage around the Hefty bags of refuse split open by the FRAC's fall. They quickly disappeared into the museum's trash and leftovers.

Joey raced back out from the courtyard.

"Got that other one before it got inside," he said between pants.

"Good job, Joey."

72

All in the Family

+62 Days – 0954 hours

Randy and I paced the perimeter of the atrium roof using scaffolds and planks assembled for a better vantage point over the parapets. Randy walked an opposite circuit with a M16 outfitted with a BARSKA 4 scope.

On the western side of the building, across Lancaster Street in the most northern of the three parking lots on that block, wandered a "family" of FRACs. They seemed to be tourists based on their clothes. The father wore long khaki cargo shorts and a magenta Polo shirt. A Nikon camera swung down his back from a strap around his neck. The woman, in a dress torn to shreds from the waist down, bumped into her partner due to a broken white patent leather heel. An adolescent girl trailed behind them. She wore a Victoria's Secret Pink T-Shirt and dirty pink flannel pajama-type bottoms adorned with black and white cartoon cows.

"What's the hold up, Walken?" Randy asked, stopping next to me. "You a family man?"

It was a rhetorical question.

Randy wound the strap of the M16 through his arm. He squinted one eye and looked through the scope. Pivoting in a slow right to left motion, he exhaled and squeezed the trigger.

The little girl with the amusing cartoon cows staggered sideways as the bullet dotted her head above her ear. She took one knee for a moment before dropping to her side.

"Gotta love the young ones," Randy mused.

I held my tongue.

He stepped closer to the edge and ventured a look over the side.

One quick shove would do it, I believe. End up splattered on the sidewalk below. So tragic.

"Pretty light today," he said. "Maybe the plague is dying out."

"One could hope," I muttered, trying to get the image of him sailing over the edge out of my mind.

In the parking lot Torn Dress Mom and Shutterbug Dad continued across the asphalt, having already abandoned their forgotten little girl.

Maybe the FRACs needed some place to develop their film from this most recent vacation. Print out some 8x10 glossies and a few wallet sizes for the relatives back home.

Two Hispanic men with machetes walked across Lancaster. Mom and Dad FRAC steered toward them at a quickened but still shambling pace.

Roy's men timed their approach and sliced their machetes on a downward angle through the walkers' heads. Their bodies crashed into each other, their heads from the lip up landing a few meters away on the pavement.

Arnold rolled over a large cart similar to a hotel laundry bin to the bodies. The machete men tossed the heads into the bin, the body parts slapping off the fiberglass walls. They grabbed the decapitated bodies and hoisted them into the bin as well.

"Another one bites the dust," Randy said before starting a fresh circuit around the roof. "Three in this case."

I stood alone again.

The machete men had not bothered to collect the young girl. A small pool of oozing dark blood expanded around her head, turning some of her Pink T-shirt a sickly brown.

A black crow landed next to her and cawed. It pecked at her eyes, bursting through the cataract and digging its beak into the eye socket. It flapped its wings and paced as it tried to get deeper into the young walker's head.

I pulled the Glock and trained the sights on the bird.

"You better not waste that ammunition on a bird," Randy warned. "Just saying."

A breeze kicked up, sending dust into the air. He coughed and took a swig of Poland Springs water from a bottle in his jacket pocket. He spit before pulling the bandanna around his neck up over his mouth and nose.

"I guess the dust got the last laugh," I muttered.

"What's that you say?"

"I said the crow's getting the last laugh," I said in a louder voice.

The crow cawed again, happy to have the entire optic nerve hanging from its beak. The bird flapped into the air. Once it caught a good cross current it spread its wings and glided westward.

73

Fist Bump

+62 Days – 2027 hours

We returned to Hiatt Hall.

Randy wiped his forehead with his bandanna, having pulled it from around his neck on the walk back to the barracks. He peeled off to the other side of the exhibition space.

Joey raised his hand for a fist bump.

"Not now."

"Sorry," Joey said.

Making his way to his cot, Randy leaned his M16 against the cot, plopped down and covered his eyes with his elbow – the bandanna still clenched in his fist.

Joey shrugged and came over to me, sitting on an empty cot.

"He's looking a little peaked," Joey confided. "Rarely passes up a fist bump."

"Rarely?"

A slight irritation flared at the back of my neck.

"Yeah." Joey grinned, scratching his greasy hair. "I usually get some love from him. It hot out there?"

"Yep."

"Figured. He's probably got heat stroke or something."

"Maybe," I replied. "How you feeling?"

"Me?" Joey's grin got bigger. "I'm right as rain. Thanks for asking."

"No coughing?"

"Nah. I'm healthier now than before things went into the crapper. Must be because there's no one to clog up the air with exhaust from cars and power plants and stuff. No wheezing. No watery eyes."

He beamed at me with his newfound youth and vitality.

"It's a beautiful thing," he said.

"Amen, brother."

Randy wiped his mouth and face with his bandanna before taking a swig of water from the bottle he had brought back from guard duty.

"Poor guy," Joey said, standing. "I should see if he needs anything."

A faint buzzing seeped in from the common area outside Hiatt Hall, coming from the library or the café.

I grabbed his wrist.

"What?"

"Let him get some rest," I answered, thinking about how the young FRAC girl had crumpled to the pavement with a bullet to the side of her head. "He's had a difficult day."

"Alright. I got to get on work rotation anyway."

"Safe shift," I said. "Don't get ambushed by any rats."

"Ha." he smiled. "I'll try."

74

Nursery Rhymes

+63 Days – Night

Ring-a-round the Rosie...

Five faceless children skipped around in a circle, holding hands. Strange gauze hid their features. They pranced around a smoking black pulsing mass.

... a pocket full of posies...

The darkness solidified into a barely formed shape of a skeletal man. Once whole, the Gaunt Man raised his pale hands up from his pockets and threw flower petals into the air. They swirled within the circle, none escaping past the fast moving kids.

... Ashes! Ashes!...

The falling petals sparked and burned. As the embers touched the children's clothes, the material lit on fire and burned off. Their skin sizzled and bubbled. The cottony shrouds over their faces melted away.

... we all fall down!

The children fell to the ground in unison, their skin smoking and charred. The young girl in the Pink T-shirt and cartoon cow pajama bottoms lay there. The little girl in the gauzy nightgown who had come into the Rainier Island plaza was there, eventually shot by the then-deputy Jared Garrett. Jacob was there – the headshot bullet wound from a Desert Eagle still taking a sizable chunk of his skull away.

The Gaunt Man stepped out from the broken circle, straddling over the smoking form of a young boy.

It was Donovan.

The boy I had left behind.

The Gaunt Man leaned down and stroked what remained of the young boy's hair, tracing a long bony finger down his ragged cheek and exposed jaw.

Shouldn't have left him on the island, John.

"Wasn't a choice."

There is always a choice. You chose poorly.

The Gaunt Man moved on spindly legs to the last child. This one was a girl. He gently scooped her up in his arms, leaning her blackened head against his shoulder. Clumps of hair were missing, revealing angry pink patches of skin and of white skull.

He turned his body to reveal her face.

Summer lay motionless in the Gaunt Man's arms. Embers ate away at her clothes and skin, feeding on anything flammable.

Always making bad choices, aren't you John?

75

Bad Choices
+63 Days – 0139 hours

Wretched buzzing woke me with a start.

I actually slept?

Finally.

A nearly forgotten melody to a children's song chimed faintly in my head.

Hiatt Hall was dark.

The lights had been turned off in order to save power on the generators. Two small battery-powered lanterns lit the space. Snores, farts, coughs and the occasional squeaking cot were the only sounds to disrupt the quiet.

Always making bad choices, aren't you John.

The images of children dancing around dense black smoke assaulted my vision. All in sticky flames, the children in my nightmare cried out to me.

Did I fail Donovan? Did I fail Summer?

Are they both out there dead because of me?

Was the little FRAC girl in the cartoon cow pjs ultimately my responsibility?

I should have stopped Randy from shooting her.

Bad choices.

Bad choices landed me here in the castle filled with a garrison of anointed knights in service of a paper king.

Bad choices cut me off from my unit.

Cut me off from my friends.

Cut me off from a damned scruffy dog, the only gift left from a now dead lover.

I sat up on the edge of the cot, looking at the other dim human shapes clutching saggy pillows, rolled up blankets, or half-full backpacks.

The glass doors were again locked from the outside, a bicycle chain around the handles. Apparently, even a beloved king with loyal subjects worries about usurpers to the throne or a possible serf uprising.

The cots around me were empty. Even Joey's accolades of my barehanded FRAC decapitation seemed to not sway any of the others to rack close to me. Maybe the story kept them away. One can never tell.

A few muffled coughs came from the far end of the exhibition hall. Whoever it was turned over and returned to a deeper snoring sleep.

Why?

Donovan sat on the cot across from me. His hair was burned off on one side. The exposed flesh pulsed a fluorescent pink. In spite of the charring of his skin, his teeth were pearly white and his eyes piercing.

Why?

"What?" I whispered.

Donovan looked around the hall. The cartilage and skin of his ear lobe was a melted lump against his head. He returned his sharp stare to me. A single tear escaped the corner of his eye, hissing as it carved a canal down his ruined burnt cheek.

Why did you leave me?

He stared through me as he waited for an answer.

"I couldn't stay, Donovan," I mumbled. "I have to get home."

What home? You don't even know where you are headed.

"I do."

Well, maybe you should stop fucking around and get back on mission, Marine! Ooh rah?

His eyes lost a bit of their luster as they clouded over.

"Ooh rah, Donovan."

But Donovan was gone.

Much in the same way the Gaunt Man flitted in and out of my

216

life, would Donovan become another albatross to my canon of recurring apparitions?

I half-expected other specters to come haunt me.

Apparently the rest of the ghosts of civilizations past, apocalyptic present, and wastelands yet to come had decided to take a respite for one evening.

I lay back on my cot.

Maybe a couple more minutes of dreamless rest wouldn't be so bad. Sleep seemed to be a token idea now. I shouldn't be functioning at this capacity with the sleep I have been getting. The restless minutes of slumber every few nights should have brought me to my knees weeks ago.

Of course, I had been making bad choices lately.

76

Appetizers

+63 Days – 0250 hours

A scream.

Followed by a yell.

A pain shot up my neck and joined the buzzing in my brain.

I popped up from the cot with my Glock at full draw. My fingers switched on the tach light by muscle memory.

A snarling Randy stood in the end of my light. His mouth was covered with blood and the bandanna was still clenched in his fist.

Randy had turned.

I shot him in the forehead.

"Gotta love the young ones," I muttered as the retort echoed through the hall.

More snarls from my left.

Three more FRACs staggered toward the noise of my gunshot, knocking over cots to get to it.

More screams.

Ms. Staff threw a cot at a walker as it reached out at her. It was Joey's larger friend, Donny, from the apartment ambush. He got tangled in the nylon and aluminum piping. She picked up her Benelli and drove the shotgun's stock into his face. After three more cracks to the face he went down for good, still caught up in the cot.

"Goddammit!" she yelled. "The fuck's going on here?"

Francis, another one of the marauders, grabbed at her collar.

I shot him cleanly through the right ear.

"Shit. Shit. Shit." Joey cowered under his cot.

"Get up, Joey," I ordered.

He crawled on his hands and knees, ducking under several more cots in an effort to get to me.

"Shit… shit… shit…," he chanted.

"Ms. Staff!"

"I'm a little busy here, Walken."

I squeezed off three more shots, dropping a trio of walkers between her and us.

Staff leaped over a gurgling woman tangled up in a sleeping bag. She looked like the server from breakfast. Her throat had been torn out and blood had stained the collar of her shirt. Staff turned around and stuck a butterfly knife into the kitchen help's ear.

Another FRAC lunged at her.

She spun the Benelli up and blasted away his face. I didn't get a good look at him before he was reduced to a shredded pulp.

The blast and the resounding echoes were deafening.

I fired on four museum survivors-turned-FRACs.

Three more shots rang out.

A trio of walkers with bloody ragged bites on their necks collapsed to the floor.

Staff shot another walker as he crawled toward us. A large stain on the tiles replaced where his head had been.

We moved to the locked doors.

"Hey!" Joey banged on the glass.

"Shut up, Joey!" Staff hissed. "I'm workin' here."

I fired once more.

Five shots left. I did not have another magazine.

Over a dozen walkers left.

"Ammo count," I called out.

"Three shells," Staff confirmed, "We can shoot the glass."

"No," I ordered. "We keep them in here. We're going hand-to-hand when we run out of ammo."

"Fuck," Staff and Joey said in unison for different reasons.

Joey continued to slap against the glass.

"Ready?" I asked Ms. Staff.

She answered by squeezing the trigger of her shotgun, lighting up the dim space.

Half of a walker's face sheared off from the blast

I shot the three closest walkers in their foreheads.

They toppled onto a cot.

Two 9mm rounds left.

Only two shotgun shells remained.

We emptied our weapons into four more walkers as they stumbled around the cots and the center wall.

I holstered the Glock and pulled my machete.

Staff turned her Benelli around and wielded it by the stock like a baseball bat.

"Come on." She taunted them.

I swung my blade into the bearded Arnold, clipping it into the side of his skull. As he sunk to his knees, I pulled the blade free and thrust it into a second walker reaching over him.

Staff gave out a yell and cracked the shotgun tailstock into the jaw of an unfamiliar young man with a hoop earring. She swung again and crushed the bridge of his nose. He tumbled forward at her feet.

"Hey? We're in here!" Joey screamed.

Staff and I closed ranks and waited for the rest to advance.

I tightened my grip on the knife.

Chains rattled.

The doors opened.

"Down!"

I instinctively grabbed Staff and covered her on the ground.

Joey was already there beside us.

Gunfire erupted over us.

Bullets ripped through the remaining walkers.

The gunfire ceased but the echoes continued for a few moments before dying down.

"What a mess this is," Duke said, several gunmen beside him.

"Yeah," Joey mumbled, still cowering on the floor with his hands over his head. "Maybe it was something they ate."

77

First Moves
+63 Days – 1011 hours

Duke escorted me into the library.

Roy sat in the same chair at the same table as before.

"Come, Mr. Walken," Roy gestured. "Duke, you can leave us."

Duke said nothing and left.

"Please sit," Roy pointed to the chair to his left, "Duke has plenty to keep him occupied with the pile of atra mors and blood scattered throughout Hiatt Hall. He has to reassign men and women from other work."

I pulled out the chair, banging it against the chair next to it.

"Please, please," Roy warned. "Show a little respect for the facilities. This is a place of learning and reflection."

"My apologies."

"No harm." Roy dismissed with a wave of his hand. "No foul."

Roy shifted in his chair, crossed his legs and squared his shoulders to me.

"A nasty piece of business last night, my good sir. It is very fortuitous that the lovely Debra and you returned unscathed. Joey, though, is a bit worse for wear. Even though he is not too brave or bright at the best of times, his brain may be somewhat more addled by this event."

"At least they were corralled in one space."

"I would have to agree," Roy interjected. "Imagine if we did not have capable people like you and Ms. Staff to stave back the atra mors. An unlocked door would have led to them having full access to the museum. And that I can't allow, no matter the security risk to the people under my roof."

"Can't be too careful, I suppose." I offered. "It was best to keep them isolated."

"Exactly." Roy beamed. "One must protect the castle at all costs."

It was true. If those doors had been unlocked and we weren't there, the majority of the museum would have been quickly overrun.

Roy got up and pushed his chair in square to the table and started pacing in front of the index card filing cabinets. Behind him was a bust in a plastic case and a circle of plush cushioned chairs for more relaxed reading.

"A Black Plague uprising right under my feet," he murmured. "Locked down. No infection. No exposure."

Roy stopped pacing and looked at me.

"How did they get into my house, Mr. Walken?"

It might have been something they ate.

Was that Joey's voice or the Gaunt Man's taunts?

The specter's morning meal appearance at the café dripping rat entrails into the bowls of powdered eggs still added a knot in my stomach.

"Difficult to say," I replied. "Anyone bit before lockdown?"

"No. No."

He started pacing again.

"I make it a strict rule to have all incidents reported. Duke would never have allowed a lights out without segregation of anyone suspicious."

Screening process?

There had been no screening process on my return from my outside jaunts with either Joey or Ms. Staff. Duke was nowhere to be found for either of those ends of shift.

Roy sat down again.

"Retrieve that box, please," he asked, pointing to the index card cabinets.

On top of one of the cabinets was a lacquered wooden box the size of a child's suitcase record player. It had a leather handle and two metal clasps.

I brought it back to the table and placed it in front of the grinning Roy.

I guess he thinks you are his errand boy, too?

Roy rotated the box around ninety degrees at a time until the handle and clasps faced him. He opened the case with something close to reverence.

He lifted out a satin lined tray.

"24 Karat gold and silver plated solid bronze pieces." He beamed, admiring the two rows of chessmen inside.

He set the tray down next to the case. Underneath was a marble inlayed chessboard.

Roy lifted it out and held it up in his hands.

"Move the case, please," Roy asked.

I did as instructed, careful to show the same care as Roy.

Once the case was out of the way, Roy placed the board gently on the table between us. He picked each of his chessmen out of the tray and set them on the center of their appointed square.

"Exquisite."

As he admired his players on the board, I reached into the tray for my queen.

Roy slapped my wrist.

"I will take care of it, Mr. Walken."

The corner of his left eye twitched for a moment.

"Randy humored me by playing me in the library every so often. He seemed so healthy yesterday. A shame what became of him. To all of them." Roy fell silent for a moment before continung. "Anyway, you seem a bright young man. I have a hunch you may be a reasonable substitute for a fallen comrade."

"We will see," I said with a shrug, knowing my chess skills were a bit rusty.

Roy started to set up my chessmen. "This Medioevale themed set cost quite the pretty pound a few years back. But nothing is too rare or expensive if one is a connoisseur."

"As you certainly are."

223

He clapped his hands together once when he finished setting up my pieces then outstretched his arms palms out.

"I most definitely am." Roy agreed, grinning as he looked upon the ornate chessmen lined up in front of him. "I believe white goes first."

78

Blood Brothers

+63 Days – 1545 hours

"What the hell, man?"

Joey took a swig from a half full bottle of Coors Light and ran his fingers through his hair. We sat on the atrium roof and looked out over Salisbury Street.

"They were inside the room, John," Joey said before taking another swig. "Shit. Inside a locked room."

"It was a shit storm for sure," I commiserated.

"I don't think I will ever get used to it," he said, his hand gripping the beer bottle tightly. "It ain't natural."

"But it is the world we live in, unfortunately." I sighed.

The men who had cleared the Shutterbug FRAC and his wife walked across the parking lot. They took out three FRACs with quick bladed precision before heading toward Lancaster Street.

"Those boys friends of yours, Joey?"

Joey leaned over the wall.

"No way," Joey shook his head. "They came in after I did by a week. Duke brought them in. They were all bloody and their clothes and packs were all tore up. Looked like they had seen better days, for sure. Wouldn't let anyone take their weapons."

They did have an affinity for their blades.

And seem to enjoy the slaughter.

"They got names?"

"I'm sure they do," Joey replied, "but I don't know what. Duke should know. Definitely Roy should know if you want to ask him. They keep to themselves. Eat their own food. Bunk down where they like. Pretty sure they're related to each other."

"Uh huh," I said, throwing in something to fill the pause.

Joey shrugged and looked at the Lutheran church on the corner before continuing. "Why you askin'?"

"No reason, Joey."

"I might not be the brightest bulb like Duke and Debra point out to anyone who'll listen," Joey admitted, "but I ain't a complete moron."

"You're right, Joey," I apologized. "There's just something about them I don't like."

"Well, that makes two of us."

"They have any other interesting tendencies besides killing walkers?"

"Besides the FRACs?" he said with a grin.

I gave him a grin right back.

"Yeah," he continued, "I like what you call them. Better than what Roy decided to go with. Festers or mortius or atra mors. What a strange dude."

"Yeah, he is," I said, "So?"

"So what?" Joey asked, his smile disappearing into a frown and burrowed brow.

"Do the machete men do anything besides killing walkers?"

Joey clucked his tongue several times against the roof of his mouth. He stared off at the church again.

Its central entrance cut into a rectangular façade with a gabled roof, circular windows on all its faces and thin pointed arch windows rising to meet them. The wood doors were bookended with carved ornamental reliefs of columns holding up a header engraved with Trinity Lutheran Church.

Joey's lips moved, mouthing something.

Above the church's name, joining the mantle of the doors and the base of the narrow arched window was another engraving. This one read, 'The Word of the Lord...'.

"Endureth forever," Joey finished in a whisper.

He looked at me with brighter eyes and a knowing spark.

"I do know that Roy hand picks them for a lot of wet work."
Joey smiled again, seemingly pleased with his choice of words.

Or pleased that he knew the words at all.

"Always wet work," he mumbled.

"What makes you say that?"

He licked his lips and added another cluck for good measure, his sharpness already fading.

"Always blood on them," he said to nobody in particular. " Can't seem to get the blood off."

With that, his eyes lost their intelligent spark. He took the last swig of his warm beer and sighed, his eyes following the path of a plastic grocery bag swirling in the breeze across the church's parking lot.

79

Breakdown

+63 Days – 1959 hours

I returned from my perimeter sweep.

Climbing the steps, I headed toward the museum's Lancaster Street entrance. On the mezzanine above the doors, four FRAC children leaned against the windows. They head-butted the already smeared surface, aimlessly moving along the panes.

The power to the sliding doors at the entrance had been cut off but handles had been bolted into the inside of the frame. Duke and another man muscled open the doors to let me in. They did the same for the second set of doors.

"Anything good out there?" Duke asked.

"Not much," I replied. "No dead around. I heard some moans coming from the other side of the auditorium, but didn't come across anything."

"Good," Duke said. "Maybe we're catching a break after that massacre last night."

"Maybe."

"Hope you enjoyed your chess match."

I went inside the lobby without a word.

Across the tiled floors, behind the chained doors to the Higgins Educational Wing, two more young FRACs looked through the thin vertical meshed security window. The young girl clicked her Hello Kitty painted fingernails against the glass while the older boy licked it through a hole in his cheek.

Ms. Staff looked at me from the front sign-in desk. Her Benelli lay on top of the station.

"Hello, Ms. Staff."

She didn't answer, staring at the children behind the locked doors.

"You holding up?"

She slowly focused on me.

"Don't know anymore," she shrugged, her eyes drifting back to the doors. "I just don't know."

The chains around the door handles rattled.

A third, larger teenager shoved the girl away as he squeezed past her and pushed against the glass. The doors held easily but my hand found its way to the grip of my holstered Glock anyway.

Staff hurried around the station, sliding her shotgun off the desktop with a scrape and raising the barrel toward the double doors.

I caught up to her two meters from the doors, wrapping an arm around her waist.

"Let me go," she cried as I spun her away from the entrance. "Those things need to be put down."

I hugged her, prying her finger away from the trigger with my free hand.

"Stop!" she screamed.

Duke and the other man looked on from the vestibule, grins on their faces and no interest to get involved.

"Stop it, Deb," I whispered in her ear. "You shoot that door and we'll have a hell of a lot more walkers to contend with than just the three against the door."

She fought against me.

"It's okay we survived the night," I reminded her as I hugged her tighter. "You can't carry the guilt of living."

You do.

Am I living? Am I even alive?

"Your daughter's death isn't your fault." I counseled her with my arms still around her. "You won't dishonor her by leaving those children alone."

She stopped struggling.

The Benelli dropped to the floor, clanking against the square tiles. She dropped to her knees. I dropped with her, my arm still

229

around her.

She let out a wail.

Duke and his partner stopped smiling, the entertaining portion of today's events now replaced with something more visceral and raw. Their discomfort caused them to turn around and look out to the street.

Deb's shoulders hitched twice before they slumped down. She curled up in a tight ball on the floor, protecting herself against the loss of her daughter and from the fingers of dark despair that were desperate to pry at the cracks of her broken heart.

I knelt over her.

Hovered over her.

Protected her.

It was some time before either of us moved.

80

Brothers Grimm

+63 Days – 2138 hours

The corpses had been removed.

The Hiatt Hall barracks was barren of the dead.

The smell of bleach and pine cleaner weighed heavy in the air, the taste of the disinfectants on my tongue. Most of the cots had been folded and left leaning against the wall. A scattered few were occupied by some of the marauders who had escaped the overnight – either because of overnight shifts or skipped breakfasts.

One unfamiliar survivor stared quietly at a bleached out spot on the red carpet.

I slid down to the floor as far from the others as possible, a couple empty cots between them and me.

A dried splatter of blood hung on the exhibit wall next to my shoulder. Small fragments of bone were embedded within it.

Against the wall that created the ring of the first gallery space, several backpacks were lined up like a row of miniature nylon coffins. Someone was rooting through them, stuffing interesting and useful items into his own duffle as he came across them.

Always a scavenger, I suppose.

Opportunity didn't hold respect for the dead. I had seen it too many times in the desert. People were like vultures. If there was something of value to be claimed, the most honest man could become a pick pocket.

Isn't that what we were all becoming now? Were we just vultures picking at the rotten flesh of the world?

Vultures are designed to corral the spread of disease from the bloat of carrion, you know.

So we were vultures. Keeping the disease of the undead from spreading too far or too fast.

I could accept that.

Cradling my assigned rifle in my arms, I closed my eyes. Sleep was a fleeting notion these days so I simply breathed deep in an effort to relax.

Don't eat the food, Johnny.

With a sigh, I opened my eyes.

Are the cots not comfy enough for you?

The Gaunt Man sat on the closest cot with his knees high against his chest. He wrapped his arms around his long legs and leaned forward.

Quite a night, huh?

Blocking him out of my sight, I couldn't see him but I could still hear him.

You dispatched them with utmost efficiency, I would say. Wouldn't you say? It was truly quite thrilling.

"Comfort breeds complacency," I whispered in response to his first question. "What do you want?"

Oh. John. I am here for you. You can count on me to be at your service.

Feeling his hot skin burning like a furnace in front of me, I reluctantly opened my eyes one more time.

He leaned forward even more, his knees absorbing into his ribcage. His spindly legs morphed into his chest, his neck extending and his face looming over me like a pale cobra. His hands tapped where his knees should have been.

You do know you should not be here.

"Yeah? Why?"

Surely you do not condone the wholesale slaughter of men, women and children.

"No."

Yet you stand idly by and watch as your sniper friend put a bullet into a child's head.

"She was dead," I replied. "The girl was a FRAC."

An innocent lass with her whole un-life ahead of her.

232

"And I'm sure she'd have no problem skipping past a warm body once in a while."

Well... a girl's gotta eat.

"My point exactly."

You're full of good points, Johnny.

"Do you have a point?" I asked, emphasizing the 'you'.

I feel a disturbance in the force, as if millions of voices cried out.

Behind the disturbing conjoined bony mass that was the Gaunt Man the machete men came in. They mingled with one of the other marauders sitting cross-legged on his cot. He nodded a few times and stuck a thumb in my direction.

Looks like we have company.

"Looks like," I answered as the Gaunt Man disappeared.

The two blade wielding men strolled my way, stopping a few times to look at the calendars on the gallery walls. They cocked their heads at the last of them before shrugging in unison.

The pair were dressed in ripped denim jeans and tan DeWalt work boots. Mud and what looked like dried blood and brain matter caked the toes of the leather. Each carried two sheaths on their belts for their black composite handled machetes.

"You Walken?" the one on the left in a lightweight blue flannel shirt asked. His skin was pock marked from acne and leathery from years of working in the sun.

"I'm sitting, actually," I replied. "Who's asking?"

"Someone who is not amused with wise asses," the other man in a red T-shirt added.

"Then how about more proper introductions?" I asked.

The blue flannelled man flashed a yellow-toothed smile.

"Alright. My name is Hector Ortiz," he said, then slapped his partner in the chest. "And this is my brother Raul."

"Sup," Raul said with a nod.

Raul was younger by several years, lacking the facial scars and road weariness of his brother. Or maybe he had managed to avoid the troubles of life that Hector had found himself in.

"Well?" Hector insisted.

"Well, Hector and Raul," I answered. "I am John Walken."

I stood, pushing away from the wall.

"What can I do for you?"

"The boss wants to see you."

"And it took both of you to fetch me?"

"We like to do things together," Raul commented.

"I see that."

Hector grinned and waved a hand toward the door.

"After you, of course."

I passed between the brothers, both of them smiling and giving me a nod.

"Of course," I replied.

81

Pursuit

+63 Days – 2152 hours

I led Hector and Raul down the short hallway to the open stairwell next to the library. From what Joey had mentioned during one of our perimeter sweeps this part of the museum was the original structure. The atrium, the cafe and the learning annex were added over the years.

Hector bumped me on the right side, herding me toward the library.

"Thanks," I said. "I know where the library is."

Raul opened the door.

I ushered myself through it.

The Ortiz brothers stayed in the hall as the library door clicked closed behind me. I stood with my hands clasped behind my back. Roy did not look up, instead gazing with his chin in his fisted hands at the chessboard set up for a new match. After several seconds, he glanced up and waved me over.

I joined him at the table, sitting in my usual chair to face him and his soldiers on the squares of marble between us.

Roy didn't smile, continuing to look grimly at the game top.

"Another game sits before us," he said from behind his hands. "We stand at a precipice. Always tempted to move that single step that would tip the fulcrum toward oblivion."

He leaned back, dropping his hands to his lap and staring at me over the game pieces.

"What say you?"

"About the state of the world?" I asked.

"Yes."

"Any cliché would do," I said with a shrug. "Survival of the fittest. Strength in numbers. Only the strong survive."

"That's fair," Roy replied. "Very Darwin of you. Of course, 'Survival of the fittest' doesn't pertain to the survival of a species due to its proclivity to beat all comers."

"No?"

"No," he lectured with enthusiasm, "it pertains to the species' ability to adapt to the changing climate, whether it be a change in temperature, the tectonic plates, Noah's flood–"

"Plagues," I interjected.

"Exactly," he exclaimed, slapping the table. "You do indeed have a grasp of the state of the world."

"But what of religion?" he asked, repositioning his chair to better face me. "Of the State?"

I shrugged, unsure of what point he was trying to make.

"Sure," he started, "a man can stand alone with his brawn, brains and cleverness. But how long can he stand against the hordes of the returning dead on his own?"

Roy moved his queen's pawn two squares forward to D4.

I matched with my queen's pawn to D5 to block it.

"The Church struck fear into the hearts of believers and heathens alike, attributing their sins as the cause of plagues and wars. Fear has always been the determining factor for most things. From the incessant need for organized religion to the next infomercial's must-have product, fear has always been the cornerstone for motivation."

Roy slid his King's pawn two squares forward to E3.

I challenged his move with my king's pawn one square forward to E6.

"It goes millennia back. The ancient Mayans and Aztecs sacrificing virgins and warriors in the hopes of good harvests or warding off the gods' solar eclipses. High priests adorned in gold and feathers proclaimed to the world that blood was a necessary natural element to be shed."

He moved his king's side bishop to a position behind his queen's pawn. I didn't mirror his move, moving my king's knight next to my king's pawn.

"On the other side," Roy said as he moved his king's bishop pawn forward two squares, "the State used the behemoth slag of power in politic to instill compliance of their populace with fear."

I returned to mirroring Roy by moving my king's bishop in front of my queen.

"Have you heard of Stonewall?" he inquired.

"Jackson?" I questioned.

"No."

"There was a drag bar in New York, I think."

Roy waved the answers away and dismissed his own question. He changed tactics and matched his king's knight to mine. I quickly moved my queen's knight's pawn forward one square to B6.

"In the medieval era the King ruled over his lands, using both his serfs and the Church to his advantage. But all for the welfare and prosperity of everything he governed."

Roy moved his king two squares to the right before moving his king's side rook two squares to the king's left side, castling two pieces in a single move. The king was now away from the center of the field and the rook was in a better offensive position.

I castled my king and king's side rook as well.

'When in Rome' as the saying would suggest.

He responded with his queen's bishop's pawn moving one square forward.

"The people are very important, John," he said. "Rulers and priests come and go. The people are eternal. They are the drivers, the backbone."

I moved my same pawn to C5.

"People like Duke are instrumental in keeping the peace," Roy acknowledged as he moved his king's knight to E5 in front of and between my bishop and knight.

I quickly moved my queen diagonally away one space to C7.

Roy moved his queen's knight to protect his queen.

"Protect the leaders and they will provide for and protect the masses."

I pulled out my queen's knight, placing it in front of my relocated queen. Roy moved his castled rook forward two squares.

"It's all about sacrifice, John," Roy said. "The people here have sacrificed. I have sacrificed."

My queen's side bishop retreated to D7.

His king's rook moved sideways to the edge of the board.

I took his pawn with my pawn, crossing to E4 behind his king's knight. He countered by taking my pawn with his king's bishop. I thought to sacrifice my knight but took his queen's pawn instead. Roy removed the pieces from the board and rested them in the satin-lined tray as each was struck down.

He slid his king's bishop all the way to my second row, taking the pawn there.

"See?" Roy commented with a smile. "More sacrifice."

"I guess religion has its place," I said, focusing on his words more than his gamesmanship.

"Indeed," Roy replied, taking my pawn off the board to join his piece already in the tray.

Using my king's knight, I took his bishop.

It also went into the tray.

Roy brought out his most powerful piece, the queen, on a diagonal tear to the edge of my side of the board. My knight was safe. I moved the queen's rook over a square.

"It seems you have played before."

"A little," I said. "My dad taught me a few things along the way."

Roy moved his queen forward a square to face the pawns protecting my king.

"And did he survive?" Roy said as he took my king's knight. Shit.

His king's rook loomed across the board. The queen was in an aggressive position. If I started sacrificing my pawns, I would eventually be defenseless on that flank.

I moved my king right one square just out of reach of his queen.

Roy responded by taking my pawn at D4.

"Well?" Roy asked.

I watched the pawn go into the tray.

"I have no idea," I said as I forwarded my king's bishop's pawn one square.

"Did he live in the city?"

"The suburbs, actually."

He moved his king's knight closer to his queen at G6.

Roy was closing the noose on my king.

Damn it!

My king was tucked up behind my king's bishop's pawn, safe from Roy's queen and king's knight. I moved my queen's knight to B5.

He moved his king's rook one square to his left.

"Any other family?"

"Yes," I replied as I moved my king's rook to G8 for more reinforcement.

"Me too," Roy admitted.

His queen's knight moved next to his king's rook.

Taking another of Roy's pawns, my queen's knight went into a position to take his king's knight.

His queen's knight moved toward the edge of his side of the board at H4.

I took his king's knight.

He took my queen's knight with his.

I thought my king to be safe so I moved my queen's bishop to A6.

He moved his to D2.

"Any of them survive?" I asked, getting aggressive with my queen into Roy's territory.

"No," he said as he moved his queen's rook to a more

offensive position.

I took his queen's knight's pawn.

White knight moved to protect his queen's back.

Black queen's rook slid to my right corner.

White knight to H6.

"Check," he announced.

My king's knight's pawn took his knight.

He moved his queen over one square.

"None of the them survived," Roy admitted. "I am not sure if that is fortunate or not.

"Checkmate, by the way."

I had left my king completely open to Roy's king's rook.

"Fortunate for me," Roy said, placing his index finger on the crown of my black king. "Unfortunate for you, I suppose."

82

Bearings

+64 Days – 1941 hours

After the quick chess match trouncing by Roy I faced another typical sleepless night.

Morning came and, after an early afternoon subdued meal where most of the survivors available for a meal wearily picked at the bread and SPAM offered as the main course, I was scheduled for sniper duty on the roof with Joey.

The silhouette of the residential skyline was interlaced with church spires and gables. It was still surreal to see the urban landscape so dim and still.

"Strange, isn't it?" Joey mused.

"What's that?"

"Everything."

I left Joey's comment hanging in the air.

The silence of the night weighed down on us.

"I mean how we got to here." He continued. "What's it been? Only a few months? It feels like Road Warrior out there. Roy has his guys out scavenging for supplies like The Humungus had his guys looking for gasoline in the Australian wasteland."

"Good movie." I agreed.

"I think he likes being king."

"Who? Humungus?"

"No," Joey said with a laugh. "Roy!"

"Is that a problem for you?"

"Sometimes."

"Why stay?"

"Where should I go? What skills do I have to make it out there?"

"You made it here, didn't you?"

"Barely."

"Barely?"

"Came in with a group of five. It was a strong group. We had done pretty good up 'til then. It was a miracle I got to tag along with 'em."

"Where are they now? You don't seem to hang out with them."

"Sent out on a scavenge run with the Hector and Raul. Didn't make it back. Ran into a mass of festers."

"None of them?"

"No," Joey said with a weak shrug.

"And all of them were capable?"

"Yeah. They were all ass kickers."

"Sorry for your losses, kid."

Boom.

An explosion bloomed to the east, lighting up the surrounding area for a flickering moment. The cloud of fire and smoke mushroomed and dissipated, leaving licks of angry flames casting their yellow and orange light around the area.

"Damn," Joey said. "Oil tanks?"

"Hard to say. Definitely smaller than an oil field tank."

The thought of an exploding gas tanker truck soured the pit of my stomach. Sebastian's heart attack and Basia's searing engulfment flashed through my mind.

"Maybe it was a car or truck," Joey wondered outloud. "Or someone's propane tank."

"Maybe."

Hope it didn't burn too far or for too long.

That was something we didn't need.

The silver lining was that the FRACs should be drawn to the fire, keeping them away from the museum for a little while.

"Why are you still here?" Joey asked, emphasizing the 'you'.

I stared out at the fires.

"I mean," he said, "you don't seem to need this place. You're capable. You aren't a sheep."

I thought back to the Gaunt Man's warning to leave.

"I don't know, Joey. Maybe I just need to get my bearings."

"I've been trying to find my bearings since I got here. It's even worse since Baker and my crew got killed."

Below us, a WAM truck pulled in to the delivery area. It turned around and backed up to the dock nearly out of sight from our position.

We heard the chattering of both the truck's and the delivery bay's roll-up doors.

Duke barked orders.

Several boots stomped into the back of the truck.

The rumble of motorcycles echoed off the buildings as the marauders drove into the handicap parking lot in front of the garden's fence. The gate swung open and they drove through, their single lights spearing the darkness in front of them. They disappeared and quickly the rumbles and sputters of their engines died.

"I guess they found some good stuff," Joey said.

"Yeah," I replied, not comforted by the marauders' return.

83

Deliberate Shots

+65 Days – 0655 hours

Another day was beginning.

Another shift on the roof was ending.

Joey had wrapped himself up in a wool Army blanket, snoring lightly.

I didn't mind covering for him. Sleep was a fleeting notion for me these days and Joey was a good kid. The downside was all the hours I had to think.

The dark held its secrets close to its bosom, unwilling to reveal any solid truths. Instead, it only offered vague promises of the unknown, preying on the hopes of irrational fear.

Most of the people here were good people, just trying to survive. They had been pushed outside their natural elements and thrown together under unwarranted conditions. They were a testament to the enduring strength of the human condition.

Even Debra Staff, wholly fueled by anger, loss and denial, was a good person.

Duke, Hector and Raul, on the other hand, seemed to take pleasure in their brave new world work. But they did bring much needed skills to the table.

Roy was right about that.

Joey had asked why I was still here.

The Gaunt Man had warned me that I should leave.

My group was still out there somewhere.

If I left now I wasn't sure I would ever find them. Where would I start looking? I wasn't even sure I could retrace my route back to the point where I ordered them out of the back of the truck.

I'm sure the overturned panel truck would still be there.

It would be a stretch to think they would still be there.

Maybe they left a clue... an arrow... a pile of rocks.

Maybe it was the fear of the unknown that kept me here.

Or could it be that you are tired of feeling responsible for failing everyone?

The less personal connections I make, the better.

And here you are guarding over a new group of people. Watching over the now slumbering Joey.

I looked at Joey warm under his oversized blanket. I felt for him but I didn't consider myself part of this group, either.

Roy enjoyed schooling me in the art form of chess and in his philosophy of the class system as he saw it. Duke enjoyed imposing his control and chores onto the rest of whom he deemed inferior members of the museum survivors. Even so, most of the others continued to give me a wide berth.

Except for Joey, of course.

He is your spunky sidekick. I hope I am not to be replaced.

Debra seemed to have taken a kinship to me, maybe like a mama bear.

A little romance, perhaps?

"Keep that shit to yourself, ghost," I warned.

Everything was uncertain.

Not everything is uncertain.

The weight of my Glock comforted me. I felt complete with the tactical knife and machete snug in their sheaths.

The Gaunt Man was right. He had become a familiar and constant companion, whispering in my brain as often as I would allow.

And even sometimes when you don't allow.

True. Annoying, but true.

The streets were empty.

I could slip away now without notice; put miles between me and the kingdom of Worcester before anyone realized I had gone missing.

The king would not take it well.

245

Agreed.

Roy wouldn't appreciate my desertion, especially after his talks of a ruler supporting his people and the peoples' requirement of gratitude in return. The king of the museum would not look upon me abandoning my duties to the fiefdom favorably. Roy would probably have Duke and the Machete Men track me down and return me to the museum as a prisoner and an example.

Or maybe they would just cut their losses, pun intended.

The rumble of several motorcycles echoed off the walls of the auditorium, amplifying their throaty straight pipes' exhaust.

Missed opportunity now, daydreamer.

Three of the riders roared into the courtyard parking lot. The other two drove down to the delivery bay.

"Where the hell have you been, Richard?" Duke's voice boomed at the riders in the bay. "We got too much going on right now to worry about you shit heels. Capice?"

The scraggily bearded rider in the leather jacket mumbled something I couldn't make out.

The three riders from the parking lot walked down to join the others.

Richard continued to defend himself.

Duke hopped into view on the pavement.

He grabbed a motorcycle helmet from one of new arrivals and cold cocked the outspoken Richard in the side of the head. The biker dropped like a stone to the oil-spotted concrete.

"Damn," the sleepy Joey said, yawning behind me.

He stretched his arms over his head, letting out a few more yawns for good measure.

"You didn't wake me up for my turn," he said.

"Nope."

"Up to you, I guess," he said. "I'll take all the sleep I can get. Shit loads safer sleeping on the roof."

"True."

Below, the biker who lost his helmet to Duke's temper was

pleading for him to go easy on the unconscious Richard.

"Todd better be happy Duke don't give that helmet back to him the hard way," Joey said to himself. "Guess Duke ain't hearing good news."

"About what?" I inquired. "Food?"

"Food is always top of the list," Joey mumbled. "Duke don't usually get this bent up."

"So then what?"

"Probably fuel for the gennies."

"The oil tank fire probably causing all sorts of havoc."

"For sure."

The other two from the courtyard each grabbed an arm of their unconscious friend and dragged him out of sight, the downed man's cowboy boots scuffing against the oily pavement.

"Steve and Chris are good people, too," Joey added to his assessment of the events unfolding below. "Duke would've left Ritchie on the asphalt, I'm sure."

Duke strolled toward the street and lit a cigarette under a cupped hand. He snapped the lighter top closed and pocketed it. After a long drag he blew out a slow satisfying drift of smoke.

After the wisps dissipated he looked up and gave us a salute with two fingers. The tip of the cigarette reddened as Duke waved it around. In the darkened light his ebony face was almost a silhouette. His white teeth cracked open his shadow like Wonderland's Cheshire cat.

"Duke scares the shit outta me," Joey said in a low voice. "Don't he scare you?"

"Nothing really scares me." I sighed. "Not anymore."

84

Clue

+65 Days – 1911 hours

Joey started snoring as soon as his head hit the pillow on his cot in Hiatt Hall. Apparently, even after sleeping through our overwatch shift and an afternoon of intermittent napping in the café he could sleep anywhere in spite of earlier safety concerns about accommodations lower than the roofline.

Ms. Staff sat cross-legged on a cot not her own between the slumbering Joey and me, her Benelli resting across her thighs. Her fingers tapped against her knees. The jeans she wore had ripped and darkened in several spots.

"What're you looking at, soldier?"

"Your glorious face, Ms. Staff," I replied.

She snorted and looked away, a smile creeping to her face without her knowing it. Maybe there was hope for her yet.

"You okay now?" I asked as she turned back to me.

"Why do you care?"

"Why not? I'm sure sympathy hasn't become a lost art."

"The world has gone to shit in case you missed it."

"Hadn't noticed. Doesn't mean that everything has to die along with it."

"Ha," she retorted, "then you are an idiot."

"Don't mince words, Ms. Staff. Tell me what you really think."

She smiled again, quickly putting her hand over her mouth to hide it.

"You don't want me to do that, John," she mumbled through her fingers.

"Probably not." I smiled back.

"You're a shithead."

Joey continued to sleep, his deep breaths giving way to a series of snorting snores. They cut short as he woke up enough to turn himself over to a more breathable position.

"Useless kid."

"Why?" I asked.

Staff looked at me with a furrowed brow and a hand clenched on the shotgun in her lap.

"Do I really have to answer that?" she asked, leaning in and speaking in a lower voice. "He was only in the way during the outbreak in here."

At least she was compassionate enough to not want Joey to hear her talking about him.

"Not everyone is a warrior like you," I said.

"Damn right," she answered, this time patting the shotgun's stock. "No one get's between me and my Benelli."

"You ain't so tough," I teased.

"Wanna test that theory, soldier boy?"

"Nah," I said, throwing my hands up in surrender.

"Thought not," she growled playfully. "At least you are marginally more useful than 'hit-the-deck' behind me."

She smiled openly now.

"You should still give the kid a break," I said.

"Yeah, sure," Staff replied as she stood and slung the Benelli. "I'll take it under advisement."

She took two steps toward me before Hector and Raul burst into the room. They hollered and laughed at each other as they made their way to a pair of cots in the far back corner.

Staff's face went neutral as she tightened her grip on the shotgun's strap. She changed direction and walked past the still sleeping Joey to a cot closer to the door.

"Hey, soldier," Hector shouted from his creaking cot.

"Yeah?"

"His Royal Highness is looking for a rematch in the library."

"With a candlestick." Raul laughed at how clever he was.

85

Rematch

+65 Days – 1933 hours

Roy sat in the same chair looking at the newly reset chess pieces. He held his head up with his fingers under his chin. The only difference between this trip and the last was that no one had bothered to escort me to the library.

"My illustrious opponent has returned." Roy beamed, looking up and waving to the usual empty chair to his left.

How many matches had Randy sat through with Roy?

Had Randy ever won?

He may have been a decent sniper but chess was an entirely different skill set.

"I must say," Roy complimented, "you have become a wonderful addition to the group."

"Thanks," I replied as I sat down.

"Up for another match?"

"Sure. Even after my last beating."

"But you have to persevere, do you not? One doesn't become an expert in their field overnight. It takes months – maybe years – to become a master."

"Umm hmm."

My mind went back to sniper training.

Boot camp had been child's play compared to Scout Sniper Basic Course in Quantico. At the Crossroads of the Marine Corps, Drill Sergeant Reavers had been as brutal and tactless as anyone I had ever come across – including my father. I had both feared and loved the old gristled vet, wanting to impress and earn respect from him through superior fieldwork.

"If you want to beat me," Roy said, "you have to get back on the horse."

"Only way." I agreed. "Like the suit of armor on the horse in the stairwell."

"Then let's begin." Roy quickly slid his king's pawn two squares.

I countered with my queen's bishop's pawn one square forward.

The white king's knight hurdled over Roy's front line of pawns to take up position in front of his king's bishop.

Sitting back, I stared at the white knight and wondered why Roy was pushing his knight out so quickly.

"Duke has been very busy lately," Roy commented. "The group is fanned out on the hunt for all of the important goods. Food, gasoline, supplies. They have been bringing in quite the haul the last few days."

"Yeah," I replied, moving my queen's bishop's pawn two spots. "I saw the truck backing into the loading dock the other night."

Roy mirrored my queen's pawn, moving his own more aggressively two squares.

"All very important things," he said. "Keeping the kingdom safe, as it were."

I took Roy's queen's pawn with my queen's bishop's pawn and handed it to Roy to put back in the satin game piece tray. Roy smiled wider as he moved his king's knight to take my successful pawn all too quickly.

"Remember, John," Roy advised. "Chess is not just reactive. You have to think five or ten moves ahead."

I knew how to play chess.

My father had taught me.

Although true, my father had not taught me chess in the traditional sense. He had sat me across from me and scolded me for every incorrect move. What did I know? I was just a kid used to playing checkers. Memories of painful slaps to the side of the head coupled with comments like 'you can't move the knight that way, dumbass' or 'the bishops only move diagonal, stupid' flooded back to me. The hurt would always come before he would take one of my pieces off the board.

My father revealed only enough of the game for me to never be able to beat him in a fair match. But he revealed enough of himself to allow me to build up an adolescence full of resentment.

Snapping back to the present, I moved my king's knight out in front of my king's bishop and its pawn.

Still moving reactively.

The self-appointed King of Worcester swept out his other white knight over his line of pawns. Both knights were out in front of his line of foot soldiers, still in his territory.

"Important to have strong men and women working toward the greater good."

Black queen's rook's pawn out one square.

White king's bishop's one square forward.

Black king's pawn to E6.

White queen's bishop diagonal two squares.

Roy was forming a nice aggressive spearhead in front of his royalty. I moved my queen's knight's pawn out to the borderlands of my side of the board.

"Duke, Raul and Hector, and the marauders – as Duke calls them – have been excellent at working toward the greater good," Roy said as he pushed out the white queen to the second row.

I frowned.

"Sometimes royalty does need to get their hands dirty," Roy grinned. "Can't appreciate the spoils of war if you didn't have a hand in it."

I hopped my queen's knight directly in front of her for a little security.

Roy pinched a thumb and forefinger on both his queen's rook and his king, castling them.

The man loves that move.

Rubbing my stubble, I pushed my queen's bishop diagonally

forward.

Roy moved his king's bishop's pawn.

I slid forward my king's rook's pawn.

He did the same with his king's rook's pawn, pushing it out two squares.

My queen's knight's pawn was the first into white territory as it took up position at B4.

"Enemy territory," Roy exclaimed. "Now we are getting somewhere. Of course you will have to do better than that to strike down my most trusted soldiers."

His knight moved back in front of his queen's rook.

My king's rook's pawn slid to H6.

Same white knight to B3.

Black king's bishop's pawn to G7.

With that he moved his knight to the edge of the board.

With the thinnest of smiles, I slid my queen diagonally to take it.

Unfortunately, that move did nothing to rattle Roy as he quickly moved a pawn forward one square. If I took the knight with my queen his pawn would take her without any trouble. Not really a fair trade of death. Instead, I moved my knight into a position to hopefully negate the effectiveness of the pawn.

"I like a man who isn't afraid to get his most powerful players into the fight," Roy said as he moved his queen's rook's pawn up to A3 in support of the white knight. "Although a couple lowly pawns seem to be giving you fits, huh?"

I didn't care about the pawns.

White queen's knight's pawn to B3.

My advancing black knight moved, taking out Roy's white knight.

Roy's pawn took my pawn at B4 in retaliation.

Black queen back to my second row.

Roy took my black knight with his pawn.

"I guess your advance was not very successful," he

commented.

The black queen's pawn moved forward one spot.

As to not be taken, the white king's pawn moved forward one square to my side of the board.

Now I was on the defensive again.

That pawn could take my remaining black knight. I moved the horse back to the middle of my advancing line of pawns.

I was exercising safety in numbers.

"I love pawns, John," Roy said, moving one of his forward another square and advancing his line. "They are considered cannon fodder, but can be indispensible when directed correctly."

I moved a piece to the other side of the black queen at C6.

Another white pawn slid into my territory.

I took the dormant white pawn at A4 who had taken my other black knight.

"Tit for tat, John?"

"Something like that."

Roy slid his king's rook forward two squares.

My remaining black knight slid into striking distance of Roy's white queen.

He didn't seem to mind, advancing his pawn to take another one of mine.

"Check."

My king was in check by a pawn – by a fucking pawn.

So I took it with my king.

I wasn't averse to getting my hands dirty, either.

A smile crept up on Roy's face again. He moved the other white pawn closer to my king by taking my pawn, his piece now centered between my knight and another pawn.

I took his queen.

White bishop to H6.

Black pawn to G6.

I move a pawn to G3.

Roy's bishop took it.

"Check."

I almost took the bishop with my king.

"Definitely getting dirty," Roy quipped.

I realized the white knight was laying in wait to checkmate me so I moved my king back to my first row between my bishop and rook.

"Well done," Roy commented without cheer.

He moved his bishop without further comments.

I guess we were back to business.

The bishop that my king had retreated next to took it upon itself to protect his king the best way he knew how. It wasn't religion that moved him, but malice. The bishop slid diagonally up and across the board until it took one of Roy's remaining white pawns.

In a defensive move, Roy moved his queen right across the pawn row to the edge of the board. I took advantage of the retreat to move my black knight to A2 to attack the white king.

"Check," I announced.

"You are getting bold, sir."

Cornered by my waiting bishop and the knight in check, Roy moved the king closer to the knight to get under my horseman's reach.

I followed by moving my queen out again to the edge of the board in case Roy decided my knight was ripe for the slaughter.

As I was chasing and cornering the white king, Roy moved his white queen to F4 to get clear of the row of white pawns. I could see that he was aiming for a clear shot at my king.

The black knight moved to C3.

"Check," I advised him.

With my queen blocking two of the four squares that the king could move to, the white king opted to tuck itself behind a pawn and next to a rook.

My black knight moved across to the pawn's row to put the white king in check again.

"Check."

The white king slid out of reach.

Fine.

I used my knight to take another of his pieces.

"Fuck!" Roy shouted, slapping the table.

The heavy chessmen barely moved.

Roy took my valiant knight with his bishop.

I accepted that sacrifice and moved my zealot bishop to C3.

Using exaggerated movement, Roy moved his remaining knight next to the bishop at B3. He was attempting to distract the fact that my queen was in jeopardy.

She was moved in front of the knight at B3.

Roy studied the board for a moment.

His rook moved left two spots.

I slid my rook across my first row to protect my king.

White bishop moved back next to its king.

Interesting.

I moved my rook's pawn forward two squares, waiting to see what would develop

The white king moved left.

Pawns were good if directed wisely, he had said.

I pushed the rook's pawn forward one square to box in the white king.

Roy slid his rook across the board to take mine.

"Check." He beamed with pride of his work.

In my excitement to put Roy on the ropes, I neglected my own king's protection. I pulled my queen back to take the bastard tower.

Roy pulled his knight back to his pawns' row.

Black queen to E7.

White knight to B1.

I moved another pawn forward.

The zealot black bishop fell to Roy's flanking knight.

My queen took a white pawn out of spite.

"Check," I said again.

Roy pulled his king back out of reach.

I took a move out of Roy's playbook, taking his knight with a foot soldier pawn.

"Goddammit," Roy spat, his cheeks flushing.

He positioned his remaining bishop to take my queen.

If I took his bishop, his pawn would take her.

I slid her away from the onslaught.

Roy resorted to moving a pawn forward.

My king came out of hiding.

The white bishop rushed in.

"Check."

A move of my king to stand beside its bishop negated the threat.

The white rook slid over.

"Check again, young man."

Shit.

The black king's day in the sun seemed to be short lived, but I moved it in retreat anyway.

Roy's other bishop moved to the edge of the board.

"Check."

Damn.

My king continued his retreat.

The board was clearing, all of the fodder swept back to the tray. I still commanded a queen, a less adventurous bishop and a rook that hadn't moved all game. Roy had lost his queen but had active bishops and a rook.

Roy looked at me with a cocked head.

He was dominating the game but seemed perplexed by the status of the board. He touched a finger to the top of the tower, clucking his tongue off the roof of his mouth as he teetered the chessman from side to side in its square. After several seconds he nodded to himself and started moving the rook left.

Duke rushed into the library.

The glass doors rattled shut behind him.

He approached Roy and bent close.

Without taking his finger off the piece, Roy leaned back.

I heard Duke say *troublemaker*.

Roy sighed.

He returned the rook to its square from the start of the turn.

"I am afraid," Roy announced, standing and slapping his hands together in an 'all done' gesture, "that we will have to finish this game another time. It seems there are matters requiring my immediate attention.

"Duke will show you back to Hiatt."

Roy brushed past the cross-armed Duke and headed toward the door.

"You are much more worthy an opponent than Randy," he said, turning back as he grabbed the door handle. "A pleasure."

He slipped into the hall and headed down the stairs, the library door clicking closed with his departure.

"Hey, Bobby Fisher," Duke commented after an awkward moment of silence, "let's get you back to bed."

86

Killing the Cat

+65 Days – 2037 hours

Duke escorted me back to Hiatt and pointed me inside.

After I stepped inside he locked the chains on the door and abruptly left toward the main stairs. His dark skin and clothes faded into silhouette all too quickly.

The exhibit hall was a symphony of deep breathing and snores. Small candles flickered at the darkness but did little to illuminate the space.

Good thing you can see like a cat now.

A quarter of the cots were filled with the remaining members of the museum community not out on assignment. The air still smelled of bleach and copper.

I returned to my wall of the exhibit hall.

The Japanese calligraphy calendars stood out as white rectangular sheets on the warmer colored walls. The squid ink of the cursive brush strokes leapt off the parchment, the thin lines crisply dividing the days into the structured grid of the month. The artists had used bold and colorful designs of birds and historical scenes to border each month.

Across the space Joey continued to sleep like the dead. Of course the dead did not sleep theses days.

All the slang using 'dead' will have to be revised.

My shoulders slumped.

The weight of several days' worth of sleeplessness pushed down on me. Even with my body needing less and less rest I wished for the days where I catch rack time like Joey.

I closed my eyes, hoping for the blackness to fill my mind with the void of sleep. I exhaled a long breath, the pulse of my heart slowing. Behind me scattered scratching could be heard. Several rats scurried through the hollow partition walls.

Hope they are not carrying any more of the dead with them. That would be a shame for all involved, I would think.

I sighed.

As expected, the Gaunt Man sat on the empty cot nearest me. His suit was impeccably pressed, his white dress shirt crisply starched and his teeth looking incredibly sharp and white. He picked at his sleeve, always with a keen black eye on the hunt for a stray hair or white speck of lint.

"Back for more?" I mumbled.

Oh, John. I am always around.

He cast his arms about the room.

"What do you want?"

Nothing of consequence, I assure you. Just wondering why you are still here, is all. Even after my earnest warnings.

"Just need to stay here a bit."

I can respect your instincts.

"If I left today," I whispered, defending my inaction, "where would you propose I look?"

If you don't know where to start, start somewhere.

I shook my head.

It's part of very important teachings.

"Yeah," I said. "You're a fount of wisdom."

I am. Of that there is no doubt.

"Then why don't you tell me where Jude is? Where are Bowers and the rest? I'll go wherever you tell me."

Well. I wouldn't want to ruin the surprise. Where's the fun in that?

"Yeah. You're a fucking peach."

That I certainly am, John.

Both of us looked across the space as Duke returned to unlock the bike chain around the door handles. He came in and rousted the slumbering Hector and Raul.

Hector grumbled something unintelligible.

Duke told him to shut up.

Raul chuckled as he bounded off the cot fresh and alert.

Duke pushed them toward the exit. At the door he stopped and looked around the room. He squinted at a few of the residents before straightening up and heading out.

He didn't see me.

I was buried under a cascade of shadows.

He does seem off today, doesn't he?

Yeah, he did.

Definitely distracted.

As proof he left without re-chaining the door.

Duke's behavior had been becoming increasingly erratic over the last few days. I'm sure that Richard was still feeling the sting of that motorcycle helmet to the ear.

Looks like the show has moved elsewhere.

Maybe.

You know, John. Curiosity killed the cat.

"And satisfaction brought him back."

87

Breaking Down
+65 Days – 2050 hours

I crept into the Egyptian Gallery.

From the atrium a warm flickering glow came from a few lit torches mounted around the mezzanine.

Duke's shadow disappeared down the steps into the atrium, heading right toward the Chapter House.

More victims for the torture chamber, perhaps?

There were no sounds of dragging chains or hissing FRACs.

Two lower level exhibits flanked the Egyptian Gallery. I moved down the steps to an antechamber as part of the medieval wing, paralleling Duke's movements and keeping the walls between us for cover. This room was empty except for a few cordoned off exhibit pieces.

To my left a hall led directly to the quiet Chapter House. Duke was not in sight.

Another opening from where I stood led to a second room dedicated to the same period. Murmurs came from inside.

I moved toward the four-foot thick entryway and stopped for a quick line of sight. In the middle of the room was a carved figure of a monk at a pulpit. At the back of the room Roy and Duke faced a stone bench and an ornate carved object like a trough or crib.

"Nothing but trouble, Roy," Duke said. "We should cut loose the whole lot."

"Now, now," Roy cooed. "I don't think that is necessary. I am sure your powers of persuasion are up to the task at hand."

"Sure. If you want me to get my hands dirty."

Roy gave his lieutenant a sideways glance.

"You really think staining your hands is going to be the right response?"

"It might be. For what you want it might be."

"Well," Roy finally said, straddling the stone bench and leaning his arms back over his head. "If that is what it takes to get to the end, use whatever means you see fit. It would be a shame, though, if something were to be broken along the way."

"Understood, Boss."

Duke nodded and walked out through the other end of the room. I backed up into the antechamber far enough to see Duke crossing the Atrium from the corridor.

I moved back to check on Roy.

He was no longer on the bench.

"It's a rather large shame," Roy said.

Shit. I froze.

"Life is not always like chess," he warned. "Just because the king is surrounded, don't think he can't hurt you."

Roy stood in front of a life-sized carved wooden monk, facing the pulpit. He patted the statue on the cheek.

"That was Ron Livingston who said something like that. An American actor." He turned to the rest of the room. "Maybe Duke has his bloody hands full these days. Do I need to step in to take control of things again?"

He turned back to the pulpit.

He didn't realize I was there.

"You know that Denis Diderot said 'Man will never be free until the last king is strangled with the entrails of the last priest'?" Roy laughed. "I guess we will just have to wait to see who wins. But I have a feeling that God and Man may come up short this time."

With that he turned away from the figure and walked out the other exit.

I crept through the exhibit he had just vacated, creeping to the columned corner of the mezzanine to follow his movements. Roy walked with purpose across the atrium in the same direction Duke had gone.

He is a bit full of himself, isn't he?

Back in the exhibit space, the Gaunt Man leaned against the pulpit next to the wooden monk with his chin resting on his fists.

"He seems to be."

You ready to leave now?

"Not quite yet."

Good. I love a good adventure.

88

Hardy Boys
+65 Days – 2107 hours

Roy's right hand reached out toward, but did not quite touch the railing that separated him from the mosaic in the floor. He hummed something as he walked, his posture straight, his shoulders back and his chin up.

I waited by the wall at the end of the corridor across from the Chapter House, covered in shadows by the column and the mezzanine above.

Roy fell into darkness under the mezzanine on the far side of the atrium. The echoed licks of his wing tips faded. The sound of his footfalls cut off after the hiss and the click of a door. No guards were in the space, only the same flickering of mounted oil torches.

The hall was quiet again.

We're like the Hardy Boys. I got dibs on Shaun Cassidy.

The Gaunt Man grinned while I shook my head.

What? He was the cute one. The fun one!

"Come on," I said.

We walked across the atrium, careful to keep quiet. The Gaunt Man strode next to me. His black wing tips made no noise at all. I wasn't even sure if his feet touched the floor. There was a glamour about him that made some of his features always a little out of phase with reality.

On the wall in the corner where Roy had disappeared, a placard denoted a cartoon man hovering over a line of jagged squiggles.

Not unlike my hallucination next to me, I supposed.

Well?

"Well what?" I whispered.

We going into the dark unknown? Into a grand adventure?

In response I moved my hands to the door bar. With the softest of clicks, I unlatched and opened the door. The other side held empty silent darkness and a set of stairs. A breeze of the faintest of wet rot puffed passed my face.

I drew my Glock and stepped onto the landing. The fire door hissed. I reached behind me to quiet the door's return into its frame.

My eyes adjusted quickly to the new deeper dark.

The Gaunt Man, who I had left in the atrium, now stood on the landing below me.

So slow! You are very tentative these days, aren't you?

I said nothing.

Even with friends like me. And with all your wonderful gifts. A shame. Truly a shame.

He smiled his devil's grin.

I half expected horns to morph out of his forehead, but was disappointed as he bound out of sight to descend to the second part of the stairwell.

"Christ," I whispered, following him deeper into the black.

89

Twist and Shout

+65 Days – 2124 hours

At the bottom of the stairs was a second fire door, emptying into the end of a long corridor lined with red metal doors. The Gaunt Man wandered several meters ahead, stopping at each door and cupping his hands through each narrow window.

Johnny, I think I may have found something. Hurry!

He waved me over.

With only a few of the security lamps operating to illuminate the corridor, I walked through the irregular pools of light past two other closed doors with labels of Archives – Asia and Archives – 18th to where the Gaunt Man stood.

He tittered from foot to foot with his grin plastered to his face. Neither ominous nor menacing, his show of thin peeled back lips and sharp teeth just looked silly now.

You would think my apparitions would keep their dental hygiene consistent.

Take a look.

I cupped my hands against the glass. The security lamp stationed on the wall across from the door cast a harsh glare. The inside of the storage room was pitch black.

Slam!

A FRAC snarled against the window, smearing her stringy hair and bloody lips against the security glass.

I backed up a step and raised a fist.

The Gaunt Man had disappeared.

The FRAC continued to scratch against the door.

Stepping right, I left the undead prisoner to her fate. As I walked away, she lost interest in the now steadied glow from the security light that had shone behind me and faded back into the darkness.

The Gaunt Man appeared again at the end of the hall, leaning against the concrete brick wall with a huge grin on his face.

"You proud of yourself?" I asked.

I'm happy with myself, yes.

"What was the point?"

Amusement, I suppose. It was pretty funny to see the look on your face.

"Why did she react to me?"

She didn't. She was reacting to the shift of shadows when you blocked the light.

"Wonderful," I said. "A hallucination with a sense of humor."

You would miss me if I were gone.

He stepped off the wall and joined me in the intersection. His smile faded into a grim, thin line.

There is nothing good down here, John.

"That I would agree with."

Both sides of the corridor were dark, the glow from the security ballasts in the main corridor spilling a weak cone of light.

Which way did Roy go?

"Shut up a minute."

The Gaunt Man held up two fingers and squeezed his lips shut. It was a comical gesture that I couldn't stifle a smile against. His lips thinned under his pinch and crept upward at the corners while his dark eyes glimmered in the low light.

To the right was a freight elevator with its up arrow button lit next to a swipe card reader. On the other side of the short hallway was a set of steel double doors. This was the corridor Duke had originally brought me in through upon my arrival.

A murmur drifted from behind the doors, a low buzzing and clicking masking another deeper muffled sound in the dark. The opposite end at the elevator remained dark and quiet, save the call button.

"Looks like we are going that way," I whispered with a finger pointed toward the rattles and humming.

You are quite the detective.

"Fuck you very much," I responded with a middle finger scratching against the side of my nose.

Classy. Very classy.

"Figured you would think so."

I brushed past my uncooperative apparition and ventured toward the noise. The hum was both beckoning and menacing.

Aren't you glad you can see so well?

"Quit reminding me."

I looked back at the cross corridor, the pool of light warm and inviting. And safe.

I pressed an ear against the cool gray steel, the door vibrating with activity.

There were no handles on this side. A brushed aluminum panel with a numeric keypad and a raised PUSH panel jutted out from the wall at waist level. I wiggled my fingers, debating whether to press the button to open the door.

Had Roy kept power flowing to the mechanism? You would figure so since the elevator call button was lit up.

Just as I put slight pressure on the panel, there came a loud click. I slipped behind one of the doors as they swung open. With me behind it, the door couldn't latch against the stopper at the top of the wall.

One of the Marauders walked out.

It was Richard – called Ritchie by Joey and his friends. He was the one who got cold-cocked by Duke with the motorcycle helmet. He stopped beyond the swing of the doors and adjusted his worn biker jacket. The doors hissed closed, leaving me exposed.

He turned, his bruised eyes widening.

"You ain't supposed to be…"

Lunging forward, I covered his mouth and nose with my right hand and spun him around with my left. I locked in behind his neck with an arm bar.

He uselessly struggled against me, his pale arms trying to pull my arm away from his face.

His hand went to his holster.

I drove a knee into his ribs.

Then I did it again for good measure.

He let out a muffled grunt as his ribs cracked.

Controlling his body, I drove his forehead against the wall.

I looked at the closed doors, the hum with the metallic clicking undertones distant behind the steel and insulation. The other end of the corridor was quiet.

We were still undiscovered.

The Marauder reached for his weapon again. His other hand dug into my wrist in a vain attempt to pry it away.

The edges of my night vision faded into crimson.

With a forward thrust, I slammed his head against the wall again. He let out a forceful exhale, even through my cupped hand.

Boom!

I spun toward the noise from beyond the double doors.

A twist and a crack followed.

The Marauder's hands dropped limp to his sides.

I pulled away to see his eyes flutter before rolling back into white.

His legs gave way.

Dead weight.

Fuck.

Well, that was exciting. 'Fuck' indeed.

The Gaunt Man looked on from his post against the door.

Lucy, you gots some 'splainin' to do.

I propped the Marauder against the wall with my right hand against his shoulder blades.

You didn't have to kill the man, Johnny. Guess you still don't know your own strength.

"I don't need your bullshit right now," I replied, angry at my sloppiness.

That may be, but you did just kill one of Roy's men.

I sighed.

The dark unknown would have to wait.

Disposal of the body was now first priority. The archival storage units were locked with mechanical numeric pads. No help there. Taking him up the stairs and across the atrium would be dodgy and ill conceived at best.

The Marauder started to stir, a low growl humming from the base of his throat. I pressed him tighter against the wall and pulled my knife from its sheath.

"I thought the virus had burned out," I reminded the Gaunt Man. "You're supposed to come back only when attacked. Like Jack was. When you're bit."

There are no absolutes, my dear John.

"You kidding me?"

No, sir. Apparently death is just the beginning.

The Gaunt Man walked closer and swept his fingers across locks of hair from the Marauder's forehead. Ritchie tilted his head slowly toward the door, a low moan exhaling through his widening jaw.

Interesting.

"What is?" I poised the knifepoint against the side of Ritchie's head.

Apparently the virus is more prolific than previously assumed.

"Fine," I shrugged as I pressed the tip of the blade into Ritchie's ear.

Wait.

"For what?"

Just wait. Please.

I continued to press Ritchie tight against the wall. He slapped weakly at my arm with his still re-animating limbs.

The Gaunt Man leaned closer to FRAC Ritchie, gazing into his eyes with something akin to love. Or maybe it was akin to some sort of appreciation.

271

Also, I wouldn't stick that knife into his ear if I were you.
"Why not?"
It is much more difficult to explain a found body with a knife wound to the ear when you are trying to conceal it under the guise of accidental death.

As much a pain in the ass as my now constant spectral companion was, he was tactically right. Hiding a body with a knife wound would raise too many eyebrows.

I guess I needed more training on the criminal pursuits of body disposal, evidence tampering and crime scene staging.

See? I know you know I'm right.

I didn't respond.

And we can dispose of him relatively quickly, now that I am thinking about it.

"What are you talking about?"

I looked back at the double doors, expecting more Marauders to come through.

With our friend in the archival room.

"And I suppose you have the numeric code?"

He looked at the squirming Ritchie before grinning at me.

I do now.

90

Security Measures

+65 Days – 2201 hours

Back at the room marked Archives – 18th, I held the back of Ritchie's neck with his face pushed toward the door. The FRACarvist inside hissed at the door, tapping her rotted and whittled fingers on the window.

"You going to give me that code, Carnak?"

Of course.

The Gaunt Man went silent again.

"You're killing me, Smalls," I said, continuing firm but controlled pressure on the squirming Ritchie.

The Gaunt Man leaned against the side of the doorframe, the numeric pad next to him at waist level.

"The code."

You are no fun.

"The code."

He pouted before smiling again then pointed at the four numbered buttons on the metal housing.

3. Then 1. Then 2 and 4 pressed at the same time. Then turn the lever after the click.

"You're shitting me."

He waved a hand at the number pad.

Give it a try.

I pressed the numbers in the sequence he provided me. After pressing the #2 and #4 pins together, there was a click.

Told ya.

I was surprised as the lever turned freely. Opening the door quickly, I swung Ritchie through it before the FRACarvist had a second to escape. Ritchie bumped into her and they both staggered back toward the center of the room.

They bounced their hips off an examination counter with a rattle. The table didn't move as its legs were bolted to the floor. A broad sword of uncertain medieval lineage slid off the table and clanked off the tile floor. The FRACarvist and Ritchie growled at the noise, leaning over to investigate whether the weapon held anything good to eat.

The FRACs preoccupied, I looked around the room. Aside from the examination table, the room was lined with metal baker's racks filled with tagged artifacts and cardboard boxes with Sharpie marker descriptions of their contents.

The window.

At the far wall was a large window coated over with white paint. On closer inspection, the window had not been the victim of random or haphazard coats of whitewash for the sake of a cheap sprucing up. The windows had been "blacked out" in order to preserve the privacy and integrity of the artifacts in the chamber.

A latching system kept the window secure. I pushed the lever and the window cracked open, letting in a sliver of moonlight and a puff of cool fresh air with a hint of oily smoke.

I opened the window wider.

A welded iron security window guard separated the room from an exterior walled-in concrete enclosure. The window sat a meter above a grated floor with cracked concrete walls rising up five meters toward the moonlight and freedom. On the grate were abandoned wooden palettes, coils of wire and layers of damp dead leaves. The museum's lawn edged to the top of the wall, the tall grass waving between the wall's cap and an iron pipe railing.

Another problem solved.

As a narrow river of water dripped down a storm drain at the center of the floor under the grate, I realized what the Gaunt Man was driving at.

I unlocked the hooded latches for the security bars and swung it open. The hinges squeaked too loud for the quiet night. I gritted my teeth and waited

274

Only crickets responded.

In the center of the room Ritchie and the FRACarvist had lost interest in the now silent broad sword. They stood slack-jawed next to the table swaying back and forth, bumping into each other a few times before they started moving in unison. It was mesmerizing, like watching a cobra in a basket under the command of an Indian snake charmer.

After hesitating a few more seconds, I grabbed Ritchie by the shirt collar. He fought against my grip, arching his back. I pulled harder and he finally relented to being dragged to the window.

Wait a moment, Johnny.

"Now what?"

It has to look like he had been killed by the fall.

"Yeah? And?"

A twisted neck is not the order of the day.

"Goddammit."

Irritated, I slammed Ritchie face first into the wall. His forehead cracked, and already blackening blood spotting the painted blocks.

Bravo!

Ritchie was still animated.

See? You are getting more control of yourself.

I grabbed his belt at the back of his jeans, lifted him off his feet, and tossed him into the sunken courtyard where his bloody face broke his fall.

The effect was comical, making me smile.

As Ritchie slowly got his hands under him, I closed the iron security bars with less of a distressed cat yelp and locked it. Ritchie turned his neck to the sound and grumbled. I cut off his complaints by swinging the window closed.

The FRACarvist, alone again except for me and the smiling Gaunt Man leaning against the examination table, wandered back to the door in pursuit of the shining light that she could not reach.

Isn't she adorable?

"Sure," I said. "Let's leave her to her history and find out what Roy's up to."

Do something. Lead, follow or get out of the way.

"That's the Army," I corrected.

Whatever you say, Johnny Boy. Those branches of the military are all the same to me.

"Yeah," I replied, "you black hat guys are a special breed."

Well thank you very much.

"I didn't say 'special' in a good way. Let's go."

The Gaunt Man stood up razor straight and saluted.

Sir! Yes, Sir!

"I work for a living, asshole."

91

What Lies Beneath

+66 Days – 0749 hours

The Gaunt Man was gone.

Again.

Blessing me with a moment of silence inside my head.

Hours had passed and the labyrinth beneath the house of antiquities had been left undiscovered and unexplored.

I sat against the exhibit wall.

A few of the Marauders sat on the other side of the converted barracks, laughing and playing some sort of card game – maybe Spades or Crazy Eights. Whatever the game, they would hoot and holler in turn with each slap of a card to the discard pile on the floor.

Deb stood in the corner by the door, sharpening a Bowie knife with a whetstone. She gazed at the edge of the blade as she slid it deliberately along the sharpening surface. At the end of one of the strokes, she looked past the knife at me.

A thin smile crept across her lips and she nodded.

I returned the gesture.

She lifted the knife and poked it in the air at me before returning to her task of making it a quicker killing instrument.

Joey came in, bee-lining between the cots toward me and breaking my sightline of Deb.

"Hey, John."

"Joey."

"You seen Ritchie?"

"You seem to think I know everyone in this place."

"You ain't the mayor of museum town?"

"Hardly. I'll leave that to Roy and his merry men."

"True. True."

"Roger."

"What about Roger?" Joey's brow furrowed in confusion.

"I meant affirmative," I corrected. "Never mind."

"Ritchie is one of the Marauders." He shook his head. "He was on basement watch last night and no one has seen him since mid-shift."

"What does he look like?"

"Black hair. Ghostly white. Wears a motorcycle jacket sometimes. He was the one that got cold-cocked by Duke the other day. Remember?"

"Oh, yeah," I responded truthfully, then lied, "but I don't think I've seen him lately."

"Bummer," Joey frowned. "Ok."

"What's so important that needs to be guarded downstairs anyway? It's not like art theft is a lucrative profession these days."

"Right?" he chuckled. "Not a huge call for priceless paintings."

Joey didn't say anything for a few seconds, his tongue pressing into his cheek. His face went through a series of contortions, sliding from slightly amused to slack to worried.

"What, Joey?"

He shook his head and looked over his shoulder to Roy's shouting foot soldiers.

"I don't know what they do down there, John," he whispered, continuing to shake his head. "Don't think I want to know."

"Why not?" I pressed, leaning forward.

The corner of his eye twitched. It was as if it took effort to keep them from looking toward the Marauders.

I shot out an arm and grabbed his bicep.

He squeaked with surprise then covered his mouth.

Deb glanced up from her knife for a moment but quickly lost interest in Joey's antics.

"What?" I repeated.

Joey leaned in, his hand gripping mine.

"I hear screaming," he whispered. "Lots of screaming."

92

Roger That!

+66 Days – 1910 hours

The sun set slowly in the west, casting a fiery orange through the haze on the horizon. To the east still burned a section of housing on the hillsides from the recent fuel tank explosion, sending up dark smoke and its own flickers of weak amber.

Enjoying the fresh air?

"Reminds me of Rainier," I replied.

That life seemed years ago, not the mere weeks it actually was.

Isn't it strange?

"What is?" I finally took the bait.

How surreal the world is now. Chaos and death surrounds you. Every day is a fight for simple survival and existence. Makes you appreciate the beauty around you a bit more.

I ignored him and walked the perimeter of the atrium roof with a sniper rifle cradled in my arms. Gravel crunched under my boots as a warm oily breeze puffed in from the direction of the rampant blaze.

A flick of white raced across Lancaster Street.

I snapped the rifle to my shoulder and looked through the scope. A plastic grocery bag floated to the sidewalk before getting snagged on a lamppost with its base covered with differently colored WAM stickers.

I nestled the weapon in my arms again and watched the bag flap against the pole. Before I could speculate how long it would take for the bag to escape the clutches of the stickered post, a yell came from the other side of the building.

"Hey!"

I trotted over to the Tuckerman Street side of the roof.

"Hey," the voice called again.

Raul stood on the grass with his machete in one hand and the other cupped to his mouth.

"It's Ritchie," he looked up at my position. "Ritchie's in the maintenance well."

He pointed to the concrete walled service corridor outside the barred basement level windows. Ritchie, complete with his biker jacket and long greasy hair, bumped into a discarded palette. He slapped against the gray damp sidewalls, gurgling his protests as he reached up at Raul's shouts.

"I found him," he yelled. "It's Ritchie."

"Points for you," I called down. "You may want to stop shouting."

I put the rifle in full draw and fired a shot.

Raul ducked.

A former businessman's forehead imploded as the brain matter pushed out the base of its skull. True to his type-A personality, his body continued for six more steps before it got the message that his brain had passed. He collapsed to his knees and pitched forward on his chest and face.

"Christ, John."

"Word to the wise, Raul."

Duke, Debra, Raul's brother Hector, and three other Marauders spilled out from the delivery driveway. The Marauders fanned out and set up a well-rehearsed perimeter. Deb stood behind them with her Benelli. Duke and Hector walked over to Raul.

"Any reason why you are being so loud and stupid?" Duke asked.

Raul threw a thumb to the service pit.

Hector stepped closer and looked over the edge.

"Oh shit, it's Ritchie," Hector shouted. "Hey, Ritchie? Where you been, man?"

Duke walked up to the edge and grabbed Hector by the back of the neck with a dark meaty hand. He pushed Hector to the tipping point. Hector flailed out his arms in an effort to grab the railing and brace against toppling into the well.

Raul tensed and stepped one foot forward.

"Stay put," Duke hissed.

Raul put up his own arms in surrender, taking one step back.

"Hector," Duke ordered, "shut the fuck up or I'll toss you in."

"Okay, boss." Hector surrendered. "Okay. It's all good."

Duke pulled him back from the edge and let him go.

"You want me to put him down?" Hector asked.

"Still being stupid?" Duke asked. "You know how he died?"

Raul peered over the edge, more confident that Duke wasn't going to push him into the pit.

"His neck is twisted. Bloody forehead," Raul pointed out. "No obvious punctures from bites. No bullet or knife wounds that I can see."

Duke looked at Raul and shook his head.

"You're both idiots?"

"What?" they asked in unison.

Duke glanced up at me.

"John?"

"Yeah?"

"Can you kill a man without a weapon?

That's a curious question, isn't it?

I looked out over the empty streets before answering.

"Yup."

Across Institute Road, the white plastic grocery bag had indeed escaped the WAM street light pole, sailing through the light breeze as it wandered aimlessly on its way to nowhere in particular.

93

Employment Opportunities

+66 Days – 2133 hours

Hiatt Hall was empty.

I sat alone against my section of wall reading the Worcester 'Knights' Exhibit pamphlet for what seemed to be the hundredth time.

"Roy wants to see you."

I looked up from the pamphlet.

Joey stood in the doorway with a hand on his hip.

Did they suspect that I killed Ritchie?

"What does he want?"

"Dude, I don't know," he shrugged. "No one tells me anything."

"Seems to be the trend," I answered. "You escorting me?"

"Yeah," he mumbled, shuffling his feet a little. "That okay? I just do what I can to stay in his majesty's good graces, you know?"

"Fine."

I met him at the entrance and patted him on the back.

"Want me to go alone?"

"I really am supposed to take you." He looked away.

"Where is he? The library?"

"With his stupid chess set."

"Alright. You're off the hook."

Joey frowned. "I really should walk you."

"I'll tell him I told you I didn't need any stupid escort to walk fifty feet."

"You sure?" Joey lighted up a bit. "You'll tell him that?"

"Yep. I'll be good. In the library?"

"Yeah. It's over there." He pointed, grinning at his own cleverness.

283

"I'll find it okay." I laughed.

"Just be sure to tell him I was gonna bring ya, ok?"

"Ok."

"Can you make him laugh for me? He usually wants me to do something stupid to make him laugh. Always asking me to 'entertain' him."

"I'll make him laugh, Joey." I promised, with a heavy dose of sarcasm. "Don't worry."

The soft taps of my boots echoed off the walls of the renovated original structure. I saw Roy through the glass. He sat in his usual spot with his lips pressed against his intertwined fingers, staring at another reset chessboard.

He is definitely a creature of habit, isn't he?

He noticed me, smiled and waved me in.

"I see the darling Joey has deserted you," he said as the door closed behind me. "A pity."

"I don't need a chaperone to walk twenty meters."

"And I am sure you mentioned that to him."

"I did."

"So I suppose I cannot be too cross at the young man."

"No," I replied, "you can't."

"Very well, then." He dismissed the conversation with a wave of his hand, gesturing me to my assigned seat with the board between us. "Come. Play another round with me."

He pushed forward the white king's pawn two squares before I even settled in my chair. I scooted the chair toward the table with a loud squeak. Roy gave me a cross look as he waited for my opening move.

I ignored his glare and countered with my black queen's pawn one space.

"I am sure you have heard a guard was killed," Roy speculated.

"Saw Duke figuring things out when I was on the roof," I replied, careful to not call the shift 'overwatch'.

"I am sure you have a theory or two," Roy pressed, pushing his queen's pawn to the square next to his King's pawn.

With gaps around Roy's king and queen, I pushed forward my king's knight's pawn one square. I left my finger on its top for a moment before leaving the move to faith and chance.

"I have a few ideas."

"Enlighten me," Roy said.

"May have fallen during the night."

His queen's bishop's pawn moved to join the other advanced pawns. They made a line that served as a broad shield in front of the king and queen.

And now his queen's bishop was left exposed as well.

Without a clue to his strategy, I slid out my king's bishop.

"Could have fallen over the side rail and broke his neck."

Roy said nothing but moved his queen's knight out to C3.

My king's pawn wandered out to E5. If Roy took the bait I could break open the wall of pawns he was building.

But Roy did not take the bait.

Instead he moved the king's knight and centered the piece in front of the defenseless king and beside the queen.

"That could have happened."

I moved my knight again, this time to F6.

"Any other theories?" he asked.

His king's bishop's pawn moved forward one square.

I countered with my queen's bishop's pawn two squares to meet up with Roy's wall of cannon fodder.

Bad move.

"John?" Roy inquired again as he took the pawn.

"You have any in-fighting?" I asked as I took his pawn in return.

"There is always bickering," he mused, "but we try to keep it at a minimum."

"You can remove that pretty lady," he picked up his queen and touched it to my queen, "if you please."

I couldn't believe I fell for that.

With a flexing jaw, I removed my queen from the board.

"Check, by the way."

I tapped his queen with my king and took her off the field of battle.

"And what of the bickering?" Roy asked as he slid his queen's bishop out to my side of the field.

"Any one of your more capable men –"

"Or ladies," he reminded me.

"…or ladies could have snapped his neck. That is, if we are pursuing this line of conspiracy theory."

I moved my king's rook's pawn out to defend against the invading white bishop.

Roy swapped his unmoved rook and king, leaving open a straight line for the rook to take my king.

"Check."

I had nothing but defense and reaction on my side of the board. I moved my queen's bishop in front of my king, blocking Roy's rook.

"There you have it," I said.

"Have what?" Roy slid his invading bishop back onto his side of the field.

"My theories." I moved my queen's knight out to C6.

"Ah," Roy said with a sigh and a move of his aggressive knight to D5.

Another invasion.

I moved another pawn to G5.

Roy moved his bishop again. This time he slid it all the way back to his second row, stacking the piece in front of his other bishop.

I took his forward knight with one of mine.

A momentary victory as Roy took my knight with a pawn.

In order to keep my remaining knight safe I moved it past the pawn and into Roy's territory. Roy moved his knight away to keep it safe from my advancing horse. I decided to create my own blockade, moving one of my pawns to F5.

"No other theories then?"

"Not a one," I replied.

Roy pushed his bishop in front of my knight.

I moved my rook for a better line of attack.

"No other individuals or parties looking to attack us?" Roy asked as he moved his rook's pawn to H4.

"I wouldn't think so," I said as I took his pawn with one of mine. "I haven't seen any other living souls to challenge you."

"That's true," Roy replied as he moved his knight to threaten my bishop. "It has been very quiet as of late."

I moved the bishop to my corner.

Roy slid his own bishop to take my last pawn at H4.

"We have managed to eradicate all the atra mors and have rounded up as many survivors as we can house," Roy said with pride. "I must say we have done a pretty good job."

"And now you have room for more survivors."

"Because of that little outbreak in Hiatt Hall?" Roy asked. "Yes. That is true."

I moved my king over one space to avoid Roy's bishop.

"Oh, yes," Roy exclaimed as he left his own king alone by moving his rook across to F1, "that last move was Check, wasn't it? My apologies."

I continued moving my king, this time one space forward and diagonal to front my own rook. I'm all about doing my own wetwork.

White pawn to G4.

Black pawn forward to F4.

White bishop to E4.

Black pawn to B5.

Roy caught me moving and not strategizing by taking my pawn at B5 with a pawn.

I took it with my bishop.

Roy moved his rook left one square, keeping it out of harm's way from my bishop. I hadn't realized I had moved the bishop into a larger attacking campaign.

"Agreed," Roy said, clucking his tongue, "I don't think there are too many people still out there to bother us."

I moved my last unmoved pawn to A5.

Like a halfback through the line of scrimmage, Roy moved a pawn into my open field of battle to D6.

"We have enough men and women to keep our little kingdom secure. I am content with that knowledge."

Unwilling to let Roy's pawn get the best of me, I moved my bishop back to flank it.

"We definitely have the fortitude, patience, strength and intelligence to take on all comers."

Roy gently slid his bishop into mine and removed my piece from the board.

I responded by taking his bishop with my knight.

"Good show, Mr. Walken," Roy smiled. "I see you do have the fighting spirit in you. That's why I like you."

He lined up his rook next to his king to trail his advancing pawn.

I advanced my king to the space beside the pawn.

Roy pushed his little pawn that could to D7 and one move away from my back line. Realizing that my king was useless to take the pawn and remain clear of checkmate, I threw my knight into the mix to block the back line rook from serving as the pawn's security detail.

Roy moved the pawn to my back line.

"King me, please," Roy grinned. "I will take a queen, but I figured use of the simpler game of checkers to be apt in this situation."

I gave him his queen back and placed the pawn in the tray.

"Thank you, sir."

Roy's goal line advance to reacquire his queen was short-lived as I took her off the board with one of the two rooks that had been guarding the line throughout the pawn's advance.

"Oh well," Roy said with a mock frown. "That was exciting, though, wasn't it?"

Then he smiled as he took my rook with his forgotten bishop. Shit!

I took the bishop with my other rook and he moved the pawn's trailing rook in front of my knight. He didn't take the knight, knowing it would be taken by one of the two pawns that were flanking the horse.

Roy taunted. "Now that was fun!"

I moved my king back a space, trying to regroup.

Roy's other rook slid across his back line.

I pushed a pawn into white territory.

Roy countered and moved his other rook.

I advanced my remaining rook to the square behind my knight.

Roy's rook confronted the advance of my pawn. But he wasn't stopping the pawn's advance. He was lining up kill shots for my other pawn and the knight beside it.

To counter, I lined up my rook to retaliate if he decided to pull the trigger.

He moved his king instead.

Trying to figure out the new tactic, I moved my king closer to his white knight.

Roy's adventurous rook retreated.

I advanced my king next to the knight.

Roy's other rook slid one square closer to his king.

I advanced the stalked pawn one space forward, even though it was a futile exercise.

"Check," I said.

"Not today, my friend," he retorted.

Roy took the pawn with his rook.

"At least I get a rook out of the deal," I replied, taking his warrior tower.

"Actually," he said, taking my rook, "that may be the most you get of the deal."

I moved my knight away to keep from having that piece taken by the king as well.

His remaining rook marched forward a step.

I did the same with one of my pawns.

"Check," I said again.

My bishop was now in a sniper's position with a clear spot to take down the king.

He calmly moved the king forward to C4.

I took his pawn at G4 with my king, finally able to do so without putting myself in Check.

Roy moved his threatened knight away to G7. His smile withdrew to a narrow line.

I pursued with my knight to G5.

He evaded his horse to E8, a furrow to his brow.

My pawn to F3.

He moved his rook away to C2.

My second pawn to E3.

He brought his king closer to my second pawn.

The pawn moved to E2.

Roy swallowed as his rook retreated to guard the white front line in case one of my pawns made it there.

With the white king a no-joy kill, I took the diagonal long shot against one of the two white pawns with my bishop.

I sat back in the chair and smiled at my good fortune. Roy was left with an unmoved pawn, a knight completely away from the defense of his king, and a busy rook. I had a remaining bishop and knight in close quarters combat, able to defend my king and attack Roy. In addition, I had two pawns on the verge 'to be kinged' and two more slowly advancing across the open field of waning battle.

"You play reactively, but hard."

"Thanks," I said, waiting for his next move.

"You know?" Roy thought out loud. "I may have a job for

you."

"Another job?"

"Yes, yes," he said excitedly, his frown turning upside down. "This game can wait. I have a more important job for you. I know of a position that just opened up!"

94

Gears of War

+66 Days – 2229 hours

Roy led the way across the atrium.

Hey. I remember this stairwell.

The Gaunt Man's voice echoed through my brain. He chose not to make an appearance, although he certainly would've been better company. He tended to speak in semi-veiled riddles and half-truths, but at least the ghost – or a trick of my mind – seemed to have my best interests at heart.

"Ritchie was a good man," Roy said. "He was loyal. A shame what happened to him. But the gears of war and the engines of progress must go on, don't you think?"

"I would have to say yes."

"Of course," Roy answered. "You are a practical man. A man with skills."

He opened the fire door and started the descent down the steps.

"Sorry to cut our match short. This is much more important." He turned the corner at the first landing. "We will finish our game, most assuredly."

"Whenever you're ready."

"Very good."

Roy stepped into the corridor and, as expected, turned left and walked past the archival rooms. He slowed at the door where the FRACarvist mewed behind the wired glass.

"It's such a shame," he said without expanding further.

The Gaunt Man, now invested enough to pop into view, paused at the door.

He knew that woman.

Seemed so.

Probably more broken up about her than he is about Ritchie.

Poor Ritchie.

Yeah. Poor Ritchie.

I thought it in jest, but I did feel remorse for his death. Not having a handle on my strength or rage troubled me. It took much less effort to snap his neck than it should have.

Did I even put any pressure on his neck?

I couldn't remember.

I didn't think so.

You were surprised by the noise. Remember?

Yes. I was.

I am sure you will figure it out shortly.

"…this corridor and the warehouse behind these doors," Roy instructed. He pressed a series of numbers on the keypad next to the doors. A mechanical chirp was followed by a hiss and the slow swishing swing of the opening double doors.

"Follow me, dear sir," Roy said as he stepped into the larger concrete storage and receiving area.

It reminded me of Rainiers Island's municipal building basement, but on a much larger scale.

Ah… the good ole days.

The floor was concrete covered with a sky blue epoxy coating. A forest of I-beam columns supported a joisted ceiling of corrugated metal. Shipping containers and steel warehousing racks were packed between the columns, effectively adding separation to the space.

Roy stopped at the second column.

Duke, Hector and Raul stood at the open delivery bay door. They didn't snap to attention when we approached, only pausing their conversation long enough to appraise us.

All hail the king. Or not.

To the right was a space between the shelving, free of containers and used as a cross corridor.

Roy turned back to me.

"It's important to know if you have the fortitude for this type of work."

"Meaning?"

"Meaning that we have a system here to protect our citizens and to keep what we have… ours. We have taken the brunt of others' greedy and vile natures. And we have prevailed. But not without loss."

Roy stepped closer.

"I mentioned that I wasn't above getting my hands dirty. And many of us have blood on our hands. It is a terrible business but we have done what we had to in order to keep the peace.

"Ritchie was one of those who safeguarded this level from both outsiders and from those in our company who do not need to understand the nature of what is 'behind the curtain' that keeps them secure."

Roy tossed a nod to the area beside him beyond the crates.

"If you say yes to this post you will be privy to our mechanics and our way of doing things that ensures a solid foundation for our house."

He is always so dramatic. Say yes so we can pierce the veil of this mystery.

"Let's take a look."

"Bully!" Roy beamed. "Come then, and see."

Roy walked on. I glanced at Duke and the others. He gave me a grim nod. I nodded back and followed the king past the crates.

95

Private Tours
+66 Days – 2245 hours

Roy prattled on about the history and additional renovations of the museum through the years, marveling about how the different structures had come together in a perfect amalgam of history and architecture. I caught the gist of his tour lecture but paid more attention to the layout of the subterranean warehouse.

He loves to talk.

The Gaunt Man walked next to me, taking in the surroundings as intently as me.

Ohh, is that a Picasso?

I shook my head and continued to follow Roy through a zigzag of aisles with crates and artwork. Survival gear, luggage, clothes, weapons and non-perishable foodstuff also took up space on the racks. It was quite an eclectic inventory.

"Listen to me going on and on," Roy finished. "Suffice to say I am very proud of what we have built here. Blood or no blood."

"You do what you have to do."

"This is your last chance to turn back, my friend," Roy said, stopping before another turn through the crate-filled racks. "After this, you are truly into the inner sanctum of our works and will become a keeper of our secrets."

I locked onto his unwavering eyes.

"Lead on, Roy."

No turning back now. So exciting!

"Come!" Roy smiled brightly, disappearing into the darkness through the opening in the racks.

It wasn't necessarily a crossway, more of an opening in the shelving where they had removed the palletized inventory.

I followed.

My eyes adjusted a bit but couldn't pierce the utter darkness of a space with no windows and only the intermittent lamplight through slits between crates.

Flashes invaded my mind. A basement concealing a newborn stealing father. A barn filled with the smell of dead cattle and an undead lover.

I shook my head against these thoughts of what seemed a lifetime ago.

In the present, the smell of death permeated through my nostrils. It was old death. Dried up death. But there was a layer of metallic spilled life on the surface of it, coating the rot like a fresh coat of red paint.

A series of clicks led to an increasing buzz in my ears.

I tensed up.

The darkness thinned as cones of weak amber light brightened. The yellow glow whitened. The space was clear of all debris and storage save a welding curtain placed at its center between two columns. The silhouette of a circle lit the curtain fabric.

Roy returned and pressed a hand into my arm.

"Remember," he said in earnest, "extreme measures lead to the best results. Keep that in mind."

We walked to the curtain.

The smell of metal was stronger here.

So was the acrid scent of urine and sweat.

"1966. The artist is Arnaldo Pomodoro." Roy lectured. "He was an architect and a stage designer who also was a goldsmith and sculptor."

In the center of the room under a fluorescent lamp was a huge sphere with several geometric cutouts hollowing out its sides and center. It was circled with heavy chains.

"Cast in bronze," Roy said as he walked around its perimeter to the far side. "The *Rotante Del Foro Centrale*. Pomodoro used geometric shapes quite a bit in his work."

One of the chains ended in a leather cuff. Through the cuff was a ball of bloody bandages.

Roy stopped at the back of the sculpture and placed his hands on his hips.

"Quite an accomplishment," Roy said as he smiled and admired his work. "See how the highly polished surface is interlaced with fissures to an eroded interior."

Cast with a wash of sickly downward light, a female was chained to the side of the sphere, her boots dangling a meter above the floor. Her jeans were damp and red. A bleeding gash blossomed in her shirt. Her arms were held high in the cuffed chains, stretching her body back against the surface of the globe.

Gazebo.

Her hair covered her face, the light casting her downturned face into shadows.

Lucy.

Roy picked up a broad sword that had been leaning against one of the columns. He whipped it about in expert fashion before approaching the woman.

"Wakey, young lady," he announced as he poked her in the ribs near the still bleeding gash, then spoke to me. "You can see in this work, much in the manner of Cubists and Surrealists, that Pomodoro has broken through the smooth surface of the spherical form to reveal the infected areas inside."

The woman hissed, strained against her bonds, and raised her crimson and swollen face. Wet strands of hair stuck to the drying blood on her cheeks.

Her eyes opened wide at Roy.

My heart pounded in my ears.

My breath hitched.

My hand twitched toward the handle of my Glock.

"Fuck you, psycho," Jude said in defiance.

96

Methods

+66 Days – 2321 hours

The marbling on the floor in Roy's office was speckled with golden flakes and darker swirls.

Black eyes. Like doll's eyes. Like FRAC eyes.

Roy sat behind his large oak desk. A placard sat on one edge, the slot for the brass embossed nameplate empty.

Should have shot him.

I nearly did.

Shock – in spite of muscle memory – and the smallest of headshakes from Jude stayed my hand from drawing my weapon and spraying Roy's brains all over the concrete wall of his torture chamber.

"What do you think, John?"

"About what?"

"Really? Surely, you have an opinion on what I showed you."

I shrugged, but asked, "Why?"

"See? That's a solid thoughtful question."

I had meant 'why' as in 'why did my opinion matter to him' but I let him lead the conversation without correcting him.

Should have killed him.

It was all I could do to keep from killing him, even now. This time I wouldn't worry how little effort I needed to snap his neck.

He leaned back in his executive leather chair, clasping his fingers behind his head.

"I assure you it is completely necessary..."

Never trust a man who asks you to trust him.

The Gaunt Man stood behind Roy, his hands behind his back. He looked around at the diplomas on the wall. Edges of brighter wall peeked from behind the frames. One certification was missing altogether, the rectangle of sun-protected wall on full display instead. At one point, the Gaunt Man swiped across the top of one of the frames and showed me a clean index finger as a result.

"...was found trying to sneak into the compound. Duke and Raul had some trouble when they first went to round her up. Like a feral cat, that one." Roy smiled at his last words. "Very feral."

"Still haven't heard why."

Roy leaned forward and placed his hands on the desk.

"We have discussed this before," he stated slowly and deliberately. "What I have built here requires hard work, forward thinking, and the ability to adapt to any situation.

"This wild woman forced her way into my domain for some reason. She passed by weapons and food. Walked by gear, fuel and paintings. She was looking for something that she had not found by the time we stopped her.

"And now we are in the midst of an inquisition to find out what or who she knows. I have to know what she sought... and for who."

"So torture is your answer?"

The Gaunt Man perked up his ears and leaned against the brick wall.

"We tried to be persuasive with food. Then we offered her an overnight stint in the Chapter House with the alta mors. She was neither charmed nor scared. You remember your time in the center of that room, don't... ?"

I nodded mechanically, hoping the FRACs did not get close to her. How did I miss that Jude was in the Chapter House?

Probably when you were locked up in the gallery.

"... you came out on top as a respected member of our group. Of course, your release from the Chapter House was probationary to start but you redeemed yourself quickly by saving the lovely Debra"

So that was a punishment for Debra and a test for us?

I nodded absently, to both Roy and the Gaunt Man.

"Anyway," he said, waving the thought away, "it was unfortunate for this new lovely woman that she got through the pat down with a knife in her boot. Duke wasn't cut but he took offense and took it upon himself to put her into a more uncomfortable position in the basement to work on her a little bit. With my authorization, of course."

"Of course."

Of course.

"This lovely warrior still is silent, though." Roy leaned back again and looked over my shoulder. "Very resilient."

The Gaunt Man leaned down near Roy's shoulder and squinted one eye to sightline what he thought Roy was looking at. The pale specter shrugged and shook his head.

"No others?"

"Hmm?" Roy shook out of his thoughts. "No. No one else has come. That's no guarantee that there are not others in her party."

"Understood," I agreed. "Nothing to flesh out her story?"

"Flesh out her story?" he smirked. "She tells no tales. Like dead men."

"Nothing on her person to clue you in to her intent?"

"I am afraid not. I feel we will just need to continue her education so that, in turn, she can educate us."

"What method are you using," I asked with restraint, "to educate her?"

"Duke has his ways I assure you. He seems to have a knack."

"Does he?"

"Well," Roy replied with a knowing nod, "I have to admit that he has had better results before this."

"What methods?"

"We tried the honey. Now we are using vinegar. First food, now famine. Sensory deprivation and delicate poking and prodding."

"Saw the bandages and blood."

"Yes indeed. All necessary."

"My advice would be to redress those wounds if you intend to prolong your methods." I choked on the last word.

Roy tapped his fingers rhythmically on his deck blotter. After all of his fingers had a chance to chime in several times, he leaned forward with a squeak of chair springs.

"Of course. We certainly can't get blood from a cold stone."

I leaned back in the canvas visitor chair and slowly exhaled.

"I will let Duke know," Roy announced. "Unfortunate that we lost the one person with any real medical training. Poor Ritchie."

Poor Ritchie?

Poor Jude.

97

First Day on the Job

+67 Days – 0630 hours

It was quiet.

Too quiet.

Shut up.

The fluorescent floodlights washed the tiles and painted the concrete in cool stark white.

Roy had left me explicit but simple instructions.

Very simple, really.

'Don't let anyone past', he had ordered.

You shall not pass!

I looked at the grinning skin-covered skeleton. His paper thin and flaky flesh peeled back in all the wrong ways as he smiled.

Remember? Gandalf from 'Lord of the Rings'. Remember?

"You are a strange bird."

That's certainly true. But no less so than you, of course. I'm just better looking.

There was no one in the corridor.

No cameras.

No other obvious intrusions.

I paced the length of the archival hallway from the fire door to the intersection. Stepping over to the receiving doors I crouched down and took a look at the numeric keypad.

You planning on a little safe crackin'?

"Maybe. You should have extracted the code for this door from Ritchie after getting the archive room code."

Geez. Do I have to do everything?

"No."

I didn't intend to start becoming reliant on my sarcastic imaginary friend.

And what are you going to do about that strength of yours?

"Still working on it."

Work harder. Or smarter. Or we will be disposing of more bodies.

I sighed.

A creak.

Followed by the hissing and click of a door lock.

Drawing the Glock and stepping to the edge of the long corridor, I cleared the corner. Duke lumbered down the center of the hall, a briefcase in his left hand and a look of determination on his face.

I lowered my weapon.

"Welcome to the mines. Roy's got you working all over the place these days." Duke gave me an appraising look. "Don't be slacking on your other duties just because Roy wants you down here."

He drew closer.

"You still have perimeter this afternoon with Joey. Having you on the roof is way more damn important than guarding an empty hallway because of his stupid pet project."

I thought Roy said that Jude was Duke's pet project?

"Couldn't agree more," I replied.

"Maybe Roy is punishing you again," Duke wondered out loud.

"Or maybe showing off a little," I admitted.

"There you go. Keep up the good work."

"Yeah, right."

Duke left me and headed to the receiving doors. His large body hid the keypad from view.

beep... beep, beep... beep

The doors hissed open and Duke disappeared without another look back. The doors closed behind him and I was left alone in the corridor.

Doing a bang up job, aren't we?

"Don't remind me."

98

Broken Promises
+67 Days – 1149 hours

My skin welcomed the warmth and fresh air of the early afternoon.

Joey sat on the edge of the roof, leaning back with one leg dangling over the edge. A scoped rifle sat across his lap.

"You better get a handle on that weapon before it goes over the side."

"Hey, John," he said without opening his eyes.

He did, however, remove the rifle from his thighs and leaned it against the wall.

"Thanks for the advice."

"No problem."

We looked out at the city of Worcester. Other than the faint wisps of whitening smoke from the various explosions over the last week or so, the streets were barren.

"Where you keeping yourself?"

"Roy has me doing other work."

"Wetwork?"

"No. Why would you say that?"

"That's the word on the street," Joey said.

"Word on the street?"

"Yeah." he chuckled for a moment before his face fell. "People are muttering on about Ritchie and maybe that you had a hand in what happened to him."

"What do you think?"

"If you did do it," Joey said, then paused before continuing, "I figured he had it coming."

"You think he deserved what he got?"

"He always seemed to be a good guy. Patched me up once.

Probably needed to be patched up more than that one time but he did a good job when he did."

"So? No?"

"I don't know. Everyone has done something to deserve what they get, I guess."

"Even you?"

Joey stared out at the city.

A few sparrows chirped in a tree by the auditorium.

The house on the opposite corner stood in stark contrast with its overgrown yellow grass and unshaped bushes. Eventually the auditorium would fall prey to the same elements and same relentless growth as everything else.

Except for the FRACs. Maybe they were part of Mother Earth's plan.

"I didn't mean it," Joey said.

I thought to ask what he meant, but kept silent.

"When the shit hit, we were glued to CNN. Probably like everyone else in America. Probably you, too, huh?"

I nodded, even though it was much less than the truth.

"We did what they said. Stayed inside. Locked the doors. Stayed away from people. It must have been a few days – maybe a week – that we stayed indoors. Then one morning we woke up and the TV was nothing but static. Nine hundred channels and nothing to watch.

"We still hunkered down and waited. A few people tried to break into the house but we managed to run them off before they busted in. It was more about us making a lot of racket than brute strength, you know? Everyone was scared. Us and them.

"Anyway, we stayed inside as long as we could. But the food ran out. We had a few cans of green beans but then the opener broke. Can you believe it? The damn can opener broke! I tried to get them open with a knife but all I managed to do is make a few holes and cut myself up pretty good. Can't live on bean juice for long.

"When we couldn't take it any longer, my mom convinced me that I had to try to find some food, or at least a new can opener. I wanted to leave the block, but Mom wanted me to stay close so I started by darting out to the houses around us real quick. Knew the neighbors had left. They were the smart ones. At least that's what I thought at the time.

"It was quiet. No festers or people on the street. I took a chance on the next-door neighbor's house. Doors were locked. Windows locked. Had the same luck with the houses on the other side of us. Went across the street and tried there. One was wide open but was already ransacked, you know? I found a few can openers but they all were the electric kind.

"Don't know how long I was looking but the sun had already set. Must have tried a dozen houses, maybe. Managed to find a screwdriver and hammer for the cans plus a few boxes of cereal and a box of pasta. I got back to the house just before the festers started wandering the streets. Thought they had an aversion to sunlight in those days. Like vampires, you know?

"Anyway, I made it back home. Was worried about getting back in before the festers got at me. Mom and me had made a pact that the house would be barricaded once I left.

"But it ended up not mattering." Joey finished.

He picked up the rifle and looked through the scope at something he found of interest. He panned the weapon before returning it to its position against the wall.

He looked down at the streets, no longer interested in talking.

I looked out over the cityscape with Joey, knowing that he wouldn't reveal more.

99

Clairvoyance

+67 Days – 2019 hours

With both jobs done for the day I sat against the wall of the barracks and closed my eyes.

Jude hung from chains in the basement while I sat against a gallery wall with no practical exfiltration plan for us.

Feeling impotent?

"A little," I whispered to thin air.

I exhaled and let the sounds of the other people on their cots flood in.

"…thinks he's all that…"

"… probably bumped off Ritchie…"

"…why? So he could get more work to do? I think he worked 18 hours straight today…"

"…leave him alone," Deb's voice ordered.

Footfalls approached.

The soft thumps got louder as Deb closed in.

"Hello, Ms. Staff," I said without opening my eyes.

"Psychic now?"

"Maybe a little." I smiled weakly.

She kicked the sole of my boot with the tip of hers.

I looked up at her.

"May I help you?"

"You're the center of attention again."

"I do what I can."

"Apparently."

"You think I did it?"

"Did what?"

"Off Ritchie?"

"I don't care what you did or didn't do."

308

"You above all the conjecture?"

"It's fruitless and draining."

"Yes. It is," I answered. "So... what's up?"

"Nothing. Roy is preoccupied with that new girl these days."

"Roy's got no time for you so you go around kicking people out of frustration instead?"

"Maybe," she smiled.

"Oh," I replied, closing my eyes and folding my arms for emphasis. "Ok."

"Shit head."

"Psychic now?" I asked, pleasantly distracted and amused.

"Definitely more than a little."

100

Coverage

+68 Days – 0823 hours

I stood at parade rest as Roy shuffled through the papers on his desk.

Even the Apocalypse has too much paper pushing.

"So," Roy asked, tapping his fingers on the spread of documents, "what is the issue here again?"

"The lights in the basement corridor."

"What about them?"

"You don't need them. Not all of them, anyway."

"How so?"

"The hallway is too bright. Some of them are already burned out, but I would turn off at least half of what is left to save on your generator. Should probably do the same for lights throughout the whole museum. Keep the priority for the HVAC and other electrical."

"That's smart," Roy finally said, continuing to tap his fingers. "I don't want everyone to get too comfortable or complacent."

"There you go. Good plan."

"Good. Good."

I turned to leave.

"John?"

"Sir?" I faced Roy again.

"Do you like it here? Enjoying the responsibility?"

"Idle hands are the Devil's playthings."

"True." Roy brightened. "Good to see things are going well."

"How's the patient?"

Roy frowned for a moment, then laughed.

"Ah, yes!" He clapped his hands and slapped them back down on the desk blotter. "The patient. Very good, John."

He paused as if remembering something from long ago.

"She is as tough as ever," he finally answered. "But I did institute a change of her bandages. Don't want any premature exits."

"Good. Smart."

"I thought so, too." Roy perked up. "Oh, I may need you inside the receiving area tonight. Duke is leading a scavenge and seems to see the need to take the Ortiz brothers and more knaves than I believe he needs. But what can I do? I'm just a simple administrator trying to do the best he can while he's got the boots in the field."

Knaves? What a character this guy is.

"I'm sure you're dealing with the challenges as they come."

"In acceptable fashion."

"In grand fashion, I would say."

"Correct you are, sir," he beamed. "Can I count on you for tonight inside the dungeons?"

"Of course, my liege," I acknowledged with a fist over my heart and a curt bow.

Roy grinned so wide that I hoped his face might crack in half.

101

More Promises

+68 Days – 1952 hours

The warehouse was darker than before. Roy had instituted my suggestion – now his own brainstorm – to cut down on the lighting usage throughout the complex.

I stood in front of the welding curtain, the shape of the spherical structure silhouetted as a dark blot against the red canvas. Steeling myself I walked around to the front of the sculpture.

The base and the coated concrete floor were stained with sloppily cleaned up bodily fluids. Jude's T-shirt had been removed completely, leaving her in her sports bra. Her bandages were whiter with less red blots, gauzed with fresh medical tape.

She leaned against the curve of the sphere, her hands still cuffed. Her head slumped against her chest, hair matted and damp against her skin. The sharp bitterness of urine and sweat was partially masked by a stale metallic smell. Jude was skinnier than before, her ribs starting to protrude against her dirty skin.

Jude stirred.

Maybe she sensed that I was here.

"Get away from me," she whimpered.

"Jude," I whispered back.

"Get away," she cried.

"Jude," I said louder. "It's me."

She lifted her head with some effort, trestles of hair still covering her face.

"It's John."

She looked through me.

"Prove it," she muttered. "Come into the light."

I stepped forward, closing the gap between us by half.

She smiled weakly before contorting her face into a struggle against tears. Slapping her restrained arms against the steel of the sphere, she leaned her head back and to the side.

"John."

"It's me. I'm here."

"You're why I'm in this mess," she spit out. "Some rescue mission this was. Not sure you were worth it."

I went around to the other side of the sculpture, wrapped both hands around the massive chains and pulled. The cords stood out on my neck but the chains did not budge.

Interesting. I figured you were stronger than that.

"Fuck," I hissed. "I'll get you out, Jude. I promise."

"Won't hold my breath," she mocked me, the corners of her mouth upturned slightly. "Actions, not words, are the call for the day."

I examined the chains and mounts, looking to find a weak spot. There had to be a way to get Jude out without breaking her wrists from the shackles or forcing her to drag the heavy weight of links with her.

Weapons fire would alert others.

The fire axe, perhaps?

"Get me out of here," Jude pleaded.

"I'm assessing the situation here."

"You're an ass, alright." she chuckled into a cough.

Footsteps came from the other side of the welding curtain.

"Shift change," Duke called out, getting closer. "Quit ogling the woman or Roy will have your head."

This will have to wait.

102

Mindless

+68 Days – 2014 hours

Jude was still captive.
My fault.
Voices and formless shadows sped past me as I walked.
I think I was walking.
Four straight shifts.
Was I walking?
Failed her.
Chained and in pain.
I bumped off one of the shadows.
"Watch it, asshole," the shadow spewed.
"Idiot," agreed another.
"Leave 'em be," a familiar voice.
"Fuck you," the shadow retorted.
A cackle of laughter came from all directions.
Something like iron clamped around my arm.
I couldn't break free.
Did I want to?
"…out of it," the familiar voice said.
Snap.
Followed by a second one.
Sharp and razor-edged, painful sparks of light.
Dull pain pulsed against my palms and chest.
"John…" the familiar voiced pleaded one last time.
Murky darkness felt more comforting.

103

Dream a Little Dream

Time unknown

My body was surrounded by gauzy comfort.

The sweet and bitter smell of warm chocolate chip cookies filled my nostrils.

A soft melody played.

I somehow knew it but the composer eluded me.

Warbling birds chirped their approval, every so often flapping their wings in applause.

Light invaded the cocoon of security and serenity, but I did not fault it. Its soft white ensured that I didn't feel cheated from being rousted.

"It's time, John," a cooing voice beckoned.

"Petra?" I muttered.

"No," the voice said, "I could never take that lovely woman's place."

I pulled the white fuzzy cover down from over my head.

The halo surrounding the form focused and sharpened, the silhouette gaining color and substance as the brilliance of the light receded.

A young girl sat next to the couch in a padded high back chair. She could have been mistaken for someone in her late teens if she had wanted.

Her blonde hair flowed past her shoulders, moving with a breeze that I could not feel. She wore a simple gossamer gown, maybe meant for sleeping.

"How are you, John?" she asked, crossing her legs at the ankles with cupped hands in her lap.

"Who are you?"

She smiled sweetly and shrugged.

"Don't remember?" she finally asked with a playful pout. "Has it really been that long? Now that's a shame, really."

"Where do I know you from?" I asked, knowing I should know the answer.

"We met just a little while ago," she answered. "I am sure you will remember soon."

"Where is this place?"

"Full of questions, aren't you?"

I looked around the room. It wasn't a room but a screened in porch. My Grandma would have called it a Florida room. Probably would have called the couch I was on a Davenport. Graying paint covered the columns and beams, white planks running along the floor and angled ceiling. A large brass birdcage hung from a rafter in the corner where the wall of windows intersected, several small finches inside skating from perch to perch.

Outside the screens were the sights and sounds of a pounding ocean. It looked like the Atlantic but not the angry North Atlantic with its cold roiling and gray/green waves, feeling more like the endless South Pacific or Gulf of Mexico with their waters full of relentless hopes.

"John?"

The girl captured my attention with small delicate fingers to my cheek. I glimpsed a long thin scar running from her wrist to her elbow before she covered it up again with her gown sleeve.

"John," she repeated.

"Yes."

"Do you know what you are?"

"I know who I am."

"Do you?"

"Of course."

"Then tell me."

"Sgt. Jonathan Walken, United States Marine Corps sniper."

"That's a label, not who you are."

"What more is there?"

"*What more* is infinite."

She smiled again. The innocence in her bright eyes had not yet succumbed to the ravages of bitterness and cynicism. The girl put her hands on my arm and squeezed lightly.

"John," she asked, "has the tall man in the black suit told you?"

She knew the Gaunt Man?

"Told me what?"

"Told you who you are?"

I shook my head, searching her bright blue eyes for clues.

"He is a crafty mischievous one, he is," she sighed. "Is he being helpful, at least?"

"Sometimes," I answered. "What does he know that I should know?"

"He will tell you when he's ready, I suppose," she shrugged.

"Can't you tell me?"

"It is not my place to tell you these things," the girl replied, shaking her head. "And I do not think you would believe me if I did share what I know."

"Why not?"

She waved the question away, her sleeve falling back to reveal that same scar. She pulled her sleeve down and placed her hands back in her lap.

She opened her mouth to say something but snapped her lips tight a moment later.

The skies over the ocean darkened, threatening rain.

This time when the breeze blew through the girl's hair, I felt it and smelled the saltiness it carried.

"I have probably said too much," she added with a frown. "Maybe if you remember when we met things will become more clear to you."

"If you say so."

"I do," she replied, "but it is still just a maybe."

Thunder rolled, shaking the floor beneath us.

"I must go," she said, quickly standing and stepping behind the chair.

"Wait."

"I can not wait. I have stayed too long."

Lightning flashed beyond the screen, blinding me.

As the thunder followed, my eyes adjusted to the now darkened and empty space. More lightning crackled across the sky, outlining a new shadow in the room.

"She was always the imp," the Gaunt Man said with his sinewy arms spread too wide.

He surged forward, his face inches from mine. The smell of dirt and damp rot puffed out of his mouth.

"A storm is coming, Johnny."

As the lightning flashed again, he disappeared.

I loosened my grip from the comforter, anxious to exit this dreamscape.

For that is what it was.

A dream.

Not because of the appearance of a strangely familiar young woman with words spoken as riddles, nor because of the Gaunt Man's theatrics with his use of the lightning and roiling ocean as a backdrop.

As surreal as the surroundings were, it felt more real than a certain hospital gurney from what seemed a lifetime ago where the entire recovery room shook as if cradled in the heaving bosom of Mother Earth. A room that defied physics as it dropped meters at a time only to be slammed into something below it like an anvil.

Breaking free of the gurney straps had exhausted me to the point where I had welcomed the release of my tenuous grip on the firmament of the living world. But a not-so-long-dead woman named Petra had spoken soothing words of calm to ground me and direct me back from the dead.

No.

This was not death. It was not near death.

This was a dream.

This young blonde girl was like Petra, calm and kind.

Here she had held the light.

But now she was gone and the light and life was gone. Only ominous clouds and throaty skies reared up. If the young girl was the light was the Gaunt Man was the dark?

Ying and yang of something, I suppose.

But of what?

"…John…"

The voice had no direction but crept in from every surface and from every corner. It was not the girl or my ethereal Guy Friday or a voice from the real world.

"…John…"

Slap!

My cheek flushed from an invisible sting. I covered it with my own hand.

I looked at my scar-free wrist.

The little blonde girl had scars.

'I had to do it,' the deputy named Garrett had whined. *'Sheriff's orders.'*

That same girl had wandered into the plaza of Rainier's Island that day.

My shoulders rocked with invisible hands.

"…wake up!

104

This Little Piggy

+72 Days – 0635 hours

"Christ," Joey exclaimed. "I thought you went into a coma or something."

"I'm fine."

"Yeah?" Joey leaned in putting two fingers to his temple. "Deb and Duke were arguing about putting you down. Thought you got bit or infected or something. Like everyone who festered out in quarters did that night. I almost believed it, too."

"I'm fine," I repeated.

"Yeah. You keep saying that."

"Just too many shifts in a row, I guess."

"True. You worked like thirty-some hours in a row. I mean, you barely sleep as it is. I don't think I've ever seen you lay down for more than a couple, but damn."

"I'm good."

I struggled to sit up and get an old pillow to prop myself up with. Joey clumsily assisted, sitting next to me like Florence Nightingale caring for an infirmed patient of the war.

"Promise?"

"Promise," I assured him.

"Ok," he said, standing and grimacing as his knees popped. He cracked his neck and rolled his shoulders.

"Ok," he repeated. "By the way, Roy says you can take another shift off."

"How many did I miss?"

"Five."

Christ.

Five shifts.

Another three days since I saw Jude.

I bolted to a seated position, whipping the wool blanket off of my legs.

The room swam.

"Wait!" he exclaimed. "Calm down."

The dizziness did not recede.

Others became more interested in what I was doing.

My ragged breath matched the pulsing of my heartbeat behind my temples and eyes. Red crept into the corners of my vision, where most of the curious onlookers stood.

Joey grabbed my arm, wincing in anticipation of retaliation.

I swung my feet out from under the rest of the blanket, placing them purposefully on the floor. Joey's hand was still on my bicep, even as he moved to let me up.

"Brave man," I said, glancing at Joey's grip before glaring into his eyes.

He raised his chin and stared back.

We stood up together, eyes still locked.

The spectators continued to watch.

"You going to behave?" Joey asked with a grim look.

I gave the look right back at him.

It was several long seconds before either of us relented.

"Ah," I finally replied with a ragged exhale and a measure of appreciation, "the audacities of the young."

"Well?" he asked with his still-fueled determination.

"Yes," I said as I slightly bent back his pinkie with my thumb.

"Ouch! Ouch!" he grimaced, trying to combat the pressure on the littlest digit but only succeeding in dropping to one knee.

"I'll be good," I answered. "Just need some air."

105

Blue Light Special
+72 Days – 0856 hours

The courtyard was empty.
I sat under the umbrella of one of the plastic patio tables.
Seventy-two hours.
Christ!
I needed a plan to get Jude out.
Now seventy-four hours.
"Don't remind me," I mumbled. "I blame you for this."
Moi?
"Yes," I said with venom. "The inability to sleep... the dreams... whatever fugue state I ended up in as a result..."
Can't say that I had a hand in any of that. I am only around for the ride – and for the wonderful conversation, of course.
"You remind me of a kid I knew in middle school."
Was he handsome and brilliant?
"He was a thorn in my side," I replied. "Constantly following me around and pestering me."
And what was this young man's name?
"Robert McGill."
Maybe I will meet this man one day.
"Doubt it. He was killed in a car accident on his way back from the mall after Christmas shopping."
A shame. Truly.
"Yeah."
Maybe I can be your 'Bob'. Or, at least, I'll be your huckleberry.
A wide, but thin sliver of sun devoured the shade on the lawn, leaving the footprint of a sharpening block of shadows.
"Sure," I shrugged dismissively. "It's better than what I call

you now."

The Gaunt Man is also very fitting, and debonair.

A reflecting glimmer of light bounced off the mirrored windows behind me and shimmered against the tall windows of the educational wing.

The children behind the glass shook from their stupor, the closest ones bumping against the windows in pursuit of the reflected sun. The light seemed to make their milky eyes glow.

They noiselessly yawned.

A younger boy – complete with stained overalls with a bright green WAM sticker peeling off them – slid past the larger boys and pressed his cheek against the glass.

Compared to the others he seemed completely normal and alive.

He then turned his head to snap his jaws towards one of the boys, revealing a ruptured eyeball and massive gash in his cheek.

I looked at my feet and swallowed back bile, taking slow breaths until the urge to throw up passed.

The strobing lights caught my attention again.

The blue and red lights intermittently blinked three times each. The little girl wandered in meandering sloppy figure eights in front of the open doorway between the intersecting hallways.

The lights flashed red three times.

The lights flashed blue three times.

A little longhaired brunette girl made a fashion statement as she sported a lone failing pigtail on the left side of her head. She wore a horizontal striped sweater and plaid leggings.

I hadn't noticed her in this wing of the annex before.

Maybe she bumped open the bar release on the door?

Maybe.

Red lights.

Blue lights.

Her furry boots were adorned with matching furry pompons.

Unfortunately it was too late for her to enjoy the novelty of the footwear.

The lights in the boot's soles blinked.

She circled twice more before wandering toward the rest of the mob. Her flashing boots caught the attention of three of the less distracted boys. They stared at the FRACdancer's pulsing feet, shuffling and bumping against each other in pursuit of the dancing lights.

A scuffle broke out as one of the pursuers lashed out at one of the others. They snapped their jaws at each other, circling in an unceremonious uneven stagger.

I sat up straighter.

The two combatants did not look at each other or recognize that the other was an undead compatriot. They were reacting to movement and the new stimulus of the morning sun and the flashing lights.

Curious.

The Gaunt Man, aka Bob, noiselessly plopped down in the chair across from me at the table.

"What's curious?"

You can see it.

He pointed across the courtyard to the belligerent pair.

"What's wrong with them?"

Hard to say. He shrugged.

"Take a guess."

Have not ever eaten. Could be restless.

"So you're saying they're cranky because they're hungry?"

Definitely hangry. He smiled. *As good a guess as any.*

"And how do you know they haven't eaten?"

He put his hands up in surrender.

My apologies. I meant to say they haven't eaten in a long time. Most of them do look a little…

"…chewed up." One of Roy's men struck a match to his half-smoked cigarette beside me on the path from the museum doors. "Damn cigarettes not gonna make it much longer. Already having to root for one that's not all bent up."

I looked back at the now empty chair where Bob had sat a moment ago.

"The kids acting up again?" he asked as he acknowledged me with a nod.

"Seems like it," I replied, worried that he had caught me talking to myself.

"It's a shame."

"Why's that?"

"Most of us can't look at them too long. I know it hurts my heart to see them shuffling around and rotting in there on a daily basis. But no one is all that eager to take care of the problem. I mean, they're kids for Christ's sake."

"Why are they here?" I had to ask.

"Dunno," he shrugged. "Roy says it was a field trip. Infection went rampant and the kids were caught up in the annex. Says that they had to be quarantined before it spread."

He took a deep drag on the cig, closed his eyes as he held the smoke in, and finally exhaled in one long blow. He stubbed the end of it in his palm and returned it to his crumpled pack of Newports.

"It's a filthy habit," he admitted as he tapped the pack in his hand before returning it to his shirt pocket, "And it's my last pack. That's why you only saw that one drag. Gonna have to kick the habit eventually."

"John." I stood up and extended my hand.

"I know," he clasped my hand in his. "You're quite the celebrity around these parts. Name's Percy."

"You're one of the cooks, right?"

"One of the last cooks," Percy mumbled. "Lost the other two."

"Sorry."

"Can I take a load off?"

"Sure. It's a free country."

"On that I would have to disagree."

"Yeah?"

"Of course," he pointed at the education wing. "Look at them. They ain't free. And as long as they exist we ain't free neither."

"I suppose."

"Can't barely sleep at night anymore. I thought it was safe inside. It was, anyway, until that fester attack the other night."

"Yeah. That was a bit much."

"Uh… yeah! You were right in the thick of that one. Can't believe you were locked in and still survived to tell the tale. Never agreed with Roy on keeping the doors chained every night."

"It did keep the infected from getting out."

"It did. But I think Roy's more worried about us wandering around than isolating the dead."

"Have to admit being locked in made the fight a little uneven."

"I'm sure you were glad to have your gun back that night," Percy conjectured.

I patted the grip.

"Feel a little bit better with it."

"Lost a lot of friends." Percy sighed, running a hand through his hair. "I didn't have an appetite for a couple days after being assigned to the cleanup."

"I know the feeling." I sympathized, thinking of losing Rosalita in the deserts of Afghanistan, Lucy and so many others on Rainier Island, and not knowing about Bowers and the others along the Yankee Division.

Percy took out the cigarette and lit it up again. He took two very long drags before tapping it out again and returning it to the pack.

"I had to palm a knife from the kitchen myself."

"Sounds like a plan."

"It's all I could get my hands on. We got an exhibit full of swords, but no weapons to wield. Well, those long staves are available, I guess."

An ocean of water but not a drop to drink.

Bob the Gaunt Man leaned against the educational wing wall,

tapping on the glass in the hopes of agitating the children. They continued their aimless wandering through the annex halls, oblivious to his mischief.

He sure did lean a lot for a black hat company man. A figment of my imagination should be more energetic.

You would think so, wouldn't you?

"… the rats?"

"Say again?"

"I said, 'Do you think that the outbreak in the barrack was because of the rats?'"

I thought back to the FRAC pinned behind the dumpster and the rodents feeding on his exposed intestines before scurrying away to parts unknown. Actually, the parts were known. They had escaped to somewhere inside the building.

"It's a very good possibility," I admitted.

"Shit. I thought so."

"That's assuming we knew shit about how the transfer of this infection happens."

"True," Percy replied, crestfallen.

"I saw a pack of rabid wolves, foxes and dogs once," I clarified, thinking about the day I met Holly. "They got feverish and crazy. They even attacked the walkers."

"You kidding me?"

"No," I replied. "Saw one of them rip the arms right off one of the FRACs."

"Christ."

"One of our people got bit by one of the dogs."

"Did he turn?"

"No."

"That's good."

"Yeah. All I'm saying is that we don't know anything. All we know is don't get bit."

"That's the number one rule I live by."

"A rule we all need to live by."

"Amen."

Percy and I didn't speak for a while.

Life was more and more a gift.

I turned my face to the sun's rays, acknowledging my gratitude for the simple things.

Bob stood across the courtyard with his fists on his slight hips.

The simpler the rules are the better.

Don't know anything? Don't know what killed the people? I all but showed you. Actually, I did show you.

I would've eaten the powdered eggs.

My appetite had disappeared when Bob decided to dance between the cafeteria tables with bloody rats hanging from his fists.

Bob had done all he could to show me the truth.

But even with that truth, I didn't save anyone from a fate worse than death.

106

Best Laid Plans

+72 Days – 0912 hours

Percy had dragged a couple more puffs from his dwindling cigarette before finally returning inside.

I sat in the courtyard under the umbrella while Jude continued to suffer in chains. The moment she needed me most was when my body decided to shut itself down completely for three days.

I had forgotten what more than a few minutes of sleep felt like. Why now?

And did the strange dream with the little girl and the threat of a brewing ocean storm hold some puzzled meaning? If sleep now led to fevered undecipherable visions I would rather go without sleep altogether.

And I was no closer to an exfil plan.

Issues to contend with.

No keys for the padlocks on the chains.

I couldn't free Jude without breaking her wrists.

My strength wasn't enough to break the chains.

Her injuries and lack of food would be a liability if we needed to fight our way out of the basement. I didn't have enough ammo for the Glock to be effective if I had to carry her.

Once outside the museum we would not get too far before the roof snipers put a bullet in our heads or the Marauders ran us down.

There were too many precision points that needed to be worked out.

Needed more weapons.

Needed a running vehicle.

More help.

A distraction.

Or you could kill them all in their sleep.

I tried to shake Bob the Gaunt Man's suggestion away.

Images of white tiled corridors with bloody, dismembered soldiers staining the walls and floors flashed before my eyes.

Pre-emptive strike.

"There are civilians that deserve to live."

Bob sat in the wire chair next to me picking at his yellowed fingernails.

And you decide who lives or dies?

"I can choose to not kill more people."

Not unnecessarily, at any rate. There are always acceptable casualties. You were and are still a Marine.

"It's not acceptable."

Then Jude continues to rot? Suffers because of your indecision and self-righteousness?

"I'll figure it out."

When? After she dies? You can rain death and destruction down on this kingdom at any time. Ride in like a white knight, slay the dragon and rescue the damsel in distress.

"Where to start?"

Doesn't matter where you start. Just start somewhere.

107

Failed Attempts, Revisited
+72 Days – 1207 hours

My reprieve from another shift was rescinded when Duke and his men were sent out again to hawk for supplies.

I stood in the warehouse basement looking at the sphere.

Jude lay against the giant round sculpture as she had before. Her bandages had been changed. This time they did not have any splotches of yellow or red. Someone had changed her into fresh underwear but her sports bra was now ripped down the center to the elastic. She looked cleaner even though her hair still fell limp in front of her face. She looked thinner than she had the last time I saw her.

I touched her arm lightly.

She recoiled.

"Get away from me," she hissed.

"It's me," I whispered in her ear.

"I wanna go home, John."

"I know," I replied. "I'm getting you out of here."

"Kay."

"Can you walk?"

"Yeah," she croaked. "Roy and his goons walk me out of here whenever Roy wants to…"

She didn't finish the sentence.

I pushed the hair out of her face revealing a purple, swollen eye and a split lip. She looked at me with her good eye, her vision sharpening on me.

"John," she said.

"Yeah?"

"I don't like you much."

"Sorry. I'm going to get you out of here."

"Yeah? What about the others?"

"Who?" I asked.

"Bowers. The sisters. The kids. Holly."

"We'll find them," I assured her, not knowing how I would keep that promise.

"They have to be here somewhere. The place ain't that big."

"They're here?"

"They were close when I came in." She shook her head. "The same guys in the WAM truck that took you took us, dork."

"Shit."

A single exfil had now become exponentially more difficult.

"Can you hang in here for a bit longer?" I tested the chains again, without success

"No pun intended?" she asked with a stray tear glistening from her damaged purple eye. "I'll make it. Just hurry the fuck up, will you?"

"Who has the key?" I asked as I looked at the massive padlock combining several chains together inside the center of the sculpture.

"Who do you think?"

"Roy?"

"Smart fucking man," she snickered. "There's hope for you yet."

108

Encyclopedia Brown

+72 Days – 1536 hours

Joey joined me outside the courtyard gate.

"Sorry I'm late, John," he mumbled, fumbling his rifle as he closed the latch.

"Don't let it happen again."

He studied my face for a moment, his teeth chewing on his tongue as it tried to poke out of his right cheek.

Then he laughed.

"You almost got me there," he pointed at my stern stare. Thought you were gonna kill me."

"When you're right, you're right."

"Knew it." He beamed.

"Can't get anything over on you, can I?"

"Read you like a book."

"If only you weren't illiterate," I added. "Such a shame."

He cackled as he got the joke. His snorts came dangerously close to the hee-haws you would expect from a donkey.

"Alright. Alright," I ordered. "We have work to do."

"Sir." Joey saluted. "Yes, sir."

We moved to the street and headed toward the church where Ms. Staff and I had meted out some undead street justice. The bodies were still there, rotting in the sun. The buzz of flies and other insects droned in the air, thick and unnerving. We crossed over to the auditorium sidewalk.

"They usually pick up the bodies," Joey commented.

"Maybe they're too busy these days."

"Maybe." He chewed on his lip instead of his tongue this time. *Apparently Joey likes how he tastes.*

"What?" I asked, snapping him out of his blank stare.

"Dunno," he shrugged. "Duke's in a mood these days. Always pissed off. Everything's hush-hush. Keep hearing about 'others'."

"Others?"

"Something about reallocation of food and assignments," Joey struggled over the bigger words. "Duke bitchin' about the cost of a bullet versus the cost of his men, gas and time. Shit like that."

"Reallocation?"

"Yeah. That's what Duke keeps muttering on about."

"I haven't heard anything like that."

"Of course not! You ain't in the inner circle."

"Neither are you, my friend," I responded with a twinge of regret, knowing that I was way closer to the center of things than he realized.

And you still don't seem to know anything, do you?

"Ain't that the truth?" His smile was still plastered on his face and he was laughing again. "I ain't nobody important or special."

"That's not what I meant."

"I know you don't mean nothing by it." He waved me off. "It's still the truth. You know the difference between us, John? You are someone special and they fear that. I ain't nobody. Period. I'm okay with that. Too much responsibility at that level anyway. I'm too lazy for all that. But since nobody takes me seriously no one notices I'm even in the room half the time. So, I hear shit I probably shouldn't. Duke ain't the most quietest guy even when he's thinking straight. Too many distractions these days to keep him from knowing to keep his yap tight."

"And you know better when to keep your yap tight?"

"Hell no," he exclaimed. "I just know well enough who to tell."

"Well, I guess you know when to keep your yap tight then, don't you?"

"I guess I do at that."

109

Plastic Bags

+72 Days – 1536 hours

The rest of the perimeter sweep was uneventful. I knew enough to not push Joey much further on the subject of Duke and his strained resources. Something was afoot and it definitely wasn't just Jude chained to a stainless steel sphere.

Probably the rest of your group, hero.

Bowers and the others weren't in the Chapter House or strung up beside Jude. I doubted they were in the learning annex with the school children. That was too risky.

We came up on the corner next to the Lutheran Church.

Joey stopped and squinted his eyes to look at the scripture engraved above the door.

"Really like that saying."

"I know you do, Joey."

Just then a flash of white darted out of sight around the corner of the museum atrium.

"Come on." I walked with purpose to the corner of the building, Joey trailing closely behind.

No white.

"What did you see, John?"

"Maybe a plastic bag."

"As long as it ain't a fester… or a bunch of festers."

We walked the perimeter past the delivery area.

Duke and Hector stood at the loading dock, stopping their conversation when they saw us.

"What you staring at, Joey?" Duke growled while Hector grinned.

"Nothin'," Joey said, lowering his eyes to the ground in front of his feet.

I wished Duke would say that to me. There would definitely be a different response to the question.

"Shake it off, Joey," I whispered to him. "Consider the source."

He said nothing and kept his eyes down as we approached the courtyard gate.

"I hate that man a little bit," he finally said when we were at the fence.

"At least you feel something. Don't let him get to you, Joey," I said. "Like you said, men like that get what they deserve."

"Ain't soon enough in my book. Heard him bragging 'bout killing a kid recently. He was very proud of it. Gunned a guy down who was trying to protect his girlfriend. The end of the world don't mean you have to be a savage."

"Pretty sure he was one before all this."

"Good one," he snorted as he unlatched the gate.

"Just remember to keep your eyes and ears open and your yap tight."

"Great advice, John. Thanks. I'll have to remember that one."

The Gaunt Man sat at my spot on the mesh courtyard chair. Joey walked past him, waving goodbye to me as he went inside.

That kid is about as sharp as a sack of wet mice.

I paused in front of my frequent apparition.

He's as dense as a bagful of cast iron bowling balls.

"Bob, do you ever do anything useful?"

Once in a while.

"What's that, John?" Joey asked from the door.

"Nothing, Joey. I'm coming."

Bob snapped his fingers.

The two most common elements in the universe are hydrogen and stupidity. Guess which one Joey...

I walked away, half expecting his voice to continue to press into the soft tissue of my brain. Luckily, even Bob knew when to leave well enough alone.

110

Tilted Corridors

+72 Days – 1852 hours

The basement had taken on a decidedly dim, haunting look as more of the spotlights had been turned off to conserve the museum's power supply. Pools of light illuminated the hall in an awkward, haphazard dotted fashion. Its asymmetry itched at the strict order of my mind.

"What you waiting for?"

Duke's voice echoed from the far end of the corridor, his silhouette hulking and dark against the white backlit concrete wall behind him.

I didn't bother to respond as I walked over to him.

"Better late than never, I guess," Duke said sarcastically.

"Waiting on you, now," I answered.

"Got quite a mouth on you, you know that?"

"That's the word on the streets."

"What streets?"

"Ford Road and Telegraph."

"You're a dickhead," Duke snorted, shaking his head.

"Right again."

"Let's go."

Duke punched in the numbers on the keypad and stepped back as the double doors opened.

"Ladies first." He waved me ahead.

The warehouse was bustling with activity.

Hector and Raul were barking orders to some of the other Marauders who were carrying boxes from the panel truck, only pausing long enough to flip a nod to Duke as we walked past.

"No! No!" Raul yelled. "Christ, Percy. Take that to the food cooler. Use your head, damn it."

"He's cruisin' for it." Hector commiserated with his brother. "Duke, when you goin' recruit some real talent? Can't just keep sweatin' to keep feedin' the dead wood."

"Shut your trap," Duke said sharply.

Hector looked at me and back to Duke.

"Sorry, Boss."

Duke led me away from the off-loading operation.

He suddenly stopped.

Spinning, he swung a meaty roundhouse left fist.

I brought up my forearm.

The blow deflected but connected above my ear.

My shoulder slammed against the shelves.

Duke lunged at me and grabbed my face with his other hand, forcing me harder into the racks.

"You ain't fooled anyone, Johnny Boy," he huffed as he connected a knee into my ribs. "Time to rejoin your friends."

The Chapter House FRACs?

I crumbled into his arms.

He spun me around in a chokehold.

My shoulder holster was ripped off, gun and all.

"Too bad I couldn't kill more of ya," Duke said as he grabbed the machete from its sheath on my belt. "You got some tough bitches."

The chokehold tightened.

The blade clattered off the floor.

"You think I didn't remember your friend at the apartments?"

Bowers.

My vision went red but I couldn't take a breath.

My vision dimmed.

Don't fight it.

Was that me? Or Bob?

Regardless, I listened.

"Roy sends his regards," Duke whispered. "Nitey…"

111

Reunions

unknown

Something tingled from far away.
Soft taps in the darkness.
"...don't know..."
More taps, sharper and stinging.
"...what if..."
"...give me a sec..."
Something familiar.
My cheek erupted in pain.
"Wake up, for Christ sake!"
I jolted out of my stupor.
Black forms swayed away from me in the dark.
My eyes adjusted.
"About time," Bowers said.
"Sergeant," I acknowledged, almost as a question.
"Sergeant," he replied.
Others were here too.
They came into focus.
Victoria clung to Melissa as they looked on with furrowed brows and wet cheeks. Melissa's jeans were tattered with blood staining one thigh.

"What a fuckin' waste of time this rescue mission was," Melissa said with disgust.

"At least we're together," a small voice said from the corner.

April scooted forward into my field of vision. A nasty gash ran from her temple to her chin, clotting with reds and yellows. Her mascara and eyeliner had streaked completely down her cheeks.

Lenny did not appear at her side to comfort her.

Instead, Summer crawled forward to wrap her small arms

339

around April's waist.

I leaned toward Bowers and he crouched closer.

"Lenny?" I whispered.

He shook his head.

April erupted in sobs.

Summer held her tighter.

Bowers almost touched his forehead to mine.

"The big black guy shot him," he whispered. "Lenny tried to protect the women. You would've been proud."

My heart sank.

"I loved him," April cried.

"Jude's gone, too," Melissa scowled. "Just gets better and better."

"Stop, Lissa," Victoria interjected. "You aren't helping."

"Jude's here," I told them. "They have her chained up."

"Fuckin' animals." Melissa hissed. "Should have killed them all when we had the chance."

"Enough," Bowers ordered.

"At least Holly got away," Summer added hopefully.

"Yeah," Bowers continued, "they chased her around for a while before trying to snipe her."

"She was too fast." Summer smiled. "Those assholes didn't have a chance."

"Summer," Victoria said, "Watch your language."

"It's the end of the world, mom." Summer rolled her eyes. "Gawd."

"The girl's got a point, mom," Bowers offered before Victoria could say more.

"Melissa, are you okay?" I asked, pointing at the blood on her jeans.

"It ain't mine," she replied. "That's all you need to know."

"Is Jude okay?" Summer asked. "I think they may have taken a shot at her."

"She's patched up," I answered. "And ready to get out of

here."

"What happened, John?" Bowers asked. "Why did they throw you in with us?"

"I don't know," I shook my throbbing head. "I thought I had gained their trust enough to get Jude out. Looks like I was a sucker for it."

"What about us?" April asked. "Were you gonna get us out?"

"Didn't know you were here until Jude mentioned it yesterday."

"Fuckin' great," Melissa said. "One disaster after another."

"We'll get out of here," Bowers said.

"Just like we got in here?"

"I was trying to get to John," Bowers said, defending his actions. "Jude agreed with me."

"We'll get out," I promised.

"Bullshit," Melissa countered. "This has been a cluster…"

"Language in front of Summer, Aunt Melissa," Victoria warned.

I finally realized why Bob wanted me to get in here.

"I said we'll get out," I repeated with more force. "I took a beating to get in here."

"Idiot," Melissa smiled thinly.

"So," Bowers asked, "do you have a plan?"

"Simple," I answered with determination. "We kill them all."

That's my boy. An eye for an eye.

"That's the first good thing I've heard today," Melissa agreed.

112

Ready, Set, Wait
+73 Days – 1925 hours

"They feed you, right?"

We stood around a steel observation table in the center of the storage room. This was not an archival room as far as I could see. The door was solid without a window inset. There were two blackened out narrow slit windows high on the opposite wall. Tiny peels in the paint allowed just light to let us make out each other and the surroundings. Empty steel wire racks lined the walls.

"Yeah, John," Bowers replied. "Just enough to keep us upright."

"They gave us a pot to piss in, too," Melissa added, pointing to five-gallon joint compound bucket. It sat under one of the windows with a piece of plywood covering it. "All the amenities of a five-star hotel."

I smiled.

"Ain't actually funny, John."

"Sort of is," I answered Melissa. "I said the same thing when I got here. And I didn't even have a pot to piss in."

"Gross." Summer wrinkled her nose.

"Do they have a set schedule, Sean?"

"Hard to say," Bowers replied. It's later in the day."

"Yeah," April chimed in. "It's always a pain to see what we're eating. Starts getting dim at that time."

"Yeah," Victoria agreed.

"They have guns, John," Bowers added.

"Do they come in?"

"They usually roll the food in on a cafeteria cart," Summer said. "It's funny."

"Why?" I asked.

"Because they don't come in," Summer added. "The door opens, we go blind with the light, and all of a sudden a cart rolls in all by itself. Funny to me, anyway."

"What happens to the cart when you are done?"

"Eventually, they bang on the door and yell for it," Melissa answered. "Threaten us with gut shots if we are thinking of trying something."

"We roll it to the door and slap the door a few times," Bowers added. "They grab the cart and double-time it out of there."

I tapped my index finger on the metal examination surface, running through scenarios for an escape plan.

We rush our caretakers and someone is bound to be hurt. None of them signed on to take a bullet – but this world wasn't one that waited for volunteers.

We could break out the window, but only Summer would be able to get through. The rest of us would be trapped. I wasn't sending out a child to save us. It was too heavy a burden.

I could take a few rounds, I was sure of that. Maybe if we break the table legs loose from their bolts in the floor we could tip the counter top on its side as a shield for the others.

Straight assault was risky.

Click.

An ambush was also risky.

The guards would already be on high alert during dinnertime.

Click-ity click.

I went to the door and tried to turn the knob. It strained in my grip and started to twist. I put my other hand above it, feeling the key entry to a deadbolt. Damn!

Breaking the one lock wouldn't help with the other.

Click. Click. Click.

Coupled with a low whimpering sound.

Summer went to the window and looked up at a shadowy lump on the other side of the already darkened pane.

"What are you doing?" Melissa asked.

"Don't worry about it."

"You need to talk to your kid about her insubordination," Melissa said to her sister.

"Let her do her thing." Victoria waved the comment away.

Summer repositioned the bucket, sloshing its contents. She tested the plywood with one foot before stepping up on the lid. She strained on her tiptoes to reach the window latch, getting one, then a second finger on the latch. After a squeaky pull of the handle the window opened and tilted in and let in the last rays of the afternoon sun.

Stepping down from the bucket, Summer backed up for a better look of the now opened window.

We all stared at the slit of the window, enjoying a moment of brightness and a slight breeze that aired out the stuffy and sour space.

"What are we waiting for?" Bowers asked.

"For whatever was making that noise, silly," Summer answered.

"Probably a dead-head," April murmured. "Probably Lenny coming to blame me for leaving him."

"Stow that shit, girlie," Melissa blurted out. "Ain't your fault."

Whimpering drifted down from the window.

We all quieted down and stared at the open window.

More whimpering.

I blew out two short sharp whistles, startling April and Victoria.

Holly poked her face through the opening with her front paws gripping the top of the tilted in windowpane and her dirty muzzle and ears resting on top of them.

A pink tongue darted out and licked her nose before she erupted into a series of low throaty demanding growls for attention. She even rolled onto her back with her ear flopping down over the edge for emphasis.

"Don't worry, mutt," Bowers responded. "You're always the

center of attention."

"And the cavalry has arrived," Melissa snickered.

"Yes it has," I said with a smile.

113

The Cavalry

+74 Days – 1830 hours

A day had passed.

We all sat around the room, some of us with our backs against the walls. In the center of the room was the now overturned examination table that we had spent the night ripping away from its bolts.

"This is a stupid plan," Victoria said.

"It will work if you give it a chance," Melissa answered.

"Come on, mom," Summer added. "Lighten up."

"It could work," April said in a small voice as she hugged Holly tight. "Lenny would have loved this idea. It would've been right up his alley."

"Is it time yet?" I asked Bowers as we stood by the door.

Bowers looked at the fading light and nodded.

I nodded back.

"Okay." Bowers clapped. "Let's get ready."

The Russell sisters crouched behind the turned over examination table, Summer between them. April cowered in an alcove behind a structural concrete pillar, running her finger over a wall receptacle.

"Figures," she snorted through tears. "A perfectly working outlet and no phone. And no Lenny."

There was no time to comfort her.

Bowers stood next to the knob side of the steel door, his ear close to the frame.

I knelt down between the steel table and the door.

Holly padded over to me and stood up on her haunches with her front paws waving at me. I scratched under her left ear.

"I missed you, too, little girl," I whispered. "Lucy would never forgive me if something happened to you… so don't get dead, ya hear?"

Holly snorted and licked my hand before gnawing on my palm for good measure.

"Same as it ever was."

Bowers snapped his fingers.

I picked up Holly and reset her on the floor facing the door. I scratched her on both sides of her neck and leaned down to whisper into her ear.

"Remember," I told her, "don't be a hero."

Holly responded by craning her neck and burrowing a tongue into my ear.

A key was thrown into the deadbolt and the bolt was thrown back. The doorknob wiggled.

"What the fuck?" was heard from the other side of the door. "Damn thing's sticking."

"Well, put your back into it," said another disembodied voice.

"Stay put," the first voice shouted at us through the door, "or you'll see the business end of my rifle barrel."

The knob wiggled again.

A heavy weight slammed into the door, popping it open.

Light from the hallway blinded us just as Bowers and Summer had warned.

"Now," I whispered to Holly. "Go!"

Holly launched out of my hands and scampered toward the light. She barked happily and rushed out the door.

"What the hell?" the first voice yelled.

Holly barked again, her claws clicking against the tile floor.

I rushed the doorway.

One of the guards saw me, but not in time.

I tackled him under the armpit and slammed him into the opposite wall.

He exhaled forcibly as two of his ribs snapped.

My vision darkened to its familiar red tint.

His rifle fell loose from his grip.

I grabbed the falling rifle with one hand.

"Freeze!" The other guard shouted. "Stop...urmp!"

His words cut short as I hurled his companion five meters headlong into him.

I drew up the weapon and trained it on our former jailors as I approached them. They lay in a heap, the arms of the man on the bottom of the pile above his head and his Beretta hanging from his pinkie.

"I don't –," he started.

"Don't what?" I dared him.

Don't believe that a man could throw another grown man fifteen feet?

Bob the Gaunt Man walked off the distance heel to toe between where the guards lay and where I had thrown the top one.

Definitely fifteen feet, for sure.

"Don't want any trouble, John."

"Good. Let's keep it that way," I replied, a twinge of regret that I didn't even know their names.

They know you, though, don't they?

I lifted off his groaning companion.

"Bowers," I called.

The sergeant came out of the storage room. He grabbed the Beretta and waved the barrel at the guard until he gingerly got to his feet.

"Help your friend inside," Bowers ordered.

"All clear," I ordered. "Everyone out."

The women and Summer poked out from the doorway before stepping into the hallway. They gave the guards a wide berth as Bowers escorted them inside.

Summer broke away from her mom and wheeled the cafeteria cart into the room behind them. Before she let it roll forward, she grabbed two Poland Springs water bottles from the top tray.

I picked up a key ring from the tiles and shook them.

Bowers backed out of the storage room and closed the door. It popped open a few inches. He pulled it closed again but it didn't latch.

"Watch out," I said.

He moved aside.

I slammed the door closed hard enough to shake the frame.

On the fifth attempt, I found the correct deadbolt key and locked the bolt. I put the large key ring on the doorknob.

"Everyone ready?" I asked.

They all stared at me.

"What?"

Bowers looked at me and shrugged.

"What's the deal, ladies?" Bowers chimed in.

Holly padded back over from the other end of the corridor and lay down at my feet.

"Well?"

"You threw that guy," April said as she cleared her throat, "like he was a rag doll."

"Yeah," Summer said. "He went sailing."

"Is there going to be a problem with that?"

"Nope," the young girl smiled. "It's chill. Ain't tryin' to cast any shade your way."

"Good." I smiled back as the red bled back to the corners of my vision. "We have more rescuing to do, don't we?"

"Hells, yeah," Melissa agreed.

"Ooh rah, Sergeant," Bowers said.

Holly barked.

Victoria and April exchanged looks of dismay but shrugged and waved us on.

114

The Great Escape

+74 Days – 1843 hours

"Once we go through," I directed as we grouped together at the security doors that led into the warehouse area, "the loading docks will be on your left with a door next to it. Bowers will lead you out. There's a flight of stairs on the right. Take them up to the parking and stay along the fence to keep out of sight of the roof sentries. At the corner go across the street to the rally point."

"We want to get Jude, too," Melissa said.

"Better chance if we divide and conquer," I said.

"Bullshit!"

"Melissa, you have a niece to get to safety. And your sister and April."

"But…"

"You have no idea what's inside," I replied and pointed at the ominous orange painted steel doors. "When it becomes a shit storm I will take it on, not you."

Melissa must have seen something on my face or in my eyes because she shut her mouth and put her hands up in surrender.

"Bowers,"

"Yeah, Boss?"

"Take the rifle."

He exchanged weapons with me.

"Take them to safety."

"Ooh rah."

I went to the entry keypad. Holly sat at my feet. Bowers stood in the middle of the corridor while the others hugged their backs against the wall.

Punching in the code I was recently given, I hit ENTER and backed away.

Nothing happened. The doors stayed closed and silent.

I rekeyed the code.

Nothing.

"Maybe they changed the codes," April whispered. "Figures."

"John?" Bowers queried.

I punched the code in once more.

Nothing.

I huff and I puff and I blow this house down.

Kneeling at the doors, I curled my fingers under the edge of the right one and wedged my boot against the other. Taking a deep breath I arched my back and pulled.

My muscles flexed.

I gritted my teeth.

My biceps flared and burned.

The red returned.

A high-pitched metallic squeal started, growing in volume.

Suddenly the corner of the door buckled and the locks snapped.

Bowers shouldered his rifle.

I pulled the door and peered through the opening.

No noise.

No sentries.

No guns.

I pulled the door open the rest of the way.

Bowers took point and led the way inside. I stood in the doorframe and waited. The sergeant cleared the corners before waving us in.

"Okay," I said. "To the door and out."

The women ran to his position.

Holly and I brought up the rear.

Bowers peered through the window in the dock door.

"Looks clear."

"Ok," I ordered Bowers. "Clear the way."

The sergeant opened the door and went out, checking the

atrium roof for the any sentries.

He waved to us.

"Ok," I said. "Go."

Melissa went first. Victoria clutched Summer's forearm and dragged her out. April hesitated, looking at Holly.

"Come on, girl."

Holly stayed behind my feet.

"Come on, puppy," April plead.

I grabbed April's arm and turned her toward the door. "Go."

April stiffened but allowed me to push her outside. Melissa came back and wrapped an arm around April's waist and led her away.

Once Bowers cleared the roof sightline, they all double-timed it up the steps to the upper handicap parking lot next to the courtyard.

When they were out of sight, I went inside and closed the loading dock door.

Holly slapped her tail against the concrete floor.

"Okay," I said. "Just you and me again."

She woofed.

What about me? What am I, chopped liver?

I ignored Bob's phantom voice and focused on the next part of the plan.

115

Two Thousand and Late

+74 Days – 1851 hours

The Beretta had a different heft in my grip than my Glock.

I missed my Glock.

Seemed to be one of the constants of my life to have it repeatedly taken from me. The weapon could be replaced. Human life could not.

Not so easily, anyway.

The quiet of the warehouse was unnerving.

With each step I took Holly paced after me, stopping to sniff the air and cock her head.

Each corner leading to Pomodoro's *Rotante Del Foro Centrale* was quiet and empty.

The final turn through the shelving cross corridor led to the open area with the metal sphere behind the welder's curtains.

Holly stayed at the opening and whimpered.

I checked the dark corners for movement or sounds.

Nothing.

Satisfied, I approached the curtain and flanked around to the right.

The chains lay at the base of the spherical piece of artwork, the cuffs attached to the ends damp and crimson. Fresh blood dripped down the metal surface. Fresh urine soured the air, mixing with the coppery metallic taste of blood in my mouth.

Everything was exactly as I had left it.

Everything except one thing.

Jude was gone.

116

Sphere of Death

+74 Days – 1903 hours

I retraced my steps to the receiving bay. Holly padded along beside me. I glanced out to the loading dock. Both the ramp and street were empty.

The door to the archives corridor still hung open, nearly off its hinges. The lights were out in the short hallway. Light flickered from the longer corridor, the last ballasts desperate to keep providing light.

Or maybe the generators had run dry.

That was probably why the lower level was a ghost town.

All hands on deck!

Maybe there was a mad scramble to scavenge fuel now that flames from the oil field explosion had died down.

The Gaunt Man leaned against the steel door next to the keypad.

Moved Jude because there isn't enough manpower.

"Maybe, Bob," I agreed. "The question is where did they take her?"

To the highest spire of the highest turret.

"You're of little use."

Or speaking only the truth in a series of riddles.

"Yeah," I said, "you're the life of the party."

He shrugged but continued to smile.

Be careful out there, Marine.

"Ooh rah."

Holly sat and watched me. Her head was cocked and her tongue hanging out.

"We're going. We're going."

The strobes continued as we approached the intersection.

I drew up the Beretta as I checked the corner.

BOOM!

Concrete chips splattered across my face, temporarily blinding me.

"John!" I heard my name in a loud and shrill scream.

Another boom.

Pain like fire ant bites on my belly.

I rolled back toward the delivery doors.

Holly's barks echoed, already deeper in the warehouse.

My vision cleared, my eyes still stinging from the shrapnel.

I made my way past the delivery bay.

The lights were off here completely now.

I felt my way along the shelves.

A sharp pain in my side.

My shirt and skin were ripped open from a nail sticking out of a jagged piece of plywood.

"Shit!" I hissed.

Holly barked from ahead of me.

"John!"

The same high-pitched yell from behind me.

A faint light illuminated the aisle ahead of me, leading back to the sphere and the empty chains. The lights were still working there, at least.

I double-timed it to the other side of the welding curtain.

Holly lay at the base of the sculpture on her belly with her muzzle in her paws, whimpering.

A patch of red was spreading from her left rear haunch.

I put the Beretta in the back of my waistband and leaned closer to examine the wound.

"Okay," I said in a soothing voice. "It's going to be okay."

Her whimpers softened.

I felt around the entry wound.

She growled from deep in her throat but did not flinch.

"Good girl."

Steel against my neck.

"Yeah," Deb said. "My girl was a good girl, too."

I slowly raised my hands.

"It doesn't have to be this way, Deb."

"That's Ms. Staff to you, pussy," she said as she disarmed me of the Beretta. "And, yes, it does have to be this way."

"You sure?"

"Damn sure."

"Why?" I was still hunched over on one knee, Ms. Staff's Benelli pressed against the back of my neck. One shot would decapitate me, regardless of my enhanced DNA.

Holly lay still with shallow breathing.

The red on her coat was not spreading, the seeping blood slowly clotting.

I glanced back.

Deb was in darkened silhouette with the emergency light behind her. Holly's blood glistened on my fingers.

"It could have been different, Walken," she clarified. "But when I found out that your bitch was taking all of the attention from Roy that I deserved…"

She tensed up, the shotgun barrel pressing harder into my muscles.

I leaned forward and spun around.

Deflected the barrel with my forearm.

Boom!

The shotgun discharged, deafening me.

Holly yelped.

"No!" Deb punched me in the nose with the side of the stock.

I fell to my ass.

She swung the barrel, catching me on the cheek with the still hot metal.

Deb backed up and pumped the shotgun.

I dove behind the sphere.

Another boom.

Sound like loose gravel thrown against a metal sheet.

More bee stings. This time in my calf.

"Don't make me hunt you down, Walken."

I gritted my teeth and looked around for anything handy to defend myself with.

No tools.

No welding equipment.

No knives.

Deb had the Beretta.

And the Benelli.

Jude's prison of chains may become my tomb.

"I saved you, Ms. Staff."

My words echoed.

So did her footfalls.

My side was damp.

Blood dripped down to my jeans.

And ran down my arm from my shoulder.

And spread through the denim on the back of my leg.

Holly squeaked in a weak whimper.

"Sorry, puppy," Deb said, pumping the Benelli with a resounding click.

I grabbed the end of the shackle and launched over the sphere.

Deb looked up in surprise.

She swung the shotgun up and fired as I tackled her like a wrestler from the top rope.

More stings.

We landed hard on the concrete, me on top.

The shotgun clanked and skittered away.

I closed a fist around her throat.

Deb couldn't recapture the breath I knocked out of her.

"It didn't have to be this way, Deb," I whispered into her ear, emphasizing her first name.

Her fists punched against my forearms. Her eyes bulged as her lips turned blue.

My vision went crimson.

The capillaries in her eyes burst.

Tears ran down both of her cheeks. For different reasons.

I heard her heart beating.

Felt it throb through my hands.

It raged in my head.

Everything was sharper with adrenaline.

Deb's hands weakened from the lack of oxygen.

Foam spit from her lips.

Holly growled at me.

Deb's eyes rolled back.

Holly's wet tongue licked my wrist.

A soft whimper was followed by more licks.

The red receded.

I released Deb's throat.

The indentation of my grip was clearly delineated on her neck.

She gasped weakly.

Her eyes regained a fraction of focus.

I dragged her to the sculpture and slapped the chained shackle around her wrist. It clicked and locked, her meaty wrist tight in the cuff.

I knelt down next to her.

Grabbing her shirt collar, I propped her up roughly against the steel orb. Leaning close, I could still hear her heart beat weakly.

"You were saved again," I confirmed as I retrieved the Beretta from her waistband and the keycard clipped on her shirt. "This time you got your reprieve from a dog. I don't have enough compassion for you. Not anymore."

I stood and went to collect the shotgun.

Turning around I whistled for Holly.

She stood up gingerly and padded over to Deb, giving her tentative sniffs.

"Get away, bitch," she hissed through damaged and swelling vocal cords.

With that Holly growled in response.

Then as the piece de resistance and to prove she was no bitch, Holly lifted her leg and emptied her bladder on Deb's thigh.

Deb started to sob.

Holly finished, turned and kicked imaginary dirt onto Deb's leg before slowly padding over to me. She woofed up at me, her tail only wagging right and center.

"Come on," I said. "You've more than proven yourself today."

117

Going Up?

+74 Days – 1929 hours

I retraced my steps to the receiving bay.

Holly padded along beside me until we passed the roll-up bay. She whimpered and sat down against a yellow barricade pole next to the door.

"Taking a rest, girl?"

She whined and licked her chops.

"Alright," I agreed.

She woofed then dropped to her belly.

I put the Beretta in my waistband and strapped the shotgun over my shoulder.

"Rest up for a bit," I scratched her floppy ear.

Pulling the pulley chains I opened the roll-up door six or seven inches.

"If you get a spurt of energy go find Bowers."

She licked my hand again.

"I know the Sergeant is your biggest fan."

She ruffed, wagging her tail twice in agreement.

I pet her head one last time before standing up.

"Ooh rah."

Woof.

Leaving Holly behind, I moved through the short corridor and cleared the archives hallway before continuing to the elevator door at the other end. I swiped the card through the magnetic reader and waited.

Nothing happened.

Isn't the power out?

I looked at Bob. He had a good point.

"Usually elevators go to the lowest floor and open in the event

360

of a power outage."

Ooh. You continue to be a fount of useful trivia, don't you?

"Yes I am."

I swiped the card again.

Still nothing.

No motors. No whirring.

Would you like to hit the call button?

I glared at Bob's grin but tapped the button marked with a star anyway.

The hydraulics hissed to life and the elevator car thrummed down from the upper floors.

I backed up several steps, swung the Benelli off my shoulder and up to a full draw. The elevator thumped to a stop and the doors slid open. The narrow but long car was empty, its overhead light bright and steady.

After you, kind sir.

I entered the elevator and turned around.

"You coming?" I asked.

Bob was gone, leaving me to the task at hand.

The elevator doors slid closed again.

The interior was eerily quiet and sterile.

It reminded me of the recovery room of my second death before the tiles started shaking off the walls and the tremors started to crack the structure's very existence.

I hovered my finger over the floor buttons. Holly's blood stained my hand. My own blood dripped in rivulets over it. I finally pushed the main level button, leaving a smeared red fingerprint on its backlit surface.

Hydraulics came to life and the car ascended.

The hum of the motors replaced the uneasiness of the former quiet. At the main floor the car eased to a stop and the elevator announced my arrival with a single electronic chime.

I breathed deep and brought up the Benelli.

The doors slid open.

It was dark outside the car.

And quiet.

The light from the elevator only cast out a few feet.

I waited.

The doors started to close.

I broke the electronic plane with the stock of the shotgun.

The doors relented and retracted.

I continued to wait and listen.

I heard a heartbeat, soft and steady.

It was my own.

Not everyone would be out looking for fuel.

It would be absurd for Roy and Duke to vacate the majority of the complex. It is hard to power a facility if it ends up being overtaken due to inadequate security.

The doors started closing again.

I brought up the shotgun to break the plane again.

A large dark arm lunged in.

Meaty fingers grabbed my shirt.

Lifted me off the ground.

I was hurled across the gallery space.

Slammed into a display cabinet.

Shattered glass.

Broken wood.

Destroyed artifacts.

I landed in a heap on the floor.

Sharp pain from glass stuck into my back.

A shard of hammered copper pierced through my side.

The same dark fingers grabbed a handful of shirt and lifted me up off the floor and close to his dank coffee-ridden breath.

"Hiya, John," Duke said. "You interrupted my work for Roy, so I guess its time to see what you're really made of."

118

Dark Matter

+74 Days – 1942 hours

My feet dangled off the floor.

Duke tossed me into the darkness.

I landed on my back.

Searing pain.

The glass shards already embedded in my back dug deeper into my flesh.

"You ready for some pain?" Duke asked from nowhere – and everywhere – his voice echoing off the walls.

I rolled to my side and up onto one knee.

"Damn. Roy thought you would be good sport."

A fist slammed against my cheek.

I stumbled, seeing stars but not much else.

My eyes stung and blurred, my vision failing. Probably scratches on the corneas from the concrete rubble. Or maybe it was from the shards from the glass cabinet.

Or both.

I spit out blood.

"Don't see the big deal."

A knee appeared.

I partially blocked it with my palms.

It still connected with painful force.

"Not much of a fighter, are ya?"

A powerful straight kick blasted against my chest.

I lost my feet and slid across the tiles.

The clouds moved.

The moon shone brightly beyond the archways from the skylights in the main atrium.

The black blur lightened into a hulking dim shape.

It lunged at me.

I pivoted and drove a knee into the side of his face.

He dropped to one knee as his momentum carried him past me.

"There you go, hero," he coaxed as he wiped a drop of blood from his lip.

"I'm no hero," I whispered.

That's no way to think of yourself.

Bob stood a few meters away, Duke between us.

The specter illuminated the space, casting Duke more into light. My knee had swollen up the big man's cheek nicely.

Duke lunged with a flash of silver.

Time slowed down.

I blocked him at the wrist, forcing him to my right.

As he drove his body forward, I chopped him in the throat with the edge of my other hand.

He gasped and fell to his knees.

The room brightened more.

I swung behind Duke, one arm under his with my grip against the back of his neck. My other arm went around his massive throat, the crook of my elbow at his windpipe.

He gasped again.

His meaty fingers curled around my wrist and forearm, trying to break free of my stranglehold.

"Asshole," he croaked.

He stood up, taking me with him.

My feet left the tiles again.

I tightened my grip.

Duke broke into a run toward the broken display case.

He launched himself at it, twisting in mid-air.

Crunch!

I took the brunt of the impact.

More glass embedded in my back and shoulders.

I didn't break my grip.

Duke picked himself – and me – up again.

"Damn it," he groaned.

He roared, backing me into the adjoining wall.

I screamed in pain.

The tips of the glass shards in my back broke off.

Every cut opened wider.

My back was slick with sweat and blood.

My grip finally broke.

Duke pressed my arm under his and swung me into the wall again.

I slumped to the floor against something hard.

Duke took two hands full of shirt.

It ripped up my back.

"Tough," Duke glared into my eyes, "but not tough enough, I guess."

"...sure?" I asked.

"What did you say?" Duke pulled me closer.

I bit down and ripped off the tip of his nose.

"Arrgh!"

Duke released me and held his hands to his face.

"Fucker!" he screamed. "My face!"

I spit out a mix of blood and his nose at his feet.

Just to spite him.

Dampness trickled down the back of my thighs.

The room was bathed in light, like daylight.

Duke stood out in sharp contrast, his flesh thrumming against the whitewashed walls. His heartbeat pounded like a tribal war drum, its pulse vibrating out from him in a rhythmic aura.

Thump... thump.

Thump... thump.

Duke brought his hands away from his face.

The center of it was bathed in red with a dark crater at its core.

He yelled and rushed me with both fists up.

I front kicked him where his nose used to be.

More blood exploded from his face and mouth.

Duke hurled back and slammed against the wall, collapsing to the floor.

"Fubber," he gurgled, getting up to his feet.

He brought something up with him.

Turning, he swung the tailstock of the discarded Benelli.

I caught it in my left hand and pressed my finger into the trigger guard.

His eyes got wide as he stared down the barrel of the shotgun.

Before he could let go, I squeezed the trigger.

Boom!

Agonized screams.

His hand still gripped tight to the barrel.

I backed up.

Duke held the stump of his elbow with his remaining hand, hunched against the wall.

"Am I tough enough now?" I asked quietly.

The room started to darken again, Duke's aura fading along with the moment of extreme night vision I had experienced.

I peeled Duke's severed hand off the barrel.

The fingers curled closed again but not before I showed Duke his own middle finger.

A bell dinged.

Turning away, I tossed Duke's fist over my shoulder at him.

I had to find Jude.

Duke's Bowie knife was ahead of me.

I bent to retrieve it.

"Wadden," Duke sputtered out my name.

I turned as he rushed me again.

A gunshot echoed through the alcove, surprising us both.

Duke dove to the floor and slid to my feet, a gaping hole in the back of his head.

Behind him, barely out from the elevator doors, Joey leaned against the wall with the smoking Beretta in his shaking hands.

"Did I get him?" he asked in a low voice.

We looked down at the limp form in front of me.

It no longer vibrated or pulsed with life, now cooling and darkening as just another inanimate lump.

"You got him, Joey," I answered. "I don't think he's going to hurt you anymore."

He looked at me as he lowered the weapon.

"He hurt you bad enough," Joey stated, emphasizing the *you*.

"I've seen worse, Joey."

"Not sure how."

I turned to the darkness of the Welcome Center.

"Christ, John. Your back."

"I'll live."

If you're even considered alive. By medical standards, that is.

Ignoring my annoying companion – The Gaunt Man, not Joey – I picked up the knife and listened for signs of life.

"Where is everybody, Joey?"

"Most are out scavenging for juice for the generators," Joey confirmed. "The rest are locked in the gallery."

"Roy still doing that?"

"He says it's for safe keeping," he shrugged. "Says 'the game is afoot'."

"And how did you get out?"

"Didn't get out."

The room was enveloped in blackness again, only the fluorescents from the elevator shedding any light into the space. Joey was backlit as a silhouette against it.

"Why? Because nobody pays you notice?"

"Usually," Joey answered. "But not this time."

Tingles started at the base of my neck, glass digging in with each turn of my head.

I looked through the darkness.

Don't forget us.

Tapping from outside the room.

I could hear the children of the Higgins Education Wing

pressed against the barricaded doors, slapping against the steel.

Be careful.

"This time I'll be remembered."

"Why's that?" I asked without turning around.

Traitors.

"Roy said so."

I turned.

A flash.

Echoes.

Judas.

Burning in my chest.

A hiss escaped my teeth.

"For the history books," Joey muttered.

Another shot and flash.

More burning, now in my shoulder.

I heard a scream before realizing it was my own.

10 pieces of silver

The children slapped harder against the door, chains rattling through the handles.

"Immortalized," Joey recited mechanically.

He walked closer with the Beretta drawn.

Flash. Echoes.

More pain.

I dropped to my knees.

Boiling tears fell down my cheeks.

The victors write history.

More insistent slaps against metal.

"Held in the highest esteem."

Joey stood a meter away with the Beretta trained on me.

"I hope history recalls you well, Joey."

"I've been promised."

I lifted my head and gave Joey my full gaze.

"And promises are always kept, aren't they?"

Joey's face fell a bit, his tongue finding its way to his cheek.

His eyes wavered and watered.

"I'll remember you well, Joey."

The angle of the barrel dropped from my forehead to my chest, revealing more of Joey's face.

Jude is waiting.

Joey pressed the trigger.

I lunged at him.

The bullet ripped through the meat of my bicep.

The bowie knife blade embedded up to the hilt.

Under his ribs.

Through his lung.

Into his heart.

I caught Joey on his way down to the floor, cradling him in my arms. He looked at me with surprise and shock.

And fear of death.

I held his face close as his heart pulsed through me and his aura brightened for a moment before dimming.

"I promise I will remember you well," I said to him in earnest. "Your mom is waiting for you."

119

Interlude

+74 Days – 2017 hours

I sat on the floor with Joey in my arms, holding him and rocking him gently. As his form cooled, he did not become a dark hunk of flesh like Duke had.

A thud resonated from somewhere.

A few meters away, Duke's corpse was a dense hole of black.

Joey's form was lighter. His body resonated with something less empty. Maybe it was a faint illumination of the soul.

Maybe you're getting too metaphysical.

I sighed.

Wasted life. Wasted death.

I looked at the new red stains on my hands.

I continued to weigh down heavily on the wrong side of the scales, regardless of my efforts.

Another hard slap came from the Higgins Wing door.

I kissed Joey on the forehead and lay his head slowly on the floor. Taking the knife from his chest I gently inserted it through his ear canal into his brain. I extracted the blade with care and wiped it on my jeans before putting it in my waistband. The Beretta was still clutched in Joey's grip. I peeled his fingers away from the weapon and folded his hands on his belly.

I staggered to my feet.

Everything hurt.

Badly.

One of the three gunshot wounds administered by Joey was lodged in my chest between my heart and clavicle. The second was a through-and-through higher in the shoulder muscle. The third had cleanly burned through my upper bicep. Deb's shotgun blasts were burning and bleeding, entry wounds peppered throughout my side and mid-section. Good thing she hadn't been using slugs or flechettes. The glass and wood fragments were well embedded in my back at this point, making removal impractical and pointless.

Jude.

Deb and Duke, Roy's big guns, were now removed from the board.

I grabbed the Benelli.

It was my big gun.

The rest of the museum's residents were under house arrest or out scouting for replacement fuel for the generators. The exfil should be easier now.

Where would Roy be?

I started down the corridor to the oaken stairway.

Rattle.

Staggering and dripping blood over the tiles, I passed by the barracks and its chained doors. People stared at me from behind the glass. Some of them knocked against the glass and yelled to get my attention. I didn't have the strength to focus on their faces or their plight.

Jude was my only thought.

I made it to the stairs –

So proud!

– and clung to the rail as I dragged myself up the stairs toward the café and the lobby beyond.

Up the next half-flight of stairs to my left the library was dark.

Roy doesn't seem to be at home.

I stumbled toward the doors leading to the café. My weight was the only thing that pushed the door open. I slapped at the doorstop with my foot until it fell into the down position. As I slipped off the door, the glass was smeared with my fresh blood. The rubber cleat of the doorstop grabbed at the tiles and stayed open.

Please come to us. The little girl pleaded.

I dragged myself toward the lobby.

Moonlight from the windows facing the courtyard lit my way.

The security doors to the Higgins Education Wing pressed as far open as they could with the weight of the children against them and the locked chains.

The little girl with the flashing shoes pressed closest to the latticed glass.

Please let us out. We didn't do anything wrong.

"I know."

He did this to us.

"Who?" I whispered as I pressed a tired hand against the cool metal.

The man who would be king.

120

Highest Spire

+74 Days – 2033 hours

The glass doors to the café lay in front of me, with two matching windows. All were framed in under ornate brickwork topped with arched reliefs.

Jude.

I know.

Three painful deep breaths later I passed the welcome center counter. I pressed my shoulder into the glass door, letting my weight push it open.

I used the chair backs to keep me upright as I passed the eating area and kitchen. Looking back at the lobby, I saw the faint but obvious trail of blood my boots were leaving behind.

Jude.

The little girl was doing her best to keep me focused.

The security checkpoint to the left led to the stairways connecting to the rest of the galleries.

My vision blurred.

I grabbed the edge of the security station desk.

Crunch.

The wood splintered.

I held on until the wave of faintness passed.

The door I propped open beckoned me like a gaping mouth.

The library and Hiatt Wing were up the stairway to my right. Those were Roy's favorite places.

The library was still dark.

I didn't see any light from deeper into the Knights! exhibit.

The highest spire on the highest turret.

I went through the door and up the right stairway.

A suited knight held vigil atop an armored pale rust red

stallion, watching my painful climb but being otherwise useless in my quest.

With the Benelli slung and the Bowie knife at my belt, I chose to draw up the Beretta and ascended the steps to the third floor.

Three large potted trees framed a stone bench in an alcove with skylights. This lower level was dedicated to Early American art with galleries on each end. Their doors were dark and locked.

The upper third floor galleries – this level dedicated to Mid 20th Century American art, American Sculpture, Decorative Arts and American Impressionism – were also locked and dark.

Continuing upward, I cleared the stairway to the fourth level.

I was running a fool's errand.

My breath was ragged.

Some of the buckshot must have perforated my lung.

It was difficult to take in a solid breath.

It was more painful to exhale.

I leaned against the wall next to a plaque denoting that this was McDonough Court.

Next to the stairwell was another elevator.

Don't do it.

Was that Bob or the children?

"You sent me on this goose chase," I said, shaking my head against the fog and stars in my vision.

Just warning you. It's your funeral.

Which voices should I listen to?

The elevator beckoned me.

"Fuck it."

I limped to the elevator and fished around for the swipe card I took off Deb.

It was gone.

I panicked.

Calm down.

The little girl with the strobing shoes spoke to me in a melodic singsong.

Look again.

I took as deep a breath as I could and exhaled slowly before searching again in a more methodical way.

The card had been in my back left pocket.

I pulled it out. The dried blood was stark against the white plastic. The blood stood in higher contrast stained against my skin. Viscera clotted under my fingernails.

It will be okay. The little girl cooed. *At least it will be for a little while longer.*

Swiping the card in the magnetic reader, I pressed the elevator's call button. A quiet click, ding, and the hum of hydraulic pistons were my reward.

The stainless steel doors slid smoothly open.

That was too quick.

You may have blacked out for a moment.

The soft light from the car welcomed me inside.

I was already pressing the button with the 2 etched on it before I realized I was inside the elevator. The lift paid no worry to my absent-mindedness as the doors closed and the car descended as instructed. The enclosure hummed with electronic life, its close quarters like a safe and familiar metal womb.

The elevator announced my arrival to the second level with its light ding, letting me know that it was always here. Prompt and reliable, it said.

The doors slid open.

I stared into the darkness.

The elevator waited patiently.

I strained to listen to sounds other than the pounding in my ears.

The elevator still waited.

I did not want to move.

Waiting long enough, the doors started to slide closed.

I stopped them.

The elevator relented to my decision to see into the unknown

375

dark even while its cool fluorescent lights and warm colored walls promised shelter and safety.

I drew the Beretta up, thankful for a moment's respite before exiting the light and entering the dark.

121

Crime and Punishment

+74 Days – 2050 hours

It was quiet.

Too quiet.

"Shut up, Bob," I ordered the Gaunt Man. "You haven't helped much lately."

It really seemed like where Roy would keep his maiden.

"Jude's no one's maiden."

And don't forget you were on board with the idea.

"Don't remind me." I spat out red. "Must be the blood loss."

You may need a few stitches.

I stood in the stairway, blood dripping down my fingers onto the floor. My T-shirt was ragged and red. My jeans were stiff with drying blood.

I believe a few stitches, I am quite sure.

A murmur.

"Quiet."

And some gauze to wrap it all up…

"Shut up," I warned.

Bob pantomimed buttoning his lips and throwing away the key.

If only it were that easy.

A noise.

Something indistinguishable.

Tapping?

Stomping?

The others.

The children reminded me.

Don't forget the others.

"Fuck."

I went down the stairs back to the first level.

Behind the gallery glass in the space that doubled as the barrack the museum residents still stood. They were pressed against the tempered wall – four deep and wide eyed.

And terrified, I would imagine.

They retreated a few steps as I approached, the front line of people closest to the glass bumping into the ones behind them.

You must be quite the sight.

"You think?" I asked sarcastically.

Chains were wrapped through the handles to the double doors.

Roy is always thinking about security.

Or imprisonment.

I took the chains in my bloody hands and spread them apart. They slipped in my grip. I tried again with the same result.

My vision was starting to dull again.

Don't punk out now, John.

As I glared at Bob I was sure that the people behind the glass wondered who the hell I was looking at.

I dropped the chains.

I raised the barrel of the Benelli at the handles.

Waste not, want not.

Instead of using the shotgun, I pulled off and spun the remnants of my shirt like I was prepping a bath towel for snapping someone's ass. I wrapped the shirt through the handles and knotted it, leaving as much slack as possible. Using the fabric and the Benelli, I created a tourniquet and started twisting the shotgun like an oversized lever. The fabric tightened. My muscles ached as the shotgun struggled to spin free of the winding shirt.

The shirt is starting to tear.

"No," I demanded.

I turned the shotgun another quarter rotation.

Chink.

Thunk.

The right side handle snapped off its bolt.

The entire assembly crashed against the glass and out of my hands. I pulled the Benelli out of the cotton and chains and opened the doors.

The people of the museum colony stared at me, but didn't move. Their fear of the unknown was overshadowed by their fear of me.

They will never understand greatness.

I ignored Bob's unwise words and focused on a familiar face in the crowd.

"Percy," I said.

"Wha… what?"

"You need to take these people out of here."

Murmurs started.

"Go where?" came a voice from someone.

"Anywhere," I answered. "It's going to go sideways in here. I want you all out of the cross-fire."

"We're defenseless," Percy reminded me. "What about the festers outside?"

"All drawn out to the oil tank fires. You should be clear until you find another spot. Try the church or the auditorium. If you stay close you can flag down and join up with the scavengers when they come back.

Or stay here behind chained glass.

"Take this," I thrust the Benelli in Percy's unready hands. "Its better than a steak knife. I'll take you through the lobby. You take them the rest of the way."

He nodded.

"Ok," he said to the others. "Get your gear and let's go. You heard the man."

The rest responded to Percy, gathering their packs and bags. A few had makeshift weapons ranging from mop handles to hand tools.

It would have to suffice.

I led them up the stairs and through the café.

"Okay," I told Percy. "Get them out and away until the coast is clear."

He nodded to me and motioned for the others to head out through the framed entry under one of the archways. They filed out into the lobby and toward the doors.

I sighed.

Feel better?

"Barely."

After the majority of the crowd had exited I returned to the stairway in Salisbury Hall.

The Library and the Contemporary Gallery were dark.

You keep expecting Roy to be waiting with a final game of chess.

"Agreed. But I'm not looking for him."

Aren't you?

"No." I said, but wondered if he was right in some small way.

He is the self-proclaimed king of this castle.

"And?"

Maybe he is sitting on his throne.

We walked through the corridor toward the Renaissance Court under the atrium.

The Knights! exhibit stood behind its own wall of tempered glass. A faint amber glow – unseen from the hallway – flickered from inside. In contrast to the other gallery, these doors were unchained and wide open.

I cleared the entry with the Beretta at full draw.

The first section displayed several forms, suits of armor with shiny steel reflecting the flicker of candlelight. Several portraits hung on the opposite wall, content to start at me. Two archways were cut out in the wall on each end, leading deeper into the gallery.

I moved left through to the next space.

Dozens more fat tall candles were lit and placed on the floor along both walls of the longer exhibit hall. The armored helmet display cases were still arranged in an oblong circle in the center of it.

The opposing figure of the Batman, standing on his perch and backlit with more candles in front of a drawn velvet curtain, stared at me from the opposite end. His familiar yellow and black insignia served as a beacon, a target and a symbol of fear.

Roy's throne, where I first met him, was behind that curtain.

Two additional figures stood silent guard on either side of the caped crusader. I stepped into the gallery and crossed the floor between the encased helmets from different eras of metal armament. When I stepped onto a circular etching depicting a famous painting the two figures flanking The Batman swayed.

Strange faint music filled my ears.

The figures stepped away from the dark superhero and moved their arms away from their sides. They wielded machetes.

Hector and Raul.

"You think?"

Always a pleasant distraction, don't you think?

"Not likely."

"Oh," Raul replied. "We don't think its likely, either, punto."

"Easy, bro," Hector warned. "Don't get yourself excitable."

"Yeah," I agreed. "We wouldn't want that."

"You look like shit, essay," Raul continued.

Probably couldn't write an essay, essay.

I smirked.

"You think I'm funny?"

"Not in the least," I answered, shaking my head. "Where's the boss?"

"Busy, bitch," Raul grinned. "Busy with your bitch."

"Cállate," Hector ordered his brother. "Muerte tranquila, Mr. Walken."

Hector rushed forward with his blade already swinging.

I squeezed the trigger.

Click.

Empty.

Fuck! How did I lose count?

Because you are slowly bleeding out, John.

I stepped back and to the left.

His blade swung past me.

I punch him in the jaw, my shoulder screaming in searing pain.

Raul raced in.

His machete jabbed into my ruined shoulder.

I dropped the gun and jumped back.

Raul drew the blade out and lunged again.

I slapped the blade away and front kicked him in the chest.

Raul fell onto his ass.

Hector sliced his machete across my back.

I blindly back kicked.

Something cracked.

"Arrgh!"

"Punto!" Raul yelled, scrambling to his feet.

He swung again.

I arched back but caught a slice across the cheek.

The amber candlelight deepened to red.

Raul double-fisted his weapon and swung it straight down.

I clapped my hands together, catching the blade.

"Mierda," Raul exclaimed with disbelief.

He tried to pull back the blade.

His heartbeat quickened with adrenaline and effort.

And fear.

Another heartbeat pulsed loudly behind me.

I kicked behind me, catching Hector square in the face.

His face crunched, exploding blood.

His machete clanked to the tiles.

"Hermano!"

Hector slumped at my feet, Raul still trying to pull his machete free.

The room took on a decidedly bright crimson cast.

My hands still pressed together.

I forced Raul's machete down, pulling him closer.

He leaned in.

I drove my forehead into his nose.

Like his brother, his face exploded in red.

He dropped like a stone at my feet.

Thump... thump... from behind me.

Thump... thump... from in front of me at my feet.

Both were weak but steady.

I looked at the hulking statue of the Batman.

He swore to never take a life.

I flipped the blade around and caught the handle.

Hefting its weight, I drove it down into Raul's skull.

A sick thunk.

The sound of ripe cantaloupe.

His pulse blotted out.

I left the machete sticking out of his head.

"Hermano" Hector whispered weakly.

His heartbeat was weakening, becoming thready.

"Muerto tranqila, amigo," I nodded.

Then I crushed his skull under my boot so he could join his brother.

122

Pay No Attention...

+74 Days – 2116 hours

"Roy!"

I could hear more heartbeats.

"Roy!" I yelled again.

The velvet curtains swept aside.

Clap.

Roy appeared.

Clap. Clap. Clap.

"Bravo, my friend." Roy continued his applause, stepping forward "Bravo! You are truly a wonderful opponent."

"Where's Jude?"

"Safe, I assure you."

"I don't want your assurances."

"Surely. I can see that you do."

"Your kingdom is burning, Roy."

"Is it?" he said with a cock of his head. "Like when Nero fiddled?"

I pulled the Bowie knife.

"A trophy! Apparently Duke was not a match for you. A pity."

He seems way too happy.

"No. He didn't make it."

"And the always lovely Debra is apparently gone, too, based on the fact that the elevators have been running and you are the one standing before me. And my affectionately named Machete Men lay here at your feet."

"And... your prisoners have been set free."

His brow furrowed, but only for a moment.

"Ungrateful knaves, all of them."

"Jude." I demanded. "Now."

"Ah, yes," he replied. "Back to the task at hand. Always mission oriented. An excellent trait."

He turned away and disappeared back through the curtain.

I reversed my grip on the knife to point the blade out and pursued the current and soon-to-be-past king.

123

…The Man Behind the Curtain

+74 Days – 2121 hours

Behind his throne was an alcove with brightly colored children's art and kid-sized tables and beanbag chairs. My stomach turned as I thought about the children in the learning annex.

Jude.

I'm on it.

I caught a glimpse of Roy's back as he slipped past the throne and into an adjacent gallery space.

He is a quick one, isn't he?

Pursuing Roy, I entered the cramped gallery chamber.

A display cabinet was mounted on a wall directly in front of me, making the gallery into a corridor. Weapons from the medieval period adorned the walls with plaques describing each one.

Roy appeared from my right. He thrust a very large ornamented curved single edged blade at my mid-section.

I blocked it.

Roy drew the weapon back, snagging and ripping open my side with the blade's decorative hooked barbs.

I hissed in pain.

Roy plunged it at me again, driving me back deeper into the gallery.

"This is a Bodyguard Glaive from the 1700s," Roy instructed as he continued his practiced thrusts. "From Venice, Italy."

He thrust it again.

I dodged the blade.

It embedded into the drywall.

Roy immediately abandoned it in favor of a wildly curved sword.

"Kondo sword," he swung at me.

I blocked it with the Bowie but the blade still sliced across my fingers.

"Central Africa. Nineteenth or early twentieth century."

He swung it high over my shoulder.

I caught the sword at the hilt with the knife.

Roy retracted upward, slicing my back with the tip.

He swung the Kondo diagonally, flaying my bare chest.

I screamed as I jabbed at him with the Bowie, catching him with a blade tip to the shoulder.

"Ahh," he cried, backing off.

Instead of pressing his advantage, he flitted out of sight.

Staggering against the wall, I left a wide swath of blood on it in my wake.

I reached for a strangely bladed axe with a talon at the top of the handle.

A steel fist crushed my cheekbone.

I fell to my knees, axe in hand.

Quit being distracted.

"Aha," Roy said, punching me again. "The Musele. It's a ceremonial knife from Central Africa. It's considered a bird-headed..."

Fog.

Pain.

Jude.

Darkness.

More pain.

Ju...

"Finally on your knees," said a whisper to my immediate left.

I lashed out with the talon of the Musele.

"Godammit!" the voice cried, followed by retreating footsteps.

No more punishment came.

Only the welcome embrace of darkness.

124

Wake Up Call

+74 Days – 2153 hours

Blinding pain returned.

A heart beat loudly in my ears.

It was my own heart this time.

And it beat painfully through every slice and hole in my body.

My chest and back were covered in red paint.

That is blood, dear John.

"Right," I muttered. "Blood."

My left eye had swollen shut. My left arm didn't want to work. I couldn't stand up straight.

Roy had not finished me off.

I limped back through the Knights! exhibit.

Past the throne, the Batman, and the cooling dark lumps of Hector and Raul.

Two words were written in blood on the glass wall.

Center Court

Such the artist, Bob said sarcastically. *Apparently he has been too busy to deal with you.*

I was in no shape to face him.

My strength was gone.

My body was failing me.

Jude.

A new voice replaced the old one. The little girl with the light-up shoes called out a reminder to me.

"I know," I cried out in despair. "I know. How?"

The Gaunt Man was gone. No help there.

Jude. The little girl sang again.

I limped to the corridor.
The Renaissance Court and pain waited to the right.
Salisbury Hall and freedom beckoned to the left.

125

Hey, Jude

+74 Days – 2207 hours

I made the only decision I could live with.

The pain was so vivid and sharp, even through the slowly ebbing out of my life blood. What could I do?

Blood continued to trail behind me, a reminder of the choices I had made.

Limping to the Renaissance Court Balcony, I was armed with Duke's Bowie knife and whatever strength I could still muster.

Blood loss is a bitch, isn't it?

Shut up, Bob.

The torches around the atrium were all lit, flooding the court in a wavering wash of amber. Roy stood in the center of the huge mosaic inlayed into the floor.

"Welcome to The Worcester Hunt, dear Mr. Walken," Roy announced with his wide spread arms.

He left hand was still adorned with the metal gauntlet glove, my blood on its knuckles. In his other hand was a broad sword. He wore my shoulder holster with the familiar grip of my Glock poking out.

Behind him, shackled to cuffed ropes between two columns under the massive wall mural depicting the bloody feast with a dripping dead stag, was Jude. She was bloody and bruised but stared defiantly at the back of Roy's head.

"Hey, Jude," I called out weakly.

She rolled her swollen red eyes.

"Haven't heard that one before, smartass," she replied.

"I try to be original," I answered.

I limped down the stairs, leaning against the wall for support. Roy frowned.

"Have respect," he yelled. "Look at the trail you are leaving behind. Do you know how much work it takes to remove blood from stone?"

"Blood from a stone," I said with a chuckle, pressing harder against the wall. "That's funny. You're funny."

"I am in charge here!"

"In charge of what?"

"Everything."

I reached for the center railing and made my way down to the court floor.

"You ready?" I asked, raising the Bowie knife.

"Of course," Roy answered. "You must know by now that I am more than a match for you."

"Always the pawn?" I asked.

"Exactly," he said excitedly. "Now you understand your station in the grand scheme of things. A glorious day has come that you have finally made that realization."

"I haven't always been that quick on the uptake. Just ask my dad."

I stepped over to the steel pipe railing surrounding the mosaic.

"Early 6th Century, I'm told," Roy explained, stalking me while he glanced lovingly at the mosaic. "Rebuilt here in the 1930s. If you walk around the room, you will see that there are several different scenes."

He pointed to a scene with the sword. "A tigress and her cubs."

He rushed in and swiped the blade at my shoulder, slicing the skin.

"John," Jude cried.

I didn't move or react.

Nonplussed, Roy continued.

"If you look at the center you might notice the hunter surrounded by speared animals. It is all very intricate and beautiful."

He drove a gauntleted fist into my jaw.

I fell to my knees, dazed.

"Get up!" Jude yelled.

Roy put the sword tip to my chest over my heart.

"Always a worthy knight," he explained, "but in the end just a pawn. You are isolani."

"Go ahead," I said.

"As you wish," Roy said.

He pulled the sword back and drove it down, a mad grin on his face.

The blade hit the hilt of my Bowie knife with a spark.

Roy pressed the sword blade down, gritting his teeth.

I slowly got my feet under me, driving the broadsword blade up with the Bowie knife.

He backed up, tossing the sword away and trying to draw the Glock with his gauntleted hand.

He stopped and stared with his mouth agape.

"John," Jude yelled again. "Behind you."

The tingling had returned to the base of my skull.

Not unlike the sound of cicadas in the dusk of deep summer.

I didn't look back.

I didn't need to.

I grabbed Roy by the collar and pulled him back to the railing, his toes dangling off the mosaic artwork.

Grumbles.

"Don't just stand there," Roy cried, staring over my shoulder. "Save me."

I put the knife in my teeth. Grabbing the holster, I yanked it from his shoulders. He spun around. I grabbed the back of his shirt and tossed him over the railing. He landed hard on the lower steps.

And painfully, I think.

I was okay with that.

A familiar strobe lit up the walls between the torchlight.

I did finally look back.

The little girl stood at the top of the stairs.

Locked us in. She said to me.

Behind her on the upper steps and on the balcony were all of the children who had been chained in to die in the Higgins Wing. They swayed but did not come down after us.

Killed us.

"Yes," I agreed.

I picked Roy up by the collar and dragged him halfway up the upper steps toward the waiting little girl.

She clicked her teeth.

The other children did not move.

"No, John," Roy yelled. "This is barbaric!"

I pulled him close and whispered in his ear.

"We're all pawns to someone. The dead are your kings now."

With the rest of my strength, I tossed him up into the throng of dead children like he was a ragdoll. He landed on the waiting children, punching them with his metal fist as he fought to regain his feet.

"Have at it, kids," I offered.

The little girl may have nodded.

It was hard to tell.

The entire crowd growled in unison and started tearing and biting at Roy. He fought back with the gauntlet, breaking a few jaws and caving in a few faces before the rest overpowered him.

I quickly put on the shoulder holster, dragging myself back to the main floor and using the rail around the mosaic to make my way to where Jude was held.

"Come on," she said, watching the kids tear away at the King of the Museum. "Come on."

I struggled to use the knife to cut through Jude's restraints.

Her arms dropped onto my shoulders.

"I got you," I said, wincing in pain.

We half-dragged each other around the mosaic and up the main steps.

Roy screamed.

Jude stiffened.

It is like music to my ears.

"Come on," I said.

The children occupying the balcony and the tops of the stairs looked our way but made no move toward us. We went straight through the arches to the old stairway leading to Salisbury Hall. With Roy and the children behind us, the exit and freedom was only a café and lobby away.

Roy wailed once more before being cut off abruptly in mid-scream.

Thank you.

"You're welcome."

"I didn't thank you," Jude said. "But a thank you is in order."

We reached the doors to the café.

So close, I thought as we crossed the threshold.

A chair slammed into us.

I twisted as we fell to the deck, Jude landing on my chest.

Ms. Staff – Deb to her friends – hulked over us.

"Sorry, lovebirds," she muttered, her wrist torn and bleeding. "Should have killed me when you had the chance, asshole."

She raised the chair up for another swing.

Jude suddenly rolled off of me, taking a part of me with her.

A gunshot lit up the lobby, echoing off the walls.

Deb snapped upright with a spray of blood from her chest.

The chair dropped to the floor.

My holster was empty.

Jude fired the Glock again.

Deb took the second shot to the belly.

"Arrgh," Deb groaned, clutching her stomach.

She staggered and fell against the chair.

Jude got to her feet while I could only manage to get up on one knee.

"Yeah," Jude agreed. "I should have killed you when I had the chance."

She hovered over Deb, straddling her with my Glock pointed at her. Deb put her hands up, warding her off.

"You know what they say?" Jude asked.

Deb shook her head.

"If you keep doing what you're doing," Jude recited, "you'll keep getting what you got."

"Bitch," Deb spat.

Jude fired two shots through Deb's palms into her face.

"Maybe," Jude shrugged. "Maybe not."

Jude came back to me and helped me up.

"Can you make it?" she asked me.

"I remember asking you that," I replied, emphasizing the 'you'.

"Yeah," she acknowledged, wrapping her arm around my waist. "Ain't we a pair?"

126

White Shadows

+74 Days – 2232 hours

We staggered out of the main entrance of the Lancaster Lobby of the Worcester Art Museum for the last time. The full moon's cast softened the otherwise deep night.

"You gonna make it, Sergeant?" Jude asked again. "You're bleeding like a stuck pig."

"I am stuck like a stuck pig," I said with a chuckle.

Each step was filled with painful shards and threatening tears in the skin but did not seem to be debilitating. I just needed rest and recovery.

"Maybe we should wait inside. We can block off an area where the walkers can't get us."

"They won't be a problem," I assured her, "but we need to rendezvous with Bowers."

"They're alive?"

"Yeah," I answered. "All except Lenny."

Jude stopped short. "How did April take it?"

"She's trying to get through it."

"We all are."

Jude rotated her arm, listening to the clicking in her shoulder.

"Yeah," she assessed, "that's not a good sign."

"Come on," I coaxed, my vision blurring and the night taking on even more darkness in spite of the moon.

We headed south, slipping along Lancaster Street and the Higgins Education Wing to the back of the property where it connected to Institute Road. I didn't bother to look back toward the front of the museum, choosing to forget about my first task for Roy.

My stomach churned with the thought of ripping a woman's

head clean off.

Institute Road was empty.

"The others should be at the other side of the auditorium," I commented, hoping Bowers was able to get the rest to safety.

"Cool," Jude replied. Then we get you stitched up somehow."

"Sure."

"Glad to have you back, Sergeant. In spite of the fact that you command a shitty rescue op."

"Whatever you say, dear."

"Damn right, whatever I say," Jude grinned. "Smartest thing you said since I met you."

She tightened her grip around my waist.

I exhaled sharply.

"Sorry," Jude apologized. "But quit being a pussy."

"Yeah, yeah."

Rustles came from the bushes.

I drew the Glock with my free hand.

The bushes sat deep against the high concrete abutments of the museum's extension. A blot of dark gray drifted low out of the recessed shadows, whitening as it zigzagged towards us.

Woof.

Holly favored her front left paw, whimpering with each step.

"Oh, baby," Jude empathized, quickly leaving me to my own balance as she rushed to the dog.

Jude examined the dog for a moment before sweeping her up in her arms. Holly licked her face.

"Ok. Ok, stinky breath. I love you."

Holly's tail slapped against Jude's arm.

"Let's keep moving, Jude."

"Sir. Yes, sir," she replied. "Don't worry. I love you, too."

I smiled as far as the pain would allow me.

"I work for a living."

"Yes, Sergeant," Jude corrected. "Geez. Soldiers are so sensitive."

I raised an eyebrow.

"Marines. I meant Marines are so sensitive," she corrected again with a wink. "Let's get going to where we're going. This fluff ball is heavier than she looks."

"Just another block."

127

Reunions

+74 Days – 2249 hours

The intersection of Institute Road had Tuckerman to the left and Harvard to the right. The United Congregational Church – where I saved Deb from the FRACs – stood quiet on the next corner. The massive concrete monolith of the Worcester Memorial Auditorium took up the entire block ahead to our right. The street map of the area was clear in my mind.

A few more steps and the Worcester Art Museum would be behind us.

"John."

Bowers and the rest of our group would be ahead. Even Alex and the rest of the museum residents could be there as well.

"John," Jude repeated.

"Yeah?"

"A light just flicked on"

She nodded up the block toward Salisbury Street and the entrances to the museum courtyard and the delivery bay.

A faint glow lit up the corner of the Renaissance Court atrium building. The street between the light and us was littered with large dark bags of garbage.

Holly growled.

"It's not a fire," Jude said.

"And it's not light from the museum."

"Something new? Should we check it out?"

"Better to rule out more problems."

I drew up the Glock and stepped onto the sidewalk.

Jude, with Holly in her arms, followed at arm's reach.

We walked quickly up to the handicap parking lot along the courtyard fence, staying quiet and keeping low.

399

Thank you.

The children sang in unison from inside the walls.

You should have bugged out.

Bob echoed a warning from nowhere and everywhere, not making a physical appearance but leaving his words in his dreadful dripping spectral voice.

We moved back to the sidewalk through an incline of dried bushes and mulch.

"Christ," Jude whispered.

The large lumps in the street were not garbage.

Amid the backpacks and shopping bags of supplies and food the bodies of the museum residents lay bleeding out in the street.

I moved closer.

Jude stared from the sidewalk, her face half buried in Holly's fur.

Double tap shot to the chest. And a single shot to the forehead.

The same was true with the next former museum resident.

My stomach turned.

The Benelli lay on the asphalt.

Percy stared at me from his side, his finger still on the trigger.

This may be your fault.

Bob pointed out something I already knew.

Every member of Percy's party – all the people I told to leave for their own safety – lay in the street in their own blood.

They were all shot military style.

Triple tap – two rounds to the chest and one to the head.

Make sure they don't get back up.

There were so many faces.

Most of their eyes were open.

Looking at me.

Blaming me.

Rightfully so, I would think.

"…lights."

"What?"

"There's movement in the lights."

Shadows danced from beyond the corner of the atrium wall.

"Sergeant John Walken," boomed a voice through a megaphone.

"What the fuck?" Jude and I said in unison.

"I suggest you come forward to the front of the museum," the voice ordered, echoing off the walls of the building.

"You and your friend," the voice asked politely. "And the canine, if you please."

"Do we run?"

Motion came from our high 10 o'clock.

Snipers on the atrium roof

I looked at Jude and Holly.

Run.

The little girl said.

"No," I shook my head, weary and defeated. "No more."

I walked toward the voice, careful not to disturb the bodies or the rivulets of blood in the street.

Jude and Holly followed, more slowly.

"Good," the amplified voice coaxed. "Very good."

When we reached the driveway, several red laser sights clicked to life. They trained on my bare chest. A couple found their way to Jude's forehead and one even to Holly's chest.

"Keep coming," the voice ordered. "Hands up, if you please."

"Very polite," Jude sneered.

My Glock went into its holster and my hands went to the top of my head. Jude did the best she could to comply.

We rounded the corner of the building. The searchlights from three HumVees bathed the area in white, blinding us.

When my eyes adjusted, I found Bowers and the others.

On the top step of the museum entrance, in front of the revolving door and its flanking single doors, were the remaining members of our group. All were in a kneeling position with their legs crossed at the ankles and their fingers interlaced on top of their bowed heads. Tears streamed down Summer and April's faces. Melissa muttered something indecipherable. Victoria simply stared at the pavement. Only Bowers glared straight at the firing squad that stood on the driveway in front of them.

"I need you," I whispered. "Now."

Two mercenaries in black tactical gear peeled away from the vehicles, intercepted us, and escorted us to the bottom of the steps.

My muscles tensed.

"Please no drama, Sergeant," the voice anticipated. "The others will not fare as well as you, in any event."

One of the mercs pulled out my Glock and pocketed it.

"I may kill you with that," I warned.

He scoffed at my comment and they both moved back to the row of Humvees.

"Should have run," Jude told me.

I looked at the snipers on the roof.

"Wouldn't have mattered."

"Young lady and puppy," the voice behind the searchlights ordered. "Please join your friends on the steps."

Jude held Holly tight while the dog growled. She stood defiantly until one of the soldiers put a M4 barrel to the back of her neck.

"Ok. Ok."

She climbed the steps and knelt down next to Summer.

"What do you want?" I yelled.

"I thought that was obvious," the voice answered. "We've come for our property."

"What are you talking about?" I asked.

"You are truly dense sometimes, Sergeant."

"Now," I whispered.

"The fact that you –" the voice was cut short.

Boom.

The large ornate single metal doors to the museum vibrated.

Boom. Boom.

A dent appeared in the middle of the metal.

Glass broke from farther away.

A chorus of mews and growls could be heard.

The mercenaries trained their weapons and laser sights onto the doors.

"Now," I repeated.

Boom. Boom. Boom!

The doors rattled.

Safeties clicked off.

The mercs backed up a few steps for a better angle.

Bowers, Jude and the others were in the crossfire.

The growling stopped.

The banging stopped.

It was quiet.

A soldier screamed from the opposite side of the parking lot.

His gun discharged into the air.

The little girl with the pigtails and strobing boots leapt up and bit into the soldier's exposed neck, ripping out skin, muscle and his carotid artery in one tear.

The other soldiers turned their guns to the little girl.

Thank you.

Thank you.

I tackled the closest guard.

His back broke as I slammed into his spine.

We both fell into another solder, taking the second soldier out at the back of the knees. I drove an elbow into his throat, crushing it.

More children appeared from around the corner.

The soldiers opened fire.

Practiced marksmanship dropped many of the small walkers with a single headshot each.

Still they came.

April panicked and screamed. She raced down the steps, straight into the crossfire. A bullet tore into her neck. She gurgled and slammed to the pavement.

"No!" Jude yelled.

"Stay put!" I yelled back.

I grabbed a discarded M4 and fired at the backs of the mercenaries.

They staggered but did not go down.

Instead they turned toward me.

Body armor.

I shot two of them in the head. That put them down.

The others continued to fire at the children.

A familiar pop.

A pain in my thigh.

I went down.

The children dragged down two more mercenaries to the grass.

Good.

More yells.

Victoria screamed.

A stray teenage FRAC clamped his teeth into her arm.

No!

The bully from the Annex stumbled away from Victoria to stalk the soldiers.

He was taken down by one of the rooftop snipers.

I pivoted and shot the offending sniper in the head.

Another two shots took out the other one.

The second sniper slumped dead against the parapet.

Victoria howled, holding her bleeding arm.

She glanced at me with blank haunted eyes.

Victoria was in shock.

Then she lunged at the closest soldier with a shriek.

"Mom!" Summer cried, held back by Jude.

The merc turned smoothly and shot her in the heart.

She skidded to a stop on the bottom step.

I shot the soldier through the ear.

Bowers joined Jude covering Summer and Holly.

"Motherfuckers!" Melissa searched the ground wildly for the closest weapon.

"Enough!" the megaphone voice yelled. "Finish this nonsense, please, my dear."

A whoosh.

An explosion and a wave of heat rushed at my back.

RPG.

Another whoosh and whistle.

Heat. Flames. Burning rotten flesh.

The children were ablaze.

Screams in my head.

I turned toward the vehicles and shot out two of the searchlights. I pivoted to take out a third.

A fist came out of the light.

Pain.

Fog.

I arched back, sweeping my leg.

It connected with nothing.

Another fist connected to my temple.

I rolled out and onto my numb legs.

They didn't support me.

I fell to my side.

"John!" Someone called out with concern.

All I saw was shapes and silhouettes in the remaining lights.

Two slender forms wavered closer to me.

One moved right.

The double-click of a pump-action shotgun.

A barrel pressed against my temple.

"Douse the floods, please," the now unamplified voice commanded.

The remaining searchlight darkened, the space lit only by the Humvees' headlights.

The slender black form sharpened but was still dark. He wore a suit with a stark white dress shirt and a narrow black silk tie. He wore polished black wingtip dress shoes, even here in the field.

He crouched down, pulling up the creases of his dress pants.

The Gaunt Man examined me, making tsk-tsk sounds.

"My," an all too real version of my personal specter said, "aren't you are a sad sight to behold? At any rate, it is good to have you found again."

"Let's clean up," he said to the others as he stood up.

I dove at the Gaunt Man.

A powerful fist to the back of my neck drove my face to the asphalt before I halved the distance to him.

Coming up on my hands, I spit out blood.

The Gaunt Man continued to walk back to the Humvees, paying me no mind.

I just registered the movement of the soldier to my right before a kick caught me in my midsection, flipping me onto my back. A boot quickly pressed square on my chest before I could roll away, the shotgun aimed at my face.

"Move and I clean up like the man said," a soft voice warned from behind the barrel.

The remaining searchlight came back to life, illuminating the dark raven hair and tan Latina skin of the familiar Marine over me.

"Rosalita?" I whispered in disbelief.

"Not anymore," she answered.

About the Author

Charles Ingersoll is a Detroit area native who transplanted to New York City for the Great American experience of contributing to the local economy.

A lover of comics, comic cons and cosplay, movies and television, the supernatural and all things undead; writing happened to be a lifelong passion that has become his next personal adventure.

He currently lives on Long Island, New York.

Other Books by the Author

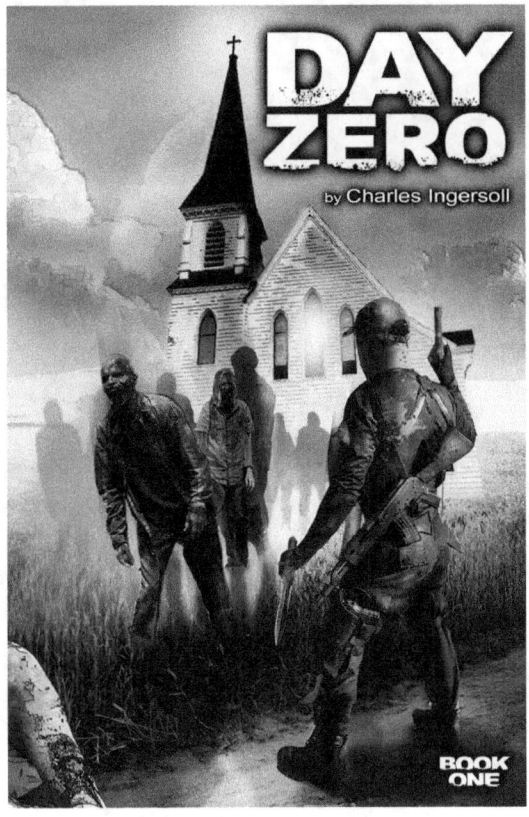

Interested in knowing how it all started for John?

Day Zero available in paperback and eBook!